THE SKY CLUB

Published by SSI, Inc.

SSI, Inc. , 880 Holcomb Bridge Road, Roswell, Georgia 30076, U.S.A.
SSI Publishing, Inc. (Puerto Rico), 208 Ponce de Leon Avenue,
Suite 1800, Hato Rey , Puerto Rico 00918-1009

SSI, Inc., Registered Offices: Hato Rey , Puerto Rico 00918-1009

First Edition Printing, October 2003

LIBRARY OF CONGRESS DATA
Feldman , Ian
The Sky Club
2003095644
1. Second World War - Fiction. 2. Nuclear Scientists - Fiction.
3. Nazi Germany - Fiction I. Title.

ISBN 0-9743673-0-3

Printed in the United States of America
Set in Adobe Garamond
Cover Design by AlphaAdvertising
Cover Photo by Pat Connell Photography

PUBLISHER'S NOTE

THE SKY CLUB

Ian Feldman

Epigraph

*"The atomic bombs at our disposal represent only the
first step in this direction. . . . . .there is almost no
limit to the destructive power which will become
available in the course of their future development. . .
opening the door to an era of devastation on an
unimaginable scale."*

*- Petition from the American Atomic Scientists,
to the President, 1945*

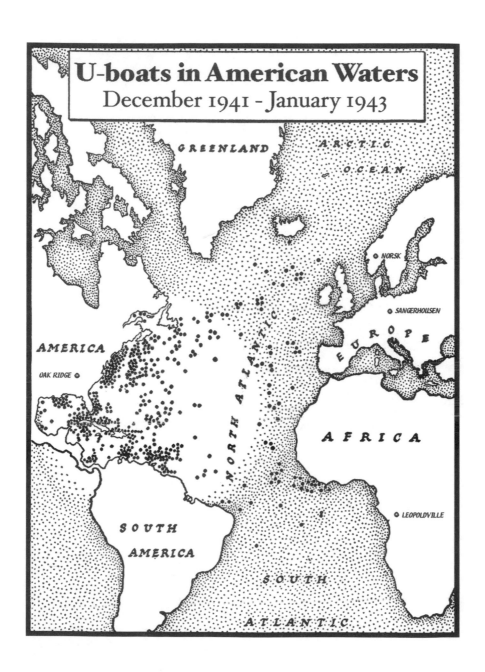

U-boats in American Waters
December 1941 - January 1943

GREENLAND

ARCTIC

OCEAN

NORSK

SANGERHAUSEN

AMERICA

EUROPE

OAK RIDGE

NORTH ATLANTIC

AFRICA

SOUTH AMERICA

LEOPOLDVILLE

SOUTH

ATLANTIC

PROLOGUE

Cape Lookout - Near Harker Island, North Carolina

On a cold black winter night in 1943, a sleek dark form broke the surface of the Atlantic about twenty kilometers off the North Carolina Coast. The war weary skipper of UX-506, a new type IXB German U-boat two-hundred and fifty-two feet in length, climbed out of the control room and onto the sea washed conning tower deck, as a special radio tower was hoisted by three of his crewman. He wasn't looking for freighter targets. The Kapitan donned his binoculars and checked the horizon three-hundred and sixty degrees, then gave an all clear and lit up a Turkish cigarette while his First Officer waited beside him in the pitch dark for a response from their recent radio transmission.

The night was clear and the new diesels hummed quietly as the sub ran at about nine knots into the rolling seas pushed by a northeast wind. When the high frequency signal came in, it was quick and lasted only a few minutes. The official signoff response would be the same as before, two static growls, silence, then one five-second continuous growl to signal received and complete.

Moments later the Unterseeboot was moving due east at a Flank Speed of eighteen knots along the surface to rendezvous with a another Long Range Attack Boat, Type IXC U-109, one-hundred and twenty kilometers northeast of the Azores. UX-506 had delivered it's message, high into the mountains of North Carolina, to a place only known to them as *The Sky Club*.

PART ONE

A Present Time

September 1972

Chapter 1

British Tortola

The late summer heat was subsiding and the winds pushing in from the eastern Atlantic and North Africa were more temperate now. Within the small islands and Cays of the upper eastern Caribbean, the warm luxurious water temperatures of mid-summer remained until the late fall.

This small isolated island group, known as the British Virgins, provided a perfect setting for travel magazines and photographers to shoot their swimsuit models in the near buff without the prying eyes of tourists to distract their crews.

Two main inhabited islands, Virgin Gorda and Tortola, plus about fifty small unnamed islands and Cays and some highly restricted areas controlled by the British Government, made up the island archipelago. The region was sparsely populated and maintained a lazy serenity compared to the nearby U.S. Virgin Islands and Puerto Rico.

Things had always remained very quiet except for an occasional Pirate's lair in the British Virgin Islands for the last three Centuries. Pirates had figured out a way to effectively shelter among the numerous tiny islands.

There, Pirate ships hidden amid rocky coves and dangerously shallow shoals and reefs were provided perfect spots to hide. Then without warning they would ravage unsuspecting ships carrying the riches of the New World back to the Crowns of Europe.

Over time, the islands became the favored hangouts of scoundrels such as Blackbeard, Bluebeard and Sir Francis Drake.

Until the 1960s, the British Virgins were mainly uninhabited. Then, in a joint venture with the British Government, Laurance Rockefeller and Charlie Cary were given the first limited development rights to control the fledgling tourism industry on the two larger islands of the British Virgins. Both industrialists recognized the tourism potential of the islands, but each took a different course.

Rockefeller developed the posh Little Dix resort on Virgin Gorda while Cary established an international marina complex on the nearby island of Tortola for large ocean going yachts and sailboats.

Both efforts were for high-end guests and restricted to prohibit an influx of visitors to the main two islands and beyond.

In addition, certain islands were completely off-limits to anyone, but officials of the British Government. Although the British Commonwealth had handed some autonomy to the BVIs in the 1960s such as a constitution and a local legislative council for island affairs, it was the governor who had control. He was ceremoniously selected by the Queen of England, but was in reality, a British Official charged with command of both external affairs and island security.

Since 1945, Jost Van der Vort had been known on all marine charts as a totally restricted access area of the British Government. Lying due south of the mainstream of the Sir Francis Drake Channel and across from the larger more mountainous island of Tortola, Jost Van der Vort Island was nestled between Peters Island several miles to the southwest and Coopers Island nearby on the northeast.

It was occasionally patrolled by medium sized Naval Destroyers and smaller British Corvettes to prevent encroachment by tourists or unsuspecting mariners. On this particular morning, it was unprotected as the eleven-hundred ton Royal Navy Hunt-class escort destroyer,

HMS Juno, a late WWII vintage ship at two-hundred and sixty-four feet assigned to the BVIs, had gone to Tortola for supplies and fuel.

Except for two armed British SAS guards occasionally moving around on a hundred-foot hill overlooking the secluded main house, the island was eerily still as the morning sun began to climb out of the eastern Caribbean Sea. Only a gentle sound came from the surf as it lapped against the white powder beach just fifty yards below a thick barrier of sharp-needled bougainvillea foliage.

Blocked from being seen from the beach, the beautiful flowering bougainvillea vines crawled up the walls of a castle-like structure that was the main house on Jost Van der Vort Island.

Two medieval styled stone and mortar turrets guarded the massive main doors of the structure as it faced eastward into the sun.

At its flat shoreline, the island had a surreal look of a Saharan desert oasis filled with luscious palm trees and gleaming white-sand crystals rearranged in a turquoise blue seascape instead of mountainous sand dunes. Only the thick bougainvillea shrubs and rock out-croppings covering the hillside behind the camouflaged main building broke the tranquil line of the horizon.

At each compass quadrant on Jost Van der Vort Island, a ten foot high red and white buoy drifted lazily within thirty yards of the shore proclaiming, Off Limits - No Trespassing: By order of the Governor of BVI.

Lieutenant-Colonel Robert MacCurry had spent the day before meeting with the Head of Section, Viscount Dalton Ramsbotham, at his Military Intelligence Post in London. His latest assignment, which in fact was his mustering-out assignment at age forty-eight, was to be a simple clean-up and dry-cleaning.

As always, these last mustering out jobs as they called them, were to ease top agents into nice remote locations of their choice for retirement. So, at the Crown's expense and in payment for extraordinary services beyond the call of duty, a quiet final duty station was usually chosen.

In the case of Lieutenant-Colonel MacCurry, he had chosen the BVIs as his last home station, after twenty years of service in Her Majesty's Military Intelligence Section.

During the Korean War, as a Captain in the Dover Light Infantry, he had received the Victoria Cross for mining an area under the cover of darkness from which he expected a massed Chinese night ground attack would be launched. His actions prevented the annihilation of over a thousand men of the 3rd Brigade whose ammunition was almost expended. MacCurry's men then carried out a successful counter-attack that held up the enemy until reinforcements arrived the next morning.

After Korea, he spent the next twenty years with Section 6-PAC - Post Action Clean-up, of British Military Intelligence.

His team was highly trained in after-action assessments and removal of espionage evidence that might implicate the Crown in any event worldwide. His authority to take any action came directly from the DMI - Director of Military Intelligence. Whatever had to be done to protect security and intelligence assets was approved without question at all levels of British Military or Royal Naval forces throughout the Empire and Commonwealth.

In this latest assignment and hopefully his last, he had received a sealed envelope directly from the Assistant DMI Ramsbotham. It was curiously coded,

MOST SECRET - EYES ONLY:
P.M.'S TUBE ALLOY FINAL MISSION

What made this very unusual was the P.M. - Prime Minister was never to be listed or implicated in any document dispatched to a field agent such as himself.

So for the first time in twenty years of service MacCurry felt this was the deepest they had ever taken him in a Clean-up Operation, even though this was supposedly his final task for 6-PAC.

MacCurry had endured a long day of flying from London. Plus, the final flight leg into Tortola had arrived late that night from San Juan. Robert knew from previous experience that it was impossible to get anything done safely after dark in the Caribbean, so he chose to rest up at the Royal Naval Officers quarters in Road Town for the evening.

The next morning, he requisitioned the Royal Navy Provost for a flight over to Jost Van der Vort since all commercial boat traffic was restricted from access to the secure Island. Only one Royal Navy plane was actually based at Tortola. It was docked in the harbor of Road Town.

The twin engine Grumman Mallard was a hardy 1940's vintage seaplane used only for special assignments, security patrols and VIP visits.

This particular RNG18 was about four-hundred pounds lighter than conventional Mallards built in the late 1940s because it had no need for deicing equipment on board, being used only in the Caribbean.

The Mallard was a favorite of the older Royal Navy pilots because it was versatile enough to drive right up onto any flat beach directly from a water landing.

The greatest problem with the Mallard was prop erosion caused by seawater and impact damage brought about by its nose dipping in rough water landings. MacCurry's particular RNG18 had a throttle lever break off inside the overhead quadrant during a rough landing the previous week.

Since it would require a major overhead disassembly, plus salvaged parts to change-out the lever/pulley assembly and properly fix it, the pilot had taken a piece of aluminum and lashed it to the broken throttle in an attempt to ready the aircraft for Lieutenant-Colonel MacCurry's sudden requirement to be flown over to Jost Van der Vort Island.

MacCurry climbed aboard the Mallard and noticed that the makeshift throttle piece for engine #1 was only loosely attached at the interior headliner.

As he began to buckle his safety harness, he looked at the contraption and questioned the aircraft's pilot, "Lieutenant Codrington, what have we here?"

"Aye Colonel," he replied, "I had a throttle lever break away from me last week on the #1 Engine. Was coming in with a blinding sunset in m'ah face. The wind was right, but the waves were a bit high, so I used the throttle to brace m'ah self on impact. Sure 'nuff it broke away and now I've got a temporary fix 'til the part arrives."

Colonel MacCurry could see the exposed throttle cables and was concerned that the cable loop would break away from the fix, but the flight was a short hop to the Island, so he simply agreed with Lieutenant Codrington's assessment.

"Well I suppose that will have do to then, Codrington", MacCurry was obviously somewhat vexed at this possible dilemma created by his urgent need to visit Jost Van der Vort.

"How long do you think the flight over will take?" The Colonel added.

"Not more than fifteen minutes from the time we taxi and get off the water," Codrington replied in a matter of fact manner.

"By the time we rotate, we will be turning across the Drake Channel and putting down on the beach side of the Island." He turned and smiled at the Colonel.

"All we will need to do then S'ah, is run up the beach a few yards and you can put off, right away, at the front door of the Castle, Colonel."

The Colonel replied back with a sense of concern in his voice. "Does everyone around here know about the Castle?"

"Well, it's not too easy to disguise from the air, Colonel, and you should know we over-fly the place at least once a month when the Juno is getting supplies out of San Juan. Besides, I heard that the mission's over anyway since the old man died", the Lieutenant causally remarked.

"When did you find out about that, Lieutenant", MacCurry quickly snapped?

"Well S'ah, the Juno's back here in Road Town this morning, and the crew's already passed the word that the old man's been in the meat cooler since Monday! That's two days, so I guess he's not comm'in out, wouldn't you say so, Colonel?"

Shocked at the Lieutenant's nonchalant attitude and the complete breach of security in the matter, MacCurry's irritated response was obvious.

"My God man, haven't you people got any sense of the confidential violations you've breached here, somebody needs to get control of this situation before we end up with a few General Courts Martials!"

Suddenly there was a serious silence in the plane's cockpit as the Lieutenant opened his flight manual and focused on his pre-flight by-the-numbers for the first time in about six months.

"Who's the Captain of the Juno", Lieutenant?" Colonel MacCurry demanded quickly, in a very serious tone of command.

"Lieutenant-Commander Philip Wickes, S'ah!" Codrington replied with an aire of attention in his response."

Then he questioned as a suggestion, "Do you want me to taxi over to the Juno's anchorage, S'ah?"

"No, Codrington, let's get on with it! Time is of the essence, now!" MacCurry spoke with a compelling concern in his voice, well aware that even without the High priority of his orders, he still outranked Wickes.

"I'll deal with those problems later, and for your information, this conversation never took place! Is that clear, Left ' Tenant! "

"Aye, aye S'ah, that is perfectly clear, Colonel!" Codrington responded very seriously, then immediately shut up and refocused on his pre-flight check.

Not another word was spoken as both engines began to roar at full throttle, drowning out all sounds within the cockpit. Instantly, the little seaplane lurched forward and they began surfing across the light waves pushing against the bow and under the boat-like hull as they made for open water.

The throttles held perfectly as they lifted off the water and banked across the Drake Channel toward Jost Van der Vort Island. It felt like they were floating along slowly in a hot air balloon ride as they leveled off and seemed to glide directly for the turquoise shallows on the eastern face of the Island.

Lieutenant Codrington then radioed the SAS officer in command at the Guard Post on Jost Van der Vort Island to identify his flight approach and announce the arrival of his VIP passenger. The SAS officer acknowledged him and identified the wind approach vector for the Mallard.

In the next moment the aircraft's manifold pressure boost began to drop as pilot Codrington adjusted for his water landing approach.

Smoothly, the seaplane made its final bank over the Island, and Lieutenant-Colonel MacCurry could clearly see the fortress-like castle and the mass of thick bougainvillea vines with the island's rock out-croppings covering the hill behind the shrouded building.

The water below appeared to be calm and flat, but the Lieutenant seemed to be breaking a serious sweat as MacCurry caught a glance of him making their final approach for touchdown.

Caught by surprise, the Colonel realized Codrington's quandary. The throttle for engine #1 was not responding. The cable loop had slipped off and retreated back into the overhead headliner making the throttle useless for adjusting the starboard engine speed. They were too close to the water to react differently, so Codrington went to full flaps, adjusted the rudder to compensate and flew the seaplane's hull hard down directly into the surf.

He immediately jerked the plane to Port and out of the first trough in the water, but the opposite reaction dipped the plane to his starboard. The Mallard took a severe hull pounding as suddenly, the starboard engine left the aircraft's wing.

Exploding off in a bizarre flash of light, the engine flew forward for about two-hundred yards ahead of the aircraft before it stalled and hit the water. It was almost comical.

There it just floundered, circling in a geyser of water like a beheaded island chicken running around blindly in a death spasm, then it slowly sank to the bottom of a sixty-foot deep coral head.

By this time the Colonel realized the landing could actually get worse, the aircraft climbed slightly to port away from the water, then it began to roll over.

Time suddenly went into slow motion as MacCurry shouted.

"Oh shit, this thing is going to rip apart Codrington", as he tried in vain to grab the co-pilot's yoke and help return the plane to level flight.

With the Mallard almost inverted, somehow Codrington nosed the bow-heavy Mallard back into the water and prevented 'God knows what' from happening?

Without the departed engine, Codrington quickly throttled the port engine down, as the plane seemed to glide directly for the beach toward the stunned SAS welcoming party.

There was no time to lower the Mallards hull wheels, so Codrington simply yelled.

"Colonel, watch out! We may hit that wall solid on, I cannot brake m'ah wheels!"

As the SAS team scattered out on each flank of the wounded Mallard, the plane roughly slid up the beach and slammed into the mass of thick bougainvillea vines bulging toward the shore creating an elastic buffer that abruptly stopped them before the nose hit the outer Castle wall.

Suddenly it was all over.

Codrington again with his confidence restored, addressed the Colonel.

"Well S'ah, its 0915 Hours and we've arrived safely at Jost Van der Vort Castle."

"Sorry, but we were unable to serve beverages on this run, however, don't hesitate to fly our Royal Naval door to door seaplane service again, whenever the need arises of course."

The Colonel pale faced and stunned, turned and grinned from ear to ear at Lieutenant Codrington as he spoke.

"You know you're one hell of a pilot, young man! Plus you got me here in record time. That calls for at least a wee bit of the MACALLAN I have stored away in your hold Lieutenant."

"Now let's get out of this bird and get on with Her Majesty's work!"

"Aye, aye S'ah, that will make a perfect welcome to this little Isle, a wee bit of the Highland's finest Malt Whiskey, Colonel! Aye, I have not had that one in years!" Codrington responded with overwhelming relief as he opened the hatch and turned to attention, hand saluting the Colonel.

However, a growing sense of urgency was building up within him as he exited the Mallard behind the Colonel. Codrington's mind was panicking. He realized he couldn't waste time on a formal welcoming. . . salt water was working it's mischief on his sunken engine, and in less than 24 hours, it's whole magnesium casing would be eaten away!

"But S'ah, I'll have to take a rain check on that whiskey offer for now. First I must get m'ah engine up from the reef, right off Colonel!"

"Very well then Codrington, we'll see about that Highland's Malt later on."

The SAS officer on duty and serving as the senior welcoming party then saluted and added his innocent observation for the new arrival as he inspected the right wing.

"Colonel MacCurry, Sir, the rest of the Mallard appears to be okay except for a seam fracture in the starboard wing."

MacCurry replied back to him with a wide smile on his face, but still somewhat pale from the ordeal. His voice had an obvious sarcastic tone in it.

"And you really think I'm going back on that thing again, Captain, with a perfectly good Royal Navy Destroyer in the neighborhood! I would have to be daff'd! And, no offense to the fine flying of Lieutenant Codrington!" He turned and grabbed his briefcase.

"In fact, for me to fly another Mallard, it would really have to be a rather cold day in hell, young man. Now, let's get those bags out of this old hulk, boys, and get this party operational."

"By the way, where's the Grand Ballroom in this Castle, anyway Captain?"

Chapter 2

Jost Van der Vort Island

Lieutenant-Colonel Robert MacCurry had very seldom found so-called simple clean up operations to really be uncomplicated. In fact, they were often more complex 'Matters of State', which needed immediate attention to avoid any likelihood of detection by outside observers, the press, or enemy combatants. This was such a situation.

Now that things had settled down, with the SAS boys back on perimeter patrol and Lieutenant Codrington fishing around the reef for his accursed engine parts, MacCurry could get down to reading his detailed orders.

First he went to the kitchen with his briefcase and located the door to the meat cooler. Inside and propped up in the back corner was an old man whose skin had turned purple from the 34°F temperature maintained in the cooler. He was dressed in a full length burgundy house coat having a Royal English Family Crest emblazoned on its left pocket and a gold cravat properly stuffed around his neckline. His eyes were closed, but his face seemed to hold a smile of final satisfaction.

MacCurry did a complete survey of the situation, initial cause of death analysis, and finally a check for objects of interest to assure final disposition of the subject person.
Then he exited the cooler and laid out his work items on a large butcher-block kitchen table centered in the middle of the room.

He then broke the seal on the coded envelope he had brought from London. As he opened it, the red block type on the inner envelope again flashed into his mind,

MOST SECRET - EYES ONLY:
P.M.'S TUBE ALLOYS FINAL MISSION.

His interest had been building since seeing the P.M. listed on the initial field orders.

Operations at 6-PAC had always concealed direct orders of the P.M. from anyone but the higher ups, so this one was going to be fascinating.

As he drew out the inside document, it appeared to be somewhat faded, but the Office of the Prime Minister's Seal was obvious. The letterhead was pre-1950s and displayed the Crest of England on a green and white background field with a silver shield below it that stated, The Right Honorable Prime Minister of Great Britain, Winston Churchill, dated April 10th, 1945.

Suddenly, Colonel MacCurry's mind stepped backward in time to the last year of the Second World War, as he began reading the twenty-seven year old document, revealing its shocking secret from the past . . .

TO: SUPREME COMMANDERS ROYAL NAVY,
ROYAL AIR FORCE AND ALL GROUND FORCES
GREAT BRITAIN
CC: ALL SECURITY DIRECTORATES OF THE
COMMONWEALTH
FROM: PRIME MINISTER -
WINSTON CHURCHILL (MOST)
DATE: APRIL 10, 1945
STATUS: (MOST) SECRET - EYES ONLY
RE: THE MATTER OF GERMAN
SS-GRUPPENFUHRER HORST DEEKE

NOTE: MAJOR GENERAL AND KOMMMANDANT OF SSI (SCHUTZSTAFFEL INFILTRATION) - SS-GRUPPENFUHRER HORST DEEKE IS TO BE CONSIDERED AN (MOST SECRET) ASSET OF THE HIGHEST ORDER TO ENGLAND AND THE COMMONWEALTH OF BRITAIN - BY ORDER OF THE PRIME MINISTER - WINSTON CHURCHILL FROM THIS DATE: APRIL 10, 1945 - FORTH AND FOR AN INDEFINITE TIME OR UNTIL SUCH EVENT AS HIS NATURAL DEATH.

SUB-NOTATION 1: UPON THE DEATH OF SS-GRUPPENFUHRER HORST DEEKE HIS REMAINS WILL BE DISPOSED OF ACCORDING TO HIS LAST WILL AND TESTAMENT WITH THE FORMALITY OF THE VIKING ORDERS OF NORWAY.

SUB-NOTATION 2: SS-GRUPPENFUHRER HORST DEEKE WILL BE AFFORDED THE HIGHEST LEVEL OF PERSONAL SECURITY NOW OR AT ANY FUTURE TIME EQUIVALENT TO THAT OF THE CROWN OF ENGLAND OR THE PRIME MINISTER OF GREAT BRITAIN - WITHOUT EXCEPTION.

SUB-NOTATION 3: THE BRITISH VIRGIN PROTECTORATE OF JOST VAN DER VORT ISLAND WILL BE THE SOLE AND ONLY INHABITATION AREA FOR SS-GRUPPENFUHRER HORST DEEKE -

AN AREA TO BE KNOWN ONLY AS BAMBURGH CASTLE SOUTH.

SUB-NOTATION 4: SS-GRUPPENFUHRER HORST DEEKE SHALL BE CODE-NAMED - LORD SUNDERLAND OF NORTHUMBRIA. ALL SECURITY AND LOGISTICAL SUPPORT FOR LORD SUNDERLAND IS THE (UTMOST) RESPONSIBILITY OF SAS AND ROYAL NAVAL ATTACHMENTS TO BE MANAGED BY GOVERNOR BVI.

END: AS REGARDS ANY INFORMATION - THIS MATTER IS CLOSED AND MAINTAINED (MOST) SECRET - BY ORDER OF THE PRIME MINISTER - ON THIS DATE: APRIL 10, 1945, FORWARD.

"Incredible", MacCurry said out loud as he thought about the events that could have lead up to this arrangement with a known Nazi SS-General and actually the highest known untried Nazi since WWII. This man was actually the commandant of the Ultra-Secret German Schutzstaffel Infiltration teams that were feared but considered so obscure that very little was known of them. SSI had been assumed to be operational throughout Europe and England from the mid-thirties until the collapse of Germany on VE Day in June 1945.

He began wondering what SS-Gruppenfuhrer Horst Deeke could have done to get the Prime Minister of England, Winston Churchill, to give him this kind of protection indefinitely. He knew he would probably never get to the real truth with the layers of security in this maze, but his interest was peaked.

For now, however, his objective was to completely clean Bamburgh Castle South, and dispose of, Lord Sunderland of Northumbria in the manner described by his Last Will and Testament. But where was the Will?

As a top cleaner specialist Lieutenant-Colonel Robert MacCurry had very few equals in either finding all incriminating evidence or disposing of it. MacCurry's methods had established the original Ramsbotham Military Intelligence Manual for MI-5, MI-6 and SAS Disposal Squads and most of his past assignments were limited time events.

With Bamburgh Castle and the BVI Protectorate of Jost Van der Vort Island, plus the SAS security team assigned on Post, the duration of this search and clean was almost indefinite.

Besides, he was retiring on this island or at least someplace nearby and a leisurely pace was more appropriate here. The only urgency was getting the frozen Lord Sunderland so to say, buried according to his wishes.

Just as he began pondering his next step, two items seemed to stand out on the block tabletop. A small black pouch and an SS lapel pin depicting the Dragon prow of a Viking Ship.

MacCurry opened the leather pouch and found a double-sided key, typical of a safety deposit box, but more likely to be Lord Sunderland's hidden safe. Then, as he turned over the SS lapel pin, he saw the initials inscribed, SSI-EF. Both items were now part of MacCurry's process as he began anxiously to discover their connections.

The key was clearly relevant to Lord Sunderland's hideout for his Last Will and Testament, but the SS lapel pin seamed to be related to his final thoughts prior to the heart attack that killed him.

Both would fall in place, as MacCurry discovered the mystery of Bamburgh Castle over the next few days, but for now he needed to locate that safe.

He spent the next several hours mapping the likely zones throughout the castle that Lord Sunderland would have treated as his prime living space and from that he was able to analyze the man's lifestyle and movements as well as the likely areas for locating his safe.

It was actually mid-afternoon before he discovered the vault located in a Library hidden at the base of a small staircase below the main entrance hall. Access to the staircase required that a black iron lighting sconce be turned to its side, then a doorway was revealed at the back of the left rounded turret guarding the inside of the main entrance door. The slab of marble that formed the door was narrow and the staircase behind it was metal and spiraled down into a hidden library below.

The safe was actually behind a detailed painting depicting a Viking Dragon Longship drifting offshore, while its crew of Viking raiders attacked and raped young women villagers somewhere along the north coast of England. As Colonel MacCurry, pulled the picture frame forward, the safe was revealed. He then tried the double-sided key.

It worked flawlessly as he turned the control handle and opened the safe's door.

Inside the safe were several books. One was a massive diary that had Lord Sunderland on it. Another was a journal with SSI & VTI inscribed on the cover and a third had The Sky Club. All were written in English with gold lettering.

A jewel case with several Nazi War Medals, ribbons including Waffen-SS lapel pins, two Knights Crosses with Oak Leaves and finally an Olympic Marching Medal from 1936 with an inscription on the back 'Das Fuhrer Adolph Hitler to Kommander of SS-Wiking - 1st Place'.

Finally, he discovered a folder with the words in German, 'The Last Will and Testament of the Viking, Horst Deeke'.

Now, he could get on with his immediate problem of burying General Horst Deeke code named Lord Sunderland and put the rest of his assignment on hold for at least a few days while he looked over the layout of the island.

He even thought he might have one of the Royal Navy cooks come over from Road Town and prepare meals for the next several evenings, while he set up operations for the clean-up and dry-cleaning. Besides that would give him four able pallbearers for the mock funeral once everything was set to go.

MacCurry carried the contents of the safe to a large mahogany reading table with two brass lamps at one end of the hidden library that provided an ample amount of light to examine the books and documents. He began first with an exquisitely bound gold and leather book that appeared to be the thickest, the personal 'Diary of Lord Sunderland'.

He opened the cover and viewed the inside sheet. It had three lines centered on the page in German;

The Sky Club

The true story of the Thermonuclear Bomb of the Fatherland

A Final Confession of Horst Deeke

Instantly, MacCurry's thoughts were drawn to a vision of the first 'Mike' test in the Marshall Islands on November 1st, 1952.

He knew that on Eniwetok, the first thermonuclear Hydrogen Bomb the world 'supposedly had ever known' was exploded by the United States. He remembered the image of the Life Magazine front cover showing that initial H-bomb as it created a fireball three miles wide and sixty-thousand feet high.

The article stated that the explosive force of that thermonuclear bomb was eight-hundred times more devastating than the first Atomic Bomb dropped on Hiroshima, August 6, 1945.

"Oh my God!" Once again stunned by the most incredible revelation of this final assignment MacCurry shouted out loud as he visualized the enormity of his discovery.

Could this known Nazi SS-General have controlled the keys to a bomb that would have instantly changed the world order in 1945?

Suddenly for the first time in over ten years, Colonel MacCurry was nervous. Even his hands were shaking from the thoughts and excitement running through his mind.

His German language proficiency was good and his verbal German was passable, but his translation skills might be put to the ultimate test with what appeared to be about a five hundred-page hand written document; a document that just might reveal one of the greatest hidden enigmas of the Second World War; a document that very few, if any other than himself, would ever know about because this was a high priority clean-up mission, and nothing would be left to incriminate the Crown when he was through.

Immediately he tried to assess his situation with the document. For now, at least the General, SS-Gruppenfuhrer Horst Deeke, appeared to have had a decent handwriting style that could be read without too much confusion.

An official letter written by the Kommandant of the Gross Lichterfelde War Academy at Berlin in 1929 and a short biography of his beginnings were clipped to the front of the document revealing the early background of the General and how he became involved in the Nazi hierarchy.

His mother's family was called Elivagar from a small island called Leka, north of the city of Trondheim on the West Coast of Norway. The Elivagar were considered to be direct descendants from a Viking Chiefdom on the island and very few of their relatives practiced Christian religious beliefs. Mythology of the Norsemen seemed to be their singular faith as they went through life in a world of clear blue seas and white ice.

Leka was a land of rugged fjords and landscapes, the midnight sun and the flashing light beams of the aurora borealis. The cold northern seas around the island would continually lash the coast, while snow would cover the ground most of the year. Icebergs with seals on them, floating down from the Arctic Circle, would sometimes be seen near the island in early spring as its virulent vegetation grew and fed the islands few inhabitants in the summer months.

Blue skies and perpetual light filled their brief summers, while ice and snow forced them to become homebound or hardy cross country skiers in the long winter months in order to bring supplies from the mainland.

All during the cold winters the elders told the wonderful legends of their Viking past to the children as they grew up, imbedding the desire to be great warriors in the young men as they worked the land for food and sustenance.

When Horst was eleven his father Knut, heard about the Great War in Europe and decided to join the Army of Prussia.

Upon leaving the island Knut joined a group of recruits in Berlin, sending money and letters back to Leka, while on the weekends staying with a wealthy Norwegian family near the center of the capital city. Knut's fearless warrior-like style amazed his superiors during the hand to hand battles against the Tsarist Armies on the Eastern Front in 1915.

He was given a field promotion to the rank of Lieutenant, after saving a General Staff officer from being killed, during a raid on their headquarters encampment in Poland.

The entire unit was overrun yet he fought off several Cossacks, taking their swords and capturing two of their officers. His tactics forced the enemy to withdraw allowing reinforcements to help him recover the ground lost to the Russians.

Towards the end of 1918 he reached the rank of Captain and led raids against insurgent bands of communists trying to foment revolution within Germany after the war. When he decided to leave and return to Norway, the commander he saved, General von Mannheim, asked him to join the Reichwehr, the Army of the Weimar Republic.

But Knut remained steadfast and agreed to send his only son Horst to the Military Academy in Berlin, once he had returned to Leka. Unfortunately Rittmeister - Captain Knut Deeke's ship was sunk during a vicious wintry gale while crossing to Oslo, and all on board were mysteriously lost in the depths of the North Sea.

Horst was heartbroken, but he vowed to follow the gallant lead of his father. So at nineteen, against the pleadings of his mother, he also decided to join the German Military.

Fortunately, the legacy of his father meant that Horst Deeke would rise quickly through the ranks even during the peace between the wars and once again the Thorholda family in Berlin became his refuge, just like his father before him.

By 1927, after his mother died, Horst was given a minor posting in the Truppenamt; the name given to the General Staff that Germany was forbidden by the Treaty of Versailles to have.

He served as an adjutant to Colonel von Manstein and helped him devise a plan for the Commander in Chief's mobilization of the Army should Germany again face a war in Europe.

With his established expertise, Horst escorted von Manstein, who became the honorable father figure that Horst longed for, as they traveled around Europe visiting several foreign military facilities learning new and better methods for a future war scenario.

This association along with his skills were honed even more, until 1932, when the SS-Reichfuhrer realizing his unique abilities requested him for his own SS-Waffen staff in Berlin.

From that day forward, Horst Deeke was considered the most seasoned military strategist on Himmler's staff and his career took an immediate turn for even higher levels of responsibility once Herr Adolf Hitler took on the role of Reich Chancellor and Fuhrer in 1933. Colonel MacCurry's mind was running at light speed as it began to spin back in time to the years before and during World War II, when he knew this man had to be at the peak of his unimaginable power.

As he turned the next page into the diary itself, Robert MacCurry was at once drawn back into the past. . . .deep into the early beginnings of an incredible story and his own final mission to dispose of one of the deepest secrets of the Second World War.

A story flowing with deep emotions and highly descriptive mental pictures carved from the mind of this obviously very cryptic and once powerful man, Horst Deeke.

PART TWO

Rising of the Valkyries

November 1938

Chapter 1

Sangerhausen

Hitler's private Condor, a large aesthetically elegant four-engined monoplane, touched down quietly in the early morning mist at the heavily camouflaged airstrip near Sangerhausen, Germany.

The Fuhrer's special SS security team quickly escorted him into a Mercedes Command Car. They drove a short distance along a hard packed gravel road bordered by thick Norwegian Pines to the massive hunting estate. The Chateau's main building was sited directly over the underground facility entrance of Sangerhausen.

Inside the massive estate, a special operations area had been set up by SS-Reichfuhrer Heinrich Himmler. Several men anxiously waited for the Supreme Commander of the Third Reich around a large rectangular table in the mahogany-paneled renaissance library.

The Fuhrer's thoughts were as yet undistracted by the major war planning efforts of 1939, so his excitement about the preliminary Super Bomb plan made his mood, almost joyful and exuberant towards the meeting with the SS-Reichfuhrer Himmler.

His delight was obvious to the group of men that stiffened to attention as he entered the room. Their positions around the table indicated their rank and chain of command to the Fuhrer.

As he acknowledged them individually with a glance and slight smile, he turned to Himmler and extended his hand. "These facilities are much better than I expected, Herr Reichfuhrer."

The SS-Reichfuhrer quickly raised the 'Heil Hitler' salute, then shook the Fuhrer's outstretched hand while stating,

"It is your brilliance and insight that has allowed us to complete it in record time, my Fuhrer."

Himmler had been building the Sangerhausen facility under orders from the Fuhrer for the past fifteen months. Now that it was landscaped and heavily camouflaged this beautiful Renaissance Hunting Chateau of the ancient Austrian Empire was the most highly classified underground War facility in Nazi Germany.

Even the Abwehr, Nazi Germany's Secret Intelligence Division, were unaware of its existence

Three of the men at the table were the team leaders of SS-Reichfuhrer Heinrich Himmler's assembled Ultra-Secret SSI Team, Schutzstaffel Infiltration, the trained espionage members selected from the Waffen - SS.

The four German Scientists on the opposite side of the table were the lead nuclear physicists of the Ultra-Secret VTI Gruppe, Virus Technical Institute. They were members of the administrative scientists from several German industrial giants now housed at Sangerhausen and assigned to develop and test a nuclear device for the Third Reich.

Each of their salaries were actually financial grants provided by the massive German chemical cartel of I. G. Farben and Bayer's Frederich Claussmann who had been secretly approached by the SS-Reichsfuhrer Himmler to assist the Reich on it's mission for world scientific supremacy just after the Berlin Olympics in 1936.

The Fuhrer removed his gloves and sat down at the table head, while handing his hat to the attaché. The attaché then stored Hitler's accessories and backed out of the room silently closing the pair of massive entrance doors.

"Well, gentlemen, what is the first step to get the resources to complete this glorious Super Bomb for the Third Reich?"

SS-Reichfuhrer Heinrich Himmler began first.

"If I may, my Fuhrer, let me first introduce Herr Doctor Ludvig von Messerstrich."

"He is responsible for the detailed assessment of the current shortage of Aryan Nuclear Scientist in Germany needed to complete the project before 1944," the SS-Reichfuhrer clear his throat as he continued.

"His objective is to maintain control over the key scientist now on the project, such as Werner Heisenberg, and to add nuclear scientific resources to that team to meet our deadline."

Hitler with his amazing powers of memory for even obscure events spoke again.

"Herr Doctor, I remember well the comments you made in Munich at the University in 1931, against the Zionist control of that faculty. Your Aryan blood and allegiance will serve you well in this matter today."

Doctor von Messerstrich, a long standing Aryan chemist and nuclear physicist with I.G. Farben had been recruited for his allegiance to the Fuhrer as well as his administrative skill in getting the maximum results from his people in the shortest amount of time possible.

His skill at diplomatic dialogue was also the reason that the SS-Reichfuhrer had selected him to speak first to the Fuhrer.

"My Fuhrer, it is with the greatest pleasure that I join you once again to ensure Germany's place at the top of the world's most powerful nations."

"What we are about to do will require five highly disciplined teams of scientists."

"We must create these teams from our own core of German Scientists, but some must come from those scientists that originally developed these nuclear design theories. Some of these scientists that are experts in nuclear theories are Jews. They have left Germany for other Western European countries. Some are even now in the United States at various Universities, paid for by Jews and philanthropists who own or run Zionist American industries."

Immediately enraged by the issue of Jews, the Fuhrer reddened in the face, then stood up and slammed his fist on the table top.

"Why do we need these filthy Jewish swine?"

"This is an effort by the Aryan Third Reich to create an Aryan Super Bomb? How can we control these scum from taking our knowledge, our ideas, to Stalin or Churchill?"

The sudden outburst froze everyone in the room. After an unbearable silence, Hitler looked down at the table, irritated at the suggestion of using Jews to design and build the Aryan Super Bomb,

"What is your opinion Herr Reichfuhrer?"

After another pause, to allow von Messerstrich or for anyone else to respond, Himmler realized there was too much fear of reprisal in the room at this point, so he began first.

"My Fuhrer, from April 1933 to December 1938, the anti-semitic Laws and Decrees of the Third Reich have effectively rid us of many Jews that were misdirecting our young Aryan Students in Great German Institutes and Universities."

"The Decrees removed thousands of the useless socialist and Zionist rats as well as supporters of communism in Leipzig, Hamburg, and Munich."

Himmler increased his tone of voice as he looked to Doctor von Messerstrich to further emphasize this point.

"As you are aware my Fuhrer, the purge of these scientists was administered by Admiral Wilhelm Canaris and his Abwehr Military Intelligence Division up until 1938."

In reality, Himmler knew it was not only Admiral Canaris and his Abwehr Agents that had directed the sweeping purges and removals to forcefully drive out many of Germany's nuclear theoreticians.

Even Heydrich's SD and Himmler's own Gestapo units were guilty of this flawed strategy, but he was not about to reveal those facts to the Fuhrer here or now. Himmler paused and looked to Doctor von Messerstrich to add to this critical point. Himmler clearly had no desire to suggest to the Fuhrer that Jews were now desperately needed by the Third Reich.

Doctor von Messerstrich took the opening, to began with added details,

"My Fuhrer, it is true, that many of the great minds of German scientific nuclear theory like Albert Einstein, John von Neumann, Leo Szilard, and the Hungarian born, Edward Teller were driven into the waiting arms of Britain and America as a result of this seven year purge."

Hitler's eyes seemed to blacken and a hint of sweat appeared on his collar as Doctor von Messerstrich continued.

"The Nuclear knowledge of those Non-Aryan scientists in the area of quantum mechanics and thermonuclear theories gained first here in Germany at our expense, were years ahead of the United States and England."

The Fuhrer was aware that Admiral Canaris had been too widespread in his purge of the Universities, but his apparent actions were now becoming suspect and something had to be done.

Himmler paused for the effect of his next comments to set in.

"Now these countries can catch up to the position of the Third Reich, my Fuhrer!"

Doctor von Messerstrich realizing that Himmler would never make the next statement, supporting the use of Jews, blurted his added response supporting the SS-Reichfuhrer.

"We must have some of these non-Aryan scientist back in Germany or at the very least, working for us in clandestine ways in America or England to finalize our Super Bomb, my Fuhrer."

Hitler again exploded verbally.

"How could Canaris and Abwehr have let this happen?" Hitler continued to perspire around the neck, but paused to allow Himmler to addressed him and offer his solution.

He straightened and looked toward the Fuhrer, but lowered his head dutifully.

"My Fuhrer, I am always at your service for whatever solution you may choose. We at this table will correct the errors of the past, the errors of the Abwehr."

"With your personal authority, we will maintain complete control and complete secrecy from all others, including Herr Canaris, for this solution. The resources at this table will get this done quickly," Himmler carefully added.

"Our SSI team is now ready to act in Europe and the SSI espionage team is already operational in America without Abwehr's awareness."

"They will extricate knowledge, provide counter-espionage, and remove resources from America to help us here in Germany as well."

"SSI will simultaneously extract support from scientists throughout Europe and from those that have families in our relocation camps or under house arrest awaiting the final solution."

Again, Himmler paused to observe Hitler's temperament. A glow had returned back to his face and a slight smirk in his smile.

"For now, these countries can catch up to us, but this scientific team seated here today and SSI will correct this very soon, my Fuhrer."

"Our greatest single strength now is Doctor von Messerstrich and his team with our control of vast amounts of Bomb making materials here in Europe."

Taking the lead, Doctor von Messerstrich directed a sweep of his hand toward his scientists seated along his side of the table.

"My Fuhrer, besides our scientists here today, these nuclear assets include I.G. Farben and M.S. Schmidt's fifty-five-percent ownership of Belgium's refined uranium oxide now stored outside of Brussels."

"Germany also now has control of the ownership of Norsk Hydro in Norway. "

"This is the only known source worldwide, at the moment, for 'Heavy Water' scientifically known as deuterium production."

"Finally, we have a scientific monopoly over a cyclotron purchased from France and soon to be shipped here to Sangerhausen."

After a few more minutes of reasoning and critical-timing details by both Messerstrich and Himmler, Doctor von Messerstrich added a final statement.

"All we need now is the immediate repatriation of twenty Physicists and Nuclear Scientists located around Europe, and we will advance well beyond the Allies in England, France, or America."

Hitler still mentally seething about the Canaris situation, looked up from his mirrored image reflected in the polished mahogany tabletop and repugnantly directed his comment to the SS-Reichsfuhrer.

"And, how soon can we get control over these filthy Jewish swine, Herr Reichfuhrer?"

Sensing the opportunity to gain additional confidence and respect for his plan from the Fuhrer, SS-Reichfuhrer Heinrich Himmler decided to introduce the lead member of his Ultra-Secret SSI Team. Schutzstaffel Infiltration was the trained espionage and counter-espionage members he had personally selected from the Waffen - SS Division to carry out this assignment.

"My Fuhrer, the timing of events and control of these scientists is exactly our next step."

Himmler again rose from his seat and turned to his right. The SS-Reichfuhrer squinted through the lenses of his pince-nez glasses with a touch of moisture glinting on his forehead.

His nervous tension due to the sudden mood changes of the Fuhrer was evident as he shifted from foot to foot while he spoke.

"Let me now introduce, Standartenfuhrer - Colonel Horst Deeke, who will explain our extortion plan for re-control of these scientist, 'Gehorsam zum Vaterland' - Obedience to the Fatherland."

As he spoke, a mature colonel of the Waffen-SS with the Knights Cross emblazoned around his throat, stood up sharply and quickly raised the salute to the Fuhrer and stated, "Heil Hitler."

Standartenfuhrer Horst Deeke's strong Nordic and Aryan features were almost overwhelmed by the impeccable black uniform, SS runes on both collars, War ribbons with oak leafs, and silver wound medals acquired from the Spanish Civil War.

His solid six-foot frame created an immaculate Nordic almost god-like appearance that looked as though he was at attention on a Berlin military review stand.

"As you are aware, my Fuhrer, no agency including Abwehr, has been concerned with the need to reacquire Scientific Assets lost from the Third Reich over the last ten years. It is now imperative that we immediately implement 'Operation Gehorsam' to gain the edge over England and America before they can viscously strike Germany with a Super Bomb themselves. Over the last five months we have reviewed the strengths and weaknesses of our Super Bomb program and have found the following to be true."

Hitler began to relax, displaying his often hidden smile and lighten his demeanor, as Standartenfuhrer Horst Deeke's creative ideas and commitment to the Project were unveiled.

"It is true, my Fuhrer, that Germany has the refined uranium oxide ready for use in the cyclotron being assembled here at Sangerhausen."

"As well, Germany has the only worldwide source for Deuterium Oxide, which according to one Nuclear Theorist in America, may hold an even greater potential for our Super Bomb than our present assumptions."

The Standartenfuhrer then made two critical key points.

"The hard part is how to gain control of the researchers and their knowledge."

" First, we can easily extort allegiance from various non-Aryan Nuclear Scientists and Theorists throughout Europe or in Germany through the use of our relocation camps where their relatives may have been already been detained by Heydrich's SD."

"However, the bulk of the Nuclear Scientific brain trust is now in America or possibly England as a result of the Abwehr blunder. So, how do we get to them?"

Standartenfuhrer Deeke's next point was critical for all present to hear, so he raised his voice slightly and used his right fist to emphasize his point.

"Foremost, we must understand that the holy doctrine of the entire nuclear scientific community, outside of Aryan German control of course, is Bolshevism, Bolshevism of the first order."

The Fuhrer was suddenly both stunned and energize in that one-second, as he blurted out.

"Continue, messenger of The Great Nordic God Odin !"

Now fueled by Hitler's comment, an even greater passion gleamed in Standartenfuhrer Horst Deeke's eyes.

"My Fuhrer, the majority of nuclear theorists and scientist in America are proven Bolshevik sympathizers and established Communists. But all of them have two core weaknesses, they follow the Zionist social pack of swine and they are all pacifists of the first order. It is therefore imperative that we quickly exploit these weaknesses and their allegiance to Bolshevism."

"My Fuhrer," he added, " a unique moment of opportunity exists to use our SSI assets hidden deep within the American heartland."

"Our plan is to befriend, then lead specific packs of scientists and Bolshevik Jews into our control. SSI teams disguised as Bolshevik sympathizers will methodically deceive and betray their leaders to uncover the American research work needed to finalize our Aryan Super Bomb."

"With your direction, my Fuhrer, SSI will assure the absolute World Domination of the Fatherland."

Once again sensing an opportunity to gain control of the discussion, plus recognition for conceiving of Horst Deeke's Plan from his Fuhrer, SS-Reichfuhrer Heinrich Himmler quickly spoke.

"So you can see my Fuhrer, our extortion plan is both ruthless and complex. The re-control of these scientist using 'Gehorsam zum Vaterland' will require the resources of our private Reichbank in Switzerland and a special arrangement with Admiral Raeder and his the Kriegsmarine."

"We will need a clandestine way to get absolute authority over at least two of Donitz's U-boats for transport of additional assets to and from America."

As Supreme Commander of the Third Reich, two of the Fuhrer's greatest irritations were the constant infighting for Reichmarks and the coveting of authority over specialized military assets by his commanders.

Of all of his military commanders, Reichcommander Raeder of the Kriegsmarine was the most apolitical, neither extreme Nazi SS nor extreme Imperial Reichsmarine.

The Commander was also the most determined to maintain correctness and Naval purity. In this sense, he was the most difficult of all to work with and required a well-conceived subterfuge in order to gain his support for certain clandestine military activities such as this.

Beside these obstacles, Raeder had appointed the most bull headed Admiral the German Navy had to control the U-boats of the Kriegsmarine, Admiral Donitz.

For the Fuhrer, all of this meant that he, not the SS-Reichfuhrer would be burdened with several extensive political meetings to conclude this matter, at least until some success in building his Super Bomb had been realized.

Energized by these thoughts, he finally blurted out.

"Stoppen Sie!   This discussion must end, now!"

Stunned, the SS-Reichfuhrer Himmler again became cautious of the Fuhrer's sudden change of mood, and the meeting had now taken much longer than he expected. Maybe a couple hours of rest and relaxation would bring the Fuhrer a better perspective.

"My Fuhrer," he said, "Would you like to meet again this evening after cocktails?"

Hitler rose from the table and all present immediately stood up to attention awaiting his next course of action. Again he addressed the group.

"I am satisfied with this meeting up to this point, but we will need more time to consider all of these implications."

Eyeing Himmler he then firmly stated,

"Herr Reichfuhrer, you will meet me in my quarters after lunch to outline some issues that must be resolved before we take any decisive action overseas."

At that moment, Hitler's attaché suddenly re-opened the pair of massive mahogany entrance doors, as if on cue.

The Fuhrer then added a last statement directed to the scientists at the table.

"Now, gentlemen, by my unlimited powers, you will have the resources needed to complete this glorious Super Bomb for the Third Reich. But with caution, I warn you, your debt will be to me, and to me alone, your Fuhrer. That debt will be to have this Super Bomb ready to use, when I need it! "

"To that repayment, to that purpose, you will all be personally liable for the just rewards of das Vaterland, or the vile vengeance of my SS, if that task is not accomplished!"

He then turned and walked out of the meeting leaving the group clearly bewildered. His final ominous words still remained frozen in the individual minds of each man left staring, as the massive doors of the volatile room closed behind him.

It was not until the following morning that the SS-Reichfuhrer Heinrich Himmler called for Standartenfuhrer Horst Deeke to report to his beautiful 18th century Austrian Empire antechamber at the Sangerhausen Chateau.

The dramatic room provided a stage for Himmler to set the mood for the next step in the transformation of the team.

As the Standartenfuhrer entered and walked toward the SS-Reichfuhrer seated at his desk, he observed a sense of relaxation rather than the tension that existed the day before in the mood of the SS-Reichfuhrer.

"Standartenfuhrer Horst Deeke, reporting as ordered Herr Reichfuhrer, Heil Hitler."

SS-Reichfuhrer Himmler had a bottle of Couvoisier sitting on a small refreshment table to his right and a half-filled Venetian crystal glass in his left hand as he acknowledged the Standartenfuhrer's entrance.

"The Fuhrer and I had a wonderful evening last night and the Valkyries must have been singing in your ears Standartenfuhrer, for we spoke of you often."

"Moments ago the Fuhrer left our Flughafen for Berlin, but our meetings late yesterday and last night were very successful."

"He dictated these orders to my secretary this morning."

The SS-Reichfuhrer gazed through his pince-nez glasses, while hinting the admiration of the Fuhrer, as he lifted the document to Horst Deeke.

"Herr Deeke, you should be truly proud of yourself. The Fuhrer himself has authorized your promotion as my Third Deputy Adjutant, with equal powers, and fully charged with all operations and resources necessary for the completion of our Aryan Super Bomb."

"Furthermore, to enforce this authority of the Fuhrer and myself as SS-Reichfuhrer, I hereby promote you to SS-Gruppenfuhrer - Major General. Your responsibility now, will be to add to your SSI team and complete the Fuhrer's Super Bomb on time."

"With your new authority any Waffen-SS and Wiking-SS asset as well as over a thousand million Reichmarks of the Third Reich will be arranged to accomplish your goal."

"I have instructed my First Adjutant to establish a permanent address for you at the Reichschancellery Offices below mine. However, your locations will always be 'Most Secret' due to this new arrangement."

Horst Deeke's eyes surged with supercharged energy as the SS-Reichfuhrer continued.

Then in a instant, Horst was shocked into reality, as he began to read the finer details of the Fuhrer's order document handed to him by the SS-Reichfuhrer. Horst now understood why the SS-Reichfuhrer was drinking so early in the morning.

Sensing his extreme emotional transformation, the SS-Reichfuhrer added.

"The SS-Gruppenfuhrer Deeke shouldn't waste too much time now," Himmler smiled and added smoothly,

"You are now personally charged with the success or the failure as alluded to by the Fuhrer yesterday, of this entire project."

"In addition, with that document signed by the Fuhrer himself in my presence, you have absolute authority to acquire any German controlled assets you need to get it done by the designated time he wants it."

Cautiously Horst Deeke addressed Himmler in a deeper voice tone. "And just when, does, he want it, Herr Reichfuhrer?"

Once again, the SS-Reichfuhrer seemed more animated than usual gazing through his pince-nez glasses, while lifting the Couvoisier filled crystal glass to his nose to enjoy its aroma, before instantly downing it in a single motion.

The heat of the Couvoisier caused the Reichfuhrer to cough intensely, before he began to speak.

"The timing will depend on many factors SS-Gruppenfuhrer, but for now, only the Great Nordic God Odin holds the knowledge of our future course."

"Like Aryan Vikings on a misty fjord far from your homeland you will know that course just as they, the forefathers of SS-Wiking, could smell their way to the earthen shores of England and Russia in ancient times past."

Horst knew that the Viking and Norse Gods were SS-Reichfuhrer Himmler's favorite analogies for offering his views of the Third Reich and the Deity of Hitler himself.

His philosophy and views of both future events as well as predictions were not simply a result of the ever-decreasing line of brandy in the nearby bottle.

Actually the ritualistic runes of pre-medieval Celtic and Nordic Tribesmen often held his interest well into evening discussions with many

of the top echelon of Hitler's inner circle.

At last Horst realized it was no longer a joke that had been played out in the events of last night's private Cocktail Party for the Fuhrer.

Himmler had negotiated and the Fuhrer himself had authorized his promotion to the Third Deputy Adjutant, as the 'Opferziege', the sacrificial escape goat, if all is lost.

He knew well the power of position and its potential penalties, as a Black Knife SS himself.

And besides, he was himself now in a position to make all of it actually happen. He was now SS-Gruppenfuhrer and Kommandant of SSI.

At once, Horst tried to visualize how it had come to all this, as he began musing of the past. . . the deep past of SSI with Himmler, Günther and of course his beautiful Heidi, his precious Valkyrie.

The place where it all began, long-ago recorded in letters, conversations, and memories that now would both drive his ambitions and haunt his heart forever.

Chapter 2

The Crossing

Only a week before their Atlantic Crossing from Copenhagen, on January 30th 1933, Günther Anderssen and Heidi Winters were in Berlin as Guests of Heinrich Himmler. Together they were attending a Dinner in honor of the newly appointed, forty-three year old Chancellor of Germany, Adolf Hitler. At their table were two other military officers selected by the SS-Reichsfuhrer Heinrich Himmler to entertain the young lady while Günther was busy meeting elsewhere with Himmler.

One of the officers, an attaché to the SS-Reichsfuhrer, a handsome young SS-Hauptstrumfuhrer, a Captain in the newly created Waffen-SS sat across from the beautiful young Heidi. SS-Hauptstrumfuhrer Horst Deeke's Norwegian name, blond hair and deep blue eyes truly captivated the young Heidi, from the moment she saw him. He was obviously, a purely Aryan man with his impeccable black uniform, and his gold SS runes gleaming at her from both his collars.

He only had one medal on his uniform, but she could tell from his solid male frame, that he must be from the perfect Viking Warrior stock her uncle had told her about. The New Reich of Germany would be built from these men, he had said.

Waiting for the right moment, she spoke to him just after her Uncle Günther excused himself from the group and entered a nearby room guarded by two SS-Rottenfuhrers of the SS-Reichsfuhrer's own bodyguards. "So where are you from Captain?"

Trying to seem uninterested and somewhat formal towards her,

SS-Hauptstrumfuhrer Horst Deeke replied quietly. "My home is here in Berlin, but I was born on the island of Leka, north of Trondheim in Norway, Fräulein."

He could see that she was already a very beautiful young lady even at sixteen, and he knew from the dossier, Himmler had given him to review, that she was also unknowingly hand-picked for one of the SS-Reichsfuhrer's future assignments.

This young Fräulein was one of the Fuhrer's prospective breeding stocks. In fact, her dossier indicated she had tested at the top of the intelligence scale for young people at her grade level. Her only flaw seemed to be her desire to humanize less unfortunate races such as the Jews, Gypsies, and Coloreds. The dossier stated, it was clear she was too forgiving of these sub-human races and likely in need of Nazi Youth re-orientation programs in the near future as to the shortcomings of these races, as well as the threat they posed to the future of the Reich. Himmler was seriously concerned about this problem, but her Uncle had assured the SS-Reichfuhrer that it was merely a stage of her youthful adolescence as a result of her broad exposure to other European Nationals during her travels with him, that had caused the problem. It would soon be corrected.

Slightly taken back by his surprised formality, Heidi then decided to redirect the same question to the more jovial looking lower ranking officer beside him.

"And you, Lieutenant, where are you from? And what does that SD on your arm cuff mean?"

SS-Oberstrumfuhrer Claus Prien was a round faced friendly young man, a little overweight, but quite effective in his interrogation squads.

SS-Oberstrumfuhrer Prien had just joined the most aggressive man in the Third Reich next to Hitler himself, SS-Standartenfuhrer Reinhard Heydrich. Colonel Heydrich's SD Unit or Sicherheitsdienst and better known as SS Security, Intelligence and Interrogation Police had just broken away from Admiral Canaris Abwehr Espionage Unit that year.

As a result, SS-Standartenfuhrer Reinhard Heydrich had begun to create his own fiefdom directly under the SS-Reichfuhrer Himmler with his own select people, and SS-Oberstrumfuhrer Claus Prien had recently become one of those people.

Amazed that the young Fräulein had even realized he was even at the table, the SS-Oberstrumfuhrer Prien responded back to Heidi with excitement.

"My home, Fräulein, is near Leipzig in the town of Halle where as you may be aware, the Director of the SD, SS-Standartenfuhrer Reinhard Heydrich is from. I'm also a musician as well as the SS-Standartenfuhrer, but of course I'm not as proficient with classical instruments as he is."

"And, regarding your question about the SD logo on my cuff," he added, " this is the newly created Division of SS-Security and Intelligence that will assist the Fuhrer in the further protection of das Vaterland, Fräulein!"

The conversation continued back and forth between them for a while until Horst Deeke was called away to a staff meeting of the SS-Reichsfuhrer's other attachés.

When the object of her real interest left the table, Heidi ceased her attempt to further impress the SS-Oberstrumfuhrer. She then, quickly excusing herself, walked off to another table of young ladies, as if she had become bored with his long-winded bantering on his future job.

Besides Heidi thought, the young Fräuleins always had more interesting things to talk about, like their own mysterious loves and maybe even some more background on her newly discovered, SS-Hauptstrumfuhrer Horst Deeke.

Günther Anderssen had left the Dinner early for a clandestine meeting arranged by Himmler himself.

That meeting was designed to launch a Special Espionage Unit for future Operations directed only by the Fuhrer.

As Günther entered the secured meeting room, Himmler greeted him and began reviewing the trip plans.

To his surprise, upon orders from Himmler, two gentlemen also in attendance, from the Montebatten und Reichbank Bank in Zurich, Switzerland, turned over a double-keyed suitcase to Günther, the now newly designated American Director of the Fuhrer's SSI, Schutzstaffel Infiltration.

Günther's undercover police work in the years following the Great World War and his recent training of Himmler's SS Ultra-Secret Espionage network in Germany, made him the perfect choice.

Within the double-keyed suitcase, were detailed assignment orders to establish specialized American Based operations using SSI operatives, bound only to the SS-Reichsfuhrer Heinrich Himmler.

A special false bottom in the suitcase held twenty million British Pounds Sterling. Himmler's primary directive from Hitler was straightforward, but deadly. It required that Günther's new American SSI Network had to be totally self-sustaining and extremely covert.

They had to be so well concealed from all other Nazi Spy Operations, such as the Abwehr, that the Fuhrer's closest core leaders of the German Reich, had absolute deniability.

Thus, for propaganda reasons and Hitler's personal protection from possible future war crimes, they could easily be designated as German-American renegades, and not members of any German Operation or the Nazi Party.

They were on their own, but they were also very deep undercover.

So, in reality, SSI would only be used in future operations of the utmost needs of the Fuhrer himself as the SS-Reichsfuhrer Himmler put it. The true enigma with this arrangement however, was very real to Günther. He knew of course that the Fuhrer's personal Waffen-SS assassins could also annihilate them instantly, if anything went wrong, or if anything they did could implicate Germany.

Given this broad mandate by the Fuhrer and orders taken directly from the SS-Reichfuhrer Himmler, Günther could call his own shots and freely make all decisions, until the time came for his SSI operatives to be activated and utilized.

Even so, with the burden of all this in mind, Günther's first American SSI operative would become his own little blond nice, Heidi Winters, at her youthful age of sixteen.

Heidi had been orphaned upon the death of her American mother and German born father in 1929. She was returned to Germany and as her only living relative, Uncle Günther had become her guardian.

As a result of Günther's work, Heidi was raised exclusively around adults and slowly became aware of Uncle Günther's work with the Secret Police.

Her maturity and intelligence amazed her Uncle as she developed an incredible interest in his work.

Because her German was as impeccable as her English, she was frequently introduced, in jest to his associates, as his future American spy child.

Heidi was constantly moved around with Uncle Günther on his European assignments and she quickly began acquiring French and Dutch language skills in addition to dialects of Danish and Norwegian.

Her bond and allegiance to Uncle Günther grew very strong during these travels as she relied on him for everything.

Heidi naively admired her Uncle for his achievements with the SS and his new assignments in Himmler's Schutzstaffel Infiltration, not really knowing the sinister things he was actually responsible for.

But to her, it only mattered that he gave her the family that she so longingly needed at that delicate time in her life.

For Günther, however, she was a critical tool in his own future with Himmler. He knew her father's Aryan bloodline made her a Poster Child of the New Third Reich.

As such, he had no trouble convincing the SS-Reichfuhrer Himmler that Heidi was the perfect instrument to serve him in carrying out their flawlessly planned subterfuge for SSI. Himmler had always admired the concept of pure Aryan families and now together, Günther and his niece could carry his ideal into America for the sake of the Reich.

With Heidi joining him as his young innocent niece, Günther could believably maintain an upstanding image in his new homeland. A cover that would assure the Fuhrer he would always be ready when future covert SSI operations needed to be activated in the United States.

Günther had always loved the folklore of great passenger ships of the seas and had often excited Heidi about the stories of the Titanic.

Their trip to New York City had to begin in Denmark. Fictitiously, it was Anderssen's home country and they used that fact to establish their detailed cover to protect them from detection by Germany's own Abwehr Agents and Gestapo.

An organization already thought to be partially infiltrated by British MI doubles and clandestine Soviet Bolsheviks.

So Günther decided to book the outbound trip from Copenhagen via Brest in France on the great White Star Line's 'Olympic'.

Günther intrigued Heidi about the story of how the original contracts were given to the Harland & Wolff shipyards in Great Britain by White Star Lines to build three Olympic-class super liners. The first of which would be the Olympic.

The keel was laid in December 1908 and three years later she set sail on her maiden voyage. In March 1909, however, the keels were laid for two more of these grand ocean liners.

One was the Britannic, but the ship of true tragic folklore was the Titanic, and on its maiden voyage April 10, 1912 she struck a massive iceberg and sank in the cold dark North Atlantic, late on the night of April 15, 1912.

Günther explained to her that after an investigation of why the Titanic sank, a lot was learned about the construction flaws. As a result, work was put on hold for completing the sister ship, Britannic for over a year.

And as further precaution, the Olympic was immediately recalled to return to Liverpool, England where she was completely refitted.

New watertight bulkheads were built to extend all the way up to the main and top decks. Even the hull was re-fitted with a double skin of steel. All of this work was easy to do on Britannic because she was still in a dry dock frame and under final construction.

Unfortunately, the Olympic had to be taken out of service and was forced to remain in port for over six months before she was able to return to sea.

The Britannic on the other hand set sail in February 1914 and made several uneventful Atlantic crossings. Near the end of the Great War however, a proud German U-boat Kapitanleutnant of the Kaisers Reichsmarine sunk the ship on a misty November day in 1916. And so in the end, it was ironic, that the first ship of the three great liners of this century became the last to survive all of them.

Now, after twenty-one years of service and over three-hundred crossings of the Atlantic Ocean, Günther and Heidi were about to board the last surviving liner of the trinity, the White Star Line's Olympic, and thus set sail on their own portentous journey into America's heartland.

Chapter 3

The Arrival

It was mid-afternoon on February 10th before Günther Anderssen and Heidi Winters finally arrived from New York in the overnight Pullman car attached to the Southern Railways 'Carolina Crescent'.

They had completed their Atlantic crossing in seven days and after two more days on the train were now beginning to show the extreme fatigue of their trip.

Günther had made extensive plans before the trip through his bank contacts at the Montebatten und Reichbank Bank in Zurich, to have a discreet local banker in Asheville, a small town located in the Carolina Mountains, make arrangements to assist him with his massive investments.

As expected, one of the associates at the Bank and his secretary were on hand to greet him and Heidi as their Pullman car arrived at the small, but private Biltmore Station.

A colored Southern Railway Station porter placed the removable steps on the station platform under the Pullman's exit door and Heidi jumped down first with Günther just behind her.

"Were so glad to finally meet you both, Mr. Anderssen . . ." Bob Moseby said in a lazy drawl, typical of the North Carolinian accents found in the region.

Bob reached out and grabbed for Heidi's hand helping her down from the steps as she looked around at the old English Styled Station House.

Attempting to imply that the little town had as much sophistication as larger towns in the South, Moseby then added.

"We were concerned, that we had come to the wrong station. You know of course that we have two stations here in Asheville."

Günther returned his welcome in English with an undefined European emphasis in his response.

" Truthfully, Mr. Moseby, I really had no idea that this little town was large enough for even one Railway Station!"

" Now that's a real hoot, sure 'nuff Mr. Anderssen", replied Moseby as he reached out to shake his hand.

"A little town like Asheville here, with two Railway Stations. Well actually, this here place is called Biltmore. It's a independent village from Asheville . . . built by the great Vanderbilt family back at the turn of the century. Their people were originally from over in your neck of the woods, I believe, Mr. Anderssen."

Günther quickly responded to see where he was going with this so-called friendly repartee.

"And where, exactly, do you think I'm from for that matter, Mr. Moseby?"

After a short pause for effect, while looking at Heidi's long blond hair, Moseby turned back to Günther.

"Why I suppose y'all are from Holland or such, Mr. Anderssen, is that right?"

Realizing he probably meant nothing from the remark, Günther made light of his mistake, as he laughed and moved Heidi along the Station Platform toward the luggage cart.

" Well, now Mr. Moseby, at least you're on the right Continent. Heidi and I are from Denmark. It's actually a bit further north and east than Holland, and a lot dryer there most of the time."

"We don't need dykes to hold back the North Sea, like they do around Amsterdam and the lowlands of the Vanders people, as you now call the American Vanderbilts."

As Bob Moseby, was quickly tipping the Porters and pointing out the location of his car for them to load Mr. Anderssen's luggage, he replied smiling at Günther and turning to his silent secretary.

"Well now, that is funny how we tend to forget how many countries there are over there across the Atlantic. But, Ursula here comes from that part of the world herself, and she can probably even speak a little of that Danish, Mr. Anderssen."

Suddenly, Bob Moseby's secretary Ursula Vidda became animated, due to being put on the spot and not properly being introduced.

She spoke with an obvious Scandinavian inflection in her precise English, first to Bob then turning to Günther.

" As you know Mr. Moseby, my mother is from Norway, not Denmark, however I can speak a little of both."

At that moment, the youthful Heidi surprised everyone and turned to greet Ursula in perfectly accented Norwegian.

"It is a pleasure to meet you, Miss Ursula!"

Just as quickly Ursula looked directly at Heidi and spoke in a soft Norwegian tone to address them both.

"And, it's a very great pleasure to meet both you and your Uncle, Heidi!"

Frustrated, at his lack of linguistic ability, Bob Moseby hastily jumped into the conversation.

" Hey! Hey now, y'all! That's enough! I give up! I can't figure out what y'all's saying or what's going on here!"

"Ursula, you've got to switch them back to the local talk around here or were never going to get them to where were supposed to be by sunset."

Günther jumped in and responded with a sense of satisfaction at the Bank's effort to make them feel comfortable.

"Well, I must say that I am rather impressed with the international diversity that you and your Bank have presented to us already today, way up here in the mountains of North Carolina. And Ursula, is truly a refreshing surprise. I believe we are really going to like this place just fine after all. It feels a little bit like home, already!"

Günther turned to Heidi, who was now somewhat relaxed and clearly pleased that she had found a female friend to talk to. "Am I correct, Heidi?"

"Absolutely, Uncle Günther, I do like Asheville. It's rather beautiful up here, almost like the fjords of Norway with these big mountains all around."

Bob Moseby was now smiling with a sense of accomplishment as he stood at the rear bumper of the big black 1932 Buick that the Bank's president Mr.Leonard had loaned him for the VIP's arrival and pick up.

The colored Porters had now finished loading the luggage into the trunk and Heidi had already joined Ursula in the back seat. They seemed to be deep in conversation, but in English this time.

Mr. Anderssen stood at the open front passenger door and waited, while looking off in the far distance. He seemed to be thinking about something important as he looked to the mountains west of Asheville and the distant peak of Mt. Pisgah. The soft orange and red clouds were beginning to form in a distant sunset over the purple hillsides, now starving for sunlight.

The Bank's president, Mr.Leonard, had been told by his Swiss Bank contacts in New York, that very seldom would people having this much wealth, come to the financially depressed little valley of Asheville these days, at least to live permanently.

Mr.Leonard had also advised Bob before he left, that these people and this situation was a real opportunity for the Bank, so don't blow it.

Bob Moseby had been an officer of the Western Carolina Industrial Bank & Trust for the last two years and Mr.Leonard had finally begun to give him a longer leash with certain customers every few months, but this customer was very big for the bank's future portfolio and very special for his career.

He was now thinking to himself. Ever since 1929, independently owned State Banks in the general areas of Appalachia and in particular Western North Carolina had been struggling to restructure and build back from the ravages of the Great Depression. Only Federally Chartered Banks and a few small State Chartered Banks survived, and the still under capitalized WCIB&T was one of those.

Now, with Mr. Anderssen's arrival and his potential investments, Mr. Leonard's WCIB&T might just have the financial strength to complete with the bigger State and Federal Banks out of Charlotte and Raleigh.

In fact, Mr. Leonard had told Bob, with Mr. Anderssen's, help they would soon have money to loan for the first time since even he could remember.

Only time would tell, Bob reflected silently, if they could become a big player with these new funds for business development in the local economy.

But at least they now had a chance.

Plus, with this new financial strength, Asheville's local politicians could begin to attract more Government Work Projects from Washington into the region, to further raise the living standards back up.

Again he was still deep in these imaginings when Mr. Anderssen suddenly broke into his thoughts, "How soon can we get going? I need to freshen up and make a few calls before the operators go home and close down the switch board around here."

"Oh, you won't have to worry about that up at the Grand Park, Mr. Anderssen. They burn the lights all night at that first class Hotel. You can call to New York for as long as you like. It's got the best of everything, for special folks like yourselves. We do get a lot of High Rollers up here in the summer season and the Grand Park or the Battery Place Hotel has to keep 'em happy. They've got the best facilities in the entire Western Region of the State right here and Mr. Leonard has personally made sure y'all have everything you need during your stay at the Grand Park Inn."

The porters collected their tips and closed the trunk as Bob moved into the driver's seat, turned to Heidi and Ursula in the back seat, and spoke. "Well were ready to go, y'all."

Mr. Anderssen entered the car and both men closed their doors, as Bob put the big Buick in gear and moved away from the Biltmore Station.

They turned and headed across the empty railroad tracks and up the hill along Biltmore Avenue as the lights of Asheville's downtown cityscape came into view.

The car continued on for several more minutes and onto Charlotte Street, before they could glimpse the looming lady in the distance.

On a gradual hillside just above them, the Grand Park Inn came into full view as the boundary of sunlight and clouds seemed to open for her, then fade into purple.

Finally, much higher up the hill, they arrived at the Hotel's vantagepoint. It's cherished overlook allowed the last moments of light in the western sunset to be seen over Mt. Pisgah, then in an instant, it was night in the valleys all around Asheville.

Günther and Heidi were home.

Chapter 4

The First Year

Even though the Grand Park Inn was initially a temporary home for their first few months in Asheville, it grew to almost nineteen months as their new home plans evolved for a permanent location. The Inn of course, remained a beautiful place to stay while the detailed and constantly modified plans were set in motion to establish Günther Anderssen's home-site in the mountains above the city.

During the early spring of 1933, several lavish parties at the Grand Hotel had allowed both Günther Anderssen and Little Miss Heidi Winters, as the maids and bellboys around the hotel's grounds like to call her, to develop a curious group of very rich friends and politicians from around the Region.

One such man, Edward Wellington, introduced to Günther by Mr. Leonard as the Grand Art Deco Architect of Asheville, became a quick associate. Flush with Günther's investment money, the Western Carolina Industrial Bank & Trust and Mr. Leonard were freely loaning money to build new commercial and industrial projects all over Asheville and the mountainous area around Buncombe County.

A direct beneficiary of this financial windfall became the building trades and especially, Edward Wellington's architectural firm.

The tract they purchased for the estate was forty-four acres high atop Sunset Mountain, below which the Grand Park Inn was located. The tract faced eastward toward the Atlantic coastline of North Carolina.

Mr. Anderssen had stressed that the home's front windows must catch the morning sun.

So, Wellington complied and faced the main house toward the Chunns Cove Valley, rather than viewing it to the west and down to the valleys on the Asheville side of the great mountain.

It was to be hidden on a majestic ridge, sometimes called Patton Mountain, like a stone Medieval Fortress within a grove of tall Norwegian Pines strategically arranged to surround the main house.

Günther Anderssen continued to develop business associates throughout the Western North Carolina and Southeastern States, eventually expanding into the Midwest as the year went along.

He was able to become especially friendly with several banking groups in the areas of North Georgia, Northeastern Alabama and Eastern Tennessee that were highly segregationist and clearly anti-semitic.

In fact, two particular Banks located in East Tennessee had board members that were secret leaders of the local KKK. As such, they had their own private detectives or security police, as Günther was told, to assist them in protecting their regional areas from the influx or increased influence of undesirables; Coloreds or Jews.

These so called enforcers were purposely not active members of the KKK, in order to avoid the attention of the FBI or other Federal Agencies placed as government watchdogs on the Southern Boys. But in all cases, once these Bankers confidentially understood Günther's position and the kind of assistance he could offer their Banks, he was brought into their closest trust and clearly offered the services of their covert enforcers for any special situations that might develop in the near future, in particularly the Knoxville and Upper East Tennessee region or any nearby areas within the Southeast.

As the year evolved, his travels continued to be carefully planned to disguise any clandestine meetings with Americans sympathetic to the new Germany under Hitler.

These contacts allowed him to develop a network of potential agents and government moles that could later be used for future SSI activities.

Although the calm before the storm in America made everyone upbeat and complacent in the revitalized communities around the Southeast and in particular, Asheville, Günther knew that events on the continent of Europe were now evolving at a furious pace and principally within Germany itself.

Looking back, 1933 had been a very momentous year for Günther Anderssen in America and the consolidation of power in Germany under the new Chancellor, Adolf Hitler.

Horst Deeke had written to him regularly on the great changes taking place in Germany. The Communists had been rounded-up and arrested by the thousands after the Reichstag fire on February 27th, and Goering and Hitler had agreed to withdraw Germany from the League of Nations, clearly allowing them to expand the German Reichwehr and the Luftwaffe.

And now, because of mounting political pressures and Hitler's need to consolidate the party, Horst had told Günther that a major planning meeting for SSI operatives in Germany would take place in Berlin sometime in May.

Günther knew that very few people in the world and especially in 1930's America, understood what was happening by the middle of 1934 to make it the final turning point for Germany. But Horst had told Günther it was coming.

And so, by early July 1934 a secret document arrived revealing the outcome.

Horst explained the situation to Günther within the detailed document sealed in a secure air pouch and delivered to Asheville via Günther's bankers from Geneva, Switzerland on July 3rd, 1934:

First and foremost he wrote, the Fuhrer wanted German Austria returned to the great German Motherland. Dollfuss, the Chancellor must yield or Germany must make him yield in the most absolute way.

The Fuhrer then stated to us boldly,

"Austria and Germany must be one."

Günther had known that Chancellor Dollfuss of Austria had only recently signed a pact with Hungary and Italy's Mussolini, called the Rome Protocols, which suggested that all three would protect each other in the event of a threat to any one of them.

He further understood, at this stage in Germany's growing power, that Italy although a dictatorship was still refusing to join Hitler in his future plans for Europe.

Horst then added a second key point in his detailed description:

The Fuhrer then slammed his hand on the table and stated to all of us,

"It is clear to me and all of my true SS supporters here in this room and elsewhere, that we cannot continue to allow the Brown Shirts of the S.A. to expand their own form of social revolution in Germany any further. Roehm must be stopped, now!"

"We all knew that Hitler's conviction was final as he raised his voice and again shouted to make his point of merging the pre-Wehrmacht Armies of Germany:"

"He has now recruited and built a force of over three million S.A. members. These men must be merged into the Reichwehr and our own SS should continue to be used to control all of those Armies.

Otherwise they themselves will make a conspiracy against us. We must act first and without clemency. They have gone beyond pillaging just the Jews and the profiteers as we had planned. Now they are willing to destroy our core supporters, the lifeblood of das Vaterland. They see their revolution as a never ending process, attacking the privileged classes and established society of German Bankers and Industrialists, people that will assure assets and support for das Vaterland's future growth over all of Europe."

Günther Anderssen had known Roehm well. He had been Hitler's Chief of Staff of the S.A., the Brown Shirt Army of Germany for seven long years. They had been together since the beginning of the Munich Putsch.

Now as he read Horst's details, Günther realized what had driven Hitler into his rage; the Fuhrer had lost control of his own man and possibly the entire Nazi Socialist Party. Something drastic had to be done.

Finally, Horst explained that the possibility even existed that certain members of the German Parliament at the Riechstag as well as the old German Military of the Reichwehr might try to side with Roehm, just to destabilize the Fuhrer at the moment when he was most vulnerable.

"We all knew that it was not just the S.A. and the Army that had to be under Hitler's absolute control, but this event would now force the total annihilation of all his enemies and everything must happen with simultaneous precision throughout Germany, in one night."

"And so on the night of June 25th, 1934, all the Reichwehr Generals right up to General von Blomberg himself were told to confine all German Army Troops to their barracks until further orders from the Fuhrer. Ammunition and weapons were issued only to SS Storm Troopers and SS Black Shirt Regulars as well as my own SS Commandos."

"Events on the 29th moved very quickly and actually set everything in motion."

First, I and my commando trained SS Storm Troopers flew with the Fuhrer as security to Godesberg where we met with Reichsminister Goebbels."

"Upon our arrival, Goebbels falsely informed the Fuhrer as we had planned, that an impending mutiny was underway in Berlin and that a Brown Shirt rising was taking place under command of Karl Ernst, Roehm's next in command, in Bremen and Hamburg."

"At this point we began our hasty journey with the Fuhrer to Munich."

"At 0400 Hours, the Fuhrer, his immediate staff and myself with a small SS Commando unit arrived secretly at the designated airstrip near Munich in Hitler's long range four engined Condor Focke-Wulf."

"Prior to our arrival however, the Fuhrer had instructed Reichsminister Herman Goering to take control in Berlin and SS-Reichfuhrer Himmler to suppress any insurrection throughout the populace of Germany."

"The Fuhrer and my twelve man SS Security Squad along with Reichsminister Goebbels and myself, quickly drove our convoy of three bulletproof Mercedes Command Cars to the Brown House in central Munich."

"After summoning the leaders of the local S.A. to his presence, the Fuhrer had me secure them and place them under arrest. Another plane arriving at the airstrip at 0430 Hours brought my additional heavily armed twenty man SS-Wiking Commando Unit."

"Then together we all proceeded with two more armored vehicles to rendezvous with the Fuhrer's convoy for his protection on the trip out to Wiessee. Once there, and without incident, Roehm and his personal staff were arrested and returned by us to Munich for imprisonment."

"Sometime after noon, the full-scale executions were ordered by the Fuhrer."

"By the time it had ended in Munich, Berlin, Hamburg and throughout the rest of the Reich, twenty-four hours later, I estimated between five and six thousand S.A. Officers, Brown Shirt Leaders, the previous Chancellor of Germany, Herr Schleicher and his wife, as well as Karl Ernst and finally Roehm himself were all liquidated."

"Reichsminister Goebbels called it, the Night of the Long Knives. Without any prior knowledge, it was simply a massacre that ended the moment we brought the Fuhrer by air back to Berlin at about 0100 Hours on the morning of July 1st."

"Later that afternoon the Fuhrer, again as we had planned, appeared on the Balcony of the Chancellery to greet the massive crowds that had been gathering all day as word spread throughout Germany. I'm sure you heard something on the radio over there in America, since we made sure every World News Services Agency had their mikes turned on for him."

"You will probably see the movie newsreels in a few days as well, since we had news cameras rolling, and made sure that his appearance was purposely disheveled."

"Then he began. He was magnificent as he triumphantly spoke in the most compelling argument imaginable, while everyone listened in awe."

Horst then gave Günther his own personal account that the World Press failed to see as the true defining moment of the German Third Reich:

"Yesterday, some that were among us, tried to take the Reich and destroy it." The Fuhrer paused purposely to get just the right intonation, as he raised his voice higher,

"Today, the Reich stands as it will for the next One-Thousand Years."

"Sounds of the crowd's acclamations were deafening, as our beloved Berliners standing below in the streets saw him clearly as the intended victim, but now also, the victorious savior of Germany."

"The necessity," he stated as he looked to the cameras for effect, *"for acting with lightning speed, meant that in this decisive hour for Germany,"*

"I had very few men with me." Again his timing was perfect as he waited for just the right moment to continue.

"Although only a few days before, I had been prepared to exercise clemency, at this hour there was no place for any such consideration. Mutinies are suppressed in accordance with laws of iron, which are eternally the same. In this hour I was responsible for the fate of the German people, and thereby I became the Supreme Adjudicator of the German people."

"Again I watched him like the statue of a Roman Dictator as he paused to hear the roar of the crowd,"

"I did not wish to deliver up the Young Reich to the fate of the Old Reich. I gave the order to shoot those who were the ringleaders in this treason."

As the deafening yells and cheers became an almost continuous sound, he concluded in his strongest tone of voice, *"In the end, I further gave the order to burn out down to the raw flesh, the ulcers of this poisoning of the well in our domestic life, and of the poisoning of the outside world".*

That day stuck like the long knife itself in Günther's mind forever. With the Fuhrer now in absolute control of the Military and the Government of Germany, he would no longer be needed there.

From now on he would live in America to make SSI's dream become a reality. Yet somehow he knew, deep in his heart, that he would probably never see his beloved Germany ever again.

Chapter 5

Crystale

Heidi meanwhile had turned seventeen and began evolving her own unique lifestyle at the Grand Hotel, separate from Günther's. She had developed a close friendship with the several members of the Big Bands that came in from out of town and played for the parties she loved to attend during the Summer Season.

Her beautiful long silk dresses from Paris and her skilled European dance styles caught their attention, as she immediately became the newest débutante of the Grand Park Inn.

Occasionally, when she would sneak in during band rehearsals, the white band members would dance with her, showing her sleek new steps and moves from the sophisticated Big City driven American Swing dance styles.

In the process, a twenty-two year old professional dance instructor from New York was hired by the management in March of the next year, to help the Grand Park during its new tourist season for the summer of 1934. The new arrival, Crystale Marsalis, quickly became Heidi's newest confidant, and her story became one of Heidi's favorite legends.

It seems that Crystale's parents had created a clandestine marriage that was annulled by a Catholic Priest at the request of her father's family, just after Crystale was born. Her mother, Renée, had been a beautiful dance instructor at the notorious Lido Nightclub in Paris, France. While Crystale's father, Fajardo Peron Munoz on the other hand, was an outwardly reserved professional politician stationed in Paris.

He worked for the Imperial Embassy of the King of Spain.

Fajardo was instantly seduced by Renée and without his family's permission married her in Paris. The King recalled him, however, after the annulment and Renée was left alone in Paris, to care for Crystale.

Due to her limited financial situation and her constant work at the nightclub, the child was brought up in the seedy underworld of Paris street life. So, up to the age of six, Crystale grew up and actually fell in love with the bizarre underworld of her mother's life. It was finally the pressures of Fajardo's family in Madrid as well as the ransom money offered secretly to Renée, that ultimately persuaded her mother to relinquished Crystale to her father's family. Unhappily, Crystale agreed to live in the massive family hacienda in Madrid, Spain, until she was sixteen.

Her father's infatuation for the exotic Renée, however, had never died. So unexpectedly, on her sixteenth birthday, her father decided to return to Paris and agreed to allow Crystale to accompany him. It was billed as a short diplomatic trip, but the Lido in Paris became his first stop. With Crystale at his side he stayed all night at the nightclub, drunk and mesmerized by Renée, and all but forgetting about his innocent daughter Crystale.

For the next several nights they frantically searched for Crystale, but it was too late. She had met a very unusual mulatto colored man from America. He was an accomplished Jazz musician named Bébe Marsalis that had come to the Lido on a summer fling. Crystale was immediately infatuated with him and stayed with him in his hotel room until Renée found her lying nude in his bed some days later. When Crystale tried hopelessly to have her mother explain to Fajardo that she wanted to stay in Paris, for just a few weeks, he refused to listen. As she expected, her father threatened to force her to return with him to Madrid.

In pure rebellion, to him alone, Crystale then chose to marry the young colored musician, to spite her father, even though she didn't really love Bébe.

Faced with his child's ugly rebellion and pressured by The King to return back to Spain himself, due to civil unrest, Fajardo sadly disowned Crystale to avoid any further embarrassment to his proud Spanish heritage and that of his Munoz family name.

Crystale confused and disillusioned with both her father and her mother, left Paris and went to New York with her new husband.

With open intermarriage considered illegal at that time in America, Crystale was forced to become a professional dancer at the famous Cotton Club of Harlem, in downtown New York in order to be near Bébe.

Finally, Bébe left Crystale for no reason, and after that, she began touring the county with Big City Swing Bands, just to stay even financially.

At twenty-two, and after six long years on the road touring with many one-night-stands, Crystale Marsalis was ready to settle down to her new more laid-back lifestyle in the mountains of Asheville.

Now, she would just be known only as Crystale. And Heidi had become the perfect friend to make all of this work out.

By the end of the Summer Tourist Season in late September '34, Heidi and Crystale had become regular dance floorflushers at the evening parties that filled the schedule of the Great Inn. Crystale's New York styled shorter silk dresses, cut to above her calves, were more body hugging and immediately influenced Heidi to adopt them, to accentuate her dance moves more freely.

That year, the management had booked six top entertainment groups like, Tommy Dorsey, the Sentimental Gentleman of Swing and his incredible fourteen-member band. The Dorsey band alone attracted high rollers from as far away as Chicago and Atlanta, while both Heidi and Crystale got to know most of the band's best musicians and singers over their three week stay.

Then on the last weekend in September, a Kansas City based band caught everyone by surprise. The management at the Great Inn had booked them because the Band's own nightclub in Kansas City, had been shut down by the local police for two weeks and they were trying desperately to fill in.

It was the last major dance weekend before the season ended and as usual on the appointed welcoming afternoon, both Heidi and Crystale, adorned in their sleek silver ballroom dresses and were on hand at the front lobby to welcome them.

Heidi saw the three gleaming Chryslers first, as she and Crystale ran across the pavement bricks of the Hotel's massive automobile entrance, to greet them. Heidi rushed to beat one of the Inn's colored doormen, who knew both the girls well, and whisked out of her way as she past him. She wanted to be the first to greet the obviously renowned band members, and made it to the front passenger door of the first black car, gleaming with freshly polished chrome flowing down its body.

As she gripped the door handle and opened it, without any thought, she immediately hugged the big man as he emerged with a surprised smile spreading from ear to ear.

"Welcome to the Land of the Sky", were her excited words as Heidi stepped back and realized they were all colored men. Crystale having run up at the same time shouted even louder,

"Oh my God, it's The Bennie Moten Band, wow, are we in for some great cutt'in butter swing tonight."

By this time, everyone was emerging from the cars as the emotional welcome had them curious as to what all the commotion was about.

Then the big colored man, still holding his smile from Heidi's enthusiastic hug, added, " I guess this must be the finest welcome I've ever had, by two of the prettiest white ladies I believe I've ever seen."

Suddenly both the Inn's uniformed colored Doormen, realizing the situation in front of them, ran to the driver of the first car and begin an animated argument that they were purposely trying to keep quite from the girls.

Immediately Crystale picked up on it, as Heidi just watched in amazement as fifteen of the most well dressed colored men she had ever seen, stepped out of the black cars and onto the brick pavement stones of the Grand Park's Main Auto Lobby.

Crystale then looked at Heidi in disappointment, "They can't get out of their cars here Heidi, they're colored. They will have to use the lower entrance for the Hotel employees, and they can't walk through the Hotel's Lobby either."

Heidi had always thought Swing Bands were only made up of white people, and she had always loved the Jazz music on the radio, but she was not aware that most of her favorite sounds were actually from colored bands. Now, that fact became her reality as she shouted to both the Hotel's Doormen.

"Stop, you are not going to humiliate this wonderful band, you hear me!"

People near the Lobby entrance were now beginning to accumulate and jam the entrance as they tried to see what was going on.

Just then, Sammy Sinclair, the Assistant Manager flew out between the massive double doors and quickly ran over to Heidi.

"Miss Heidi, please," he begged her, "the Hotel has special rules for this kind of matter and we must follow those rules. These are colored men and we will take very good care of them at the lower entrance, but not here at our main guest entrance."

Heidi quickly snapped back at him in direct contrast to the Little Heidi he had known up to that moment.

"What are you saying, Mr. Sinclair, that these men can't receive the same treatment that all the White Swing Bands, we have had all summer long, have had?"

Heidi spoke almost in tears she was so energized.

"Every time this season, Crystale and I have met them, right here at this Lobby entrance. We have never had a problem before, and now you're going to send these well-dressed men down to the back door, just because of their skin color! I can't believe the cruelty of your actions, Mr. Sinclair!"

Sinclair was stunned, but held his composure as the entire band began slowly getting back into their cars and compiling with the Doormen's instructions.

He tried to speak calmly as she glared at him.

"Miss Heidi, I just work here and this is the policy of the Hotel, it's a tradition here in the South to enforce social separation of Whites and Coloreds, I'm sorry we didn't have time to tell you they were a colored band before this happened. It's so embarrassing ma'am, I may even lose my job over this, Miss Heidi. Please don't make it any worse."

Crystale came over to Heidi before she could speak. "Hey kiddo, he's right, we really don't want all these wonderful people to get in any more trouble with the social misfits that make these crazy rules."

" Let's just go downstairs and give them a bigger welcome, what do you say, mon Cheri!"

Crystale then looked at Mr. Sinclair as she added, "Besides, we love old Sammy here, and he could get into some very serious trouble with the big manger on this one, so let's let it go."

By now over fifty guests were filling the porch area and milling around the main doors waiting for someone to do something or at least resolve the obvious colored incident.

Heidi looked around and decided to change her tone as she watched the cars begin to drive off to the lower parking entrance before she spoke.

"Crystale, who was that happy faced man I gave the big hug to anyway?"

Crystale clearly excited to tell her, just smiled, "That young lady, was the man that wrote One O'clock Jump, that was Count Basie, the absolute smoothest and easiest keyman in Swing or Jazz for that matter, and you just wait 'til tonight, he's going to rock this place into heaven! And Sammy here owes me a dance. Right, Sammy!"

"Yes ma'am, Miss Crystale," he answered in renewed relief, "and you can be sure I'll be there tonight to pay up, come hell or high water!"

Realizing the crowd was about to leave since everything appeared to go back to normal, Heidi made one last move, as she caught everyone's attention.

"Hey everybody, we were just welcoming the band for tonight, it's Bennie Moten and Count Basie, so get ready for one of the best Swing and Jazz Bands you have every heard."

As Heidi turned back to see the last car drive off, someone back behind her in the now shrinking crowd at the doorway started clapping.

Then several others joined in, as suddenly everyone was clapping, when a tall man in the back of the crowd shouted at the top of his voice, Bravo, young Lady, Bravo, as others echoed his feelings and joined in also, Bravo, Heidi, Bravo!

Heidi simply turned back to them, slowly admiring their response and gave everyone her now famous Grand Park Inn dance floor curtsy and bow.

That night became the ultimate image that Heidi drew from.

At once, it became clear in her mind, a dream that she would eventually use to create her own masterpiece, a nightclub and a dinner club that would rival even the art deco clubs of Paris and the Big Band Dance Halls of New York.

Her club, she envisioned, would be smaller than the massive dance halls, hosting only the best sounds in Swing and Jazz, eventually becoming the center of her social world. She would call it, The Sky Club, in honor of this beautiful valley in the Land of the Sky she had now adopted as her own.

Heidi knew she could create a truly renowned nightspot here in the mountains that would make it the choice of both the rich and the famous from all over the South, as well as any of Günther's friends that joined him from Europe.

Count Basie and Heidi became fast friends that evening.

First she reintroduced herself and made sure Sammy got all of the Band Members separate lodgings at the dormitories, down the hill from the Main Hotel. The facilities were meek, but acceptable and were often used by out of town employees, hired in the mid-summer rush. Heidi then got her special friends in the Hotel's maid service to put a welcoming fruit basket in every room, plus some fresh bed linens.

By the time the early rehearsals were finished everyone had been introduced and the evening was beginning to turn into the best event of the season.

The Hotel's ballroom filled up early after the dinner hour. By Nine PM the place was packed with hotel guests and the elite of Asheville that could afford the price of admission to the last gala event of the Grand Hotel's regular season.

The elaborate room was awash in glittering ball lighting and soft ambient light beams from the art deco sconces spaced a few feet apart midway up on the twenty-foot walls, while shimmering accent lighting flushed downward into the spacious dancefloor from the high ceiling.

It felt like the intimate atmosphere of a large nightclub, yet its massive hardwood dance floor with table linens and decorative table lamps all around the wide perimeter made it easy for everyone to get up and have a good time.

Thick drapes covered the massive windows that saw Mt. Pisgah in daylight on the west end of the room, while the stage was almost a surreal arena filled with two opposing grand pianos and orchestra stands for all the instrumentalists, including a microphone for a young colored singer named Billie.

The rhythm section was clearly the heart of the Bennie Moten and Count Basie band, and real style dancers just loved Basie's smooth keyboard arrangements as he played that easy swing.

Bennie was a piano player himself, but he clearly recognized the big man's talent at the keys and it was understood that the Count's arrangements drove the band.

Heidi would always watch the drummers closely in the Swing Bands that had visited the Hotel over the past months, because good dancers relied on those guys to carry the right feeling.

She and Crystale both disliked the heavy thumping of the base drum that had been typical of most bands during the summer.

But the Count's drummer, Jo Jones was a master of the light relaxed, fluid and shimmering wave of percussion that the girl's needed to show off their dance steps.

Jo even told Crystale, he'd once been a Tap Dancer himself and because of that, he knew how to get the best effect on his two high hats and ride out the big cymbals, just so the band's soloists could slip in and talk to the dancers with their Horns or Saxes, whenever they felt like it.

Heidi saw this as pure artistry at work as she and Crystale would move from one new partner to the next, jitterbugs with their hips and swingeroos with their legs, as the men on the sidelines would call out, while they watched the true dancers in envy.

The girls would show their new partners moves and sometimes they would learn a few new ones themselves, as some of the band members got out on the floor for their Kansas City dance solos.

It was an incredible evening and even Uncle Günther, who had just arrived back from his long trip to San Francisco and the West Coast that afternoon, came down for a final Lindy Hop on the dance floor with Heidi, before it ended just after midnight.

Günther couldn't get to sleep that night as he tried to adjust back into Eastern Time from his extensive journey to the West Coast and the Mid-West by train. His mind drifted back to that ominous day in Berlin five months before, as he sat back in his adopted lounge chair in the hotel suite, and relaxed in thought.

The three objectives that Horst outlined in his dispatches on July 3rd had actually come to pass, as he had foretold. The Night of the Long Knives had consolidated Hitler's power with the Reichwehr and it's Generals, merging them with the Brown Shirts to become the new German Wehrmacht. While the SS Storm Troopers and SS Black Shirt Regulars merged into an even stronger and more virulent SS organization, adding the Gestapo's power under Reichfuhrer Himmler to fully control all elements of Military, Domestic, Juden Concentration Camps, as well as Protection of the Fuhrer above all else.

The Reichstag and Parliament were now under the absolute domination of Chancellor Hitler, and although his original rise to power came from the people freely electing him, he had always lived under the influence of the right wing coalition to maintain his control. But, that was now dismantled, and at Marshall Hindenburg's death earlier in the year, the old Democratic Republic had died with him.

The New Nazi Order embraced all of das Vaterland now, and the hearts and minds of all of it's people. The Fuhrer had become the Absolute Sovereign Power over all of Germany.

The last element of the three, Günther thought, but in the Fuhrer's mind his most precious was Austria, and although it was yet to merge with das Vaterland, the events directed by the Fuhrer and Himmler in July, had assured the eventual success of that goal in the very near future.

Günther had been informed through covert communiqués from Horst early on July 26th, that a clandestine group of SS Commandos disguised as armed rebels, had successfully assassinated Austrian Chancellor Dollfuss inside the Austrian Chancellery.

Once his replacement, pro-Nazi Chancellor Rintelen establish his own prerogatives, Günther knew, it would only be a matter of time before Germany and Austria were one, at long last.

Finally, feeling the physical effects of Heidi's last Gala event, the draining activities of this travels, and at long last a sense of comfort in knowing das Vaterland's future was in good hands, Günther adjusted his position in his soft leather chair drifting slowly off into a deep relaxing sleep.

Chapter 6

The Move

By the end of October the House was ready and the move from the Grand Park Inn was well underway for Günther and Heidi. It was sad leaving the beautiful lady, as they often called the Great Inn, but it was even sadder that Crystale's contract was up and she might not be back until the spring, or in Heidi's mind she might be lost forever.

All was in readiness on October 15th, as Mr. Edward Wellington and his staff at the architectural firm, personally awaited the arrival of Günther and Heidi at the Chateau on the mountain top, for their final walk through before turning it over to the excited couple.

The engineers and several managers from local tradesmen as well as suppliers were also on the premises to demonstrate the special modern appliances that Günther had requested for the Chateau's functionality.

Mr. Wellington had his architectural team consider many eventualities for the property. As such, he had arranged a complete external support system assuring that the Chateau would be fully independent of any local electrical or water utilities, if the need arose, on their isolated mountain ridge high above the City.

Prior to 1934, even telephone service had not arrived at the uppermost levels of Patton Mountain, so a special diesel generator system and radio transmission shack had been designed at the rear of the Chateau to provide direct communication to the Asheville fire and police stations down below, in case of emergencies.

And further assurance for their safety was derived from the fact that the single-lane Towne Mountain Road in front of the estate had been freshly paved before the winter set in, all the way from Asheville to the Blue Ridge Parkway's eastern entrance.

Günther Anderssen and Heidi Winters stood in anticipation at the Auto Lobby Entrance of the Hotel as Bob Moseby and Mr. Leonard drove up in two of the Bank's brand new black Buicks, to escort them to the final walk through of their new home.

Behind them, the Hotel's porch was lined with well wishers for the send off. Their friends at the Hotel from Managers to House Maids and Doormen, and even the Hotel Porters stood at the ready to see off two of the Hotel's most celebrated and long staying guests.

In the background, even further beside two packed suitcases, stood Crystale, as she began to contemplate her own future back on the road again with one-night-stands and without the close companionship of Heidi.

Just then, realizing there was plenty of room in the transport caravan provided by Uncle Günther's bankers at the Western Carolina Industrial Bank & Trust, Heidi made up her mind. Günther had already entered the first car with Mr. Leonard and waved a farewell as the door closed, but Mr. Moseby was still waiting for Heidi as she turned and ran back to hug Crystale.

"Crystale, you're coming with us, no excuses," with arms embracing each other, Heidi clutched the open mouthed girl tightly as tears welled up in her eyes.

"I love you doll, you are the closest friend I have ever had, and I need you to help me convince Uncle Günther to build my dream club."

Crystale was shaking and beside herself with overwhelming euphoria and surprise as she reacted.

"Oh Heidi, I love you too, mon Cheri, and nothing else would make me happier than to be with you, and see your beautiful dream finally realized."

Almost on lead, Sammy Sinclair appeared out of the crowd and stooped down to pick-up Crystale's bags, then turned to his Head Colored Porter.

" Here Fletcher, load these into that black Buick for Miss Crystale." Fletcher jumped forward and replied dutifully with a tone of real respect to his favorite manager, "Yes Sir, Mister Sammy."

Bob Moseby also realizing what was happening, ran back and opened the big Buick's trunk, while glancing to see just how far ahead Mr. Leonard was.

"Hey Miss Winters," he exclaimed with a sense of urgency, "we had better get going, if we want to keep up with your Uncle, he's mov'in away fast."

Heidi grabbed Crystale's hand and waved to their friends, as Crystale turned back to Sammy in her own sultry style.

"Thanks again, old friend, and you know where you can find me, if you ever get hungry again for another real slow dance partner."

Sammy was almost blushing, as he became overly aroused by the invitation he had only dreamed of, ever since meeting Crystale. He had only drooled about getting some of her nookie.

"You can bet on that, Miss Crystale," he stuttered, "I will definitely come look' in you up, once I get a day off from the Big Boss."

Crystale laughed, then winked at him and turned back to Heidi, who was now in a state of energized excitement as they both ran for the open door and into the backseat of the Buick.

Just as they jumped on the seat, and before Mr. Moseby had made it around, after closing their door to the driver's side, Heidi whispered searchingly.

"And what was that all about, Crystale?"

Crystale turned and looked deeply into Heidi's beautiful moistening blue eyes, "Well, remember that night we enjoyed the Count Basie Dance, he pushed into me so tight during those slow dances, well, I knew exactly what he was dreaming, and believe me, he is really big down there."

Moseby had just entered and was cranking the starter as she quickly finished. "Heidi my love, don't you worry even the slightest about that boy. I can assure you, he's never had a woman yet, and between you and me, we could really make nookie with him, when you feel the time is right, that's all."

Heidi spoke softly, as a small line of tears ran down her left cheek and Crystale took off her neck scarf and patted it gently. "I really do love you Crystale, you know that don't you?"

Heidi then took a breath, "And, I will do anything you asked me to do, as long as you will continue to love me, even including making nookie with Sammy, if that will twist you too."

Again, Crystale searched deep into Heidi's eyes, "And, I love you very much Heidi, but you have much to learn this year my young calico, and I will be there to be your expert teacher."

Heidi turned and looked out her side window as the car lurched forward and out of the Hotel grounds onto it's upward climb to the Town Mountain Road. She stared for a moment at the crowd waving to them from the Hotel Lobby as they pulled away and her thoughts became blurred with infinite possibilities.

Had she made the right choice in bringing Crystale deeper into her own life and that of her Uncle, knowing full well, how complicated the mission for das Vaterland might become?

She could now feel Crystale's hand gripping her own, even tighter, as she came back into the moment and turned to face her.

They were both unaware of the several glances that Mr. Moseby had made in the rearview mirror as he continued to rush up the mountain road, carefully driving though curves to tail the other Buick.

At that moment, Heidi was completely sure what she wanted. But just to confirm it, for both herself and Crystale's absolute knowledge, she stretched forward to kiss Crystale's cheek, just as the car hit an awkward turn in the road.

With her alignment slightly off and her forward momentum still in place, Heidi and Crystale's lusciously full lips now collided into each other with the passion of sex starved lovers.

The moment remained unbroken, until Mr. Moseby recovered the car and spoke, as he quickly glanced into the rearview mirror viewing what he assumed was their unbridled desire with his own eyes.

"Oh, uh, I'm sorry," he said somewhat embarrassed that he had caught the two of them, in such a strange and now very personally arousing situation.

Then realizing his predicament and hoping that they hadn't seen his glance, he decided to add a second thought. "Boy, that was really a switchback, these curves are the most difficult on the whole mountain here, Miss Heidi." Heidi responded not knowing what he had seen, as she sat back and looked directly into Crystale's large dark brown eyes.

"Were okay, Mr. Moseby, just keep up the good work, and don't worry about us."

Then she smiled, "Were definitely going to be just fine."

Chapter 7

The Chateau

High atop Beaucatcher Mountain, a single lane road winds even higher for about twenty miles toward the eastern entrance of the Blue Ridge Parkway.

For two years, Günther Anderssen had been building his estate, located on a forty-four acre reserve along the uppermost ridge of this route called the Towne Mountain Road. There he had created a large stone and brick Mansion carefully hidden within the trees just below the crest of the great mountain overlooking the valleys around Asheville.

Surrounding the entire estate was a fifteen-foot stonewall with black iron spikes strategically mounted across its thick three-foot top, adding an ominous medieval look to the overall appearance. A single gatehouse entrance was setback from the main road in a hidden cluster of winter pine trees. Various support structures for guests, servants, auxiliary power and a water cistern system as well as security with a small dormitory for his guards, were also set up around the property.

The main house, which they called the Chateau, could not be seen from the road below, due to the massive stonewall protecting its perimeter. Even peering through the wrought iron guard gates would only expose the closely planted mature Norway Pines that hid the actual Mansion grounds from view.

The Chateau itself had a dark and sinister look to its exterior design due to the limited use of windows, thick landscaping and mossy black stone covering the walls.

And, at over a mile above sea level, the entire estate offered an interesting possibility; with a powerful radio transmitter, a direct line of radio waves could travel unimpeded directly to the eastern Atlantic Coast of North Carolina on a clear night, without detection and without a bounce of its signal.

Here at his hidden mountain Chateau, the enigmatic Günther Anderssen would soon begin arranging meetings with a limited amount of very rich and powerful people within the region or brought from abroad for short stays at the estate. Then without interference, he could begin cultivating the key alliances designed to build the blueprint of his American strategy for SSI.

The first car to arrive for the official walk through was Mr. Leonard's Buick, as the Pinkerton Guard at the gatehouse recognizing the Bank President immediately, motioned them through and onto the serpentine gravel driveway that climbed up to the mainhouse.

Crunching along on the white gravel stones, the tire's ground their distinctive sound, as the car slowly made it's way upward until they arrived at the rear motor entrance of the Chateau. Mr. Edward Wellington and his architectural firm's staff were waiting there along with several engineers and construction managers that had worked on the project for the last two years.

Mr. Wellington was all flourishes as he ran to Mr. Anderssen's door and greeted him.

"Günther, let me personally welcome you home!"

"And, my distinguished friend," Günther replied in his typically reserved manner, "it is so good to finally be home in this superb architectural masterpiece."

It was almost noon before Mr. Wellington's staff and the others on hand, had thoroughly detailed every conceivable nuance of the estate to Mr. Anderssen.

During that time, Heidi and Crystale had arrived and were welcomed by Mr. Wellington's Senior Interior Designer, Mrs. Judy Knox. With Judy's assistance, Miss Winters had gone about selecting two of the most exquisitely decorated bedrooms on the second floor of the main Chateau for herself and her first guest to the estate, as she had introduced her friend Crystale.

Mrs. Knox had spent the last five months working with Mr. Anderssen at Mr. Wellington's direction, to select the massive furniture inventory and appointments for the mainhouse and the various support facilities at the estate.

Her most impressive work, however, was Uncle Günther's library and cigar smoking room. It was designed with a cluster of Moroccan leather settees and lushly upholstered easy chairs for his male guests as well as walls lacquered with antique-gold bas-reliefs, depicting ancient Norwegian Viking ships in various battle scenes.

Uncle Günther had personally selected over five-thousand book titles, that were now in place in the massive library shelves with their own rolling ladder assembly made from imported dark mahogany woods.

The combination room, as Mrs. Knox called it, also had its own bar and guest restroom, as well as a small bedroom with a second bath area off to one end. It was added specifically by Uncle Günther so that he could easily accommodate a special guest, or even himself, if he chose to stay downstairs for the evening.

Alive with the rustle of fine china and silverware, and the buzz of conversation, the Chateau's grand dining room was filling for the first time with the welcoming party and Mr. Anderssen.

Mr. Wellington's staff had thought of just about everything, with the estate's project budget coming in at over $1.5 million dollars, this was by far the largest private home contract in his firm's history.

But just to make sure of success for the gala welcoming party, Mr. Wellington even brought-in one of the top high-end catering firms from Atlanta, Gayle Darling & Company.

Gayle Darling was in her mid-thirties, but her experience level was very diversified. She had lived in France when she was in her teens and had worked at the Tour D'Argent, the Silver Tower on the Left Bank of the Seine and probably the most famous restaurant in all of Paris.

In her late twenties she had returned to New York and became the pastry chef at one of the most famous German restaurants in America, Lüchows on East 14th Street. And now, Miss Darling herself brought along her favorite three-piece classical musical ensemble, to complete the effect of her celebrated cuisine, plus something very special Mr. Wellington suggested just for Günther Anderssen.

His favorite styled Schnitzel a La Lüchow mit Kartoffel Klosse - Veal Cutlets with Potato Dumplings. From that day forth, she had Mr. Anderssen around her little finger, yet she never knew it.

As the Violinists accompanied the Pianist on the Chateau's newly tuned Grand Steinway with their soft melodious background, Heidi and Crystale entered from the main hallway's staircase, with Mrs. Knox trailing behind them.

"Ah there you are, my sweet little darling," Günther announced, as he spied her and purposely interrupted a boring conversation with one of the senior construction engineers reviewing the complex details of excavating the building's granite foundation.

"It's time for the Lady of the Estate to be toasted, my dearest Heidi."

"Here, here". . . Mr. Leonard exclaimed overhearing Günther, "it is with my greatest pleasure that I welcome you to your new home, Miss Heidi Winters," as the beautiful young duo came into full view for all to see.

"And, my dearest, I see you have added even more beauty to our Homecoming Luncheon with the lovely Miss Crystale here, along as well," Uncle Günther added as he winked to her in obvious approval of her decision to follow-through as they had agreed, with the clandestine recruitment of Crystale.

Günther's American SSI Operation at that point in late 1934 had only a few very close confidants in America, and those were primarily pre-identified German or even Nazi sympathizers. Günther had fully explained to Heidi during the last year, that her own progress as an agent had to include recruiting others. He had further said to her, "Heidi, the complex process of developing your own agent might require you to use more than just psychological methods to gain their deepest personal allegiance, you may even need a commitment that rivals true love. To prove that to them, you may be required to use your own promiscuity, in order to gain their deepest confidence."

"I have some exciting news, Uncle," Heidi exclaimed in a shy innocent tone, outwardly for Crystale's benefit, but hoping he would not rebuke her request.

"And, my dearest, what would that be?" Uncle Günther replied, knowing fully what she was about to reveal to him.

Once she and Crystale were finally beside her Uncle, she then spoke to him in a close whisper, while all the time making sure that Crystale was near enough to overhear her imploring request.

"Do you remember the project we discussed earlier this year, about the Private Continental Style Restaurant that you were planning to open next season on the mountain near the Grand Park Inn?"

Günther grunted, "Uh, yes of course," as he looked at Crystale while listening to Heidi's soft whispers, yet clearly observing Crystale's posture, knowing she would be willing to do just about anything to get him to agree with Heidi, as she gave him her most sultry come on look.

"Well, Uncle," Heidi became more animated as she spoke very softly, "I want to expand that idea into a complete Restaurant and Nightclub as well. And Uncle Günther, I want Crystale to stay on with us over the winter to help us design it. She would manage the Nightclub with me and we could find someone here locally to manage the Restaurant."

"Ah my dear, what a set up you have made here with Crystale and all," he smiled at both girls as he replied quietly back, including them both in his response. "It seems it would be rather impossible for me to turn you both down, now that you have brought all your ammunition to this party."

Heidi's smile and eyes were lighting up her face, even though she was somewhat unsure of what he meant by 'all' of her ammunition.

"So you are in agreement Uncle Günther?" Heidi reconfirmed, "Crystale can stay with us and we can pursue the Nightclub, then begin looking for a Chef or Restaurant Manager after the first of the year?"

Günther looked at her quizzically, now knowing she had forgot to read the letter he had sent Mr. Wellington instructing him to bring that special catering group of his, up from Atlanta for the Official Open House and Walk-Through Gala.

The plan was that if all proved successful, that group would be offered the management position at the new Restaurant, if of course everyone agreed that their cuisine was as terrific as the social crowd had raved about in Atlanta.

"The letter my dear," he urged her, "you never read my letter to Mr. Wellington, outlining the plans for the Official Walk-through Party?"

"Oh that, no, you're right I didn't see that," she stated somewhat honestly, but concerned at his agitation, since he was always so precise in everything he did, and she knew he expected the same of her. "Nothing must be left to chance, get access to all, knowing all information is critical to making the correct decision," he would instruct her time and again, "this is the attribute of a truly professional agent, never trivialize that."

"Well then, my dear," he then surprised her with a smile, rather than the expected admonishment for her oversight, "you must immediately get over and meet Miss Gayle Darling, try out some of her succulent canapés and hors d'oeuvres, and help me to make a decision this afternoon."

Heidi and Crystale discreetly looked back at each other, as they simultaneously finally realized what he meant by 'all' your ammunition. The probable Chef or Restaurant Manager was right here with them today, and what a catch she would be, since she was known to be the talk of Atlanta's Top Social One-Hundred. But as Uncle Günther had been clearly advised many times over the past two years by his esteemed banker, Mr.Leonard, money talks in these parts and anywhere in the Southeast for that matter, and in times like these the man with all the money gets to take home the prettiest things, no questions asked.

"Oh Uncle Günther, this is fantastic, I can't thank you enough for inviting them," Heidi's mind was racing in overdrive as she smiled that conniving look at Crystale, who gave her the same look back.

It was now time for them to put their well-honed skills into action, and when they got through with Miss Gayle Darling, she was going to become a true co-conspirator in their new Nightclub and Private Dinner Club concept, just like them.

Then as both girls headed off to the Chateau's massive kitchen, Günther couldn't help but think, at last the American Strategy for SSI was beginning to evolve into his design of a perfectly innocuous private social club, a club that would gain him access to agents or information vital to the final solution for Germany.

Chapter 8

Building the Legacy

Up from the city's lights and concrete skyline, and rising high along the western wall of Beaucatcher Mountain was a singular vantage point that gave a magnificent one-hundred and eighty degree sunset view of the entire valley of Asheville, all the way to the top of Mt. Pisgah nestled in the far western mountains. A single lane road flowed up the mountain from the main streets of town. Built to gain access to one of the city's water reservoirs on top of the mountain, the concrete road worked it's way past the construction site and further upward in tight curves and switchbacks every few hundred feet. It was there at this site, on a cold late January morning in 1935, that the first shovel of dirt was turned over for what would eventually be known as *The Sky Club*.

Planning and Design for the combination private dinner club and entertainment nightclub actually began in earnest soon after Heidi and Crystale set their sights on recruiting Gayle Darling and some of her top chefs from Atlanta.

As Günther had promised, money would not become a problem in putting this project together and even Mr. Edward Wellington and his architectural firm dedicated two senior architects and three top construction engineers to the effort, the moment they saw Günther's five-million dollar budget.

The intent was to fast track the whole effort for a projected mid-summer opening, but the deadline made sure that only the finest workmanship and construction methods would be used, even if that meant moving out the completion date.

Mrs. Knox, Wellington's Senior Designer dedicated her newest hire, a commercial facilities Interior Designer named Millicent Edmonds, to the project.

The thirty year old Miss Edmonds had gone to USC on the West Coast to get her degree and had recently completed a new Art Deco Styled Nightclub in Beverly Hills, so she was the most influential person beside Heidi and Crystale in the overall plan.

While the other cohort, Miss Darling and her chefs, would come up for kitchen planning sessions and dinning room design meetings, staying at the Chateau a few days every other week from Atlanta. That way they could continue their weekend catering business until the facilities were ready for fully training the dinning and kitchen staffs.

Throughout February and March, the Grand Park Inn also became a hang out for Heidi and Crystale as they recruited some of their favorite department managers, dinning room servers, busboys, and a few housemaids to provide a range of services for the club.

By May the main building was taking shape, concrete foundations had been laid into a vertical cut on the mountainside and three levels of reinforced concrete floors over a storage basement had been poured. Steel support beams for the roof were in place and a pad for upper level access and automobile parking had been completed on the five-acre location.

It was early afternoon before Günther arrived to meet with Edward Wellington and his two senior architects, Mr. Davis and Mr. Wolcott. Heidi was already there with Gayle Darling discussing the proposed Dining room modifications with Mr. Wolcott and Miss Millicent Edmonds, when Günther's chauffeur, a new SSI operative recently sent by Horst Deeke to join them, opened the rear door of his Cadillac Touring Sedan.

"Heidi, my darling I have some exciting news," Günther exclaimed as he exited onto the parking lot overlooking the vast construction site with the twin municipal buildings of downtown Asheville gleaming in the sun drenched valley, about three miles away.

"Oh, Uncle Günther, I'm so glad you're back," she said happily as she and Miss Gayle Darling strode up to the newly waxed sedan. Heidi clearly stood almost a foot taller than Gayle, a diminutive woman at barely five feet, that had proven she was nothing but pure energy and was just waiting to turn his Dinner Club into to her future chef d'oeuvre.

Like a child in pure anticipation though, Heidi was wide eyed in wait for what Günther was about to say.

"Remember I had discussed Germany's problems in securing the Olympics for 1936 in Berlin," Günther announced while opening his briefcase, " well it's on."

"Wow, that's terrific news," she reacted, while holding back her full excitement for what she knew might be even more sensational, because Uncle Günther loved dramatic surprises.

He then pulled two large ticket envelopes and her new Danish Passport from within a leather pouch, as he held them out to her.

"And, I've booked two First Class Cabins on the most beautiful ship in the world, the brand new French Liner Normandie. It's not only the newest, but it's biggest and fastest ocean liner in the world, my dear, across the Atlantic in under five days."

"Oh my God . . . ," now she was truly animated as she jumped forward to hug him and kissed him on the cheek, "that's the most wonderful gift Uncle Günther, you are so good to me."

"Unfortunately, my dear," again Günther enjoyed the dramatics, while sounding so foreboding as he lowered his voice,

" I will not be able to join you on this trip," he paused, " but I do have a fairly nice alternative for you."

"Oh no Uncle Günther," she tried to seem sympathetic as she held back even more excitement, "I so wanted you to show me Berlin, like only you could do."

"Well, my darling, it isn't to be this time," Günther added, " So, I've decided to give my own set of First Class tickets on the awesome Normandie, to your good friend Crystale, so she can join you on this experience of a lifetime."

Heidi read him perfectly, "Oh my God, Uncle Günther you're extraordinary!" she knew he was going to do it, but she was still even more animated than the first time as she latched around his neck hugging him and kissing him repeatedly on the cheek, "Crystale is going to go crazy with excitement, you know that! Wow, what a gift."

"Here now, take these my dear," he again handed her the two large ticket envelopes that read Normandie, O Ship of Light - FIRST CLASS CABIN with her Passport, plus a second set of envelopes that read BERLIN Olympics - August 1st, 1936, " and be sure to keep them in a safe spot, Heidi, these events are over a year away."

"Oh I will, Uncle Günther," she replied as she firmly stuffed them down into her large handbag, "you can be sure of that!"

For the next few minutes Günther organized some others items from his case and then turned back to Heidi and Gayle Darling, as the two of them were still gushing back and forth about Heidi's newest surprise.

"So bring me up to date," he stated in a more formal tone, "what's been going on here with the Club, Heidi?"

"Well Uncle, we have just decided on the greatest improvement, and Mr. Wolcott says it can be managed with very little change."

"And what's that Heidi?" he asked, as he bent down and lifted two more files from a case on the car's rear floorboard.

"Gayle and I agreed," she said as she seemed quite exuberant with their new solution, "that all arriving guests should enter the Club directly from the Parking level. You see Uncle, Automobiles are modern and clearly the future of America, and all of our arrivals should be able to enter at the upper level from their cars and simply step down from there, right into the dinning area or the dance floor."

"I see, and what about the elevator idea you were pushing last week, that's modern too, isn't it?" Günther exclaimed seeming to understand their modification, but wanting full disclosure.

"Well," she said, "we want that too, but for a different purpose. In fact, what the new plan has become, incorporates Miss Edmond's ideas from Hollywood, it's like a theatre in the round, Uncle Günther."

Just then a beautiful young lady walked up beside Heidi. Günther was struck by her looks and thin legs immediately.

She was as tall as Heidi, at bit older, but clearly had no breasts. In her case breasts didn't matter though, as her blond hair, jade green eyes and the chiseled features of her face held any observer spellbound in her gaze.

"And I suppose this is Miss Edmonds from Hollywood, then?" Günther was obviously interested in the young beauty.

"Oh, I'm sorry Uncle Günther, you're right this is Mrs. Knox's new commercial designer, Millicent Edmonds from Los Angeles."

Millicent quickly added as she extend her hand to shake his, "Well, I'm actually from Asheville originally Mr. Anderssen, but I've spent the last eight years on the West Coast and now I'm back," then she paused for effect, "guess I was just homesick for these luscious green mountains all over again."

Günther seemed to hold her hand a bit longer than the typical time for a professional handshake to observe her flawless complexion and delicately long fingers. "You appear to be of Scandinavian extract Miss Edmonds, is that correct?" Günther was obviously taken and Heidi didn't miss a beat in recognizing his interest.

"She is, Uncle Günther," Heidi injected, "and, I've invited her to dinner tonight at the Chateau so she can tell you all about herself. Sammy Sinclair and Crystale will be joining us as well, and I think she has finally recruited him as an assistant manger for the Club."

"Once again my darling", as Günther smiled his extreme approval to her, cleverly knowing that several midnight visits to Crystal's steamy little boudoir over the last two months had certainly not hampered Mr. Sinclair in making his obvious decision to join them, "I can see that you two have everything moving along quite nicely now."

Then looking back toward Millicent, Günther renewed his discussion with her. "So tell me more about the new Hollywood design concept Miss Edmonds?"

"The Romans and Greeks actually originated the concept, Mr. Anderssen," Millicent replied to him with an even warmer, almost submissive look, now that she had gained his full attention.

She then placed her briefcase on a nearby work table and pulled out a design blueprint. Quickly in one motion, she retrieved a pair of stylish black reading glasses and began going over the blueprint layout.

"With this concept you get the best of three worlds," Millicent continued as she purposely used the glasses to tone down her looks and appear more professional, rather than look like a New York Fashion Model, which Günther had already compared her to in his own mind's eye.

He was clearly smitten, Heidi thought, as she watched him closely survey Millicent's narrow hips. She hated that they were just as thin as hers, and of course Crystale had already pronounced them as 'calico hot' and wanted to know, if Millicent enjoyed sheba nookie just like she did, sometimes?

Whenever Crystale wanted to make her jealous, she would always find some new dish to upset her with, preferably without bubs like Millicent, and now Crystale planned to make Millicent her latest tasty little sheba.

"First, the New Design," Millicent explained with an aire of technical smoothness that easily held Günther's full attention, "has ten, one foot high, semicircle concrete tiers or levels set at a width ten feet wide. Each of them wide enough to hold Gayle's intimate Dinning Tables near the front edge of each tier and still leave an open corridor along the back edge of the tier for traffic, guests, servers and busboys without too much crowding of the intimate dinning atmosphere of the guests."

"So, if I am to understand this, Miss Edmonds," Günther asked, as he looked carefully at the blueprint, " the existing three floor reinforced concrete building now in place, will not need any major restructuring?" Then he added for more clarification, "And, of course that being the case we would not need to add more money and time to the project completion, correct?"

"Actually, Mr. Anderssen," Millicent smiled demurely towards him, as Heidi seemed to enjoy the interplay of both of them listening to her reasoning for use later, "that's true, but let me continue through the three primary advantages before I clarify costs and time."

"Very well, Miss Edmonds, carry on," Günther said, clearly more comfortable now in her ability to work through those problems later.

"Entrancing is enhanced first," she said, "since that is the immediate impression your patrons, excuse me Club Members, will experience as they enter the main lobby and descend step by step to their designated private Dinning Tables or down further to the actual Dance Floor level where smaller floorside cocktail tables will be located around the Dance Floor."

Heidi couldn't hold back as she jumped in, " Isn't it great Uncle Günther, how Millicent thinks of all these wonderful ideas, and with her tier idea, nothing will hamper the view from each guest's table either."

"Yes it is my darling," he respectfully replied to Heidi as the opportunity gave him a chance to glance at the way Millicent's summer weight silk dress was clinging to her thin thighs and luscious legs, as she turned away to listen to Heidi.

He was imagining what she might be like in his bedroom, just watching her, a soft body straight from the Nordic Gods, a perfect blond haired Valkyrie, surely with the same young and wild sexual appetite that both Heidi and Crystale displayed in their rooms.

Maybe there was hope for him after all, although he had never touched the girls, he had always wanted a beautiful young lady to complete the image of his respectability and this one, properly cultivated would certainly be unreal to experiment with.

"Next, the Ambiance is enhanced," Millicent continued after allowing Heidi enough time to strengthen her credibility with Uncle Günther, even more. And god only knew, Millicent thought to herself, her career had now boiled down to money and power and not necessarily in that order.

While her personal sacrifices were not even an issue anymore, since she had already prostituted herself to enough LA power brokers and sugar daddies to get named to the FBI's list of LA's most screwed vamps. And hopefully, at last with Heidi's help, one or both of her goals could be attained with this project sometime soon.

As Millicent regarded the situation even longer, while looking at Mr. Anderssen, she considered her own Scandinavian ancestry and now knowing a little bit about this older man from Heidi's earlier comments, and her secret conversations with Crystale, he could certainly become a very fortuitous friend, as she cultivated him in a more personal way.

"The physical array of the site is clearly the ultimate element of the Clubs Ambiance," Millicent added as she again focused on her work.

"As Club Members enter at the upper level in the late afternoon or evening, the impact of the massive curved panoramic view of the city and the Western mountains either in sunset or in twinkling nightlights through the Club's thirty foot high windows, will leave them breathless. With no orientation to either ground or sky, the Sky Club members and their guests will feel as though they are floating on a Grand Entertainment Ship traveling into the night's starlit sky.

"Incredible," Günther exclaimed out loud, "you should be in our government's propaganda offices in Washington, my dear Miss Edwards, that was brilliant."

Heidi, now knowing things had been moved up to a higher level of agreement by secretly using Millicent to make the plea to her Uncle, was elated as she spoke.

"See, once again, Millicent's experience in the high end Beverly Hills club scene and particularly in Hollywood's glitzy nightlife has without any doubt made her ideas the grandest yet, don't you think?"

"Absolutely, Heidi," Günther replied.

Then Gayle Darling added, "You're exactly right Heidi," with just enough emphasis to let everyone know that she was also on board with both Heidi and Millicent.

"The Sky Club will certainly be, with Millicent's new modifications, the most magnificent of all modern private dinning and nightclubs anywhere in the country, much less the Southeast." Then, before anyone could continue, Miss Darling added further credibility to her comments, "and I can assure you ladies, I've worked for quite a few of the best over the last twelve years."

"And that you have, my dear Miss Darling", Uncle Günther added, winking at her in a way that only both of them knew came right from his real heart, the gastronomical love of Gayle's specialized Lüchow trained German and Scandinavian cooking. She had upon his personal request, yielded her time to train Günther's own house chef, Rolf Christensen who had himself been trained in Copenhagen at Belle Terrassee.

But even so, Rolf had told Günther that he was amazed at her expertise in technique and presentation. Gayle he had said, had a well-crafted philosophy towards her gastronomy. She had explained to him on the occasion of Heidi's 18th Birthday Dinner with over seventy-five guests at the Chateau, that great food must be the nectar for all human senses . . . taste above all, then smell, sight, touch, but even the sound must become a musical harmony . . . the goblets, the wine and champagne bottles, the plates, silverware, and of course the snap of freshly laundered linens, as each new table is carefully prepared for the next welcomed guest.

Millicent waited to speak, as she observed Miss Darling with a sense of awe, knowing from many of her long time friends in Atlanta of Gayle's profound reputation in the art of fine gourmet catering and dinning.

"Finally, the Flow of Operations," Millicent began her conclusion with a simple rationale that made perfect sense to everyone, and particularly Mr. Anderssen. "It must evolve from the perspective of the club's patrons and guests, not from the perspective of the support services."

Günther was mesmerized by Millicent's jade green eyes and, as Heidi finally realized, that was why she was also wearing her body hugging green silk dress that played so perfectly with her soft flesh tones as well. The more Heidi watched her, the more she wanted to learn from her. Now, she could view her technique first hand; Millicent was clearly captivating Uncle Günther in a way she had never seen him look before. This woman was so smooth Heidi thought, almost like a professional twist as Crystale had suggested only last week, particularly with the way she could handle men with ease, in appearing so delicate and submissive to them.

Heidi wanted that kind of style too, so scrupulously she began recording in mental pictures, every move Millicent made throughout her pre-arranged spectacle. A spectacle Heidi thought, that she had obviously rehearsed and played back many times before, but with other commercial projects from her past, in California.

"As Guests arrive in their separate cars," Millicent continued, "the Valets at the security booth will greet them at the top level automobile welcoming area; next, as they walk in at that same level, they are handed off to either the Dinning Hostess or the Club's Concierge at the Grand entrance.

Then, as they wait, if that is required, they can see the spectacle of everything in the entire Club, from either the vantage point of the waiting area or while having drinks in the main Bar located alongside the waiting area at the upper level."

Heidi observed her subtle movements, as Millicent maintained eye contact only with Uncle Günther and always at just the right moment, seductively holding his attention, she would turn her neck and use a sultry movement of her hand to smooth her long blond hair back over her right shoulder.

Even the breeze from down below the hillside seemed to be at her command, as it tossed blond strands against her face or twisted them seductively as they encircled her exquisitely formed neck.

"From there," Millicent added, "they can enjoy the breathtaking panoramic view, the orchestra playing down below centered against the massive windows on the opposite side of the dance floor, and even the dancers moving to the swing beat on the dance floor itself. And along each of the ten tiers below them, they will be able see other guests enjoying the chic ambiance of the Club at their own private dinning tables."

Millicent now seemed to sense that Heidi was watching her.

Suddenly she turned directly to her, causing an excited thrill to run deep into Heidi's tummy as she bit her lip and looked shyly into Millicent's beautiful eyes.

Günther caught the look they gave one another for that brief moment, as he himself became incredibly excited at the thought of both these sexy Valkyries making love to each other in the Chateau's upper guest bedroom.

A place, that only he knew had a secret viewing mirror and chamber along side the massive low profiled king size bed. The bed on which, the well-endowed Mr. Sinclair had enjoyed unbridled exercising with Miss Crystale's lithe little body, as her supple hips would thrash about and her groans of obnoxious French phases like, je suis montee au cheval mon amour, would spew hoarsely from her lips.

Often he thought, she was extra loud on purpose, just so everyone upstairs could hear her. But that was okay too, since it meant that sometimes one of the other girls might join in at any moment. Maybe tonight would become an evening to remember, like those as well, he mused as Millicent began to wrap-up her presentation.

"Everything from the way that the Maitre d 'Roitisseur introduces himself, the arrival timing of Servers and Support personnel at the newly set up tables, and even the way the Orchestra arrives and leaves from breaks will be a scripted flow of perfectly harmonized events."

"So what do you think, Mr. Anderssen?" Millicent inquired as her well-organized, but somewhat long-winded justification ended, leaving Günther hypnotized without words.

Just at that moment Mr. Wolcott and the Construction Engineers wanting to get into the act, and of course get a better look at the high heeled dolls entertaining the Big Boss, as Mr. Wellington liked to affectionately call Mr. Anderssen, walked up.

Pausing to regain his business composure, Günther answered,

"It's all quite incredible, as I had said before Miss Edmonds," as he, yet again was distracted by a little shiver that Heidi revealed, as she looked back toward Millicent's hair again blowing freely around her delicate long neckline.

She took no action to push it back, this time waiting to see Günther's reaction.

"Let me take some time to think about all this, and in the meantime I need to review other engineering issues with Mr. Wolcott, and of course Edward, who is also coming to finalize some things today. As soon as they are finished here, I'll meet all of you up at the Chateau for cocktails."

"We can have another of Rolf's incredible dinners together and then I will give you my final decision, how does that sound, my dear Miss Edmonds?"

Everything had gone just perfectly, Heidi thought, and all Uncle Günther really wanted to do now was to see how that 'choice little calico' might fit into his plans, as soon as she had a few drinks in her and she saw the inside of the Chateau's upper facilities.

Heidi also knew, Millicent was going to get a personal tour of Uncle Günther's incredible Library with his Scandinavian art treasures and engravings, and of course his Legends of Viking Valkyries that he loved to tell about, once he had downed one or two shots of his favorite Cognac or Scotch.

"That sounds great Uncle Günther," Heidi interrupted before Millicent could try to mount another argument, possibly forcing a decision now, rather than waiting until later. But Heidi had other plans and certainly lots of experience with Uncle Günther's habits as well as his unusual perversions.

"Its settled then Heidi," Günther replied, " I'll see all of you, and especially you Miss Edmonds, at the Chateau, dressed for the occasion, I'm sure, by about Six PM."

Then Günther added, as he winked his private signal to Heidi to get things moving along for tonight's special entertainment plans,

"And, Heidi why don't you take my Cadillac now. Max can take you and the Ladies on up."

"I would love to come along Mr. Anderssen," Gayle Darling quickly interjected, " but, I have plans already in Atlanta tonight, so I personally will be leaving right away."

"Of course, my dear, I understand, maybe next time," Günther reacted, knowing her very conservative nature and feeling relieved that she was not joining them.

Then he turned back to Heidi and spoke. "Just send Max back for me in about two hours, Heidi. I need some time with the Architects and Engineers to clear up some other matters and make sure some particular design issues have been addressed."

"Of course, Uncle Günther," Heidi answered.

At that, Max instantly reacted, and in just a few moments Heidi and Millicent were escorted comfortably into the lush leather seating in the rear of Günther's Black Cadillac Sedan.

"Goodbye, Uncle Günther, and thanks again for my wonderful gift," Heidi shouted as she waved, getting the attention of most of the younger males now purposely watching as they milled about on the upper construction level.

The car turned up the hill and was out of sight when Günther turned back to the waiting group of men.

Jack Wolcott waited until he was sure that Miss Darling had gone before he spoke. "That's a fine looking group of ladies you have there, Mr. Anderssen," he commented as Günther turned to greet them.

"Yes, you're quite right about that Mr. Wolcott, I just hope that were making the right decision giving them as much leeway on this project, as I am."

Günther confided to him, as he walked back to the newly poured reinforced concrete wall that would eventually protect the parking lot and the upper levels from ground erosion.

"I completely understand your concern, Mr. Anderssen," Mr. Johnson, the project's senior structural engineer added, as they walked together in a slow stroll over to the embankment, "but that lady, Miss Edmonds spent over four hours here earlier this morning with both my top construction men, and I'll be damned if they both said they could do that change with hardly any bother at all. "

"As a matter of fact, well be able to leave the elevator in place feeding all three floors with the new Otis front and rear access door system set in the upper level lobby, and although the tiers come down almost a full story, the underside of those things in their modular design as she suggested, can include offices in the taller zones and storage units in the shorter zones on that second floor. All in all, Jack and I agree, it will really set the place off pretty dramatically. I'd say it's probably the most creative layout we've seem since we started up here in Asheville."

"Well gentlemen," Günther felt relieved now they had added their more optimistic opinions as he looked out over the hillside toward the cityscape of Asheville, "I certainly hope you're both right."

He paused, as he thought of the growing group of young attractive *Mata Haris*, that he now had in place for potential SSI operations in America. Günther realized some of them would never really know they were his operatives. That's the way these things worked out.

He also knew even more surely now, that these beautiful and exotically seductive women would soon be SSI's keys to gaining secrets and knowledge from the deepest levels of America's future war machine.

Exactly what that would be was yet to be determined, but extracting information as well as the psychological and emotional warfare these women could induce on vulnerable men or women, once their tasks had been set in place, would absolutely devastate certain people's lives.

But for now, until the clouds of War in Europe had fully formed in their proper place, no future course could be set for his growing SSI arsenal.

"Now, let's go over some of those special design changes I wanted," Günther remarked as he headed down the concrete steps to the lower construction level, "and, the arrangements that will be needed to finish out the kitchen once Miss Edmond's new modifications are in place."

Chapter 9

Swingtime

Heidi and Crystale were shocked to hear that the bandleader Bennie Moten was dead. Moten's drummer Jo Jones had called them from the Hospital in Kansas City very upset.

He told them Bennie had died from what he thought was going to be a simple tonsillectomy operation, but he didn't make it.

Suddenly, not only building delays throughout August and September, but now even the whole entertainment plan was falling apart, with only three weeks left before The Sky Club's Grand Opening, things were looking pretty bad. But, two days later, Count Basie himself called them back and said he'd formed a new band assuring them that he would personally make the gala weekend date on Friday, October 11th. Basie had taken the remnants of Moten's best musicians and quickly put together a nine-piece group with the drummer Jo Jones, Walter Page the great bassist, and the infallible guitarist Freddie Green as well as several others from Bennie's Band.

The moment the local radio station W8XOS was informed of these events, they requested to be on hand for the Club's opening gala. Maybe finally, Heidi could get enough publicity to salvage at least a remnant of the quickly ending tourist season in Asheville. The station manager, Bill Murray loved Basie's Swing style and wanted to be the first radio station in the country, to broadcast the new Count Basie Swing Band live.

The Broadcast would stretch across all the Western Carolina Mountain regions and even down into the rest of the Southeast.

Now, Heidi had things moving again flawlessly.

The final opening date had been reset as far back as September due to landscaping and final interior detailing problems, when Günther advised the girls of his plans to attend the World Series with two of his new scientific associates from Detroit. On that Monday, October 7th, the Detroit Tigers won the World Series.

Goose Goslin's single hit won the final game, with two outs and only one man on base in the bottom of the 9th inning.

Günther loved American baseball and was ecstatic about the Series ending in only six games, but the Tigers had been great all that year and winning the Series had just capped off a great season for Detroit.

It was Wednesday afternoon, when he finally arrived back in Asheville at the Biltmore Train Station, and both the girls came down to welcome him and give him the good news about the new Band. They also couldn't wait to tell him about the added publicity the local radio station Manager had offered them at no cost, just to have the first broadcast anywhere, of the new Count Basie Band.

Crystale pointed out, that even though the summer and fall season was over, the slower winter season would allow the Club to smoothly hone it's operations for the upcoming year with locals around Asheville becoming their mainstay membership, at least until April. Everything was now in readiness for the Gala Opening Night Celebration.

The girls were wearing their new sable mink jackets Günther had brought them from New York as they arrived at The Sky Club in a new Black Chrysler Sedan. Max had been selected to escort them down with little fanfare at about Five PM. Both girls had chosen long svelte satin dresses for the opening, and Heidi's was all black and bare shouldered as it contoured down to perfectly accent her small waist and narrow hips.

Because of the weather, Crystale had chosen a warmer elegant high neck style having full-length sleeves, but a very sexy open back that draped down to her hips with beige coloration. She wanted a more conservative look so she could work the front entrance area welcoming guests at the arrival concierge and still get some time later, on the dance floor. This late in the season meant that the mountains would be chilled with early winter weather, and as a result the women guests would be dressed far more extravagant for dinning and later swinging on the grand dance floor of the club than would be the case in the warmer summer months.

A lot of pre-planning and preparation for regional membership development by the girls and the staff plus some well written publicity in the Asheville and Atlanta newspapers had gained strong interest by the elite for the Grand Gala Night. Gayle Darling's society following in Atlanta alone had filled two private Southern Railway Pullman cars with new Sky Club members staying over in local Hotels, just to sample her cuisine and dance in the starlight one last time before snowfall might hamper their weekend soirees up to the mountains.

To assist in the process, Günther had also arranged for two temporary limousine firms to be added to the Asheville scene from Charlotte and Atlanta, plus some of the VIPs had even brought their own personal chauffeured cars for the event.

Night came early and the chilled air allowed the stars to be seen from the mountain side as cars and limousine shuttles started arriving from the area Hotels at about six that evening.

Sleek socialites were everywhere as the beautiful and rich began arriving near the Club's brightly-lit entrance. Limousines were backed up almost a quarter of a mile down the main road by seven.

And although the process inside went smoothly, the parking area was already overfilling.

Günther himself arrived from the top of the mountain and got caught in the jam as he got out and quickly joined a couple nearing the front gallery. He had recognized them from a private Biltmore Forest party only a month before.

The couple was typical of the September-May romances that seemed to be the latest trend with Günther's wealthy associates around Asheville. She was a young woman about twenty-five, blond and wearing a short cape-like jacket with a long silk dress fit to every curve on her thin body, while he was in his fifties wearing a dark suit and heavy overcoat.

Bill Waterman was exuberant as he recognized Günther extending his hand as he spoke. " Günther, what a beautiful event this has turned into, although a bit crowded out here with all these limousines, but that's money for you!" He laughed and Günther joined him, as well.

" I'm so glad you could make it Bill," Günther replied, equally energized by the excitement at the Club's main lobby entrance, "and who, may I inquire is this lovely creature you have with you, my friend?"

Waterman had worked for the government in Washington for years as a Civil Engineer and had been divorced for about ten years when he actually went independent and hit the big time. Massive government construction contracts and the Tennessee Eastman contract for their production facilities in Kingsport, Tennessee had grown his engineering firm into the largest U.S. Government sub-contractor in the Southeast. Then cash rich over the last few years, he had built his second home near Asheville, a ten-thousand square foot mansion in Biltmore Forest.

As events permitted, he divided his time between Washington, D.C. and his southern base here in the Western Smokies.

Bill was clearly proud to introduce his latest doll as he answered, " Günther, this is my new executive assistant, Miss Diana Morgan, and she is one hell of a swing dancer I might add!"

Günther couldn't help being distracted by her appearance now being fully exposed, as she shed her small jacket exposing her creamy soft shoulder flesh, once they had cleared the doorway. Her dress was cut just like Heidi's, but the rounded tops of her breasts swelled so close to it's upper edge, that it looked like her nipples would pop out and smile at him at any moment. 'Christ, just look at that,' at once Günther's thoughts became focused on how sexy she was as he silently scanned her down to her narrow hips, just the inward slope of her abdominal muscles alone, made her seem like a lascivious animal wanting to run naked and breed with the first erect male she could find. No wonder Bill was so proud of himself.

"My extreme pleasure, Miss Morgan," Günther stated as he nodded and caught Crystale's presence out of the corner of his eye.

She had seen him and was rushing up to hug him while they were relieving their coats to the assistant hostess as Günther continued, "and you, being a dancer young lady, let me introduce our own in-house dance professional here, Crystale!"

"Günther, you've arrived at the perfect moment," Crystale exclaimed as she hugged him and was also drawn by the vision Günther had just experienced, with the arrival of Miss Morgan.

"Crystale, I want you to meet Diana Morgan and of course my good friend and colleague Mr. Bill Waterman."

"Yes, Mr. Waterman, it's a pleasure to meet you," Crystale said first, while saving her best intro for the young lady,

"And Miss Morgan, what a stunning gown you are wearing, my God, it must be a Paris designer original, it's so beautiful. And, an incredibly perfect fit as well with your petite figure."

In alternating responses both Bill and Diana returned trite introductions back to Crystale as Miss Morgan added somewhat condescendingly, "That's so sweet of you, Crystale, and it is of course an Yves Saint Laurent couture original. Bill and I picked it up this summer in Paris, after our trip on the maiden return voyage of the French Liner Normandie."

Crystale did not even flinch at her smug remark, knowing this gal was way out of her league but she didn't even know it, as she turned just enough to add Günther into her view, while still keeping her eyes locked on Miss Morgan's erotic body.

"Everything is moving flawlessly, Günther," she added, clearly smiling brightly at Bill and Diana in tow with him, "and Heidi's out on the dance floor down there hostessing the hors d'oeuvres and complementary drinks to the overflow crowd of new members still waiting for their tables."

Günther turned to see her down below, while on the bandstand several members of Count Basie's group were playing some soft background music just to soften the initial dinner atmosphere, before the main Band began their planned Swingtime arrangements, to be broadcast live at around Nine PM.

"That may be true in here, my dear, but the crowd building up outside is what I'm worried about." Günther seemed serious as he advised her, "How fast is Darling's crew getting people to their tables and serving them?"

"I'm not sure," Crystale knew Günther could get testy if he didn't get exact answers, as she replied cautiously,

"But they seem to be getting the tables filled smoothly enough, Günther. And you know how fast Gayle is in the Kitchen. There must be more than a third of the guests seated and starting their appetizers or at best into their second courses."

"Why don't you have the Concierge and the Valets do a count of the overload, my dear, especially outside in the waiting cars."

Günther was anxious for her to get started as he added, "Also have your assistant contact the two main Hotels that are feeding the overload and put them on hold until we can get the traffic outside back under control."

Günther then returned his attention to Bill and Morgan, "I'm so sorry for this Bill, as you can see it seems we have overreached our resources for the moment and I don't want anyone disappointed with our service especially on our Opening Night."

"Don't worry about us Günther," Bill Waterman reacted in support, " you go ahead and get things under control, we'll catch up to you later."

"Tell you what Bill, why don't you and Miss Morgan take my private table for the moment and use that as your base," he snapped his fingers at Sammy Sinclair who had just looked his way.

"Sammy here is the Club's Operations Manager," Sammy was able to negotiate a path to Günther as he quickly realized from Günther's expression the importance of these guests, "and he knows just what to do Bill."

"Yes sir, Mr. Anderssen, good to see you again," Sammy reported in almost a military-like manner, clearly remembering just how Mr. Anderssen preferred his Managers to react when VIPs were in earshot. " and just how can I help, sir."

"Escort Mr. Waterman and Miss Morgan to my private table Sammy," he said as he prepared to join Crystale in relieving the current problem, " and get one of Gayle's people to set them up with whatever they need."

"Why of course, Mr. Anderssen, I'll get right on it," Sammy was quick as he turned to the couple, " Right this way, please Mr. Waterman," and in an instant he had them headed down to the lower levels and Günther's Private table overlooking the main dance floor.

Günther immediately made his way to the elevator to further check on the Kitchen as he looked back over the gathering throng of guests and tried to mentally analyze the situation inside; there were clusters of very well dressed men and women together but no one seemed left alone, he thought, that was very good; and the clusters were alive with conversation, champagne, mixed drinks, canapés and of course Gayle's incredible selection of continental hors d'oeuvres held in their hands, or floating by on the uplifted hands of Gayle's deftly skilled servers reacting to every nuance of need. The scene was just right, as Günther entered the warm elegance of the Club's single mahogany paneled elevator, custom designed with dual front and rear opening doors.

As he entered, two servers quickly slipped by him on both sides and exited with more of Gayle's canapés and hors d'oeuvres. And there, standing to the right of the door, in his smart new blue uniform with matching cap was Fletcher.

"Gooood Eve'nin, Mr. Anderssen," Fletcher respectfully offered as he greeted him, " and, what floor do you need sir?"

"Oh, Fletcher, it's good to see you again," Günther replied, somewhat relieved that he didn't have to operate this newer model Otis himself, "better get me down to see Miss Darling, right away."

In that moment, the door closed. And, unfortunately, Heidi had just missed getting on the elevator with him because of the exiting servers blocking her entry. But neither had seen each other, so she impatiently waited for it to return while observing that there didn't seem to be that many men under thirty, in fact very few were actually under forty.

It was plainly obvious at least to Heidi, that the privilege moneyed type Club members here tonight were the older more establish males in the group, 'the sugar daddies', and the younger ones were simply decoration for the dolls.

"Heidi. . . Heidi, " someone from the concierge desk called to her as she started to push the button again to urgently get Fletcher back up to the top level. She turned to see who it was.

"It's me, Crystale, I need your help, Heidi!" Crystale called to her, a bit louder than the chatter of conversations filling the nearby main bar area.

"Hey good look'in, what's up," Heidi replied as she abandoned her wait and slithered quickly along the backsides of two gray haired gentlemen, who turned and obviously enjoyed what they felt as they each one parted from their space and the ladies they were talking to.

Before she could reach Crystale, however, she spied a champagne glass on the floor dangerously near a female guest's foot. As she turned to retrieve it, she caught both gentlemen smiling in complete enjoyment of her bare-shoulders and obvious exposure of her cleavage while she was bending in their direction to snag the dangerous object.

"Are you gentlemen enjoying yourselves, tonight?" Heidi quipped in an obviously playful way, looking up at them before seductively rising to walk over to Crystale.

"I most certainly am, Miss Winters," the taller one said as he admired her cleavage while addressing the other gentleman,

"And you Alfred, what do you have to say?"

He continued smiling directly at Heidi as he added, "Time of my life, Frank. Time of my life I must say, Miss Winters, and I expect to have at least have one dance with you tonight, Miss Winters, just like the old days at the Grand Park Inn."

"And so you shall Mr. Daniels," Heidi replied unabashed," just look me up when I get to the dance floor after ten."

Crystale was grinning at her when she finally got to the desk, "You still have that incredible charm my dear," she laughed, "and ever since you met Millicent, I think your techniques with men have almost doubled in effectiveness."

"You're right about that," Heidi softly replied, so as to not attract too much of the ears of her nearby employees, now desperately trying to solve Günther's overload concerns.

"So what's the problem Crystale?" Heidi questioned as she redirected the conversation.

"Günther says were overloaded and somehow, I've got to stop or at least reduce the current stream of cars filling the parking lot, and now according to Gerald out front, they're almost a quarter of a mile back down the mountain and half way to College Street."

"Oh my God," Heidi was shocked as she half-laughed back at Crystale, "this is unreal, are we a hit or what?"

"So what do you suggest Heidi," Crystale was frantic, "I'm out of ideas except for trying to stop the incoming flow of Cars and Limousines for the time being by calling the Hotels."

"I have an idea," Heidi confided to her," but I'll need a full length coat to pull it off in those temperatures outside."

" I only brought that short jacket with me."

Crystale looked at her coat-check gal, "Missy, didn't I see someone walk in with a full length white Russian Mink coat about ten or fifteen minutes ago?"

"Yes Ma'am, Miss Crystale," Missy replied, " and it sure was a beauty, hung it myself just to get my face on that fur."

"What do you think, Heidi? " Crystale questioned, "think we could pull it off?"

"Where is the guest now, Missy? " Heidi looked into the crowd as she spoke.

"She had a table all ready, Ma'am," Missy added as if she knew she was going to be in some secret conspiracy, regardless of whether or not she wanted to be, " and they went down almost right away."

"Okay, Missy, lets do it " Heidi looked back at her and Crystale, "if the worst happens, let me know, and I'll enter from the outside into the elevator. That way it will look as though we were bringing it up from a secure vault or something."

"Sounds good to me, Heidi? " Crystale said as she directed Missy, "go get the coat, Missy"

Missy was back and Heidi was out the main lobby doorway in a flash, pumps clicking on the concrete as she located Günther's chauffeur, Max.

"Got an assignment for us Max," she said grabbing the door of Günther's black Cadillac Sedan Roadster and breaking his concentration on a new Marvel comic book he was reading, "somehow we have got to get these cars blocking the mountainside under control."

"Either they have to back down the mountain, turn around and drive down the mountain or leave their cars in place and we can take them back to their hotels for at least a while. What do you think Max?"

"We can arrange that, Miss Winters, it's not a problem, " Max replied, obviously unperturbed with the task, "let's go."

Within less than a half-hour Max and Heidi had cleared up the entire bottleneck and satisfied all the delayed guests with a special offer; that they would get the same complementary drinks, the same hors d'oeuvres and the same complementary entertainment arrangements as tonight, if they would just go back to their Hotels or Homes tonight, then return Saturday Night, beginning at Five PM, rather than Six.

That way, if they got there on time, they would be the first to be served and seated in the Dinning Room.

Heidi personally guaranteed it by signing their Private invitations on the back with her special comment and signature, noting that they would be admitted first.

By Nine PM, the place was really percolating with daddies, dolls and dames, and "everything's copacetic", as the Count himself like to say in his exuberant deep voice.

The upper bar was filled with cigarette and cigar smokers and beautiful young ladies enjoying the sounds of champagne bottles opening and glasses clinking together, while at each level couples did the same at their private tables, with everything working together in that special harmony that Gayle Darling said must overwhelm the senses.

The conversations were buzzing, Ladies had their after dinner drinks and Men had their booze, and now it was time for the real Swingers to come to the dance floor as the radio announcer tested his mike for the third or fourth time, tap, tap, tap . . .

Suddenly everyone was quieted by the announcement, and the new Count Basie Band for the first time anywhere in the America, emerged in single file from behind the bandstand and up from a staircase beginning at the rear of Gayle Darling's Kitchen down below.

The Swingers and Skirts went wild with screaming and shouts as the trend immediately overtook even the most docile Club members.

The opening number One O'clock Jump filled the dance floor with floorflushers and even the radio announcer was having trouble getting the band's sounds over the air with the crowd volume at such a frenzied level.

And that was just the first night of many weekends all winter long, as *The Sky Club* of Asheville became the hottest private entertainment nightspot anywhere south of New York City.

PART THREE

The Assassins

Late 1938

Chapter 1

Evolution

Overwhelmed by the tasks Himmler had assigned him, it was not until the following Wednesday, *Woten's Day* in old Norse Viking lore, before the newly commissioned SS-Gruppenfuhrer Horst Deeke was able to focus again, on thoughts of his own personal mission.

His mind's eye began to recreate the images of 1935. His years with Franco just before the Spanish Civil War. Back then he had created the Sicherheitspolizei Units, called SIPO, for Generalisimo Franco to rid Spain of it's Bolshevik virus.

In that year, Horst Deeke had been ordered to develop the most proficient group of terrorist and assassins ever conceived in the Third Reich. He collected the team only from previously experienced Aryan Military Specialists in Germany, Finland, and Norway. He called them 'Warriors des Fuhrer'.

The original order's mandate was based on the SS-Reichsfuhrer's paranoia. Himmler conceived of it to protect the Fuhrer and prepare for possible weaknesses or disloyalties by certain German Wehrmacht Field Commanders that even the SS-Waffen would be unable to deal with.

This clandestine fighting machine was so fierce that in truth, the SS-Reichsfuhrer's own Waffen-SS Units feared them.

Thus, the original SS-Wiking Legion, Nazi Germany's closest link to the mysterious and all-powerful Roman Praetorian Guards of antiquity, was created by the SS-Reichfuhrer. The name the SS-Reichfuhrer envisioned from his previous life's incarnation was a name honoring his Nordic obsessions of das Vaterland.

Horst remembered the monotonous train trip he had made with the core members of SS-Wiking deep into the Pyrenees Mountains of Spain.

He would succeed or fail, but even from the ashes of what remained, he would personally control or destroy the madness himself.

They had been rushed in to assist Mussolini's Italian Fascists and their friends in the Imperial Spanish Secret Police. Then Commander Franco was outclassed in his fight against the masses of Bolsheviks revolting and gaining control over the Unions.

Even Mussolini's Fascist police squads were no match for the crafty Zionists.

They were creating chaos everywhere at once and spreading the fires of Bolshevism quickly throughout Spain. In desperation, Franco had stated in a despondent letter to SS-Reichfuhrer Himmler, that Madrid was the last bastion left for him to stem the tide of Bolshevism. If it were lost, he and his family would be forced to evacuate to Argentina. And the communist would have a toe hold in Western Europe. Thus, the first trial of SS-Wiking was on course.

Suddenly Horst's vision returned to the present. He clearly knew what apparatus he would now use. His men were his most ardent core assets.

Precision killers, fluent in over five languages, Aryan militarists and Olympians of strength and endurance that had personally ended the Bolshevik purge of Franco's Madrid.

By utilizing 'The Omnipotent Orders Letter' from the Fuhrer and SS-Reichfuhrer, the Reich's Coded Swiss Bank Accounts, and the unfailing loyalty of his SS-Wiking Legion, newly promoted SS-Gruppenfuhrer Horst Deeke might just be the most dangerous man in the Third Reich.

His SS-Wiking Legion would always be unfailing, devoted and true to him alone under all circumstances. Now, the SS-Reichfuhrer Himmler's lunacy in seeking recognition from the Fuhrer had shifted the sole responsibility for any outcome that resulted from this future Nazi Hell squarely onto his shoulders.

Horst would never be able to change this course.

At that moment, Frau Bruller's voice broke coarsely into his daydream. The sound came through the metal intercom speaker mounted over his entrance door, announcing Erich Folker's arrival. "Wiking SS-Sturmbannfuhrer Erich Folkers is here as you had requested, Herr Gruppenfuhrer."

Erich Folkers had always been Horst Deeke's top officer in personal allegiance within the SS-Wiking Legion. His skills and weapons knowledge along with his uncanny sense of vigilance made him perfect for Horst's initial plan. For Erich this wouldn't even be much of a challenge, but those would come later.

Again, Horst's thoughts of Erich Folkers began to remember that ominous past.

The year was 1935 and they were traveling to meet with Franco in Madrid, but their orders required SS-Wiking members to remain in civilian clothes until they had cleared the French border. The day had been uneventful as the sky outside faded into an orange dusk.

Long monotonous train rides along with their repetitious metal clicking sounds have a way of lulling minds into a kind of hypnotic trace. The men in the Unit were no exception, except for Erich.

Once again, the train entered another tunnel on the French side of the Pyrenees Mountains, just twenty kilometers before Figueras.

Erich got up and moved silently toward the forward passenger car just behind the electric engine.

At that instant the normal electrical blackout cut off all lights in the train cars and only the tunnel roar and screeching metal on the tracks could be heard.

Before this moment, and back then only a SS-Sturmbannfuhrer, Horst had never really seen his SS-Obersturmfuhrer Erich Folkers in action, but the stories about his exploits seemed to be legendary within SS-Wiking.

Horst knew that Mussolini's Fascists and Franco's Secret Police had been advised of their arrival city, Barcelona, but no time schedule or train number had been sent, purposely.

SS-Wiking planners always knew the Italians had leaks to the Bolsheviks in Rome and you could trust very few people in Spain.

He would always remember the two events that ignited 1st Lieutenant Erich Folker's mysterious abilities of awareness and vigilance that later partially explained Erich's bizarre actions. Both of them became etched into his mind forever.

Earlier, the train had made one intermediary stop at Montpellier, France, after leaving Marseilles.

No one bothered to board until the final whistle blew. Then a couple of young French girls climbed into the forward car with an older dark haired man carrying a black sack over one shoulder. They never bothered to walk back to the conductor's station in the rear car and never moved from their forward seats. That was the first event.

The second, Erich noticed after the train exited the first tunnel. In Spain, older tunnels on electric tracks like those in the Pyrenees Mountains were designed for steam engines.

They had no electric cables overhead nor at the rail beds in the tunnel.

To reduce electrical drain from the train's batteries, only the engines had power during the short tunnel trip and for a few moments the interior cabins were blacked out without any lighting until the train emerged on the opposite end.

Generally these events were so common in mountainous train travel that no one noticed anything, just Erich.

After the first tunnel and resulting blackout, the pretty girls and the dark haired man had moved to the rear seats of the forward car without creating any attention. They had then turned intermittently and observed through the access door's window, the layout of the seats in the SS-Wiking car.

Erich Folkers knew this, but still alerted no one. They of course had no idea that he was wary of their next move. If they had known that it was he, the god that was about to take vengeance on all of them, they would have gladly jumped from the train to their immediate deaths. In the lore of SS-Wiking, Erich's Black Knife was almost as legendary as his massive upper body strength.

No one could begin to judge his movement speed.

Everything happened so quickly. Horst only realized that something terrible had happened when he was seen returning somewhat disheveled from the forward cabin.

The train had just exited the second tunnel and the light was finally restored to the cabin. Horst's Sergeant Major quickly walked up and asked if everything was okay, but he just said "Yes, Herr Sturmscharfuhrer " and sat down quietly.

SS-Sturmscharfuhrer Alex Wolfbauer and Horst's Adjutant SS-Hauptsturmfuhrer Gotz Pelkner both hastily entered the forward car.

There in eerily bizarre positions, all twelve of the passengers including the unknown trio lay decapitated in their seats. The fact that Folkers had accomplished this entire massacre in less than three minutes while the train was in complete black out was phenomenal.

Adjutant Pelkner stated that his physical kill strength and awareness techniques were uncanny to say the least, because every decapitation was flawless. There was no flesh ripping anywhere around the victim's spinal cords.

Pelkner figured it would have required over five-hundred pounds of weight from an impeccable guillotine blade to make the same slice from behind each victim, right to left.

SS-Sturmscharfuhrer Wolfbauer quickly focused on the black bag and went through it's contents. As he turned to Horst's Adjutant SS-Hauptsturmfuhrer Pelkner in surprise, he lifted three fully loaded canisters of 45 cal. Thompson Sub-machine gun ammunition and one of three US made Tommy Guns lodged in the sack.

They later found Bolshevik documents, several Russian-made grenades, and train schedules written in Italian and French. Needless to say that situation resulted in SS-Obersturmfuhrer Erich Folker's first Knight's Cross under Horst's command, but certainly not his last.

There was of course one thing that was never included in the report to the SS-Reichfuhrer Himmler. Once the team had secured the train, it made an unscheduled stop twelve kilometers east of Figueras, Spain.

Quickly, the team changed into camouflaged field military uniforms and prepared it's weapons.

After inspections and a general clean up of the forward car, SS-Obersturmfuhrer Erich Folkers asked to bury the two young girls himself.

SS-Sturmscharfuhrer Wolfbauer then observed him, as he positioned their decapitated heads carefully back onto their bodies in a shallow grave while kissing their lips. He proceeded to strip their bodies and manipulated their breasts repeatedly. Then with the dexterity of an experienced surgeon, he removed the ovaries from the lower abdominal cavities of both girls without any observable external scars.

SS-Sturmscharfuhrer Wolfbauer said he had to turn away when Folkers started this grotesque behavior with the girls, so he didn't see precisely all that happened. However, he felt that Folkers must have had the skill of a surgeon deftly hiding their ovaries somewhere, just as he turned away.

No one ever questioned Folkers on any of the final details and the entire matter was sealed as confidential by Horst's personal authority. Finally, when SS-Obersturmfuhrer Erich Folkers came down, they noticed that he had never bothered to fill their graves with earth. SS-Sturmscharfuhrer Wolfbauer's attaché SS-Rottenfuhrer Ernst Harms agreed to climb back up and finish the job. Soon after, the team was again underway to Madrid for the salvation of Franco and his Secret Police from the wrath of communism.

Again, but now with a sense of distress, Frau Bruller's voice broke into Horst's daydream through the metal intercom speaker.

"Herr Gruppenfuhrer, Herr Gruppenfuhrer, please, Wiking SS-Sturmbannfuhrer Erich Folkers has been waiting here for your requested meeting. What should I do?"

Almost jerking into the reality of the moment and pressing the intercom button with his foot, Herr Deeke responded in a surprised voice to Frau Bruller's pleading.

"Yes Frau Bruller. What you should do, is send Herr Sturmbannfuhrer Folkers into my office. Is that clear Frau Bruller."

Instantly relieved of the burden of entertaining the legendary, Erich Folkers for even one more minute, Frau Bruller's voice excitedly came through the intercom speaker again.

"Yes, Herr Gruppenfuhrer. Thank you. Herr Sturmbannfuhrer Folkers is on his way."

As Erich entered the renaissance Austrian Empire styled room, he closed the massive wood door behind him. Horst Deeke immediately rose from his chair to greet him. Without the formal Nazi-SS salutes, Horst grabbed Erich in a kind of bear hug and spoke. "God, it's good to see you again my friend."

Erich responded. " And you as well, my Supreme Commander! I have been excited to begin our new project together as soon as I heard of your promotion."

Erich opened his arms to emphasize the vast room that Horst now called the Wiking-SS Headquarters-Europe.

"This place is incredible Herr Commander, it must have cost a fortune to rebuild and now to keep it operational. And look at this grand library you have here!"

Erich gazed with awe at the three tiers of Empire bookshelves filled with many 1st edition works, the mahogany ladders on opposite walls for vertical access to the stacks, and finally the impressive reading table and the gold plated Louis XVI desk that Horst worked from.

"The lighting in here is quite amazing as well, even though those are not outside windows, Commander."

Horst smiled at his remark.

"Once again you amaze me Erich! Your uncanny ability to realize all truth in an instant still startles me."

"I won't even guess how you did it, but we back lit those walls and camouflaged their real purpose."

He walked to the wall and rubbed the velvet smooth drape tapestry in his fingers for effect, "We used these beautiful Royal Blue Drapes from a Viennese Chateau once used by Napoleon, to disguise the harsh concrete. You're right, they're as solid as the walls of ancient Rome, six feet thick to the outside earth works."

Suddenly, Erich spied a new toy and quickly walked to a backtable near a mahogany 1805 Napoleonic Field Bar.

"Ah, Herr Commander, you have obviously had Herr Follmer at Erma Armor create something new for SS-Wiking to completely overwhelm our adversaries." Erich picked up the latest custom designed shoulder fired machine pistol built for SS and Wehrmacht Paratroopers, the MP-38/SS-Wiking, often incorrectly referred to as a Schmeisser.

SS-Gruppenfuhrer Horst Deeke looked at Erich and smiled. "Erich, you now have in your hands an unloaded version of the most versatile and effective automatic machine pistol the world has ever seen.

The Erma Armor Company of Hamburg has modified two-thousand of these weapons specifically for our Wiking SSI Teams."

Erich began testing the charging handle and holding the gun in position for firing as he pointed it high into the curtained wall to his right.

" Herr Commander, this weapon is incredible, it is lightweight and very fluid in it's action response."

SS-Gruppenfuhrer Deeke then added,

"Herr Follmer took the MP-38 adopted by the Wehrmacht's paratroopers this year and made a further modification, specifically as I suggested. Notice, Erich, the front handguard. I had him mount it off the removable barrel."

"Without gloves, even sustained firing wont burn our hands in close combat. Plus, with that simple side release latch below the handguard, can you see it?"

Erich responded quickly. " Yes, yes. . . I have it."

Horst continued, "You can exchange a warped or damaged barrel in less than twenty seconds."

Again, Erich gasped with excitement. "Wunderbar, this thing is extraordinary! What is it's rate of fire?"

Horst again spoke with even stronger confidence of the weapon's unique capability. "Erich, with it's blowback in fully-automatic mode of fire, it can theoretically sustain a very controllable five-hundred to eight-hundred rounds per minute." Erich smiled with satisfaction as he listened.

"Of course, you realize that a typical Schmeisser magazine only holds thirty-two rounds of 9mm, but I asked Erma Armor to modify our SS-Wiking versions of the Magazine to fifty rounds each."

"Herr Follmer has always had a desire for perfection, so he himself added a quick release/insert on the larger magazine and a high pressure loading spring allowing the weapon to be reloaded easily even while you're running. "With a few magazines in your pack, you could take out over fifty 'schweinhunds' in a flash, Erich."

By now Erich was in complete ecstasy playing with the special underfolding steel buttstock as well as the fixed and hooded front sights.

SS-Gruppenfuhrer Deeke continued. "You can even mount it on armored vehicles and I've had them add a flippable rear sight for our assassin squad assignments with settings for one-hundred, one-hundred-fifty, and two-hundred meters."

"I've also had him make loads of a heavier charged super 'Steel-Point' nine millimeter rounds, for more accurate flat kill trajectories.

That way you can all keep a couple of these pre-loaded SSP magazines around for special assignments anytime."

While Erich continued to manipulate the MP-38/SS-Wiking, Horst Deeke walked back to his gilded desk and pulled a file of papers across it's Italian leather top.

"Erich, I now have several new and very special assignments for you and your SS Wiking 'Ende Lösung' Squad."

Promoted many times since those cold days in Madrid at the end of Spanish Civil War in 1936, SS-Sturmbannfuhrer Erich Folkers now had his original Knights Cross emblazoned with Oak Leaves for a second time in the service of SS-Wiking.

The Offizierschutzkappe that he held firmly under his left arm had the unique SS Wiking Legion markings designed by Horst. A golden SS Skull was centered on the faceplate of the cap just below the outspread wings of the Nazi SS Eagle emblem. The black eyes of the skull emphasized their deadly tasks while the ancient Dragon Prow from a Viking Longship symbolized their Nordic strength and true allegiance to SS-Wiking.

The SS-Gruppenfuhrer continued as he opened the file.

"A French contact befriended by our SSI Agent in Paris has revealed the names of two key Physicists working at the Joliot-Curie Radium Institute. The institute has effectively sequestered them from our Abwehr Agents in a hidden bunker near the Sorbonne in Paris. Apparently it was an ancient catacomb under the old city carved out during Roman Times. The French physicists have assembled a nuclear isotope cyclotron, piece by piece in this vast underground chamber."

"Electric power had somehow been drawn from electricity used for the Paris Metro System without anyone's awareness." Horst paused for effect, as he turned directly to face Erich.

"As you know Erich, we now have a massive cyclotron here at Sangerhausen. But what this SSI Agent uncovered, we need more acutely now; their knowledge. The French Zionist scientists have proven, using their cyclotron, that a new and potent source of neutrons that can be used to split Uranium-238 into U-235 much more quickly to form weapons grade uranium."

Horst knew that up to this point in time, German scientists, as well as American Scientists, were focused on U235 as the only method for creating a massive nuclear explosion. The current theories and methods for harvesting incredibly minute amounts of U-235, from literally tons of Uranium ore, would be an immense and costly undertaking that could take years to accomplish. The French had a faster way to get U-235.

On top of that problem, German physicists at Sangerhausen had triggered an accidental setback in their own experiments when they used impure sources of graphite as their primary moderator for the Uranium separation. Then, needing quicker results, as a result of the potential reprisals from the SS-Reichfuhrer, they immediately changed course and decided to use 'heavy water' as their moderator. Heavy water, however, had only one known worldwide source at Vemork, Norway.

The French physicists at the Joliot-Curie Radium Institute facility hidden near the Sorbonne had already begun using that resource in limited quantities to complete their experiments in extreme privacy. But for political reasons, they had also refused to publish anything that their American counterparts could use, to catch up to them.

Horst's thoughts then focused again. His eyes were drawn across the glint of leather of volumes massed along the upper walls of his operations library.

He then looked again toward Erich. The die was cast for the use of the SS Wiking 'Final Solution' Squad.

Erich's team would be the perfect instrument. They would clandestinely extricate this knowledge and the people that conceived it. Horst then spoke emphatically. "And so my Teutonic Knight, we must have them and their discovery here at Sangerhausen at all costs."

Without any hesitation, Erich's face brightened as he responded to Horst's medieval reference.

"Of course, 'mein Lord und Kommandant' !"

"Then let's begin," Horst rejoined, as he motioned for Erich to join him at the planning table centered at the rear of the room.

Together they sat down and worked out the details for several hours. Weapons, equipment, and logistics as well as who would be selected from the SS Wiking 'Ende Lösung' Squad for each specific action they methodically planned.

Erich of course, amazed Horst Deeke once again, as he visualized even the most remote details of human maneuvers, his own back-up tactics, and what would happen in the event of unforeseen problems.

By midnight, all was in readiness.

Dressed in civilian clothing SS-Sturmbannfuhrer Erich Folkers and his SS Wiking 'Ende Lösung' Squad members were on their way by train, to Paris, by way of the international crossroads at Geneva, Switzerland.

Chapter 2

Schutzstaffel Infiltration

Unknowingly, Severine Ventremou had befriended a very handsome Nordic officer of SSI-Wiking who was effectively disguised as a philosophy student. He had pursued her to meet him by accident back in September at a coffee shop in the Latin Quarter near the Sorbonne. Now, that casual interest was beginning to burn into her sexual fantasy to have him to herself.

SS-Obersturmfuhrer Hans Vogel's cover for this SSI assignment directed him to have influential, but as well, clandestine ties to Bolsheviks and politically connected Russians and Jews back in Austria. Herr Vogel easily convinced Severine Ventremou of his subterfuge, since at least six months earlier, she herself had been innocently drawn to Bolshevism by her Institute Advisor and friend, Professeur Ghentmann.

Severine was a very pretty, but petite girl of twenty-one that had worked for the Curie Scientists in their Radium Institute facility at the Sorbonne for over a year. Her innocence and theoretical curiosity made her the object of Professeur Ghentmann's every thought, when he wasn't in the lab. Severine's thin figure and soft dark exotic features had attracted his sexual imagination ever since she had joined his student scientists.

Often she would come to the Lab without a bra because of clothing rationing problems. Sometimes on cold mornings the effect would harden her nipples teasing Ghentmann.

Regularly without her labcoat, she would enter his office to get her morning assignments and he always seemed to delay her with extra theories or discussions.

Of course, she knew where his eyes were and she played her sensuous game with him, to perfection. Even to the extent of leaving strategic buttons undone to expose her cleavage to him from time to time. Besides she needed the job and he was too old for her anyway.

All the while his cravings for her grew, and sexually drove him into blind frustration. He would do anything to make love to her, but she only teased him more.

On the other hand, Ghentmann's cohort, Professeur Lippenski seemed to be so pre-occupied with the cyclotron project that she had to pry thoughts from his humdrum mind.

Whenever she got bored down in the cave as they called the cyclotron facility, because Lippenski never spoke to her, she would read the French Communist Newspapers.

It was at once clear to her, when she truly discovered his strange idiosyncrasy. Professeur Lippenski was gay. As such, he was typical of most French homosexual men and would never be drawn to her casual intellectual style or feminine seduction.

As she continued to reach out to him, however, she found that he was strongly sympathetic politically toward Bolshevism and uncovering this gave them a mutual topic of conversation. Sometimes she would just read the daily Communist Newspaper aloud to him, while he remained absorbed in his endless calculations in the dimly lit cave room.

For SS-Obersturmfuhrer Hans Vogel, Ghentmann was the real focus of the ruse. He and Professor Francois Lippenski, who trained under Niels Bohr in Copenhagen, were the two most innovative French Jewish nuclear physicists in Europe. And now they were working covertly with Monsieur Joliot on the cyclotron that SS-Gruppenfuhrer Horst Deeke needed.

But because of her association and close confidence with both of these scientists, Severine Ventremou had also become the object of SS-Obersturmfuhrer Hans Vogel's false pretense, since he actually preferred men himself. A fact, the SS-Obersturmfuhrer had gone to great efforts to cloak from anyone in the SS, but especially the SS-Sturmbannfuhrer Erich Folkers and his SS Wiking Squad members.

Of course, none of that mattered now, nor would anyone ever know, because he was in an isolated branch of Schutzstaffel Infiltration, and by authority of SS-Gruppenfuhrer Horst Deeke himself, SSI Agents always worked alone on their extortion assignments.

When SS-Sturmbannfuhrer Erich Folkers and his SS Wiking Squad arrived at the Gare d'Austerlitz, in Paris, it was again midnight. This time the train crossing into France had been like clockwork and uneventful.

As they disembarked from the station entrance, SS-Obersturmfuhrer Hans Vogel silently met them with a small black Citroen Van.

They quickly loaded their gear without speaking and drove off into a deserted alleyway nearly obscured by the night mist and the blacked-out street lamps.

After a couple of severe turns, they emerged into a lighted area as they made their way along the Boulevard St. Germain within the 5th Arrondissement, to Vogel's underground flat near the Sorbonne.

The Latin Quarter of Paris always held mysterious people at all hours of the day and night, and War in France was almost a year away, so their journey was again unobserved and without incident.

Once inside the flat the SS-Sturmbannfuhrer took command and addressed the SS-Obersturmfuhrer with a sinister smile on his face.

"Where is this Bolshevik Mademoiselle of your dreams, Herr Vogel?"

Awkwardly, the SS-Obersturmfuhrer Vogel, attempting to formalize the request by his Senior Officer, snapped his heels together and quickly gave the official SS Salute. "Heil Hitler, SS-Sturmbannfuhrer."

"The young Fräulein Severine, our innocent instrument of this betrayal, is waiting for me at her apartment as I had planned, SS-Sturmbannfuhrer. And it's obvious we need her because she has told me that Professeur Ghentmann's cravings for her have grown insane.

She's even afraid he will rape her if she continues to tease him like she has, and of course she says he would do anything, just to get into her silk panties."

SS-Sturmbannfuhrer Folkers again reacted with a clearly perverse look in his eyes. He quizzically starred at Vogel's face, then raised his voice in rage.

"As you planned! You like her don't you, Herr Vogel! Why are you concerned for this Jew Lover Herr Vogel? I've read your reports and she's probably screwing another young Zionist student at the lab every evening. Would you choose to dip into that Juden's fluids, after he fills her up each night!"

Folkers vulgarity struck Vogel with an instant fear of reprisal for making such a smug remark to an SS-Wiking Staff Officer.

"Jawohl mein Kommandant! "

"I understand your meaning and my comments 'were' out of line. It is your plan that will accomplish this mission, not mine. I am not at all concerned about this girl, only the complete success of your mission tonight. I simply wanted you to know that the Professeur Ghentmann's cravings would allow us to extort his full allegiance."

"Particularly if she was also abducted along with him and Professeur Lippenski. . . She could be used to satisfy Ghentmann's carnal cravings, and he of course would do whatever we asked of him then."

"So what do you want me to do Herr Sturmbannfuhrer?"

" I am at your Command!"

This time SS-Sturmbannfuhrer Folkers seemed to calm himself and stated.

"Then it is decided. She will be taken as well. You will announce to her by telephone, that you will be there momentarily and she should prepare for you tonight, in whatever way that pleases her."

" Do it now!"

"Jawohl mein Kommandant!" Vogel responded in enthusiastic relief that the subject had changed from his plan, back to the SS-Sturmbannfuhrer's mission plan. Severine was the last thing he wanted to mess with anyhow. He knew he would be out of harm's way, if he could only make the evening's pleasure visit sound believable to her.

Nodding understanding, but without asking permission of the SS-Sturmbannfuhrer, he hastily turned away and moved into the bedroom to dial her number.

In French, he greeted her as she answered in a sensual, but groggy tone. She sounded either dazed from the late awakening or intoxicated from the occasional wine she liked to overindulge in on certain nights.

Her voice was still very soft and sexy as she seemed to be begging him through the phone to come over, even through the hour was late. Han's perfectly accented his French softly back to her as well.

"I have something I must finish now, but I promise I will be there in a short while."

"Just leave your key under the door and I will delicately wake you when I get there, mon Amour."

For effect Hans added a last impression for her in his most sensuous French. "Make yourself very comfortable and this time we will make love, je promettre."

Severine Ventremou had longed for this moment ever since she and Hans had met. Now she would have this beautiful young man to herself.

"I want you deeply, mon Amour! Come to me quickly . . . au revoir, mon Amour!"

Severine replaced the phone and closed her eyes as she drifted back to sleep with her newly imagined fantasy evolving in her mind.

Chapter 3

Abduction

Since well before medieval times in the 11th Century, Paris has had an invisible underground system of catacombs, quarries and sewers built from its gypsum and limestone subsoil. Within the Latin Quarter alone, near the Sorbonne, over three-hundred kilometers of tunnels exist unused by the surface population. The entrance to one of these vast chambers and it's access tunnels was built at great expense just before the Franco-Prussian War in 1870. Now the Apartment building over the chamber housed several members of the Curie Radium Institute's Nuclear Physicist team. Two among them were Professeur Ghentmann and his vital comrade, the Bolshevik, Professeur Lippenski.

During their reconnoiter, SS-Sturmbannfuhrer Folkers SS-Wiking three man Spezialist team found a secluded access to the upper apartment above the chambers from a building across the street.

A metal ladder bridge had been constructed in the early 1900s to provide a meager fire escape from one building to the other across the narrow Rue below. Now, Wiking SS-Hauptscharfuhrer Schnee - SS-Master Sergeant and his two assassins, SS-Scharfuhrer Mahn - SS-Staff Sergeant and SS-Rottenfuhrer-Spezialist Mahn - SS-Corporal Specialist, setup the bridge and made their way across, then down into the sleeping quarters. At that hour nothing was moving in the building or in the street below.

They moved silently without challenge to the designated targets. Their entry was flawless and in moments both Physicists were subdued without harm and brought by the Citroen Van to the rendezvous point near the Gare d'Austerlitz.

The new immobilizing anesthetic drug, morphine hyoscine hydrobromide, prepared at the Nazi controlled Bayer Pharmaceutical facility by Spezialist-Doktor Claussmann, left little fight in anyone injected.

The immediate effect left the victim somewhat dazed, but ambulatory and completely subjugated to the person controlling the injector. In most cases, several injections were needed for a full twenty-four hours of control, but an interesting side effect was the bizarre fantasies experienced by the victims.

There seemed to be no long term side effects, so SS-Sturmbannfuhrer Folkers seemed to think of it as his own personal carnal aphrodisiac. Erich would always find some opportunity to employ its effects on a mission in some unsuspecting young femme fatale.

SS-Sturmbannfuhrer Folkers entered the Apartment building as arranged by Hans and briskly climbed the staircase to #410. Severine's apartment was located off the Grande Rue Monge near the Jardin Carre. As expected, he found her door key in a small envelope with a note.

However, as he read the note written in French, he was drawn into a phantasmal dream created by the young Severine. . .

> *Hans, Please surprise me, mon Amour!*
> *I will promise not to open my eyes until your*
> *kiss is on my lips. I have so wanted this night,*
> *and I'll be waiting naked under the sheets for*
> *you, even if I'm asleep when you arrive.*
> *Severine*

Suddenly, Erich found himself anticipating this new and innocent prey. She was now his ultimate fantasy. And this would be his ultimate charade.

Erich entered quickly through the doorway and saw a dim light glowing in the next room as he secured the entry door. He silently moved into the room and removed his injector case holding the syringe .

The sealed vial within the case contained 500mls.of morphine hyoscine hydrobromide, but he only removed 100mls.for Severine's injection. He wanted her to enjoy her fantasy, before he completely enslaved her in his.

Severine's features were just as he expected. She was a small delicate girl with soft glistening white skin and full exotic lips. His eyes moved quickly to view the gentle rise and fall of her chest and the rounded form of her breasts. He knew she was naked under the thin sheet pulled up to her delicate neckline and he could vaguely see the pink outline of her small nipples.

His fantasy began slowly, as he noticed a black silk scarf tied to the bedpost. Quickly he unfastened it, and with one motion, blindfolded his prey, tying it off gently behind her head, to maintain his ruse.

She hadn't moved nor given him any suggestion she was awake yet, except for a sensual movement she made, as he laid her head back onto the pillow.

Erich removed his clothes slowly as he quietly watched her. Deliberately, he placed the loaded syringe on the nearby bed table and carefully lifted the bed sheet to completely view her. Then gently, he moved under the sheet beside her. She felt warm to his skin as he slid next to her. Severine's thin body hardly took up any room in the single bed.

A sudden jolt of incredible stimulation returned Severine to the present moment with what she thought was Hans. She could now feel his massive grip around her tiny waist, while he seemed to be rubbing his thumbs in a circular motion on the tender mounds of her ovaries.

In the next moment, he pushed deep inside her.

She spontaneously grabbed him to protect herself from the incredible pain of entry, and as she did so the silk scarf came loose, but it was too late.

"You're not Hans! You are killing me! You're raping me, you bastard! Where is Hans, oh God, where is he?"

Erich gazed into her terrified green eyes now filled with fear and panic.

The surprise and the utter hopelessness of her predicament left her crying violently, as he continued with his perverted phantasm, driven by his animal urge.

Drained of all fight, she released her grip and collapsed back to the mattress. She was emotionally devastated and drained of any strength. Her eyes were transfixed on the soft light reflected off the ceiling.

Her body seemed to lie back on the bed in the form of a crucifix with her long brown hair spread out in a bizarre effect around her bewildered face.

Erich glanced back at her, as he reached for the syringe and tapped out the air bubbles. She needed the injection now, if for no other reason than to keep her quite on the long journey back to Germany.

He then popped an engorged vein on her left fore arm, without any resistance, as she lay ravaged and weakened on the sunken mattress.

Quickly he injected her with a full dose, but she never moved or said a word. She just continued to stare in a dream like state at the ceiling light above. Severine was in shock as she finally began to mumble again softly.

"Who are you? Where is Hans?" Then she turned to face him. "Why did you do this to me?"

Erich said nothing.

He just continued to watch for signs that the drug was taking hold. He moved in close to her face and checked her eyes again. The vibrant green was now beginning to turn dark.

They were starting to glaze over, without feeling. Her speech was becoming unrecognizable as she tried to reason with him once more.

"What did you inject me with, you bastard? What is . . .?"

Erich then got up and went into the bathroom to clean up as she began to drift off into a black void. Her eyes closed and she was out.

SS-Sturmbannfuhrer Folkers arrived at the Gare d'Austerlitz at about 0600 Hours.

Schnee greeted the SS-Sturmbannfuhrer and advised him that both Physicists had already departed with escorts to the Swiss Frontier before 0300 Hours.

He then inquired about the girl because she seemed to be in need of medical attention. Erich advised the SS-Hauptscharfuhrer to get her into a private train cabin on the return trip to Geneva and continue her injections. He then provided the SS-Hauptscharfuhrer with the name of a particular Doctor to attend to her when they got to Switzerland. She was to see no one until they crossed the Swiss border.

Erich knew this woman would be used to further extract support from the two French Scientists, at least until they had accomplished their goals for SSI. Then they would all become expendable sub-humans, by order of the SS-Reichfuhrer.

He then departed the Gare d'Austerlitz for his new rendezvous assignment at Niels Bohrs' Slow Neutron Fission Lab in Copenhagen.

Chapter 4

Control of the Unwilling

Horst remembered that from April 1933 to December 1938, anti-semitic Laws and Decrees of the Third Reich were being directed specifically at Jews in the Universities. The University of Berlin Physics Institute and the Kaiser Wilhelm Institute as well as major Universities in Leipzig, Hamburg, and Munich were purged of over sixteen-hundred of their greatest physicists, chemists and nuclear theoreticians.

Several non-Aryan Nobel laureates like Albert Einstein and John von Neumann, had already left Germany, while Max Planck, Fritz Haber, Leo Szilard, Wolfgang Pauli and Otto Frisch had recently moved to American Universities to escape the growing Nazi horror.

Both the brilliant young Hungarian, Edward Teller, author of the expanding applications of quantum mechanics and thermonuclear theories, as well as the Italian Nobel laureate Enrico Fermi, who was actively recruited to join the Columbia University Team, had left the Axis counties by 1938.

It was back in the early 1930s, that the most critical future players in the WW II game of high stakes nuclear warfare development evolved.

They were two nuclear physicists that took their Ph.D.s under the great German Physicist Werner Heisenberg in Leipzig, Germany.

One of these men was Mort Bruckmann and the other very key player was the Hungarian, Edward Teller.

Bruckmann had known the young Edward Teller in Karlsruhe, Germany in 1928 at the time of Edward's accident. Edward had got caught between the electric grounding rail and the wheel of a streetcar.

As he did so, his right foot was severed just above the ankle. While the amputation healed, Mort and Edward developed a close friendship that continued with them into their work at the Institute in Leipzig in 1930. They had always remained friends, but as the Nazi pressures against Jews in Germany grew, their paths began to diverge.

Edward moved first to the Institute for Physical Chemistry at Gottingen because of overt anti-semitic discrimination festering in Leipzig. At Gottingen, he personally developed over thirty original papers focused on quantum mechanics and nuclear physics.

This was the same young nuclear physicist that by 1939, would become one of the world's leading experts in quantum mechanics as well as the first scientist to describe the finite details of a hydrogen based thermonuclear bomb.

Once again a great opportunity was lost for Germany. Nazi pressures continued to build-up in Germany and Edward Teller was finally driven away to Copenhagen, Denmark, accepting a Rockefeller Fellowship to work with Nobel Laureate Niels Bohr on the next evolution of quantum mechanics and nuclear physics.

That event in 1933, left his friend Mort Bruckmann working with Physicist Werner Heisenberg for another three years on similar quantum mechanics problems, but without the vigorous conceptual arguments of Teller.

They of course, always remained close friends and constantly exchanged ideas, but nothing would substitute for the direct working relationship they had developed at Leipzig, in the past. By 1936, even Mort was under severe pressures from the Nazi's.

Unlike the very Jewish appearance of Edward, Mort looked more like his Catholic mother. He had blue eyes, very Germanic features, and thick brown hair, cut short in a military appearance.

Mort was also more physically sturdy than Edward, but he seemed to be immature socially and insecure with women.

As a good skier, mountain climber, and all around athlete, it was surprising that he was so exceptionally competent in a wide range of nuclear physics studies. Unfortunately for his future in Germany, his father was Jewish.

Because of that, he chose to follow his mother's catholic background and the nationalistic influence that her grandparents had on him.

Her grandfather, who still had a sharp mind at almost eighty-five years old, had been a zealous German and as a young officer in the Prussian Army during the Franco-Prussian War of 1871, and he wanted Mort to join the Wehrmacht.

Still, being a strong German Nationalist mattered little as the Nazis began detaining various Jewish families in Special Camps throughout Germany. And the Bruckmann's were an unlucky bunch.

As 1938 came about, his father's political enemies at the University of Kiel identified him as both as a Zionist and a Bolshevik sympathizer after he was caught aiding some students hurt at a rally near Hamburg in April, 1938.

Things happened fast after that event. By the time Mort Bruckmann knew what had happened, Herr Heisenberg had sent him a dismissal letter and advised him, for his own safety to get out of Leipzig by way of Switzerland as quickly as possible. That was the last time he saw his family, Werner Heisenberg, or his homeland of Germany.

By late 1938, Mort Bruckmann had arrived via Switzerland and France into the United States and was trying to get work at Princeton in New Jersey.

He had yet to contact his good friend Edward Teller who had left Copenhagen, but the events in Germany had shaken him so much that he had lost all sense of time during his escape.

His application to the Institute for Advanced Study was on hold, but a chance meeting with the renowned Physicist Albert Einstein at the Institute on the day of his oral presentation, allowed him a telephone introduction to Robert Oppenheimer at the California Institute of Technology - Cal-Tech.

Oppenheimer was ecstatic and they hit it off great, right away.

He immediately needed a strong theoretician in quantum mechanics as well as nuclear physics, and Mort easily fit the bill with the high honors.

A flight was arranged for Mort to join Oppenheimer at his home in Berkeley outside of San Francisco, California. From that point on, Mort Bruckmann became the most prized asset in Robert Oppenheimer's quantum mechanics faculty. Mort spent the next few years of his re-location to America with the Cal-Tech faculty and Oppy, as Oppenheimer was affectionately known by his associates and friends at Cal-Tech. He stayed in touch with his family in Germany, but outside of teaching, his secondary focus was to help Oppy get Edward Teller to Cal Tech, and that he did.

By the end of 1939, Mort, Oppenheimer, and Edward Teller had become the most important theoretical nuclear physics players anywhere on the planet.

This association formed their ultimate destiny, as it merged into the core of General Groves' massive Manhattan Project, the top secret project that began a two billion-dollar industry initially developing America's first two Atomic Bombs, Little Boy and Fat Man, in late January of 1943.

Chapter 5

Extortion

Realizing a unique political opportunity, to correct the damaging mistake of the "Scientific Purge and Purification Decrees against German Universities", Horst's leader, the SS-Reichfuhrer Heinrich Himmler met with the Fuhrer to confer on this critical oversight. Horst knew that the Reichfuhrer had conceived the meeting to regain control himself over the massive Financial Assets and Nuclear Scientists that would soon be used to create the Nazi Super Bomb.

Horst also knew that if Himmler could re-direct the blame for the Scientific Purges, it would yield him even more power in this matter in the future, and of course the "ultimate" recognition of the Fuhrer.

By emphasizing the potential devastation to the German War effort caused by this critical error in judgment and uncovering detailed evidence, he confirmed to the Fuhrer that Wilhelm Canaris and his Abwehr Military Intelligence Division had caused the 1933 Purge of key scientists. The effect allowed Himmler to ultimately strengthen his absolute control over the Nazi SS and SD Units and take exclusive control over the Nuclear Bomb Project in one decisive move.

On that particular day in November 1938, SS-Reichfuhrer Heinrich Himmler's meeting with the soon to be promoted SS-Oberfuhrer Reinhard Heydrich had but one purpose, the formation of a special containment unit for families of re-located Jewish scientists.

The program focused on Scientists that were working on crucial German Scientific War Projects or specific Physicists already working in America or Britain that could be extorted to aid the Reich at some future date.

The camp would be under the direct control of Heydrich's SD Units and would effect absolute control over all Zionist Scientists working for the Third Reich.

The chosen re-location center would be southwest of Leipzig, deep in the Harz Mountains just outside the wire fences of Buchenwald.

This unit exclusively for the Scientists Families would be isolated from the main concentration camp and would have it's own enclosed infrastructure, post office and SD Security Battalion.

It would be called Zelten Jerusalem, and would become a model of pure subterfuge to extract allegiance from the critical sub-human assets needed to develop the advance war making technology of the Third Reich.

SS-Oberfuhrer Reinhard Heydrich had conceived of the diabolical idea of Camp Jerusalem some months before this meeting with Himmler, to disguise the atrocities that might be needed in the future to either re-locate or actually eliminate the entire Jewish problem from das Vaterland.

The image of a warm place to stay, a private room, schools for their children, a medical facility, good food, plus protection from the overt aggression now existent everywhere in Germany's streets was fostered as the main reason this camp existed.

Heydrich designed a complex Post Office run by his own SD units to covertly censure all in-coming and out-going mail. The Zelten Jerusalem Post Office encouraged families to communicate this subterfuge to Jews outside the Camp in Germany proper as well as back to their Scientist Husbands, Sons, and Lovers that were forced into service for the War effort by the SS and SD of the Third Reich.

Two psychologist were even added to Heydrich's SD staff to assure the Jewish Families that they would eventually be re-located to a Palestinian homeland not far from Jerusalem in the Middle-East.

Chapter 6

Zelten Jerusalem

Horst's associate SS-Oberfuhrer Reinhard Heydrich had recently enlarged the Buchenwald facility to provide a staging area for further re-location of the general German Jewish population. Later on it would be expanded even more as Germany invaded various other eastern European domains. In that fashion the Fuhrer's Final Solution, could then allow pure Aryan Germans to re-populate areas that the Jews were extracted from. Furthermore, Juden would be removed from the cities and the conquered countries bordering Germany, thus allowing a perimeter to be built around das Vaterland of pure Aryan militia, Aryan workers, and Aryan farmers moved directly into the vacuum Judenfrei created. In the end, das Vaterland would be insulted from the poisonous ideas of the hated Zionists and Bolsheviks that had devastated Germany before, and had nearly destroyed the Aryan race. A hatred, according to das Fuhrer, viciously created on 28 June 1919 at the Treaty of Versailles after the Great War, when the Zionist and Bolshevik controlled nations had taken away all of Germany's abilities to return as a normal country, to the world community.

The initial group of families had been standing near the train car on the hard packed snow in a roll-call line-up for about twenty minutes in the freezing November wind.

Unlike the Jewish prisoners with yellow Star of David armbands recently deported from German cities in the main compound of Buchenwald however, these specially selected people were allowed to have their coats and shoes on as they waited in silence with their limited belongings.

Suddenly, a massive four door Mercedes Benz command car roared into the small rail siding where a sign overhead read Selection for Jerusalem.

Instantly, the group of forty black uniformed SD Totenkopf Kommandos holding Schmeissers at the ready and guarding the small group of families, slammed their boot heels together.

A loud simultaneous clap echoed around the nearby dark wooden buildings forming the enclosed courtyard at the railhead. A Technical Sergeant jumped out of the driver's side of the Mercedes and rushed around to the right passenger door.

As the Oberserscharfuhrer opened it, a gleaming spit polished black boot slammed to the snow beneath the door and a tall impeccably uniformed Aryan SD Officer in his late thirties emerged carefully from the car.

Near the center of the mass of frigid bodies at the train siding was a bearded gentleman in his late fifties and a dark haired young girl of only sixteen standing tensely together. Orsi Bruckmann held her father's hand tightly as the apprehension grew in the group of Jewish internees in the Central Muster Plaza of Auswahl als Jerusalem.

Ever since the untimely death of his wife Kristine Bruckmann in December, Orsi had become her father's only desire to live and he would make that promise to Kristine last until she was safe from this horror. Orsi had been born late in her mother's life, so she had very little recollection of her brother Morty. Samuel Bruckmann was a strong man, but the years since his son's escape to America, his six months of harsh imprisonment in Hamburg's Juden Work Prison for trying to save a student with a bashed head during the Bolshevik Rally at the University of Kiel, and finally his wife's painful death, had taken it's toll on him.

Samuel loved his son Mort, but he was sad that he had not seen his mother before her final agony with the cancer that ended her life. He knew Mort would have done anything to be with her, but they would have caught him too and so he never sent the letter requesting him to visit her one last time in Hamburg.

Now, it was just Samuel and Orsi, and Mort would never see them again either, now that they had been sent here to the Buchenwald Concentration Camp.

Auswahl als Jerusalem was actually further from the main Buchenwald Camp than it appeared from the air.

With a constant west to east breeze from the upper Harz Mountains into the Valley, they could neither hear the sounds of trains arriving, nor smell the air or smoke emanating from Buchenwald.

Observing the Auswahl Kamp from an overhead view clearly indicated it was geologically separated from the main Buchenwald facility by a ridge of hills about one-hundred and fifty meters high.

Also, there were no SD Death's Head Guard towers nearby and tall Norwegian Pines were packed edge to edge blocking the view of a ten-meter high wire perimeter fence, allowing the compound to look like an unassociated administrative area.

Buchenwald itself was about three kilometers away in a valley to the southeast of the Auswahl Camp, and a remote rail switching yard had been built about five kilometers to the northwest of Buchenwald to direct selected rail cars to the Auswahl area without interaction from the daily trains that fed deported Jews into Buchenwald. A Juden free, all Nordic State was the given reason for these deportations in late 1938 Germany, but all too often a greater-fear was growing in the minds of all Jews arriving into these ghastly camps.

Concentration Camps like Buchenwald would eventually become death camps and extermination centers for Jews, not re-location centers for Palestine, but Samuel Bruckmann still had hope that he and Orsi would somehow escape all that here at the Auswahl Camp.

Within the Third Reich, for the past six years, hundreds of thousands of German Jews, Bolsheviks, and Non-Aryan Races had been placed on extensively categorized lists.

However, the Lists had only two main groups. Gruppe I, Verzeichnis von Feinde - #1 - List of Nazi Enemies and Gruppe II, Verzeichnis von Wissenschaftlerinnen Familien - #2 - Lists of Scientists Families. Both these lists had been extensively researched by hundreds of SD and Gestapo Officers for the sole benefit of the SS-Oberfuhrer Reinhard Heydrich's Programmes.

Today, as he exited his private Mercedes Command Car, Heydrich was about to meet the first extractions for his Gruppe II list.

Boots stomping and crunching the snow was the only sound anyone at the train siding heard as an SS Major rushed forward to the SS-Oberfuhrer Reinhard Heydrich's door. Stopping just short of Heydrich, the officer quickly raised a salute while loudly exclaiming, "Heil Hitler, Herr SS-Oberfuhrer!"

The SS-Sturmbannfuhrer then came to a stiff state of attention as his boot heels clicked together allowing the SS-Oberfuhrer Reinhard Heydrich to exit the car and return the salute. For a moment, Heydrich stood silent as he slowly looked from side to side over the crowd of about fifty Jewish people huddling to stay warm.

Heydrich was a tall, horse faced, blond haired Aryan man that had often been called the Blond Beast.

He stood over six feet tall in an impeccable black overcoat adjusting his black leather gloves as his piercing eyes bored into each face. He seemed to know the final fate of every Jew standing before him. He even seemed to relish the pain they were all experiencing, as they stood there shuddering away from his eyes and the freezing wind, blowing down from the mysterious Harz Mountains to the northwest.

Then, SS-Oberfuhrer Reinhard Heydrich spoke with almost the gentleness of a shepherd talking to his sheep.

"Ladies and Gentlemen you will not be detained here in this freezing cold much longer. We have a warm building nearby, set up as a processing center, where you will be asked to undergo a standard medical exam. Please follow the instructions of my nurses and doctors carefully. We will then assign you to your own private rooms. Each Family will have beds in those rooms for individual adults and children. Proper amounts of bath linens and bed linens will be provided as well as a shared water closet for every two families. "

"Once this first phase is complete, I will introduce you to the protective SD officers that will provide for your security here at Zelten Jerusalem, " he continued.

"We will meet at 1200 Hours in the dining room for a hardy meal and my officers will provide an orientation to our school, our exercise facility and our greenhouse built to assure you of fresh vegetables even during this harsh winter."

Everyone was still silent. No one in the crowd had suggested any indication of recognition, of what had been said. They all seemed frozen with fear. Heydrich then became very serious as he added his ominous final statement.

"Ladies and Gentlemen you have been brought here to be relocated to your homeland in Palestine in the near future.

We want you to conduct your lives as normally as can be expected during this time of adjustment for das Vaterland. Let me caution you however! You must not try to escape from this facility, ever!"

Once again, SS-Oberfuhrer Heydrich adjusted his gloves as he looked into the crowd.

His eyes seemed to be piercing by design into the face of Samuel Bruckmann, and Samuel was frozen in place by the absolute raw fear of this man, as he again raised his voice.

"You are here for a reason, if that reason goes away you will no longer be provided with my infinite protection," he paused for effect.

"Please, for your own sake and that of your family do not disappoint me, I will only offer you this one chance to re-locate from Zelten Jerusalem to your future home in Palestine. After that your fate is your own."

Everyone knew exactly what was meant by the inferences, still silent though, they waited to be dismissed by the SS-Oberfuhrer.

Heydrich turned to the SS-Sturmbannfuhrer beside him and spoke quietly into his left ear.

No one had heard the SS-Oberfuhrer's instructions, but as the conversation ended, the SS-Sturmbannfuhrer responded out loud.

"Jawohl, mein SS-Oberfuhrer! I will move them to the Medical Clinic at once."

Then Heydrich walked off to a side entrance in the Medical Clinic used by the Doctors, leaving the SS-Sturmbannfuhrer to finalized the next step in processing the scientist's families.

As if instructed by the SS-Oberfuhrer to be extra kind to these people, now under his direct control, the SS-Sturmbannfuhrer changed his normal tone of voice and pleasantly requested that everyone follow him.

"Please listen everyone, pick-up your belongings and follow me to Bau #1, the Building with the green light over the doorway."

He then pivoted and barked orders to the SS-Hauptsturmfuhrer to his rear, to release the attending SD Security Guards to their respective posts throughout the Camp.

Immediately the area was cleared and the group of fifty, now almost hypothermic families, filed off to the Medical Clinic behind the quick steps of the SS-Sturmbannfuhrer without even a whisper.

The SS-Oberfuhrer had always been known for his womanizing and had often chosen very young girls to add spice to his somewhat perverted sexual appetite on these long trips away from home, in Berlin.

This particular situation offered him another unique opportunity, since the Medical Clinic had two exam rooms for the female patients on either side of a small closet with a one-way transparent mirror facing into each room.

Heydrich had arrived early so that he would be in place when the younger girls were stripped. That way he could chose a potential female for the afternoon. His Chief of Medical staff, Herr Doctor Rudolf Mohr had already been a willing accomplice at Buchenwald on several occasions before this. And this situation would of course be no different here, at Zelten Jerusalem, since they would be using a drug to disorient the chosen Fräulein, as soon as the SS-Oberfuhrer Heydrich had made his choice. Within about an hour, Helga Schug, a female Nurse at the clinic, had brought Doctor Rudolf Mohr about ten young female patients for examination.

Most of the young girls were devoid of any breasts, and none had aroused the SS-Oberfuhrer enough for him to tap on the mirror with his Golden Death's Head Ring, the arranged selection signal.

Then, as Helga brought in Orsi Bruckmann the SS-Oberfuhrer Heydrich began to squirm around in his hidden observatory. Doctor Mohr spoke first as the young girl entered the exam room. "What is your name my dear young Fräulein?"

Orsi responded and the Doctor continued without much acknowledgement other than instructing Helga to help her undress.

"And, what is your age young Fräulein?"

As Orsi stated "sixteen, Herr Doktor", Helga started removing her blouse by pulling it over her head. Orsi began to raise-up her arms to help Helga, and instantly her large breasts fell out of her top, exposing their perfectly formed nipples for Heydrich's pleasure.

Each one seemed to harden as the overt touching of the Doctor's hands now holding her waist and Helga's hands undressing her began to stimulate her emotionally.

"And, how does this feel to you Orsi?" Doctor Mohr asked as he purposely squeezed her left nipple several times for the effect that he knew it must be giving the SS-Oberfuhrer, now mesmerized on the girl's body, as he squirmed in the confined alcove hidden behind the mirror between the two exam rooms.

At that moment unusual new sensations were electrifying Orsi's body for the first time from a man's touch, causing her to shiver and almost jerk away from the Doctor's expert fingers, as she tried to explain her reaction.

"Oh, you are hurting me, Herr Doktor, it feels very uncomfortable there, and it's causing my tummy to feel very funny also," as she again quivered.

Heydrich stood in the cramped isolation of the observation room, as he intensely watched the scene. The innocent young girl's naked breasts began lifting and falling rapidly, as her breathing became desperate.

Doctor Mohr was somewhat surprised that the SS-Oberfuhrer had not given the signal tap from behind the mirror by now, since this young Fräulein was by far, the most attractive and obviously the most well-endowed of the group.

He was unaware the SS-Oberfuhrer had become so distracted by the scene, taking place in front of him through the protective glass, that he himself had forgotten to alert the Doctor that Orsi was his prime selection for the afternoon.

Realizing that this girl was probably going to be either the best choice or possibly the only choice left for the SS-Oberfuhrer, Doctor Mohr decided to take the young girl in her topless state of undress, right into the next exam room.

As they entered exam room #2, Helga now helped Orsi remove her skirt and underpants, as she assisted her in mounting into the stirrups of the obstetrical table for a complete internal exam.

Doctor Mohr turned the table facing it toward the mirrored wall.

The SS-Oberfuhrer Heydrich was again having a difficult time turning around in the cramped space and controlling his excitement, as he watched the naked girl being moved into position for the exam.

Nonchalantly, Doctor Mohr began another question series.

"And, Orsi have you ever had sex before?"

Orsi, incensed by the obnoxiously probing question, reacted very seriously this time.

"No, never Herr Doktor, I am still a virgin and I will remain so, until I am married!"

Without gloving Doctor Mohr began his simulated vaginal exam.

"And again Orsi, how does this feel to you?

Orsi suddenly couldn't even speak.

The sensation she was feeling was making her weak as she shivered with an unknown excitement building deep inside her.

Then all of a sudden she responded in an almost inaudible whimpering tone of voice.

"Oh! Herr Doktor, please stop, I am feeling very uncomfortable now, please."

"Fräulein", Doctor Mohr commented sternly in a military-like fashion, as he turned and looked back at the mirrored wall for any sign from the SS-Oberfuhrer, "this is a medical exam and we must conduct it according to our clinic protocols."

At that moment, the SS-Oberfuhrer Heydrich was at last able to realize, that this was his queue, breaking his concentration from the view that was driving him mad. He then made a single tap with his Death's Head Ring on the mirrored glass.

Doctor Mohr at once asked Nurse Helga to prepare the syringe with one-hundred cc's of the immobilizing anesthetic, morphine hyoscine hydrobromide. A drug that had serious proven side effects after it's two-hour duration. But an additional undocumented side effect was the long-term images that would tend to persist and often haunt the younger female subjects, which also seemed to make them more promiscuous over time. Up to now they had only used this drug on adult females over twenty years of age and the typical dose had always been only 75 cc's.

While Helga was pre-occupied with preparing the drug dose, Doctor Mohr removed his hand. The young Fräulein's eyelids were now closed in humiliating submission as Nurse Helga suddenly turned toward the mirror, certain that she had heard a man's cough or moan somewhere in another room.

The SS-Oberfuhrer knew that he could not come out of hiding until the Doctor had dismissed Helga.

He also knew, that once the drug took effect, he could probably have her exclusively without any fight, for about ninety minutes before she would became aware that anything unnatural was happening.

As the injection site on her strapped left arm was prepped by Nurse Helga, Orsi tried to again speak.

"Oh! Doktor, what are you going to do to me? Please stop, Herr Doktor."

In a moment it was done.

Orsi grimaced at first, then let out a soft breath as Helga injected all 100 cc's of the drug into her arm. Her next reaction was almost instant, as the her eyes became dark and glazed over. Orsi's entire body became warm and super-stimulated from the effect of the over-dose.

The SS-Oberfuhrer watched wide-eyed through the glass directly at the girl's naked body as her heart rate almost doubled.

To carry the ruse further, however, the Doctor advised Helga to turn up the heat in the room and use a surgical sheet to cover the girl. That way they could leave her alone in the room for the time being, while they attended to other patients.

Helga knew something was up, but once again, this was just another Juden and another of the Doctor's bizarre experiments, so why should she get involved anyway. She was always very obedient and simply did as she was told, especially around Senior SD Officers.

As they left the room, however, Helga looked back at the young girl with a gentle thought. How beautiful the child's skin was. She wondered if Orsi really was a Jew, maybe she actually had some Aryan blood in her after all?

Doctor Mohr then mechanically pulled the door closed behind them and tapped twice on the wall to signal the SS-Oberfuhrer Heydrich that his selection awaited him.

It was late afternoon before Samuel Bruckmann completed his processing and entered the private room assigned to the Bruckmann Family. He had selected two work activities after the orientation meeting as his projects at the camp, appropriated to keep all of them busy during the wait for their so-called re-location to Palestine.

Exhausted from his afternoon pleasures, SS-Oberfuhrer Reinhard Heydrich failed to attend the noon orientation of Samuel Bruckmann and the other families however, and it was explained to them that he had a sudden crisis and had to return to Berlin. In his place, the SS-Sturmbannfuhrer Walther Lohmann had completed the orientation for the detainee families.

Things were made to seem pleasant and relatively normal for Samuel and the others following the humiliating Medical Exam process, but for some reason his daughter Orsi had not yet returned from her examination and that was putting Samuel on edge.

As he tried to stay busy, beginning to inspect the new family zimmer, there was an abrupt knock at the door. A uniformed Nazi nurse, Helga Schug, from the clinic, had brought a letter from the Women's Doctor, Rudolf Mohr.

Suddenly, an ominous fear swelled in Samuel's mind as Helga greeted him. "Herr Bruckmann, I bring you this information letter from Doktor Mohr, regarding the exam of your daughter Orsi".

Helga Schug had just spent the past two hours cleaning up Orsi Bruckmann and Exam Room #2.

When she had first re-entered the room following Orsi's anesthetic injection, she had been shocked to find the young girl huddled in the back corner of the room shivering with the surgical sheet barely covering her body.

Some blood was evident on the floor and sheet, and at once Helga took the girl into the Sitz Bath room. The clinic's Sitz Bath room had a shower and a type of surgical preparation bath in which only the hips and buttocks are soaked in a warm saline solution to be cleaned prior to surgery. Helga washed the girl following her ordeal from head to toe.

"Your daughter is okay, Herr Bruckmann." Helga continued," but Doktor Mohr found a small cyst on Orsi's right ovary, and decide to perform a cauterizing procedure to prevent it from growing any further and turning into cancer."

Doctor Mohr had concocted the cauterizing procedure story after a follow-up examination of the girl after Heydrich left, revealed a severely torn hymen.

Then realizing Orsi still had no idea of what had happened, the Doctor made up the completely unverifiable story which would easily cover up the fact that Orsi was now, no longer a virgin, thanks to the thorough ravaging of her young body by the SS-Oberfuhrer.

Bruckmann fell back onto the bed and cried out.

"Oh God, Orsi's mother has just died of cancer, and now, I cannot believe God would afflict her in the same way."

Helga felt a tinge of compassion for the old man as she spoke.

"Herr Bruckmann, Doktor Mohr was able to completely cauterize the cyst and Orsi is resting comfortably now at the clinic. She will be home safely before dark, I can assure you personally, and this matter will be behind her, forever.

Believe me it is over now and she is just fine, a strong and beautiful young woman."

Helga's final words seemed as though they had a double meaning to Samuel Bruckmann, as he spoke with objection.

"She is not a woman yet, she is still my little girl and I have no intention of letting her become a woman until she and I are out of this horrible place."

Helga at once seemed shocked at his reprisal of her comment, yet she knew what he meant and she also knew what had really happened.

Not only was Orsi a woman now, she might even have become impregnated with a true Aryan child of the Third Reich, a child which would be taken upon it's birth to the Leibstandarte Home 'Adolf Hitler' in Berlin.

Helga turned and re-opened the zimmer's door.

"I must return to the clinic now. Will you be all right, Herr Bruckmann?"

Samuel seemed calmer as he reacted.

"Yes, yes Frau Schug. I must prepare this place for Orsi's return.

"Please, release her to me soon."

Helga responded as she closed the door. "I will bring her myself in about an hour, now you must go to the dinning hall and enjoy a good meal before they close it down Herr Bruckmann. Goodbye."

It took his daughter several days of bed rest in their small room, to recover from her ordeal before she began eating normally with the others in the dinning hall. During that time Samuel, although concerned about his child's listlessness and apparent flashes of delirium, settled down and adjusted to the camp's regimen.

Herr Bruckmann had been assigned to make furniture in the woodworking shop, located near the tall Norwegian pines at the north end of the compound, while his daughter Orsi had been sent to tend flowers with two other younger girls in the greenhouse building near the Compound Appellplatz.

Both of them had also been given a communications kit with stationary, pen and inkwell by the SD Postmaster. The ominous instructions were to write often to their relatives and particularly to his son in America of the good care and protection that they were being afforded here at 'Kamp Jerusalem'.

The SD Postmaster had specifically said to all of them, "And this is most important, everyone! You must assure anyone you write to, that you are confident you and your family will soon be on your way to Palestine."

Unable to sleep and to pass the time in the evenings, Samuel would sit writing letters to his son Mort and Professor Stein in Hamburg. Not infrequently, he would often notice Orsi balled up in her bed sweating and breathing heavily, and caught up in some dream-like hallucination.

On those nights he would violate the Kamp curfew and go down to the Medical Clinic to get some calming medication for Orsi.

If Nurse Helga's light was on, as she often stayed late to complete reports for the Doctors, she would spend time talking to him, asking questions about his wife's background and checking up on the details of Orsi's condition.

Helga would sometimes come back to their zimmer protecting Samuel from being harassed by the SD Guards for violating curfew and to personally check on Orsi's physical situation. She would often ask Samuel to wait outside the room, while she completed her physical exam of the young girl privately.

To Samuel, these exams always seemed like an ominous sign and his fear of what had actually happened to Orsi on that first day at the Kamp always haunted him.

The question of why she was perpetually acting in such a bizarre manner grew larger in his mind every day.

But Orsi would never talk about it and he would never ask her directly.

The whole matter was just too horrible for Samuel Bruckmann to seriously think about, beyond the boring and complacent life they were now fictitiously living here, supposedly isolated from the real world dangers of Nazi Germany. And neither he nor Orsi would initially know the real reason they had escaped Buchenwald, but their potential in the extortion of a key American Nuclear Scientist might prove even more dangerous to them as time went on.

PART FOUR

Building the Dragon
January 1941

Chapter 1

Unterseebootwaffe

By 1941, the majority of Germany's Unterseebootwaffe, known as U-boat forces by the Allies, had been moved from Wilhelmshaven and Kiel into hardened U-boat pens in the western regions of France along the Atlantic Coast of Brittany. Initially, their high commander, Kriegsmarine Admiral Karl Donitz chose Brest, France as his headquarters, but as the war progressed and the British bombers came closer to his facilities, he moved further south to the town of St. Nazaire on the Bay of Biscay.

Armed with the authority of both Hitler and Reichfuhrer Himmler, SS-Gruppenfuhrer Horst Deeke arrived to secure control over the U-boat that would eventually become a major component of his ultra-secret Super Bomb device.

It was the evening of 22 January 1941 and the hardened underground Headquarters Operation Room was buzzing with action as the SS-Gruppenfuhrer and his Adjutant, SS-Oberstrumfuhrer Otto Zahn entered. The secret Kriegsmarine Enigma coding system had just decrypted a transmission from Kiel that the massive battleships Scharnhorst and Gneisenau were moving out at flank speed, a maximum thirty-two knots, on a second attempt to breakout into the North Atlantic for an anti-convoy operation codenamed 'Berlin'.

Their mission commander, Admiral Günther Lütjens, stationed on the forty-thousand ton flagship Gneisenau had made every effort to enforce secrecy as they rapidly steamed through the Great Belt that separated Zealand from the mainland of Denmark in the dark of night.

But now, a report just received, put his breakout in serious jeopardy. Vizedmiral Godt, Donitz Chief of Staff was intensely working the problem with their communications genius, Fregattenkapitan von Stockhausen, as an Oberleutnant introduced them into the secure operations room.

"SS-Gruppenfuhrer Deeke on board, Vizedmiral Godt," the Oberleutnant announced as he pushed open the steel bombproof door of the operations room for Horst Deeke and his Adjutant.

"Jawohl, Herr Gruppenfuhrer," Vizedmiral Godt replied formally as he continued to work the problem with a communication's assistant without turning around to greet the higher level officer, "we had heard you were coming from the directives sent to us from Berlin, but I did not expect you so soon."

"That's quite understandable, Vizedmiral, as very few people in Berlin are privy to the activities of my SS-Wiking operatives."

"Ah ha, but, Herr Gruppenfuhrer," Godt laughed in a somewhat unnerved manner, as he rose and turned to face the Fuhrer's special visitors, " as you know the beautiful Fräuleins of the Left Bank are appropriately located between there and here, and quite often an extra day in Paris is always the case for General Staff of the Fuhrer."

"So true Admiral," Horst replied in a relaxed voice, "but my interests are on a strict time schedule for now and obviously that would become rather distracting, would you not agree?"

"Of course, Herr Gruppenfuhrer," Godt smiled, also realizing that Horst had not verbally expounded the usual, 'Heil Hitler', which the Kriegsmarine typically didn't use. Godt wondered, this man seems to have a professional style similar to that of Admiral Donitz, and just maybe that suggests he could eventually be confided in on other matters. "I completely understand your circumstances, then," he added.

"Thank you, Admiral," Horst remarked, as he looked for a chair to jump into, since the flight had been rather tedious through some rough and bumpy weather they had fought all the way from the Rhineland.

The Admiral watched with amusement as Horst sat in the same chair Donitz preferred, often when he would come down to observe the alignment communications between his U-bootwaffe Wolfpacks operating in the North Atlantic, as they set up their coordinated convoy attacks.

"If I may delay your situation briefly Herr Gruppenfuhrer," Godt implored, more as an informal request, "let me tell you a little of what is going on right at the moment, so you will see what has us so occupied and very concerned."

"And may of course keep me down here for a while."

"And what may that be, Admiral," Horst replied in a concerned tone of voice?

"Herr Gruppenfuhrer," the Admiral spoke cautiously to detect Horst's level of awareness, "we have just decoded a radioed report by our observation crew on U-128, that three British battleships and several cruisers had turned on their boilers and were making movements within Scapa Flow."

"I see, Admiral," Horst said, as he quickly observed the map being worked ahead of him by two naval assistants.

He noticed them moving a group of flagged German vessels to the north west of the Norwegian coastline very near what Horst knew was 'The Naze of Norway'. "And what is that group of German vessels moving north off the Naze of Norway, Admiral?"

Scharnhorst and Gneisenau and their support task force 'Ops Berlin', Herr Gruppenfuhrer," Godt instantly added.

He was clearly impressed at the quick recognition that Horst had for the little known landmark the Kriegsmarine used to set their movements either north or south toward the English Channel.

"So they are making a second break for the Atlantic, Admiral?"

Horst inquired knowing the answer, as well as more details than the Admiral expected, especially about the Kriegsmarine since they had always tried to keep their ops as clandestine as possible from either the Wehrmacht or the SS Operations people in Berlin.

"You seem quite familiar with Ops Berlin, Herr Gruppenfuhrer," Godt quickly stated with even more surprise.

"I get many reports from my own sources, Admiral," Horst replied in an almost matter fact way, " and unlike some people in Berlin, I read and analyze them with respect to future events I will be personally responsible for."

"That is quite enlightening, Herr Gruppenfuhrer," Godt was growing curious as he added, "and what can you tell us of this impending potential crisis for the Fuhrer's only operational battleships."

Horst realized that throwing in a morsel of his brilliant psychoanalysis of the two players in this unexpected event, might gain him a needed friend in the Admiral, now that one of Donitz U-boats and crew had become part of his scientist's potential deployment system for the Reichsfuhrer's Super Bomb.

"Admiral," Horst said with an eerie sense of confidence and knowledge of very current top secret information that actually shocked Vizedmiral Godt, "I believe your task force Berlin is commanded by a risk taker, Admiral Günther Lütjens, correct?"

"Jawohl, Herr Gruppenfuhrer," Godt was shocked, but he replied stone-faced without reaction, shutting up to listen further and even more intently.

"And according to my Abwehr informants," Horst knew this would really shock him, "the man on the other side of this chess board is Admiral Tovey, not Summerville as one would expect, and Tovey is a cautious man that will choose to stay close to the home islands, rather than risk venturing North of 66° near the ice pack in the Norwegian Sea."

"Your Abwehr informants, Herr Gruppenfuhrer," Vizedmiral Godt seemed more surprised that Admiral Canaris' people were informing this man directly, then he was of the revelation about the Admiralty in London and who exactly their opposite number on this one was.

"Well, there's very little benefit to anyone here, if I revealed that piece of background, Admiral," Horst replied somewhat discreetly, " so, let's just work with the assessment of your high seas problem, for now."

"Very well, Herr Gruppenfuhrer," the Admiral was beginning to wonder where Herr Deeke was going with this, as he was sure very deep 'covert background information' had been exposed to him willingly, and without an equal measure paid by himself.

"I will only make a supposition for now, Admiral," Horst cautioned," based on the premise that British Naval psychology is biased by both the Luftwaffe's battle for Air Supremacy over Britain and now your successful U-boat battle in the North Atlantic."

"Both factors have made them very paranoid in the Admiralty about allowing their homeland fleet reserves to venture very far at all from their shores. Besides, they are still not sure if or when we intend to invade, or from which direction that fleet could come from either, as yet."

"All of this appears to be a reasonable hypothesis, Herr Gruppenfuhrer," Godt replied, as he now began to see the only choice for Admiral Lütjens, himself, as Horst continued.

"Lütjens task force should make it's way into the Atlantic, only if ice and weather conditions permit, from a route just below the Arctic Circle and along the edge of Iceland, then southward through the Denmark Straits instead of using the likely planned Iceland-Faroe passage, do you agree Admiral?"

Godt was privy to what Admiral Lütjens originally had planned, but their discussions were held in Wilhelmshaven in Top Secret with only three people present, how did Herr Deeke know this, he thought as he spoke,

"So Herr Gruppenfuhrer, what do you propose I or Admiral Donitz do at this stage of the process?"

"We should for now," Horst spoke in a serious tone to emphasize his conviction, one that made perfect sense to the Admiral, "only be aware of the options, the real events will unfold soon enough, and tipping our hand or that of the Task Force too early could be just as dangerous as directing Admiral Lütjens into this hazardous northern course in winter."

SS-Gruppenfuhrer Deeke then added, "What is the status of any U-boats in that zone Admiral, particularly north of the Faroes?"

Godt addressed his two Kriegsmarine subordinates working the Map layout and setting coordinates for known Wolfpacks and Convoys entering the Atlantic from Halifax, then turned back to Horst Deeke, "Herr Gruppenfuhrer, we have only a single U-boat North of the Shetland Islands at 61° Longitude, U-118, and it is on the surface moving from Bergen towards Group ZX at about twelve knots. I doubt it could be of any use that far south."

"You could however," Horst suggested, "position it south of the Faroe Islands for the next twelve hours to provide information on any British Task Force movements and directions, Admiral."

"That way if the British cross their path, we can assume they would obviously be planning to intersect Admiral Lütjens in the Denmark Strait, if they see no one, they will either be heading for the Iceland-Faroe passage, or not coming at all."

For the next hour communications were encrypted by the Kriegsmarine Enigma team and then transmitted to both U-118 and Admiral Lütjens on the Gneisenau. Both Battleships in his Task Force of twenty ships had a combined two-thousand officers and crew on each ship.

Nine, 283 mm bore - 11" diameter, guns plus fifty additional guns of various caliber as well as multiple torpedo tubes and four He-115 surveillance planes were mounted on the Scharnhorst and Gneisenau. If this plan to detect the British Fleet worked, Lütjen's task force would create a new dimension in the German battle against the American and British Convoy efforts in the North Atlantic.

So, with the updated information in place, everyone agreed to meet back in the morning to review the latest reports and scrutinize the next phase of the unfolding drama.

As for now however, SS-Gruppenfuhrer Horst Deeke had a new and important friend in Vizedmiral Godt, that in the long term future would provide invaluable Kriegsmarine and U-boat support assistance to his SSI Super Bomb project.

Chapter 2

UX-506

U-118 saw them first at about 1140 Hours the next morning, just to the west of the Faroe Islands. Two Royal Navy Battlecrusiers and Destroyer Escorts moving at flank speed to the northwest were observed, more than likely planning to take up positions south of Iceland.

By 1220 Hours another Flotilla with a very Large Battleship possibly the King George V followed them past the U-boat's submerged position. Communications to the Ops Berlin Fleet were buzzing wildly as Horst entered the command center with both Admiral Donitz and Vizedmiral Godt in attendance.

"SS-Gruppenfuhrer Deeke on board, Admirals," the Oberleutnant announced as once again he opened the bombproof door for SS-Gruppenfuhrer Deeke and his SS-Adjutant.

This time Admiral Donitz was the first to speak with a decidedly friendly tone in his voice, "Jawohl, Herr Gruppenfuhrer, Vizedmiral Godt has told me of your outstanding contributions over the past evening to the obvious extreme success we are hearing about Ops Berlin.

"And my sincere greetings of the day to you, Admiral Donitz and as well to you Vizedmiral Godt," Horst exclaimed clearly pleased to see the supreme commander of Germany's U-bootwaffe in the command center with Godt,

"I take it then, that Supreme Kreigsfuhrer Admiral Raeder and his Fleet Admiral Lütjens have prudently decided to move the Task Force down the Denmark Straits instead of the planned Iceland-Faroe passage?"

"Well, not quite yet, Herr Gruppenfuhrer," Godt replied looking at Donitz as he spoke in a somewhat conspiratory way.

"What we decided was to maintain observation and only suggest ideas to Admiral Lütjens, as he is very independent and old school Reichsmarine, and as you correctly assessed last night, a risk taker."

"I see, so may I ask what has happened and where this appears to be headed?" Horst replied as he carefully assessed Admiral Donitz reaction to his specific line of questioning.

"Once again, to explain, Herr Gruppenfuhrer. . . ," Vizedmiral Godt started to respond as Donitz suddenly took over.

"Herr Gruppenfuhrer as you are surely quite aware, we have a very close relationship with the surface fleet of the Kriegsmarine and of course the High Command of Admiral Raeder, however Ops Berlin is totally under their control and it's success will be theirs as well, not ours, when hopefully they are richly rewarded by das Fuhrer upon the it's successful completion."

The room was quiet and totally focused on Admiral Donitz now.

"I fully agree with that, Admiral, and what has happened here stays here as far as I am concerned," Horst replied in a confident, but respectful manner to the senior officer to assure him that his intent was not to create a riff between commands nor imply that he would ever confide in the Fuhrer or the SS-Reichfuhrer regarding these events, "only Admiral Lütjens will have credit for this mission's success as I see it, so please continue Admiral!"

"Thank you, Herr Gruppenfuhrer, you have obviously made my point for me with a complete understanding of these matters," Donitz seemed relieved as he again looked to Godt, " so we will continue now, Vizeadmiral Godt."

"Jawohl, Herr Admiral," Godt spoke with the ultimate respect for his commander as he relaxed and again began his review for Horst.

"We feel that knowing Admiral Lütjens, he will probe the shorter route at least once more before he fully commits to the more technical problems of the ice shelf and the northwest coast of Iceland using the Denmark Strait."

"Very well, Admiral," Horst replied, "it appears we are now in a waiting game until both Fleets movements can be reviewed later this afternoon."

Then looking to Admiral Donitz he added,

" Maybe now would be an appropriate time, Herr Admiral, to begin our discussions on SSI's U-boat design modifications and crew arrangements."

"I agree, Herr Gruppenfuhrer," Donitz replied somewhat eagerly interested in a more private setting for that discussion, as well as Horst's perspective on matters in Berlin.

" So lets continue in my private quarters." Then turning to his chief of staff as he led the way to the door, he ordered, " Vizedmiral Godt, advise me of any changes of status in the situation."

"Jawohl, Herr Admiral," Godt again spoke formally to acknowledge Donitz transfer of control for Atlantic Unterseeboot Operations to him during his absence. Horst then joined Donitz in the hallway as they made their way to another level lower, and into the stateroom and quarters of the U-bootwaffe's High Commander.

Admiral Donitz poured himself a glass of cognac as he walked to his stateroom's bar and turned to Horst, "And you, Herr Gruppenfuhrer, care for a cognac or some schnapps?"

"I'll take cognac, Herr Admiral", as he turned and nodded to his Adjutant to return to the Operations Center, rather than join what Horst could see would be better off one on one.

The Admiral prepared a second glass and moved to a leather sofa extending his hand with the cognac for Horst to retrieve, "Have a seat, Herr Gruppenfuhrer, and let's talk about the Reichsfuhrer's Directive on UX-506."

"Ah yes, Herr Admiral", as he quickly spied an opposing chair near the conference table, Horst set down his briefcase and reached forward for the cognac, "thanks, it's been several days since I've had a decent drink. Due to my flight schedule, I like to be ready to back up my pilot, if an emergency arises."

Admiral Donitz pondered him carefully, "And you fly as well, Herr Gruppenfuhrer?"

"Only on occasion, Herr Admiral", "just to keep sharp for any unexpected events, since my Command Focke-Wulf is normally flown by my personal pilot SS-Strumbannfuhrer Grimstad. I only act as co-pilot when he is overworked or if a problem arises, but thanks to your staff he's resting up at the Luftwaffe base at Brest on this trip."

"That's a pretty impressive plane, Herr Gruppenfuhrer," the Admiral added as he looked closer into his face to see why he was so important to the Fuhrer, " even the Fuhrer does not have his yet, I understand."

"That's actually true, Herr Admiral", Horst said trying to re-direct his questioning, "but, the Fuhrer prefers a much larger staff than I need, and the Command Focke-Wulf would not provide enough seats, for now only General Rommel and Reichsminister Goebbels use it for their operations throughout the New Reich."

"I see, Herr Gruppenfuhrer," the Admiral seemed satisfied with that rather interesting answer as he sipped his cognac while eyeing the Gruppenfuhrer a little skeptically, " so, again what is this project of yours that demands a separate U-boat and crew for the duration of the war.

You know I'm short U-boats because of the Fuhrer's land and air war demands, and now he wants me to give up one of my precious Unterseeboots."

Horst Deeke knew this would be testy with Admiral Donitz, a man who, although Hitler respected him, was clearly not a willing participant in the Nazi hierarchy in Berlin. But Horst also knew, only so much could be revealed to the Admiral and his preferred approach knowing Donitz's personality profile would be logic first, honor of the Kriegsmarine next, and emotions only as a last resort," Herr Admiral, the project SSI and my SS Wiking Operations Team is involved with, has probably the highest level of authority and importance of any other to the Fuhrer."

Then without so much as a nod from the Admiral, Horst sat down his glass of cognac and continued, "This means that whatever you provide my operations now will be returned in support to you for U-boat Command itself, tenfold."

"How would that be possible, Herr Gruppenfuhrer," the Admiral again seemed a little suspicious, but quite intrigued with Horst's direction."

"Admiral," Horst continued giving him the impression he was making him privy to the Fuhrer's covert secret project in the process, " it's possible because I intend to propose the use of several more U-boats for my project directly to the Fuhrer and the Reichfuhrer Himmler, but they will of course not be needed for at least two to three years. The advantage to you is they can be put into construction now, ahead of Admiral Raeder's Aircraft Carriers, Rommel's new Panzers and even the Luftwaffe's newest technology wonders."

"Now that could be incredible, Herr Gruppenfuhrer!"

"But what type U-boats would you propose," the Admiral again was very anxious to here Horst's answer, since he personally had been relegated to the end of the line in getting more boats from the Fuhrer and with less than one-hundred and twenty U-boats, how could the Fuhrer expect him to strangle Britain, much less without adding new U-boat designs."

"You mustn't get your hopes up too high Admiral," Horst continued attempting to soften his dramatic revelation somewhat due to what he knew was the likely reality with the Fuhrer and Himmler, " the boat's would of course have to be similar to the one we are requisitioning now with certain modifications."

"I can understand that, so go on, Herr Gruppenfuhrer," the Admiral was actually now even more excited, since Horst's comments made very obvious and rational sense to him.

"To begin with, Admiral," Horst began smoothly outlining his primary design, " the boat's would be at least equivalent to your current IX-B/C Series in size; about seven-hundred and fifty tons, two-hundred-eighty feet in length, a cruising range of at least eleven-thousand miles with increased submerged speeds of from twelve to fifteen knots or higher including rubberized hulls and Danish snorkel systems."

"Specific modifications like a stern ballast system to offset an additional fifty tons of gear located in the converted aft torpedo rooms, plus an enlarged round access hatch will need to be built into the modified rear deck area. Essentially the U-boats I will need would not have rear torpedo tubes operational on deployments during SSI projects."

"But of course, until such time as I actually need them, the ten boats I will request can remain with rear tube ports installed, just not used when we take them over."

"You and your engineers have really done some homework, Herr Gruppenfuhrer," the Admiral reacted surprised at Horst's ideas, some of which were still on the drawing board at Kiel, and in some cases, like the rubber coated hull to deflect sonar as well as the Danish designed underwater snorkel for extended submerged hiding from surface ships, were top-secret even within his own organization.

"As I said, Herr Admiral," Horst remained very serious, " this is the Fuhrer's highest priority project, and as such, I have access to the brightest technical minds in all of the Third Reich."

"And what else will be modified on my, er your, current U-506 Unterseeboot, Herr Gruppenfuhrer," Admiral Donitz was now obviously committed, but needed to visualize the specific modifications for Horst's first UX boat.

"Besides the specific modifications I've already mentioned, Herr Admiral," Horst replied as he again lifted the cognac and took a good swallow as he regained his confidence, now knowing Donitz was on board so to say, "well need a twenty meter long by one meter square water tight hatch added to the starboard side rear deck area to house a specific classified device that will be mounted into the modified round hatch I had mentioned before, during the U-boat's operational phase."

"Your plans seem achievable, Herr Gruppenfuhrer," Admiral Donitz said as he finish his cognac with a final audible gulp and was now obviously ready to bring in some commanders to get a better feel for the task details and crew requirements, "I suggest then, that we have some lunch and bring in a few of my U-boat Skippers for a more detailed discussion."

Admiral Donitz and the SS-Gruppenfuhrer continued their discussions over lunch and into an afternoon conference with several prospective U-boat Kapitanleutants and one Korvettenkapitan.

All were considered good selections for the initial mission and to oversee the modifications. The final location for the berthing of UX-506 would be the hardened U-boat pens in St. Nazarene due to better protection from the potential of British air raids on Brest and increased security. Eventually all final modifications would be completed there in secret as well.

Horst Deeke now had two crucial friends in the German U-boat Command that might later prove to be his most valuable assets in the ever expanding dimensions of SSI and his Super Bomb project.

Later that evening, a Destroyer on point from Admiral Lütjens Fleet hugged the ice fog along the edge of the Norwegian Sea and spotted the same two Cruisers that U-118 had seen earlier moving southward near the channel between Iceland and the Faroes. Lütjens at that point made his decision to hug the Northern ice flows and enter the Denmark Strait at midnight. With that action, his Fleet with the massive battleships Scharnhorst and Gneisenau quietly slipped without detection into a new chapter in the North Atlantic Convoy war, that would become a legend for German sailors throughout the rest of WWII.

By the end of March 1942 upon his Fleet's safe arrival in Brest, France, Admiral Lütjens legacy had become unique in the chronicles of the German Navy. He had commanded the most successful breakout of German capital ships in the entire war.

Operation Berlin covered seventeen-thousand eight-hundred miles of the North and South Atlantic to the Cape Verde Islands in less than sixty days creating a record wartime voyage for German capital ships. Lütjens flagship, the Gneisenau sank or captured thirteen merchant ships totaling over sixty-two-thousand tons while its sister ship the Scharnhorst sank eight vessels grossing forty-eight-thousand tons.

In total, Lütjens' Fleet captured or sank twenty-two merchant vessels totaling over one-hundred-thirteen-thousand gross tons. When the journey was over, Scharnhorst was berthed alongside the Quai de la Ninon in Brest, where the famous French battleship Dunkerque had been sunk. The Gneisenau, however, was installed in the Number Eight drydock at Brest for minor repairs.

As for Admiral Lütjens himself, a special celebration took place for several days and included Admiral Raeder, Admiral Donitz, Vizedmiral Godt and a special visitor from Berlin returning to see his new U-boat, SS-Gruppenfuhrer Horst Deeke.

When the party was over, he packed his bags for a new assignment hitching a flight back to Berlin with SS-Gruppenfuhrer Deeke.

At the Reichstag, shortly after his return, he was honored by the Fuhrer with his third Knight's Cross with Oak Leafs, and the ultimate irony, appointment at the Fuhrer's request to Fleet Commander for the preeminent pride of the German Navy, the Bismarck and Prinz Eugen. By May 1942, Admiral Günther Lütjens would once more be faced with the coincidental risk of reaching the ice shelf off the Norwegian Sea and silently penetrating the Denmark Straits to successfully once again raid the North Atlantic. This time however, the outcome became a strange twist of fate that sealed forever the legacy of this great German Naval War Hero.

Chapter 3

Winds to Africa

It was decided that Horst's SSI Team would take an initial flight on May 23rd into Leopoldville, in the Belgium Congo to inspect the Uranium Mines owned by Union Miniere which was now controlled by Nazi Administrators in occupied Belgium.

Deutsche Lufthansa was chosen rather than a military aircraft since connections along the West Coast of Africa were relatively well supported by German commercial airline crews and the obvious military presence would generate too much attention from the locals.

As a result, his men were assigned Union Miniere Commercial papers and wore tropical business attire for the trip, while packing all military gear in their luggage stored under the plane. Besides, the British were heavily occupied in Egypt and North Africa and unable or unwilling to put up a fight for any air space over the region they might still control.

With all this in mind, the cruising speed of the continental version of Lufthansa's 208 mph four engined Condor seemed satisfactory for getting his initial ten man team into the Belgium Congo.

Later they would continue by train down to the mines near Elisabethville, southeast of the Capital and along the border with British held Northern Rhodesia.

The flight itself started from Paris at 1000 Hours and was relatively benign for eight-hundred miles until they changed to a special long range Condor in Lisbon, Portugal that had a twenty-seven-hundred mile range.

From there, Lufthansa Flight #309 was tedious and long, besides moments of sheer terror for those in the plane that had never flown at night near or through African thunderstorms which had to be negotiated by the pilot on several occasions due to lowering fuel supplies from the heavy headwinds.

For Horst however, he was too exhausted from the week's planning activities to be concerned, so he slept most of the nineteen-hundred miles from Lisbon to their first African stop in Senegal, at the Port City of Dakar.

That stop required three-and-a-half hours to complete refueling, some repairs to an engine, and replenishment of the plane as well as a crew change.

The opportunity gave Horst and his newly promoted SS-Sturmbannfuhrer Erich Folkers time to visit a Portugese Flagged Freighter docked in the harbor and purposely sent from Brest. The Freighter held the SS-Gruppenfuhrer's force of two-hundred SS-Wiking Commandos that would eventually embark off the Congo Coast in preparation for securing Horst's precious Uranium supplies.

The SS-Gruppenfuhrer and Erich Folkers were recognized and quickly cleared though several SS-Wiking Commandos positioned in secure locations about the Merchant Ship, when they arrived on board at about 0500 Hours on May 24th.

The first officer to see them was Skipper Klaus Lemp of the SSI's newly modified Unterseeboot UX-506, as he met them on the bridge appearing nervous, but excited to see them.

"Herr Gruppenfuhrer, its again, so good to see you," Lemp seemed relieved once he recognized who they were," we have been monitoring some urgent Enigma traffic in the secure radio room, that I'm sure you would like to be aware of."

"And I as well, Herr Korvettenkapitan," Horst replied as he checked his Swiss Chronometer to re-verify the time and date, and looked back at Erich surveying the situation carefully, "and this is my number two, SS-Wiking field officer SS-Sturmbannfuhrer Erich Folkers."

"My pleasure Herr Sturmbannfuhrer," the Skipper returned as he motioned for them to follow him, adeptly moving to the next deck past two guards and into the secure radio room.

As they entered, Lemp addressed a uniformed Kriegsmarine Unterseeboot Radio Tech that was busy deciphering the latest transmission, "Gelt, what do you have man, tell us?"

"Its Otto Schnee in U-201, he has spotted a massive German Task Force Skipper," the young technician yelled as he took the latest transmissions his assistant had handed him.

He continued typing aggressively into the bulky Enigma machine as he spoke.

"The German task force is on a southwesterly course at 220°, speed twenty-eight knots in mid channel of the Denmark Straits. They are relaying transmissions from two capital ships to Admiral Donitz and Grossadmiral Raeder's Command". As he turned and looked back he realized the room had two others with his Skipper and decided it would be prudent to immediately return a formal response," Herr Korvettenkapitan."

"Carry on Gelt," his Skipper ordered, " these men are Officers from German High Command in Berlin."

Suddenly Horst realized who it was as he spoke," That Task Force must be Admiral Lütjens breaking out with the Fuhrer's Super Battleship Bismarck and the Battle Cruiser Prinz Eugen."

Stabssteurmann Gelt quickly called out a new report, " U-201's hydrophones have detected the noise of several large propellers."

"They are running at flank speeds toward the Task Force's port side at about thirty-two kilometers to the southeast."

"Keep working it Stabssteurmann, this is like listening to the final dash in the 1936 Olympics on the radio," the Skipper added turning to Horst as everyone's mind reached a crescendo focusing on each transmission as the tech ran back over with another slip for decoding.

"I was there. . . . and I saw that dash, you know Skipper," Horst reminisced as he watched the excitement build throughout the control room, "and they 'were all' like thoroughbred race horses performing incredible feats of physical endurance to the cheers of a hundred-thousand people. . . . it was back in a gentler time for all of us Skipper, at that majestic Berlin Olympic Stadium."

In that moment, Horst began to envisioned another image. . . it was the incredibly sexy image of Heidi's beautiful blond hair blowing against his face as she sat beside him smiling at the runners on the massive field down below them.

A powerful feeling overcame him as she completely occupied his thoughts, he couldn't help thinking of those wonderful moments with her in the past . . .as his mental fatigue from the overnight flight, allowed him to drift back in time to that proud and emotional day. . . .

Chapter 4

Frozen in Time

The wonderful dream suddenly became real again as Horst's mind drifted. . . far, far away and long ago to Berlin.

Banners proclaiming *Welcome to the 1936 Olympics* were everywhere. Neatly aligned rows of red Nazi standards were unfurling in a warm breeze along the main avenue below the Adlon Hotel that afternoon, as the sound of marching bands awoke Heidi from her nap. As she grabbed Crystale, both of them ran to the balcony to view the incredible unfolding scene.

Bronze skinned Hitler Youth and Labor Corps members sinewed with muscles were goose-stepping in their leather boots.

Polished spades were mounted on their shoulders, as the whole scene contrasted with the hundreds of Nazi Olympic banners along the sidewalks.

Pre-positioned crowds were extending 'Heil Hitler' salutes as the cracking of boots on concrete and synchronized drumbeats emphasized their power, causing men's heartbeats to skip and women to become breathless as the combined sounds left all foreign onlookers awestruck in their gaze. Standard bearers of the new Wehrmacht with gilded German Eagles atop their poles glittering in the sunlight, donning starched brown uniforms, were the next to march past the Hotel as the girls stood mesmerized watching this pre-Olympic spectacular. The cheering was louder the closer the parade got to the Fuhrer's reviewing stand, and the military bands played continuous music with a new one filing in behind the next, as they moved up the expansive avenue.

All of them were making their way toward the Brandenburg Gate reviewing stand several blocks away where the Fuhrer took their salutes and repeatedly extended his own salute in proud recognition of the precision Military Machine of his Thousand-Year Reich.

Their drill movements were perfect with bodies toughened by months of Spartan diets and now full employment producing government and factory buildings, offices, autobahns, rail and highway bridges, land reclamation and food harvesting.

Günther had told the girls before they left, that Germany was now at full employment with over twenty-thousand kilometers of new electric railroads and over three-thousand kilometers of four-lane high speed autobahns modeled on American styled parkways sensitive to the natural character of the landscape.

All of this had been designed by Albert Speer, Hitler's premier architect and artistic right-hand man, to connect Germany's major cities and provide high-speed mobility for the protection of das Vaterland.

Suddenly, Crystale gasped as she looked below at the newly arriving troops and command vehicle,

"Look at that hunk of Aryan Manhood in that black convertible Mercedes command car, Heidi. Boy, would I like to hug his bare muscled body for about three of four hours."

Heidi ran to the edge of the railing to get a better look as she screamed back to Crystale in excited frenzy, " Oh my God it's Horst," she then at the top of her voice began shouting down to him as she waved frantically to get his attention, "Horst, Horst, it's me Heidi. . . up here Horst!"

Then, as if on command, he looked up to her as he smiled raising the 'Heil Hitler' salute while giving some kind of command over his right shoulder to the troops directly behind him.

Instantly they raised their banners of the SS-Wiking in a ceremonial salute toward her balcony. The roar from the crowd became deafening as they goose-stepped in precision while simultaneously looking up to her balcony. Then with a deep roar of their voices in 'accented English', they repeated her name, "Heidi! Heidi! Welcome to das Vaterland. . . Heidi!"

Crystale went wild as she screamed back to Heidi from the edge of the balcony, "They're gorgeous Heidi, I would make 'whoopee with all of them' right now, look at them Heidi!"

Heidi was overwhelmed with the recognition Horst had just given her as she ecstatically began throwing him kisses until his car had driven beyond her view and onward to the Fuhrer's reviewing stand.

"Oh God, did you see that Crystale?" Heidi was shaking she was so excited, "Do you realize what he did for me?"

Crystale laughed out loud and kept throwing kisses to the oncoming SS-Wiking Units still arriving behind the main standard bearers unit as she spoke, "Well, Heidi, I'm not sure what he did for you, but all I can say is he had 'my bubs' at full attention when he turned and looked up here!"

Then Crystale added after a long pause, "But if he's your man, then you sure as hell better hold on tight, because the dolls and vamps around this town will be after that one, for sure!"

For those that admired disciplined precision, the SS-Wiking Division Commandos were a spectacle to behold as within the crowd, even foreigners and other soldiers were impressed with what they saw.

Unfortunately they were equally worried as well about what this meant for the future. It was like watching the Roman Legions of the Germania from antiquity preparing to take over the known world and secure their Northern European Empire.

Chills were forming along the backsides of the British, French and Dutch dignitaries lining the streets below near their own Foreign Embassies as this foreboding power, in what was considered peacetime, marched past them in a robotic-like ballet of muscular Aryan dominance.

The precision movement formation of the SS-Wiking was in a class with Hitler's personal bodyguards, the 'SS-Leibstandarte Adolph Hitler'. It was if they were competing for an award from the Fuhrer against his own SS-Division of Aryan perfection.

Every SS-Wiking was at least six feet tall, in perfectly fitted black uniforms with at least twenty-percent already having Hitler's Knight's Crosses hanging from their necks as a result of action in the Spanish Civil War.

Their strides were massive as they easily stayed right behind the command car, while children trying to keep up with them along the sidewalk were running just to stay behind them, yet their movements mimicked a newsreel in 'slow motion'.

Heidi and Crystale were held completely enraptured as the two-thousand giant uniformed bodies with steel faces half-hidden by their Nazi SS-Death's Head helmets, showing very little indication of sweat, moved up the grand avenue.

Each magnificent stride resembled the Praetorian Guards of Caesar responding only to a blind corpse-like obedience, as they past them by, formation after formation.

It was almost five in the afternoon before Heidi and Crystale returned back into the study of their suite from the excitement on the Balcony.

The hotel's housemaids had already cleaned the suite and prepared the beds once again.

Since it made no sense for Heidi to return to her unrequited nap, she simply telephoned downstairs to the message center for the latest calls to be delivered and sat down with Crystale to plan their evening.

Within minutes the young bellman had delivered the messages and Heidi quickly tipped him as she began checking them for the most important first. "Nothing from overseas," Crystale asked?

"No, but Horst has left a message," Heidi announced with excitement as she looked through the list of calls.

"He will personally arrive at Seven-thirty PM to take us to a cocktail party hosted at the home of Reinhard and Lina Heydrich. After that, we are to join him at a Norwegian restaurant called the Blom of Oslo located not too far from here."

"Do you think he has made any arrangements for my escort, Heidi?" Crystale asked somewhat concerned, since she did not want to interfere with Heidi's plans, but still wanted to make sure she was either free to make her own plans or have Horst make them made for her.

"I don't know Crystale," Heidi replied somewhat anxious as well, "Do you want me to call him and find out?"

"No, don't worry about it for now," she said as she got up and went into the bathroom to prepare her own bath. "It could be that things must remain politically correct for our first night here, Heidi. You know, only the high ranking officers can mix together."

Heidi started going through the her closet to plan her outfits, "Are you sure Crystale, I'll be glad to call."

Crystale replied emphatically, "Please, don't worry, I'm sure I can easily find someone as the evening gets going, and if not, I'll just stay with you and Horst."

"If nothing turns up, I'll wait until tomorrow and then call on that handsome young SS officer at the concierge desk downstairs."

Crystale started her bath water and was unable to hear Heidi's response. While Heidi began preparing her elegant new Paris fashions for the Gala evening.

It was almost Eight PM before they arrived at the elaborate Berlin home of Lina and Reinhard Heydrich, the new head of the Nazi SD Network and Himmler's top right hand man.

Lina was a beautiful blond, but she had a sharp tongue when she observed other women, especially under the age of twenty-five. She would take immediate notice if Reinhard spent over ten minutes talking to them because that meant he was lusting for them.

So in the matter of the beautiful Crystale, her observations of the youthful girl were a bit hard as she spoke to another Nazi official's wife.

"She's a hot little bitch, a bit bony in the hips and not too much breast, but very nice legs, the legs of a dancer probably. He would like that wrapped around his head. I'll have to keep an eye on that one if she's here longer than a few hours or he'll be on top of her in the Library downstairs before midnight."

"Especially considering the way he's looking at her over there right now."

Horst was stunned by how beautiful Heidi had become now as a fully matured lady. For the first time in ages, he seemed to be focused on a woman instead of the intricate political dealings of his SSI and SS-Wiking military career.

The two of them left the crowd and went out on the grand balcony to watch the evening fireworks.

While the rest of the guests and High Nazi Officials seemed to be completely involved inside with their typical cocktail intrigues.

A butler arrived on the balcony and asked Heidi and Horst if they needed new drinks. Heidi asked for another Martini with two olives.

Horst decided to loosen up a little now that they had broken the ice of almost four years.

"I'll have a martini as well, and include two olives with that one too."

"Jawohl mein Herr," the Butler exclaimed as he quickly went back to the bar.

Heidi laughed as she looked lovingly at Horst, "You've become more handsome than I can remember, Horst."

"Oh really, how so my dearest," he replied carefully in a question to see where she was headed before he revealed himself too much?"

"Well," Heidi said, "when we first met at the Fuhrer's Celebration Night dinner back then, you seemed very serious and quite uninterested in those around you, and me in particular."

"Go on Heidi," he encouraged her, knowing she knew from her Uncle that he had been infatuated with her from that day on, "this is becoming an interesting retrospective for me."

"It was almost an immaturity of sorts," she continued in an naively innocent way, trying to reveal her own honestly to him, "but then again, I have little room to criticize, since I was only sixteen at the time."

"Now, you seem so self assured, matured by obviously some serious military encounter or something, and certainly more focused on your own future goals and maybe even desires to have a family."

"Well you have obviously seen deeper into my personality than many others have been capable of, Heidi," he replied softly.

He was quite amazed at the accuracy of her observations.

"I'll be very honest with you Horst," Heidi said as the Butler arrived and handed each of them a newly prepared Martini, then hastily returned back into the Grand Ballroom,

"I have spent the last four years waiting to see you all over again."

"In fact," Heidi spoke carefully, now somewhat unsure of how he would take her forwardness, " I have spent most of this time perfecting my own maturity as a woman, but also learning about you in as much detail as possible from my Uncle Günther, who by the way has the utmost respect for you as a man and a soldier, excuse me, a warrior."

"I'm beginning to see this visit more clearly now," he added, "and before you get concerned, I must say that I was also waiting for this moment to see how you had grown, and exactly what kind of interest we might have again, in each other, Heidi."

"And how does it look to you Horst?" Heidi asked, almost imploring him to tell her his deepest feelings while looking up into his eyes for the true answer, as he spoke to her.

"Until this moment, I was honestly unsure of how it was going to look."

"But hearing your honesty and feelings of interest in me, and watching you as I have tonight, Heidi, you are truly the most beautiful woman I have ever seen in both heart or mind. And if ever I were to love a woman on this earth, it would have to be a woman like you Heidi."

She paused for a long a moment as she looked back to the lights of Berlin.

"What you've said to me, Horst," Heidi was becoming very emotional as she again turned to look into his powerful eyes, " is enough for me to give myself to you forever, but I feel you are protecting something or someone from your own true feelings."

Heidi really wanted to know why he needed to do this and what he was protecting, but she was afraid to bluntly ask him that?

"Once again, your perception of me is much more sophisticated than your year's suggest, my dearest. My role within the Third Reich is only beginning to be revealed to me, as I continue to develop the SSI Network and the SS-Wiking Commandos for the Fuhrer. In the next few years these events will evolve to a much more steadfast point and then I will be truly ready to have what most today would call a normal life, including the family that I really desire."

" Horst," She was hoping he'd be open with her as her breathing became heavier with tears growing in her eyes. She tried her best to form the words for her critical question, "am I the person that you would want to wait for you, when you 'are ready' of course, and when the times are what they should be for making your future family?"

"I can say to you now, at this very moment Heidi," Horst was also getting emotional knowing he had to give her something to cling to, as he took the last of his Martini in a single belt, " you are the only woman I know, that I would want as my future wife," then he added, "when that time comes Heidi."

It was almost as if time stood still for both of them as Heidi pushed herself upward to his lips and closed her eyes as they made soft contact. An electrical charge seemed to hit them both at that moment and Horst pulled her into his powerful arms holding her motionless for what felt like an eternity as they deeply kissed.

Both their eyes were moist as they held each other until the distant booms of the Grand Fireworks Finale began near the New Olympic Stadium.

Then suddenly they heard the other guests streaming onto the massive Italian styled balcony for the last event of the evening's party.

They continued in their embrace as the gathering soon engulfed them. Then immediate reality set in as Crystale came up close to them and spoke softly in Heidi's ear,

"Hey you two, you're making me jealous and. . . very lonely, and if you don't take me someplace exciting soon, I'm going to scream!"

Instantly coming off her emotional peak, Heidi began to laugh out loud at Crystale's remark, "Okay, Okay, little sister, we'll take you some place exciting or at least find you a suitable escort," then Heidi turned back to Horst and kissed him once more for effect as she added, "right, Horst?"

Horst was still too stunned to react, as he gazed with absolute approval and adoring emotion at this newly matured woman that clearly made his blood boil with excitement. At that instant, he knew what it was to desire love. Yet it was still too dangerous to take her into what he knew would be an unknown future. A future surely filled with chaos and danger within just a few short years.

"Why don't we go to the restaurant then, Heidi," Horst at last suggested after a thoughtful pause, "I'm sure you're both hungry by now, and besides there's someone I want Crystale to meet?"

Quickly they made their way to Horst's command car as they offered the proper salutations to the Host and Hostess as well as some of Horst's Nazi associates, including the SS-Reichfuhrer himself, whose blue eyed and blond haired Prussian born wife Marga was trying to get him to leave also.

When they arrived at the Norwegian restaurant called the Blom of Oslo, Horst sent his driver to get the Hotel's young SS-concierge, SS-Obersturmfuhrer Hans Schiller.

Heidi had mentioned to Horst, Crystale's frustration just after they had met in the women's room, when the host, Reinhard Heydrich had asked her to view his 18th Century Prussian Library as a pre-text to getting her nookie. Heidi then told Horst that when Heydrich closed the door, he immediately turned and grabbed her crotch and tried to remove her panties in one motion.

Only her stocking garter belt stopped him, so he asked her to remove it herself just as Reinhard's wife Lina entered the door with her own key.

Without saying a word, Crystale turned and quickly escaped, closing the door behind her as she reached the main staircase in time to barely hear the woman screaming at Heydrich. After that event, she stayed clear of every male at the party, working herself into several ladies only conversations and drinking at least six gin and tonics until the Grand Fireworks Finale.

Horst then inquired if he should try to make other arrangements for Crystale, or just leave her alone for now, but Heidi insisted she was not turned off to men, she just didn't want to embarrass Horst anymore with inappropriate situations involving his Nazi associates. Then when Horst suggested Hans at the Hotel, Heidi told him she was sure that would workout just fine.

It was late when they finished dinner at the Blom, with all four of them laughing and feeling overstuffed with Horst's favorite Scandinavian salads, main course cuisine and desserts.

The ceremony of eating is a pleasure in Norway and everyone enjoyed the customs and Viking tales that Horst had told them, right down to the last Skoal of their Aquavit chasers.

He had suggested they try the Aquavit chasers first.

He felt that would put them in the right state of mind for the food, explaining they were a form of ancient Viking alcohol base wine typically referred to as firewater for the soul and dispensed from a block of ice into a tiny glass to be downed in one gulp.

Crystale was clearly the winner, when after she had gulped down her fifth Aquavit the others gave up the challenge. But now it was time to either settle in for the night or be off to more nightspots in Berlin, as Crystale and Hans decided to visit a nearby French Cabaret Club that the foreign Embassy personnel stationed in the area had recommended to Hans as very exotic, La Boule.

Crystale and Hans said goodbye to Horst and Heidi with exuberance and kisses as they began weaving their way to the entrance disappearing into the warm night air without a sound.

Horst looked back at Heidi quietly sitting beside him at the table, smoothly touching his hand to her beautiful blond hair as he brushed it back from her left cheek then leaned forward gently kissing her lips.

An energy had been building in him all evening every time he looked into her soft blue eyes, he longed to kiss her luscious lips. But until now, his discipline had held him in check, as he maintained his reserve around his junior officer.

After a long silence, Heidi spoke first with a profound sense of premonition, overwhelming Horst as he sat back watching her with a true sense of adoration and respect for her intellect, "Horst, I want you to protect me tonight, all night long, I don't want you to leave me for a moment."

"And don't tell me you must leave at some ridiculous hour," she knew he was in charge now.

She also felt strongly that they all respected him; his incredible power over all of them was evident and they all knew it. They probably would desperately fear him if he decided to take over, but she knew he was an idealist, so his honor and goals for the Reich must come first.

"I understand you now my darling," she added, again imploring him as she looked deeply into his eyes, "and just what you want for das Vaterland's future, but tonight Horst, tonight my darling, I am yours and yours alone." Heidi knew she was his for however long he wanted her and in whatever way he wanted her.

"I beg you to take me back to the hotel and stay with me all night my love," Heidi's fears were growing as she knew their time together was fleeting and the new energy that was driving Germany would carry them both into an unknown future destiny.

Horst and Heidi spoke little as they left the Blom hand in hand with the chauffeured command car following them slowly a few yards behind. They walked the short distance to the Adlon Hotel and up to the suite in a hypnotic trance of tranquil serenity, almost divining each other's thoughts as they entered Heidi's room.

"I want you to stay here Horst," Heidi repeated herself as she sensuously looked at him just to make sure he understood her gift to him meant that he must obey the one wish that she had requested of him.

"And I will my love", he replied softly back to her as he cupped her perfectly formed face in his hands. "Tonight, I will be yours, and only yours, Heidi."

Then he kissed her luscious lips again arousing the blood flow deep within him as they pushed closer together.

After leaving Horst and Heidi at the restaurant, Crystale walked as best she could, sometimes stumbling until she took off her high heels while Hans tried to get her to work off the alcohol she had consumed in mass quantities over the course of their dinner.

Their first stop was the notoriously exotic French Cabaret Club called La Boule. And probably because she was so drunk that she almost passed out, Hans took her to a dark vaporous booth in the rear of the Cabaret, so she wouldn't attract too much attention.

The dance floor was very busy and the music was loud as waiters mingled with the crowd soliciting drinks and cigarettes for the patrons. Several young very attractive ladies of the international set were already using the booth Hans chose, as a cover to smoke an opium pipe that had been provided by some military officers.

The officers had rented two rooms at the upstairs Lebensborn Facility to assure they would have willing sex partners all night long.

Just as Hans arrived with Crystale, one of the young officers returned downstairs to select another girl and offered to have Hans join them, but he declined, instead going to the bar to get another Martini for himself and a Club soda for Crystale.

Unfortunately Crystale was too drunk to realize that Hans had left her, so by mistake, she reached out in the dark to grab the young officer's hand as he was about to leave with the chosen girl.

Since Crystale was an even better looking choice and she offered no resistance, he decided to take her instead and they made their way up the elevator to one of the orgy rooms.

The Lebensborn facilities throughout Germany had initially been designed to provide care for unwed mothers, but under the Reichfuhrer they had evolved into free sexual clinics for the military.

Medical doctors and nurses administered the facilities and young Wehrmacht or SS officers were encouraged to come to the hostel-like rooms ostensibly to breed with young Fräuleins of pure Aryan blood.

The objective, as the Reichfuhrer had planned, was the further enhancement of das Vaterland by breeding more pure Herrenvolk and master race children.

Actually the bizarre situation had evolved into houses of prostitution for the elite officers of the Reich and they were allowed to perform just about any type of sexual act on the women that they desired, usually for the amusement of both the participants and the observers.

At certain times of the day or night, High Ranking Officers or so-called Officials of the Reich were allowed to observe what was going on in the rooms through one-way mirrors.

It was often their perversions that resulted in even more sexually grotesque behavior, sometimes resulting in serious harm or even death to the chosen girl.

As they entered the room and closed the door, the scene in front of Crystale seemed a little blurred. But as she began to focus, she envisioned one of the tales she had read about in the tale of the Roman Caesar Caligula, one of the most dangerous and sexually perverted men of all time. He had become so notorious that he himself was murdered by his own army.

Crystale could see the young girl between both the naked men on the bed. One was madly thrusting into her while the other was kneeling and watching in front of her.

She seemed to be in a trance unaware of what was happening as they both continued to ravage her small body with an obsessive rage in their eyes.

Then as they turned to observe the new arrival they both stood up and the big one began walking toward Crystale.

She still seemed woozy, but the young officer that brought her in held her steady, as the man looked her over.

"This one is a true beauty mein Herr," the bigger one said as his naked body came in close contact with Crystale's left hand.

"Hold me Liebchen," he added as he moved into her lips while guiding her hand down and forcing her to squeeze him.

"Put her on the bed Gerhard," he ordered, " and get those clothes off her, schnell."

Suddenly she realized this wasn't Hans. Now she was really in trouble, all because she had gotten herself smashed and left the only sure thing somewhere downstairs in a smoke filled bar. All she could imagine was the thought of being raped by these madmen as she looked for some way to escape.

Crystale reacted and screamed just as the young officer began removing her dress over her head, "Stop, what are you doing, you're not Hans, I came with Hans, he's my date, who are you people?"

The big one had already gone back to the bed to begin mounting the young girl again, when he stopped, "What's going on here," he yelled in German, "this girl's an American, she's not supposed to be here Gerhard. You're going to get us in serious trouble with the SS!"

Gerhard stopped what he was doing as he noticed the metal card fall to the floor from a pocket Crystale had stashed it in earlier on the inside of her dress.

"Oh God, Fritz," he exclaimed in German, as he picked up the SSI ID Card, "we are dead men!"

"What is it man?" Fritz yelled back as he jumped to the floor and began pulling on his trousers.

"She's got an SSI ID Card direct from the Reichsfuhrer's High Command, she's a VIP of the Fuhrer, Fritz!"

"Speak to her in your best English, Helmut," the big guy yelled to the other naked officer, as he continued to dress himself.

Immediately the naked one grabbed his own pants and began stuffing them on as he cleared his voice, "Madame, we are truly very sorry for this mistake, we thought you were one of our own ladies of pleasure."

Almost on cue, the door to the room flew open and SS-Obersturmfuhrer Hans Schiller stood at the entrance with two SS-Wiking NCO's holding fully loaded and charged Schmeissers as he shouted in German, "Get on the floor face down, all of you, now! Arms behind your head, now!"

Both SS-Wiking NCOs were instantly hovering over the top of all three men now lined up together with arms folded behind their heads. Crystale was shaking as Hans retrieved her SSI card from the only fully clothed officer, then picked up her dress and handed it to her as he spoke in English, "Miss Munoz, I am terribly sorry for this horrible situation, these men will be severely punished for the embarrassment they have caused you, and I truly hope you will forgive me for my own mistake in not staying more closely with you downstairs."

Crystale looked at the young girl now laying prostrate on the bed in a semi-state of consciousness as she turned back to Hans, "I'm okay Hans, they didn't hurt me, and in reality it was all pretty stimulating, I mean to see something like this for the first time. You will have a lot to explain to me about this, wont you Hans?"

"Of course Miss Munoz, as you wish," Hans replied dutifully as he turned to look at the attractive nude girl breathing softly now, on the bed.

"And Hans," she added, " please call me Crystale."

"Yes of course Crystale," he politely corrected himself for her.

"And Hans," she continued still a little woozy, " please don't hurt these guys, it was as much my fault when I clearly got confused, thinking it was you bringing me here, because I was too drunk to know what was going on."

"I understand, Crystale," he sounded more official now as he spoke, " but these men have clearly disgraced themselves and gone beyond the proper authority of their rank. Their punishment is out of our hands now. It's best for your own personal safety, that I take you back to your Hotel now, and we will discuss these things later."

"Okay Hans," she replied without protest, " I really am tired anyway, and this has certainly been an evening and night I will never forget."

Within fifteen minutes Crystale was returned to her Hotel suite as Hans said good night to her and returned back to the Lebensborn facilities to process the trio he had left with his SS-Wiking guards.

She entered her room without even noticing the locked door to Heidi's room as she stripped off her evening dress and silk underwear and slid effortlessly under her cool sateen sheets. Slowly she began to take her fingers and relax herself, quickly relieving the incredible hyper-stimulation she had experienced over the past eight long hours.

In moments Crystale was asleep.

On Saturday, August 1st, 1936, the opening ceremonies of the greatest Olympics ever staged anywhere up to that moment in history, began at Hitler's new one-hundred-thousand-seat stadium in Berlin.

The new fashionable class of Germany's Third Reich were noticeable everywhere that afternoon. Nazi Party bigwigs including Hermann Goring, Josef Goebbels the Gauleiter of Berlin and the Party's Chief Propaganda Minister, surrounded themselves with actors, popular national personalities and flattering yes-men as they showed themselves to the masses in the grand box seats near the Fuhrer's overlook at the stadium.

Newsreel cameras were rolling everywhere throughout the stadium and for the first time in history the entire event was broadcast over radio transmitters to the waiting world.

The immense assembly of German and International visitors had been building since the early morning as the Fuhrer entered his box, then the crowd's roar of 'Sieg Heil' became deafening as they robotically extended their right arms upward in unison with the Nazi salute, time and again repeating it, until the Fuhrer was at last seated.

Hitler's capital city had been transformed into Goebbel's one-hundred-million deutsche-mark public relations miracle. An eight mile parade route had been built from Hindenburg's old royal palace, widening the road to over six lanes and lining it with thousands of Olympic banners and oversized Nazi standards for the morning's opening procession.

Even the official posters for the 1936 Olympic Games had been printed in over twenty languages and distributed worldwide to gain attention for the New Germany; a model society bursting with an arrogance and energy that would drive it for the next one thousand years.

Both Heidi and Crystale had arrived early to their private box to observe the parade arrival. While Horst and one of his new protégés, SS-Strumbannfuhrer Rolf von Varendorff had arrived just before the Fuhrer entered the arena.

Rolf's family was descended from Prussian Royalty and his father had been an instructor at the Military College at Karlsruhe. Horst's close friend General Major, Heinz Guderian, one of the Wehrmacht most talented mechanized warfare generals, had recommended Rolf.

Today Rolf was to be Crystale's escort for the event, but from the reaction she gave Heidi after they were introduced, it was clear that she still wanted to spend some more time with the handsome young SS-Obersturmfuhrer Hans Schiller.

Horst had allowed Schiller to be reassigned from his duties for the past two evenings because he had saved her from a possible rape on the 29th, but now he was concerned that Crystale was getting too attached to him, so he decided to select a new more impressive and wealthy officer of the old Prussian aristocracy; SS-Strumbannfuhrer von Varendorff.

Heidi was excited as she recounted her latest encounter with Hitler's star architect of the Nazi hierarchy, "Horst, it was so thrilling, we met Albert Speer just before you arrived. He personally came by our booth and kissed my hand telling me to advise you that you had made the best selection of all the young Fräuleins in Germany, when you picked me for your date today."

She laughed, as he turned to her blushing, then cautiously remarked about Speer's comment, "You know what he really meant by that remark, don't you?"

"What, Horst," she teasingly asserted as she smiled happily at him, knowing what he was about to say already.

"He really wants into your silk panties, you little flirt," he joked to her in almost a whisper as he beamed proudly, observing her gorgeous complexion and dazzling blond hair radiating in the sunlight.

Once again she was laughing out loud at his concern, "You're just jealous of him. You know I would never even consider another man when I have you, you're the pinnacle of these men here, they don't even come close. But I must say, I do like it when you try to protect me from their yearning eyes."

"It may take my entire SS-Wiking Commando Division," Horst laughed, as he looked back over his shoulder toward the Fuhrer's booth several rows above them and caught Speer watching them as he waved back to Horst conspicuously, " to protect you from your ever growing list of admirers the longer you stay here, my Liebchen."

"Yes," she said as they began to start the first track and field events below them, " but you wouldn't want me to hide from them either, or you couldn't show me off now, could you Horst!"

Again he laughed at her unabashed behavior, "Well I must admit you are really fun to show off around here, with all these desirous eyes watching your every move, it certainly seems to have gotten me a lot of unexpected attention."

At that very moment the SS-Reichfuhrer Heinrich Himmler walked up with his blond haired wife Marga as Horst began to rise up to attention. "No, No, SS-Standartenfuhrer," Himmler remarked, " Don't get up, I just wanted Marga to see our little Heidi again, now that she has grown up into our purest example of Germanic Aryan Womanhood."

Marga reached over to hug Heidi as she also agreed, "It's so true Heinrich, she is truly a radiant young Aryan beauty now," Marga then looked at Horst," you both must bring children to the Reich, SS-Standartenfuhrer, don't waist time."

"We will need their strength to grow das Vaterland for the Fuhrer."

"Yes of course, Frau Himmler, you are absolutely correct," Heidi responded as she turned and gave Horst an unexpected kiss in front of his Reichfuhrer, who was now glancing to the field below to hide his own shyness in the face of any overt sexual act, no matter how innocent.

Marga on the other hand was very pleased, "That's right Heidi, now go home tonight and make a beautiful Aryan baby for our wonderful Reich and the Fuhrer."

"Of course, Frau Himmler, we will follow your wishes to the letter wont we Horst," Heidi said as she smiled her little playful look back at Horst, waiting to see if he would react, now that she had him trapped. So to play along, he gave Heidi his trademark grin and nodded to Frau Himmler just as the audience saved him by standing up for the playing of the German Anthem.

Everyone began instantly shouting 'Sieg Heil' again in a deafening roar with stiffened right arms jerking in unison to the Nazi salute, repeating it again and again, as the two German and one American Athletes climbed the award podium to receive their medals.

The crowd was euphoric with jubilation as the SS-Reichfuhrer and Frau Himmler took their cue, moving upward to their own booth next to the Fuhrer's.

Heidi continued to have fun with Horst the rest of the afternoon and even Crystale began to enjoy Rolfs subdued personality, as several visits to the refreshment areas gave them a chance to get to know each other's common interest in the arts, jazz, dancing and most of all, Rolfs intimate knowledge of Paris.

Chapter 5

Horst's Valkyrie

Even the ancient mythological runes of the Norsemen foretold of Hitler's perfect society and how the pageantry of the Olympic Games in the Empire's Capital City would fully captivate the world.

Over fifty thousand international guests, diplomats, businessmen, tourists, and even reporters from the free press in Britain, France and America were hypnotized by Josef Goebbel's enigmatic propaganda.

The subterfuge had been effective on all. Heidi, Crystale and Horst himself were captivated more than ever before by the energy and enlightenment driven by the events of the sixteen-day spectacular.

The Aryan Spell had been cast, and the world was now filled with unadulterated believers in the purity and the future goals of Hitler's Thousand-year Reich.

At long last, the ashes of WWI had disappeared as 1936 evolved into truly the watershed year for National Socialism while it blossomed to it's highest level of dignity, further energized by the Vatican's Concordat Treaty finalized by the Pope in Rome and yielding solid international respectability to the New Reich and the Fuhrer himself.

As their last evening together arrived, Heidi's desire to visit the renaissance Prussian Library at Horst's home in Berlin's new Schickeria suburb called Grunewald was finally granted. Heidi walked in beside Crystale who was holding an opened bottle of wine with an Adlon Hotel wineglass in tow, as they entered the massive room through a double ten-foot solid wood doorway.

Horst immediately got up from his chair to greet them, as Heidi ran up and planted a deeply seductive kiss on his lips before he could say a word.

" My darling," she spoke admiringly of his taste as she slowly viewed the chamber noticing the awe on the face of Crystale as she turned, "your home is so darkly handsome and very Nordic," while focusing on the twelve-foot marble statue of the Nordic God Odin.

"Odin looks so mystical here in this place Horst, it's almost like it's his Cathedral," Crystale added as she carefully noted his Crown flanked by two Ravens, his massive beard flowing onto his Greek-like warrior toga and his magical spear and round invincible Viking shield. His Viking boots contrasted against his massive calves and thighs exposed to just above his knees.

Everything seemed seductively exotic to her as she admired his French Napoleonic Cavalry rapiers mounted on the mahogany paneled back wall.

"He looks like he's guarding you and all those around you my darling," Heidi asserted as Crystale followed her observations silently. Horst's empire styled bookshelves were filled with an array of books bound in ancient leather bindings.

Two mahogany ladders were positioned behind the statue of Odin for access to the stacks and a leather topped reading table evinced his latest reading subject nearby.

Eyeing the book, Heidi again offered a question while Horst simply admired her innocent wonderment of his once secret inner sanctum.

" And, what on earth are you reading about these days, my darling?"

"Notes on the Franco-Prussian War from the writings of Prince Otto von Bismark-Schoenhausen, my Liebchen," smiling at her in genuine fondness for both her intelligence and Nordic beauty.

She was truly his Valkyrie princess.

Then he abbreviated his remark at that point to allow her to continue her candid discovery of his esoteric realm.

"You are so mysterious Horst," Crystale commented as she walked close to the imposing Statue of Odin and felt a tingle on her skin. It was almost as if something had touched her.

Heidi walked back to Horst and embraced him burying her face into his enormous chest as she drank in the musk of his masculine odors.

"Oh Horst, tell us a story about the incredible god Odin," Crystale begged while running her hand across the cool surface of Odin's thigh as she gazed up at the marble giant standing beside her.

"It looks like he's going to be my date for the night Heidi, Crystale laughed at her own remark. So at least I deserve to hear about his mystical powers over my mortal body, don't you think?"

Unfortunately Crystale and Hans had never quite made it sexually after the incident at the Lebensborn facilities on the first night. She had simply pleasured herself the entire trip choosing to enjoy Hans' respectful company, rather than get into some type of messy affair that she knew would never go anywhere.

Sexually frustrated, her current laughter reflected that feeling, as she refilled her glass with the wine bottle she had brought for herself alone, from the Hotel.

"Of course you do Crystale," Heidi quietly replied back to her trying to be sympathetic as her own excitement began to arouse her.

She made sure Crystale was not looking as her hand moved down between her and Horst, gently pulling him against her warm skin.

Horst made no attempt to stop her as his own desire for her began growing. He wanted Heidi again so much.

The leather couch he had spent many a late evening on in exhaustion, rather than returning to his upstairs bedroom was positioned along the wall opposite Odin's statute. Heidi could clearly see it as an opportunity behind Horst, as she pushed him into the soft leather cushions. A second glance across the room convinced Heidi that Crystale appeared engrossed with the exquisite form and smoothness of the sculpture sipping her French Chardonnay and playfully touching the statue, as she waited for Horst to begin his story.

But suddenly, Crystale saw them and slid behind the statue laying down on the floor silently, as she began to pleasure herself while observing them in absolute ecstasy.

Again looking over her shoulder for Crystale, who was now out of her view, Heidi cautiously decided to take a chance, since this was their last night together, and besides Crystale wouldn't mind anyway. Quickly she removed her silk panties and garter belt while pulling her silk stockings down to the floor.

Secretly Crystale continued to watch in wild anticipation, as Heidi unknowingly exposed herself and lifted her small hips onto him as they began thrusting in a quiet frenzy.

It was beautiful to see such love and tenderness as Crystale began to cry knowing she would never enjoy a man's love with that kind of innocence, ever again. For her closest friend, Crystale was happy that everything had worked out. The trip had seemed like a perfect dream for Heidi, but she wondered sadly if this fairy tale dream would really end, with love ever after?

Chapter 6

Enigma

Reality came back fast to Horst, as the sounds of the radio's high pitched crackling and excited voices broke into his thoughts once again. . . .

The crew was soon imagining what it was like, as that icy mist filled the early morning light. A different image unfolded for each man speculating what would happen in the freezing North Atlantic, just west of Iceland's shores.

The greatest battle in the history of Modern Ocean Warfare was about to evolve, while thousands of miles away they intently listened to the decoded reports minute by minute.

Again, Gelt shouted out a new report, " U-201, Herr Korvettenkapitan, has overheard an urgent request for intelligence data from the German Naval High Command regarding the disposition and movements of all major British naval units North of Scotland. And now, a major capital ship's smoke plume has been detected by the Prinz Eugen at a distance of thirty-one kilometers off it's port horizon, south-southeast."

Gelt exploded with excitement, "That's same direction indicated by the U-201's sound detection equipment, Herr Korvettenkapitan." Suddenly the transmitter stopped. The young technician couldn't seem to get back a signal as he frantically worked the dials.

"Get that thing working Gelt or well miss the fight, schnell, schneller!" The Skipper was animated as he jumped to the transmitter to assist him while Horst and Erich re-checked their watches. It was now 0543 Hours GMT.

They still had more than two hours until their departure at 0830 Hours, and this event was almost worth missing the flight for, if need be.

"Jawohl, Herr Korvettenkapitan," Gelt rushed to the high frequency transmitter listening intently for any Wolfpack signal.

Then he heard it, they all heard it, as it again blurted continuous code back to them in response to the events now unfolding.

Every U-boat on the surface of the North Atlantic or with a powerful enough receiver range was now intently listening to this incredible high sea's drama and translating events on their top-secret four wheel Enigma Machines using Admiral Donitz Hydra cipher code. Every moment, brought them closer to an action that very well might re-write Germany Naval History.

At fifty-thousand tons, the largest and most powerful battleship in the world armed with eight of the most technologically accurate 380 mm long range guns ever built was about to be tested. And, from all indications that test was only moments away.

"I have it again, Skipper," Gelt was again so involved, his formality was gone, just like all Kriegsmariners would be on board their own U-boats in the heat of battle with an enemy Destroyer prowling on the surface overhead. The scene in the room was fascinating SS-Sturmbannfuhrer Folkers as well, as he began to imagine the intensity of the German Naval Gunners straining to precisely find their targets in the icy spray, of the wind torn north Atlantic.

At 0550 the Prinz Eugen spotted another ship, as Gelt again released the decoded transmission, " A targeting solution has been made at about 20˚ forward of the port beam. Several enemy ships have been spotted ahead of them creating a slight lead on Admiral Lütjens Task Force.

Smoke has been sighted from additional British warships arriving to reinforce the identified British Cruisers HMS Suffolk and Norfolk now clearly being used in a surveillance role."

Suddenly Erich spoke, "That could be a serious threat to Admiral Lütjens Task Force, if they are trying to break out and make an escape into the wide open North Atlantic. They won't be able to shake off that many pursuers if the British remain ahead of their own course, they will need to engage them now."

The Skipper added his thought, "You're right Herr Sturmbannfuhrer, what is that man thinking, he needs to fight now, before they have him ranged, he has the advantage."

Once again the transmitter stopped. Gelt jumped to the console, but nothing happened.

Everyone was frozen with tension awaiting the next sound, but there was nothing, as the Skipper instructed Gelt to ready the decoder while he personally took over the receiver waiting for any sound to emit.

Then abruptly at 0610 Hours, the transmission went wild once again as both the Skipper and his young tech wrote down the dispatches and handed them to Gelt as fast as they could.

"Schnell, Gelt, schnell!" the Skipper implored him as they added more and more reports to his stack of cryptic dots and dashes.

Slowly he began getting caught up as he unexpectedly screamed aloud, "Oh my God, Skipper, they've killed them, they killed the biggest ship in the British Navy.

"What happened, Gelt," the Skipper pleaded to him, "tell us what happen, vorderhand!"

"U-201 reports that a large British Warship has been sighted by the Bismarck at over eighteen kilometers distant and she has opened fire from all of her 14" guns with at least five separate salvos."

"Come on, Gelt, what has happened and who is this ship!" once again the Skipper begged him to hurry, while Horst and Erich looked on, unable to believe what they were hearing as Gelt continued.

"U-201 reports a high flame has been spotted shooting skyward near the mainmast of the large British Warship, and a tremendous explosion in the aft section of the ship has now shot another flame and a massive smoke cloud up on the horizon to their southeast.

She has been dealt a mortal blow by das Fuhrer's greatest ship," he paused to again listen.

"Wait, she is gone," he reacted with loud excitement. "She has sunk below the surface in under three minutes."

Although that was the last transmission by U-201 regarding the events on that early morning, it was not until almost a month later that SS-Gruppenfuhrer Horst Deeke would find out two additional critical details from the battle of the Denmark Straits. The first was revealed by mid June in a personal meeting with Grossadmiral Raeder at the memorial services for his friend Admiral Lütjens. At that time, SS-Gruppenfuhrer Horst Deeke discovered that the shell delivering the fatal blow to the HMS Hood came from the Bismarck's fifth salvo, when it penetrated the deck over her aft magazines and detonated tons of cordite propellant stored below it's apparently lightly armored deck metal.

In the horrendous vortex created by the exploding powder, hundreds of high explosive shells detonated like a colossal fireworks display with an array of explosions seen from many miles away by crewmen and officers on the decks of the Bismarck and Prinz Eugen.

The force of that detonation caused the ship to rip apart spewing debris and human remains into the air and landing back in the water all around the remaining wreckage.

In the end, a ghostly black and yellow cloud formed over the remains for sometime.

Grossadmiral Raeder said a report by a Norwegian Officer on board the Bismarck stated, 'it was almost as if the hovering Valkyries of old Viking Legends were preparing to lift up those worthy Warriors that now would partake in the Mead of Odin in the Ancient Halls of Valhalla,' as I looked upon that horrific scene of carnage.

And so, the once great and mighty capital ship, the pride of the British Navy, HMS Hood, took with her almost two-thousand sailors to their cold and horrible grave in the unforgiving North Atlantic Ocean.

In time, the SS-Gruppenfuhrer Horst Deeke would learn the final two mysterious parts to this incredible battle: The second part was revealed at a meeting in Berlin, when the Kriegsmarine's highest ranking officer Grossadmiral Raeder elaborated on a another event in the Straits that morning to SS-Gruppenfuhrer Deeke regarding the Prince of Wales.

He explained that following the sinking of the HMS Hood, the Prince of Wales made an abrupt turn to the south-southeast on a new course of 150° while making smoke to conceal her movements, and although she continued firing at the Bismarck and Prinz Eugen with her rear turrets, none of her shots ever hit anywhere near the Bismarck because her gunners were obviously hindered by their own smoke created to hide her escape. Admiral Lütjens decided not to waste any more ammunition on the ship and ceased all firing from the Task Force. However, his commander, Captain Ernst Lindemann wanted to finish off the Prince of Wales now that the Bismarck had sighted and ranged her.

Uncharacteristically, Admiral Lütjens made the fateful decision to disengage the pursuit of the Prince of Wales.

His standing orders were to avoid any engagement with British Capital Ships unless they were engaged while defending allied convoys.

Years later it was further learned, that *had* the British Admiralty lost both ships, with the Prince of Wales being their newest Battleship, it would have change their pursuit strategy.

The additional Carriers from Gibraltar would never have been committed and the Bismarck would have escaped the death noose that ultimately held her fate.

Toward the end, Admiral Lütjens himself became conservative and decided to move the Bismarck to the massive drydocks used in the late 1930s by the once fabulous French Cruise Ship Normandie, at St. Nazarene. It was that decision that sealed the fate of the greatest ship in Germany's history.

The third and final part of the mystery, unknown at the time, to anyone in the entire Third Reich, was that the British had actually seized an Enigma cipher unit as well as broken Admiral Donitz Hydra cipher, just after the capture of his Unterseeboot U-110 off the coast of Greenland on May 9th.

Only fifteen days before the Bismarck entered the Denmark Straits, that event actually sealed it's fate.

Bletchley Park had almost a three-month record of all U-boat operational settings and could therefore decipher code almost as fast as the German wireless operators could transmit it.

In the end, this of course was the final nail in the coffin for Lütjens and his Bismarck.

The little friends, as all Kriegsmarine capital ships called their U-boats, in fact became the Trojan Horse that unknowingly exposed the fateful route into the Denmark Straits and later the Bismarck's final route to the coast of France on May 27th, 1941.

Every movement and every communication had been meticulously deciphered day by day at the British OIC in Bletchley Park then transmitted by teleprinter to a concrete bunker called the Citadel where the Admiralty's braintrust was located in the heart of London.

It was not until 1945 that Horst later learned of Britain's access into those supposed top-secrets of Germany's Kriegsmarine, but fortunately for him, his own enigma cipher 'Thor' and it's settings, that held the secrets of SSI in America and vital information about the new Nazi Super Bomb, were never broken.

Chapter 7

Leopoldville

A strong headwind caught them as their Flight headed away from Dakar by 0845 Hours GMT.

Until they crossed the Gulf of Guinea the headwind slowed their journey.

It finally subsided after almost eight hours, then turned behind them allowing precious fuel to be saved as they descended into Leopoldville almost thirteen hours later after the last leg had begun.

Green marker lights were all that could be seen in the darkness, as the four radial-BMW engines revved loudly allowing the Condor to begin it's rapid descent onto the main airfield that serviced the Belgium Congo's commercial region.

Horst's fateful trip to the mines in Katanga, almost twenty-four-hundred kilometers to the southeast, would be in a dilapidated freight and passenger train that followed the Kasai River basin to Ilebo and then into the mountains of Angola on the Portugese Benguela Railway, to their final destination at Elisabethville. It would begin in two days.

For the team, the harsh jungle conditions, the tortuous mountain rail route, the heat, and the open cars they had to ride in, would likely be the most uncomfortable part of their entire African journey.

All four engines stopped almost simultaneously just as the Lufthansa Steward, the one his men had nick-named 'the narrow faced weasel', came out of the forward flight deck almost sliding as he tried to break himself from running down the plane's sloped aisleway, bumping accidentally into Erich Folkers' seat just ahead of Horst.

Erich had tried to sleep from Lisbon, but only in the last three hours had he finally made himself comfortable in a make shift bed of cushions and pillows.

Startled, Folkers instantly grabbed for his throat and wrenched the man down to the floor in one massive movement. He screamed in pain as the terror in his eyes looking up at them reminded everyone of a deer caught in a brilliant lightbeam. Finally Folkers reacted and released his hand, now in a death grip on the man's neck, " Sorry there old fellow, but you startled me."

"Oh my God, what are you doing," he cried as the rest of Horst's men just watched the scene in amusement, well knowing that Folkers was probably the most dangerous assassin in all of SS-Wiking.

"That's enough now," Horst commanded as he stuffed several German Marks into the man's breast pocket while carefully lifting him back to a standing position in the aisle and reading his name tag.

"This should take care of your discomfort, Herr Wollmann, and there shouldn't be any need to mention this further I hope," Horst added in a serious tone.

"Very well then," he cleared his voice and looked around at the stoic faces observing his actions, then back to Horst,
"I'll just get the doorway opened now."

He quickly finished his trip down the aisle to the rear exit door carefully avoiding any contact with the others, as he opened the hatch into the humid night air smelling of animal swelter or something even more undesirable.

Another Lufthansa agent, with a substantial muscular build and short-cropped blond hair met the passengers at the portable stairway as several of Horst's men made airborne styled jumps down to the tarmac from the second or third steps.

Horst was the last civilian to exit the plane, while the others had already entered the terminal and were quickly being processed through.

When he got to the doorway, he immediately eyed the muscular man knowing he was probably the local covertly attired Gestapo Agent assigned by Heydrich to meet them and assist with their housing and transportation requirements, as well as any other needs that might be out of the ordinary around Leopoldville.

"Heil Hitler, Herr Mugler," Horst spoke in German and expertly made his way off the plane walking up to the Agent as his team waited near the entrance to the small terminal building," I'm Horst Deeke of Nordland Miniere!"

"Ah yes, Herr Deeke," Mugler spoke softly, so the ground crew working near the plane didn't pickup anything unusual, " we have chosen to use the 'Heil Hitler' greeting only in private here at the present, since there are British Agents from South Africa everywhere and we still must convert many of the local Belgique Nationals who are somewhat reluctant to support us as yet."

Adeptly, he picked up Horst's Black Leather SS Flight Bag for effect, as they began walking to the terminal.

Then he added, "And of course we do not have enough ground forces in place here, to fully effect various pograms in this remote part of the New Reich."

Turning, he then inspected the ten man SS-Wiking Unit still dressed in civilian clothing rather than their camouflaged uniforms as they stood under the airport's welcome sign, "as I'm sure you and your men here, obviously understand."

"I'm fully appraised of these issues, Herr Mugler," Horst again addressed him in German, "so, let's get on with processing and moving my men with their equipment to suitable quarters, so we can prepare for tomorrow's meeting with the Union Miniere administrator and his people!"

"Jawohl, Herr Deeke," Mugler then rushed forward to be the first to open the entrance door, as Horst immediately entered ahead of him into the open, but dimly lit International Arrival area, now void of anyone but two Belgium Congo Customs and Immigration Officials, as the rest of his team followed silently.

Chapter 8

Union Miniere

Folkers drove the French Citroen through the muddy streets down to a restricted area near the waterfront on the Congo River just before nine AM the next morning.

Both of them, for safety reasons, had decided to continue their subterfuge disguised in tropical business attire.

As SS-Gruppenfuhrer Horst Deeke got out, he carefully inspected the small concrete and tin roofed Administrative Building that housed the Company's all-powerful jurisdictional prefecture. Several armed men stood near the side of the building, while along the waterfront an armed riverboat docked nearby held several other men that were probably armed as well.

Two large Negro security guards in gray uniforms readied their British Sten Submachine Guns as they met Horst at the porch and asked him for his papers before he entered. Clearly, Horst's current observation of the situation was not exactly what the Waffen-SS or the Abwehr had assumed in Berlin from their recently provided reconnoiter reports of das Kongo situation.

A man in his twenties, probably a Belgium National and a young well built but exotically beautiful Negro woman were sitting in the outer office as Horst entered. The monotonous sound of the overhead fan slowly pushing down the dense early morning heat from the tin roof and a typewriter being used by the Belgian were the only noises evident in the room.

She looked at him in short glances as he addressed the administrative clerk in a friendly, but businesslike manner,

"Good Morning Sir, I'm Horst Deeke from Nordland Miniere, here specifically to meet Mr. Lebbeke."

"Ah yes, Mr. Deeke," the clerk turned and watched him closely as he spoke," it's Monsieur Lebbeke, he's from Northern France you know, not Belgium. I believe Monsieur Lebbeke has you on his calendar for this week, but we usually don't arrange meetings such as this so quickly after your arrival, sir."

With only one Lufthansa flight each week, it was easy for the vanquished Belgium locals to prepare the proper image for their German visitors who usually slept a few days after their grueling fights before meeting anyone.

Now, apparently Horst's change of that typical protocol had caught them off-guard.

"You're Norwegian, are you not, Mr. Deeke," the clerk said, then made some kind of motion to the girl as she quickly got up and entered what appeared to be Lebbeke's office, closing the door behind her.

"I am Sir," Horst replied as he scanned the open screened windows and a second doorway out of the office into another room or hallway, "Our headquarters is in Oslo, and where may I ask are you from?"

Almost before he could answer, the Negro woman reappeared and motioned for the clerk to join her as he exclaimed, "Oh, excuse me" "just a moment Mr. Deeke, I'll be right back."

Both of them entered the private office and closed the door back as Horst stood up and walked over to the desk. The man had been typing a document in Belgique, and beside the typewriter was another letter to an address in Northern Rhodesia, Barclay and Rothschild Bank Holding Company, Ltd.

He quickly scanned it's contents and returned to his seat as he heard movement from the private office. The clerk opened the door holding a stack of documents and moved over to his desk, as he now addressed Horst somewhat suspiciously and with a new tone of voice,

"He will see you now, Herr Deeke."

Horst didn't answer; he realized the change in his voice at once and entered Lebbeke's office shutting the door behind him.

He saw the Negro woman first as he entered, posing seductively in the right corner of the room behind Lebbeke's massive desk with her blouse now unbuttoned to a point just below the cleft of her breasts. Both her hands were hidden behind her back.

The room was over twenty feet high and at least that wide with four open screened windows and three large overhead fans running twice as fast as the one in the outer office. There were no exit doors other than the one he had just closed and the room was at least ten degrees cooler than the other office. The fans caused the papers to rattle on Lebbeke's desk as Horst watched.

Other than the main desk and chair, the room was sparsely furnished with only two other items, a stark interrogation-like chair in the center of the room and a floor lamp to the left of the desk next to a built-in bookcase.

Lebbeke looked up from the page he had been reading and spied Horst as he stood with his back to the door. He made no remark as he beckoned Horst over to him and quickly pointed to the chair centered in front of his document filled teak desk.

He then returned his glare to the item he was reading and didn't look up for several minutes as Horst put his own greeting on hold, continuing to evaluate the items within the room and checking the Negress's gaze as he caught her watching him.

When Lebbeke had finished reading, he raised his eyes toward the ceiling fans seeming to drink in the cool air blowing down in his face, as it rearranged the hair on his forehead. He then exhaled audibly lowering his eyes to meet Horst's as he spoke, "Herr Deeke, we live in a unique world down here, far from the rules and influence of those that now govern the small countries of Western Europe such as Belgium. And, as I'm sure you are aware our rules are very different."

He cleared his throat with an obvious growl as he added. "This directive from the Nazi Powers, the new Conquerors and Warlords of Europe that now control Belgique's Union Miniere on the Continent, do not understand who really controls mining and the vast mineral holdings located here and in the Southern Congo."

Horst continued to evaluate the overweight French/Belgian that clearly saw himself as in control of this little fiefdom deep in the Congo.

He focused on what Lebbeke was really saying as he again checked the Negress for any sign of movement. She seemed to be in a trance as she continued to stare toward the window near Horst's chair.

"After reading this directive from them," Lebbeke continued almost automatically pontificating his opinions," it is apparent that they have sent you to this place, thinking that you would take over administration duties."

"Ha," he paused, " my administration duties I suppose, of the vast mineral resources of Katanga with the simple stroke of the German Fuhrer's preverbal pen."

Lebbeke turned to again view the document before him on the desktop.

"Well, Herr Deeke, that is so far from the truth as you will see very soon."

"I see, Monsieur Lebbeke," Horst replied as though he was willing to accept his assessment without challenge, "tell me more of this truth, as you say, that is misunderstood by the new administrators in Brussels and Berlin."

"The German Fuhrer believes that he has conquered Belgium and therefore all of her Commonwealth," Lebbeke added as he seemed to gain energy speaking of the power he had over the various Congo Trusts, "well he is grievously misinformed by his generals."

"We will allow you to visit here for now Herr Deeke, but I, as the sole representative of the world's most powerful global banking consortium will remain here well after the German Reich has ended. "

"The Congo has three Trusts, all of which I now administer directly from this compound."

"The CCCI or Compagnie du Congo pour le Commerce," Lebbeke continued, "by which I control all of the Congo's industry, agriculture and public works. . . . In that trust alone I have over fifty-five-thousand workers who are indentured to me for one-hundred and twenty days of every year by law, which of course is controlled and enforced by my own security police. The so called German mining operations in Katanga for Union Miniere, Ha, they really belong to the Comite Special du Katanga or CSK. . . .again my secret police assure total control and enforcement over that region with the partial help of troops trained by your enemy, the British in Northern Transvaal."

"But Monsieur Lebbeke," Horst slyly interjected a weakness to his assumed control, "those British troops are mixed blood and controlled by South Africa, and the Transvaal is over six-hundred statute miles Southeast of the Katanga Province?"

"By the time the German Fuhrer has delivered enough troops into my Commonwealth of the Congo, Herr Deeke,"

Lebbeke confidently added as he exposed a weakness of his own control.

"I will have caused an insurrection of the oppressed tribes that will have destroyed all the main rail lines built throughout the country . . . .flooded the Uranium, Zinc, and Copper Mines at Katanga and blown-up the Leopold Dam east of Matadi."

"That Herr Deeke will render the Congo useless to Germany's Thousand Year Reich, while the British will have had time to arrive and destroy the remaining Wehrmacht Troops left to guard Leopoldville and Elisabethville."

"It appears, Monsieur Lebbeke," Horst again wanted to uncover Lebbeke's weakness in controlling the oppressed Congo Tribes who he clearly knew hated the Belgique as much as the Nazis hated Jews, even if Germany chose not invade or take over the Congo Region. Besides he needed to find out what this woman's role was in Lebbeke's scheme and so far that was unclear, "that the Negroes and Negresses like this one you have here will eventually cause rebellion one day sooner or later anyhow, due to your murderous and repressive methods of labor control."

"So, Herr Deeke, you have finally noticed my beautiful light skinned Negress whore. . . . Ha, if you only knew her truth?"

Lebbeke turned and stared at her as the true possession she knew she was to him. The woman dropped her gaze to the floor in submission, as Lebbeke told her story.

"Her family was going to kill her because she was too light skinned."

" When they were forced from the Kasai Region by another tribe they decided to leave her since she was too young to survive the journey. My men found her near a Kasai riverbank just before a crocodile made her his evening dinner and brought her to me as a servant. Well, over the years she has become much more as you can see."

"She can even speak some French, but I've taught her to hate Germans, that's why she looks at you so funny. I told her you were Norwegian before you came in though, so don't worry."

"But now, she is also my best enforcer and assassin. She kills without any remorse and of course is my personal bodyguard."

Horst didn't comment as he again watched her look back at him.

"But to answer your specific question, Herr Deeke, the Tribes work against each other to maintain balance in the Congo. Those that support me, I give wealth and control over vast regional areas. When I need them, they pay me with assassinations and military support by offering their forces against my enemies. The important point is that they do not see me so much as a conquering European master, as an allied force to control their own wealth and domination over this massive land of anarchy."

"So you see Herr Deeke" Lebbeke grinned, "if Germany really wants those minerals they will have to fight a highly seasoned force for them."

"It certainly appears that way, Monsieur Lebbeke," Horst agreed with him, while hopping to get more details, "so how are they organized."

"My security squads are bound by blood!"

"Blood from the original tribal lords that accepted the rule of King Leopold II's Agents. . . .we are the controllers of this godforsaken land not Germany; No Panzers, No Luftwaffe, nor Waffen-SS will drive through this land's thick vegetation, horrid heat and diseased infested jungle."

"Only the silent blade and poisoned arrow will remain as sovereign in the Congo's black of night. The day is for sleeping for the Congo's killers."

"Automatic weapons and foot soldiers that have never fought in the blackness of the jungle night will wither and die quicker than a man without water on the Sahara's burning sands."

"Mark my words Herr Deeke," he gritted his teeth at Horst, " for you will always remember this day as your last on earth, if you choose to challenge me."

"Very well then, Monsieur Lebbeke," Horst purposely acted surprised at Lebbeke's previous revelations, "what would you suggest I do now that the Germans have flown me here and assigned me the task of running the mines in Katanga; mines that they obviously thought they had sole control over?"

"By the time the Germans have realized what is going on down here the Americans will be in the war and Germany will be defeated."

"It will be just like the first Great War, Herr Deeke," Lebbeke spoke with his own brand of overconfidence, "I have been here now for almost twenty years and the system I have is flawless and simple. My clients are the richest in the world. . . . the Rockefellers, the Guggenheims, the Ryans and the Forminiere Mining Group."

"What I suggest," Lebbeke added, "is that we join together and use this opportunity to protect our own future while Germany controls Belgium, as well as ship these minerals to only the highest paying bidders in the United States or elsewhere. All of their orders are paid to me in advance by the three-bank consortium of Midland, Barclay and Rothschild. Believe me Herr Deeke, that money will never dry up and their pockets go very deep."

"But what about the shipments to Germany, Monsieur Lebbeke," Horst again decided to string him into an even deeper web of deceit, "how could you keep Germany from discovering shipments to other bidders?"

"Herr Deeke, you are Germany's only source of information here and their Gestapo Agents, if they even come at all, will never go to the actual mines in the Katanga Province. Besides, even if they did, they would never know that those trains got diverted near the border of Angola to other Ports. Everything for Germany would always come to the Port of Matadi as expected, while the other Ports of Benguela and Lobito in neutral Portuguese Angola would support the other buyers."

"And the accounting records, Monsieur Lebbeke," Horst had him going now and he felt his overconfidence would finally get him to reveal his deepest secret, the one that could truly hang the man, even if Horst's team didn't take him out, "how do you suggest we could handle that?"

"Ah, Herr Deeke," Lebbeke smiled seeming to offer his deepest sincerity as his fat rounded face portrayed the always innocent bureaucrat, while Horst saw his eyes reveal a vile and corrupt swine, who had been hiding years of hatred in the back of his mind, " there are no records, my system is perfect and no one has been able to figure out how it works, in all these years."

"Come to my house tonight," he guilefully suggested, "around seven and we will seal our arrangement over a bottle of my favorite Brandy. If you still have any doubts about how it works, we will visit again tomorrow and I will show you my ultimate secret."

"Excellent, then let's meet at seven, Monsieur," Horst accepted the offer knowing this would give his commandos another day to scout out the area as well as complete their planned contact with Monsieur Lebbeke's mortal enemy, the son of the murdered ruler of Katanga, Prince Msiri. The Prince had recently left his hiding place in Angola to join Germany in overthrowing his fathers true killers; the Belgians, Lebbeke, and his thugs from Leopoldville.

Horst left quickly and met Erich several streets away in a small marketplace as they silently melted into the crowd and rejoined the SS-Wiking commandos at the designated coordinates.

He was now sure that the mission would require the back up of Prince Msiri's men once he realized the extent of Lebbeke's empire. Even Admiral Canaris people were unaware of the depth of this man's hold on the Congo or exactly how dangerous it was to the future of SSI's primary mission.

And unknown to Horst Deeke, tonight Monsieur Lebbeke would reveal an even more sinister side of his power in das Kongo to his guest.

While Horst made plans to join Lebbeke at his home that evening, Erich scouted a Belgian Bar and Restaurant in the European part of Leopoldville where Monsieur Lebbeke's office clerk preferred to take his evening meal. Erich had earlier met two attractive German working girls in one of the local Bars he had scouted. He then made arrangements for the girls to join him in a covert scam to be played on the shy and introverted Belgian office clerk.

The plan was simple; interrogate him in preparation for the following day's tactical attack against Lebbeke and his twenty-man security force based in Leopoldville. But the results were even more astounding as the man willingly revealed the entire background of Monsieur Lebbeke's empire, without any direct physical pressure from Folkers himself.

Using the sexual attentions of his ladies of the evening on 'the mouse', as Folkers disparagingly called him, they'd effectively uncovered spicy details of his life story and that of his arrogant boss. . .

It seems that Lebbeke had worked for powerful Belgian Financial interests for almost forty years.

And during with the last twenty years of that, he had built his own empire in the Congo.

His appointment took place after the Great War because of his family's personal relationship with King Leopold II of Belgium. Several corporations had to be set up in order to control and exploit interests for Belgium in the Congo and the largest stockholders of these corporations were financial groups owned by British and French banks employed to keep their respective countries from themselves unilaterally trying to develop the Congo's vast mineral and oil reserves behind the back of the smaller and weaker imperialist, Belgium.

The first and largest of these corporations was CCCI, Compagnie du Congo pour le Commerce et Industrie.

It was created to build the lower Congo Railroad where thousands of West African Negroes, indentured Negroes from the Congo, and Chinese laborers died in the jungle and along the cliffs of the river basin over the ten years it took to complete. This rail route went downstream from Leopoldville through the treacherous mountain gorge created by the rapids of the Congo River as it dropped to the deep water Port of Matadi.

BCK, the Bas-Congo au Katanga Railroad Company was the second largest corporation. It was built to exploit the vast mineral reserves, such as Uranium, Copper and Zinc in the Katanga Province. The Rail routes themselves were built from Elisabethville almost nine-hundred miles to the lower Congo basin at Leopoldville.

It was within this BCK Corporation that the secret of Lebbeke and certain Belgian Financial interests were hidden. During construction, the line was completed from Elisabethville to Ilebo.

Ilebo however was located at the upper Kasai River where it could be easily navigated by barge down to the intersection of the Congo.

At Leopoldville the CCCI railroad took over and carried all freight and passengers to the Port of Matadi just upstream from the open Atlantic Ocean. Initially a terminal and rail yard were built at Ilebo, but once the rail line was completed into Leopoldville the railyard was abandoned.

Then a mysterious tribal uprising took place in 1931 and most of the rails from Leopoldville to Ilebo were destroyed. Although some of Lebbeke's associates were implicated in the uprising, nothing was ever proven. In addition, none of the stockholders of any of the corporations were ever aware that the Leopoldville to Ilebo railroad had never been rebuilt. In fact, only Lebbeke and the Belgian Minister du Finance knew of the concealed mystery. The private owners of the river ferry service became Union Miniere du Congo controlled solely by the Minister du Finance and Monsieur Pierre Nikolas Lebbeke. It was this device over the past ten years that had made this man both recklessly powerful and rich.

The 'mouse' would not only double bill the giant mining company, UMHK, in Katanga for freight down the Kasai River to Leopoldville, but a mercenary ex-German Reichsmarine captain, left over from the 1916 gunboat wars on Lake Tanganyika, now working for Lebbeke, would purposely removed certain barges hauling precious minerals and then resale them to the highest bidder on Lebbeke's behalf.

Shortages were never reported in the shipments at the Port of Matadi, because it was always expected that at least 20% to 30% of the shipments resulted in pilferage or spillage commonly occurring on the thousand mile journey down from the vast Haut-Katanga Zinc and Copper mines or the Shinkolobwe Uranium mine near Elisabethville.

Tactically however, the German Naval Mercenary and his boats would have to be dealt with.

And Folkers now knew he needed to get this new information to the SS-Gruppenfuhrer quickly, just in case this man appeared in Leopoldville knowing something that could entrap Horst at some point in his subterfuge with Monsieur Pierre Nikolas Lebbeke.

It was nearly 2300 Hours before Erich had secured the clerk for the night and returned to check on the SS-Gruppenfuhrer.

Horst had gone to Lebbeke's house in the European sector of town about an hour earlier.

A single light now appeared in the entrance area as Folkers moved the Citroen into a nearby alley and silently went about checking the residence for movement. The house was empty.

And, upon a more detailed investigation of Lebbeke's library, Folkers found documents indicating that a newly embezzled mineral shipment was about to be hauled by barge into Leopoldville tonight. Immediately he realized that they had all gone to the waterfront, a place that could endanger Horst if the German Naval Mercenary was there, and somehow discovered who the SS-Gruppenfuhrer actually was.

Time was critical, still he didn't want to expose any part of the SS-Wiking commando operation just yet, but Erich needed firepower, so he went directly to the team's night rendezvous point.

SS-Wiking commandos were already in night-camouflaged gear and ready for Phase I of Horst's operation, the takeover of Lebbeke's twenty-man security squad at the Union Miniere's Administration facility.

Unfortunately though, Prince Msiri's warriors had not arrived from the mountains of Portugese Angola, so Erich knew they were on their own if an uprising of Lebbeke's allied Negro Tribesmen took place.

And then, there was the unknown element of exactly how many gunboats might stalking the black waters of the Congo that night?

Immediately Erich changed into his night camouflage gear. He then took three of his best men and drove to one of the storage buildings he had scouted earlier near the Union Miniere dock and began observation of a new arrival, a WWI British Fly Class gunboat docked near the main building.

These gunboats were quite formidable in the Congo River battles of the Great War with their four machine guns and three small 4.7-inch deck guns. They could easily control river junctions and provide commanding firepower over land targets that were within one-thousand yards of their moveable positions.

Due to their one-hundred and twenty foot length, low hull design, light forty-five-ton weight, and hull tunnels for their single screw steam propulsion units, they could easily operate in shallow river zones with a draft of only two to three feet of water and still reach almost nine knots on the river.

By the last years of the Great War, they had become the mainstays of Germany, Britain and to a lesser extent Belgium for control of their colonies.

It was now obvious that Lebbeke and his mercenary ex-German Reichsmarine Captain were using these surplus gunboats to enforce their own brand of domination over this lower region of the Congo.

Tonight, Folkers armed his men with several specialized commando weapons, but the most useful for this mission would clearly be their 'silenced' Schmeissers.

A match flared in the darkness on board the boat exposing the outline of an armed guard on the foredeck about ten yards from the positions taken up by Folkers SS-Wiking team. Then suddenly two other Negro Sentries appeared across the street.

They were near the Administration Building and began walking toward the dock where the gunboat was moored.

Within half a minute Folkers' team had identified seven targets in the immediate area requiring elimination. These would have to be cleaned up before they could continue to search for their commander.

Folkers knew his primary six-man team would now be in place to take out any sentries within the Administration Building itself, as he moved into final position.

On command, a red signal light flashed behind the building to confirm their readiness.

In an instant, the smell of their own cigarette smoke was the last sensory memory that either of the two Negro boat guards had. 'Fhummp! Fhummp!'

Several silent rounds from Folkers team hit them simultaneously.

Blood spattered the metal platting as they slid off the foredeck and into the water while some rustling in the marsh area nearby signaled that the local Crocs would soon make quick meals of their mangled hides.

The guards crossing the street were now on the dock.

They froze in place and nearly pissed in their pants with fear, as they watched their comrades bodies rip apart before their eyes in a kind of soundless slow motion dance then instantly disappear backwards into the black water of the mysterious Congo River.

Turning wildly in all directions, they franticly began fumbling to get their own weapons charged, but it was too late. Fhummp! Fhummp!

Instantly the same silent impacts ripped them off the wooden dock and down into the marsh grass surrounding the boat hull. In a matter of seconds the entire open dock area and gunboat deck had been cleared of all belligerents.

Upon clearing the interior and rear of the building, two of his team appeared at the doorway of the Union Miniere Office and again their flashlights blinked the code signal clear and ready.

Now they were in position to eliminate the gunboat crew.

Folkers and his commandos boarded silently from the foredeck as Team II crossed the dock and quickly covered the stern and midship position.

Suddenly a crewman climbed out of a steel doorway at the gunboat's main superstructure from somewhere on a lower deck.

He lit a cigarette as he began adjusting his eyes to the blackness of night, while Folkers men instantly melted into the darkness. Their instincts and training caused them to become invisible to the untrained eye, they made no motion, no sound, never disturbing even the sixth human sense of awareness, as the sailor took his last deep drag on the thick full-flavor of a French Cigarette.

SS-Wiking Sturmscharfuhrer Emil Lang's hands were like lightning bolts as his stiletto sliced the vital neck artery and before blood had found it's way to his skin's surface, the twitching body was disposed of into the water below.

Quickly, two more SS-Wiking Commandos slipped into the open doorway and began their manhunt along a narrow corridor down to the lower crews quarters.

The sounds emitted from down below deck confirmed that the objective was now under their absolute control, as Team II reported no sign of their commander Horst Deeke.

Now unfortunately, Folkers would again be forced to interrogate Lebbeke's 'mouse' for details to establish an alternative plan to locate the SS-Gruppenfuhrer. He first needed to completely clean the killing zone of all evidence as he moved his men throughout the dock area.

Then as one force, rather than split them leaving some to secure the waterfront, they all left to locate Horst.

At this point his commandos had neutralized almost twenty-five of Lebbeke's top mercenaries and sailors, so if Prince Msiri's warriors arrived in any reasonable amount of time, they could easily take up control and protect the Union Miniere waterfront with very little if any opposition.

Erich went psychotic with thoughts as he scrambled into the Citroen, where was Horst and in what state would he find him once the pursuit was over. His theories were racing as he entered the car, joining his men in a rush to the safe house, believing he would discover the answer imbedded in the mind of Lebbeke's 'mouse'.

Chapter 9

Lebbeke

"**H**err Deeke," Lebbeke smiled as he held up his Brandy snuffer in an informal toast to himself and his years of deceit and power as the sole Prefecture of Belgium's well hidden international slave consortium, the Republic du Congo, " so now you understand the framework of my empire. It is neither the Congo Free State nor the Belgium Congo, it is my Republic du Congo, just like Napoleon."

" And that's just why I'm now so effective in controlling these primitives and exploiting their vast mineral reserves. The tribal leaders themselves understand how it works and their interest is controlling their people, while mine is their resources. That is why together, the Tribal Chieftains and I alone can prevent any European power, no matter how great, from incursion here."

"Once more you have surprised me Monsieur," Horst replied cautiously as he scanned the room observing the change of demeanor and location of Lebbeke's so-called Negress Enforcer, " you must realize that these people will one day rise up and destroy your empire as well as all of your henchmen. Probably in the same despicable way you have enslaved and murdered their own subjects, one hand removed at a time, doesn't that concern you?"

"Ah ha, Herr Deeke," Lebbeke again grinned at his remark, " you must know by now that I'm not a fool, I've always prepared for such an eventuality, just like any great dictator from antiquity, and as such, I have my back door always waiting."

Lebbeke then got up and walked to his bar to pour another shot of Brandy as two other men entered the room from the entrance hall.

Now Horst had three targets and as yet no indication that Lebbeke knew who he was. Then it became obvious, as Horst recognized the 'narrow faced weasel' walking slowly behind the first man entering the room.

It was Herr Wollmann, the inept steward that Folkers had almost killed on the Lufthansa Flight. This was Lebbeke's inside man, working the German Flights down from Dakar.

It now made sense to Horst, that man had been used to detect all incoming threats from Europe, regardless of nationality, and he knew, if Wollmann had overheard anything on the plane, the ruse with Lebbeke would have been up for some time.

Before he could turn, Lebbeke's six-foot Negress had her blade across his neck and her incredible physical strength was evident in the muscle pressure she was exerting across his upper shoulders. Simultaneously both men drew pistols and pointed them at Horst.

"Once more my informants have protected me as you can see, Herr Deeke," looking down at his watch Lebbeke turned to his new arrivals, " you see, like any great leader, my secret informants are always finding ways to discover impending problems, like unexpected arrivals from the Third Reich."

Lebbeke turned to Horst as both men began shackling his ankles while Lebbeke's Negress held him tightly in check. Quickly they frisked him for weapons and pulled both his hands behind him, placing handcuffs on his wrists.

"Herr Wollmann," Lebbeke added," what time do they expect us?"

"Mon Commandant," Herr Wollmann responded in a subservient manner reminiscent of the Fuhrer's own staff as they often sounded when trying to please the leader of the German Reich .

"Kapitan Schelstrum sent an old British gunboat. It's now waiting at our waterfront, while his paddle barges are positioned forty-five kilometers Northeast at Junction Island off the main channel."

"Excellent, Herr Wollmann," Lebbeke reacted as he grabbed some papers and stuffed them into a briefcase filled with stacks of banded Swiss Francs, " bring along Herr Deeke so we may allow him to further view the extent of our vast colonial holdings before his untimely disposition to the 'true gods' of our Congo."

Horst was too surprised and preoccupied with his own situation to be concerned just yet, clearly aware that both Hippos and Giant River Crocs were considered the so called gods of the Congo by the people in this Region.

The real question in his mind was the status of his Phase I operation and Folkers' fact-finding mission. If that had been successful, they would at least know where he was, and hopefully where they were taking him.

Within minutes Lebbeke's entourage and Horst were on their way to the waterfront where fortunately a boiler problem on the gunboat forced them to choose the slower conventional paddle wheel river barge docked nearby rather than the heavily armed surplus British Gunboat, Tsetse Fly.

Chapter 10

The Congo

This time Folkers handled the interrogation of Lebbeke's Administrative Clerk, himself. In less than ten minutes he spilled enough details to convinced Erich that the SSI team had been compromised, and even more serious, the SS-Gruppenfuhrer was probably trapped.

Horst had actually been vulnerable from the moment he had arrived into Leopoldville.

At that moment SS-Wiking Sturmscharfuhrer Lang broke Erich's concentration as he entered the room and spoke, "Herr Folkers, we have just received an urgent coded communication from Prince Msiri's relocated headquarters at Maquela do Zombo just across the border in Angola."

Erich needed to know where the Prince stood now that Horst's situation would require most of his men and attention as he replied in Norwegian to block the 'mouse' from picking up on their conversation,

"Go ahead Sergeant, fill me in, but speak only in Norwegian." Lang complied in fluent Wikingspeak as they called it,

"The Prince and a force of thirty-five-hundred of his loyalist warriors are now enroute to Madimba, seventy-five kilometers to the southwest of Leopoldville, Herr Folkers. Their objective for now is the control of the CCCI Rail Station at Madimba."

Erich reacted concerned, "What kind of weapons do they have Sergeant?"

"He didn't give me any information on that," Lang quickly fired back, " but he did state that from there, they intended to join forces with two other allied tribes near the Port's of Matadi and Boma."

"They intend to bring those areas under their joint control along with everything west of the capital, eventually including the entire lower Congo Region."

"Mein Gott," Erich reacted in German as he quickly returned to Wikingspeak to finish his thought,

"The SS-Gruppenfuhrer will go crazy when he hears these people are trying to take over the port region without a logical tactical plan or any automatic weapons."

"The Belgian Security forces will cut them to pieces down there and the best they could have to fight with is a few bolt-action Mausers, some poison arrows, knives and a few spears. That's so damn primitive, those tribesmen are already out of control. If they could only wait a week, our freighter from Dakar is carrying two-hundred SS-Wiking Commandos plus over eight-thousand automatic small arms and eighty-thousand rounds of ammunition as well as grenades and mortars." Frustrated, Folkers instructed two of his Sergeants to secure the prisoner, then left the room as he went into the lower radio room with Lang to further analyze the situation.

"Sergeant, we've got very little time left to assist the SS-Gruppenfuhrer. I want him out of this mess as soon as possible."

Erich collected his thoughts as he again spoke,
"Code and send Prince Msiri the following message, Sergeant;

TAKE AND HOLD THE RAIL FACILITIES AT MADIMBA, DO NOT - REPEAT - DO NOT LEAVE THAT POSITION UNTIL WE HAVE FORCES IN PLACE AT THE PORT OF MATADI TO MEET AND SUPPORT YOU.

Folkers and his commandos quickly returned to the Union Miniere docks and re-boarded the Fly Class gunboat following the map laid out by the 'mouse' to the Junction Island off the main Congo River channel.

Since two of Folkers men were ex-Kriegsmarine mechanics, they quickly made the boat's boilers operational with some kludged equipment found on the waterfront as the single screw steam propulsion unit cranked up, pushing them up river in the Fly Class gunboat at it's top speed of nine knots.

To maintain their stealth, Folkers positioned his best forward scout on the foredeck with the new Zeiss night optics binoculars, designed for U-boats.

He scanned up river as they carefully tried to muffle the old steam engine by staying far enough behind the boat that likely held the SS-Gruppenfuhrer.

"A target dead ahead, five-hundred meters, SS-Sturmbannfuhrer", Folkers Scout called back under his breath, as only he could make out the outline of the paddle wheeler, while they silently closed the distance.

On board Lebbeke's boat up ahead, the noise of the engine and paddle wheel slapping the black water behind them, blocked any indication of Folkers' approach in the heavy pitch-black night air.

With an almost circus-like look, light bulbs surrounding the maindeck and stern of the paddle wheeler caused a halo of return glare to engulf the boat. The effect prevented anyone on deck from being able to see behind the boat, as the Tsetse Fly closed the distance between them.

Folkers' scout observed only one person on deck besides the forward guide, who was calling back directions to the boat's pilot as they made a turn to position themselves in the mid-channel."

Below deck, Lebbeke was still rambling on about his empire and how even the Reich could not dislodge him now, as Horst kept a close eye on Lebbeke's Negress who was seemingly agitated as she peered out of the starboard port hole into the black night while they moved up-river.

"Herr Wollmann," Lebbeke changed subjects momentarily as he turned away from Horst, "get Kapitan Schelstrum on the radio and tell him our position on the river," Lebbeke then laughed as he turned back to Horst, " I want him to meet Herr Deeke before we conclude our negotiations."

"As you wish, Herr Lebbeke," Wollmann responded, as some movement on deck seemed to catch the attention of both Horst and the Negress.

Realizing her keen sense for trouble, Lebbeke snapped his fat fingers at her and pointed up the stairway for her to check out the situation.

Like a black leopard unleashed for the first time into the night, she lunged for the staircase ahead of Wollmann and was gone in an instant. Lebbeke returned his pistol to his right hand and pointed it at Horst as he awaited the return of his enforcer. Wollmann completed his climb and was also making his way to the pilothouse.

On deck the soundless calm indicated trouble as the Negress' senses heightened just as she turned.

'Fhummp!' With her eyes frozen in a stare of surprise, she took a single round right between them into her forehead, from Folkers silenced Schmeisser.

Lifelessly she slid into the black void of the river with the rest of the dead crew.

By now, four of Folkers commandos had control of the upper decks as Wollmann emerged from below and turned toward the bridge's ladder, unaware of his last fateful step as Folkers came up behind him with his signature movement.

In one motion with his gleaming stiletto, Folkers slit his throat and slid the body carefully over the side as the roar of the paddlewheel continued to hide any unexpected noise.

Finally, it was time for the Fat Pig, Lebbeke.

Folkers knew that Horst needed Lebbeke alive, but as they realized their situation, Folkers decided to be the distraction as his sharpshooter readied his aim from behind him on the lower stairs.

Erich had over twenty scars on his body from previous commando mission wounds in Spain and elsewhere throughout Europe, and his threshold of pain was beyond normal human capacity.

He was known by his men to fight in an even higher state of frenzy when wounded; he's a berserker they would say, as he would go wild with the enemy.

When injured, he would purposely disfigure and maim his victims before he killed them, if they happened to be the hapless soul that wounded him.

Slowly Erich stepped down into the cabin with Lebbeke and SS-Gruppenfuhrer Deeke with his silenced Schmeisser pointing at the deck floor to avoid confronting Lebbeke.

"Herr Deeke," Lebbeke turned to Folkers smiling in a vicious grin as he held his pistol on Horst," it appears that your reinforcements arrived before we were able to reach Kapitan Schelstrum."

"That does appear to be the case, Herr Lebbeke," Horst replied in a serious tone trying to determine if Folkers was going to try to capture him, rather than kill him outright,

"and I would like you to remain with us Lebbeke, as we conclude our negotiations with the good Kapitan for the Uranium ore."

At that moment, realizing he was closer to Horst than to Lebbeke, Folkers lunged to cover the SS-Gruppenfuhrer from the pistol's trajectory as his sharpshooter behind him, locked-on and fired at Lebbeke's right wrist holding the gun.

Lebbeke let out a shrilling scream as his wrist became a mass of blood and mangled tissue while the gun flew back against the rear wall. Folkers then jumped to grab him, as he remained fully distracted in pain.

"You didn't have to do that, "Lebbeke yelled at Horst grabbing his wrist as he now laid on the floor under the massive pressure of Folkers arms," I was going to drop the gun. I knew I was overpowered!"

"I knew you had control of the boat! Look at my hand! Oh God, get me something to stop this bleeding, please Herr Gruppenfuhrer!"

"I'm terribly sorry Herr Lebbeke," Horst stated in his less than condescending manner after being held captive for the past three hours by Lebbeke's Negress enforcer," but we are trained only to be certain that any situation is under our complete control, never trust anyone, especially the enemy."

Within moments one of the commandos who had medical training was summoned to assist Lebbeke as they continued up-river to eliminate Kapitan Schelstrum and his jungle mercenaries.

The gunboat remained out of sight in a trailing position with five commandos crewing it and all of it's weapons loaded and charged.

Within hours, a major firefight with Schelstrum's boats near the mineral barges at Junction Island had erased any other opposition.

During the trip up stream, Lebbeke had revealed the full extent of his association with Kapitan Schelstrum to Horst Deeke. They had split the profits of one-third of all the shipments from the vast Haut-Katanga Zinc and Copper mines and the Shinkolobwe Uranium mine near Elisabethville, three ways.

In fact, one-third of all shipments simply never arrived. They were treated as pilferage or spillage and were in fact re-routed to holding areas forty-five kilometers up-stream from Leopoldville on the Congo River by Kapitan Schelstrum. The barges were easily secluded in small tributaries and bayous at the Junction Island hidden off the main Congo River channel. Sailors and gunboats previously controlled by Schelstrum protected the area for the joint venture formed by Lebbeke, the Belgium Bankers, and Schelstrum himself. Now that was gone.

At the time, knowing that he was going to kill Horst Deeke anyway, it provided Lebbeke with a sense of power to explain his dominion in precise detail to the conquerors of the Belgium Empire in Europe. But now the SS-Gruppenfuhrer was back in control, and Horst understood completely the potential British Commando problem as well.

Horst now knew that it was only practical that the Belgium Congo should remain under control of Lebbeke and presumably the old Belgium Administration, so that the Brits would maintain their stand-off boundaries and not attack the Uranium mines in Katanga. However, it was clear that as soon as Lebbeke was deposed or failed to continue as the administrator of the Congo Region, Britain had planned an invasion from Rhodesia and South Africa to completely destroy the Katanga Mining operations for the duration of the war with Germany.

Chapter 11

Norsk Hydro

$\mathbf{F}$ive weeks dragged on before Horst's Portugese Flagged Freighter returned with its initial five-hundred ton load of Uranium into the harbor of Brest, France from the Port of Matadi. It was quickly unloaded, then place on a secure freight train that rushed it across the occupied countries into Germany and on to the outskirts of Sangerhausen without incident.

Unfortunately for the SS-Gruppenfuhrer, further shipments over the next two years were to become much more problematic due to increasing Allied interdiction near Gibraltar and the North African coastline, as well as obstacles created by British SAS Commandos stationed in Rhodesia and penetrating the mining defenses of the Katanga providence in the southern Congo.

Nevertheless, the next critical piece in the SSI Super Bomb Project became clear to Horst by the end of September of 1941. With Germany's successes in occupying Norway, das Vaterland now had the lion's share of industrial assets and total domination of the major cities from the Port of Narvik on the Norwegian sea coast near the Arctic, to the Port of Oslo in the south. The world's only heavy water production facility at Vemork, deep in the central mountain valleys west of Oslo, was now under the administrative ownership of I. G. Farben with the industrial support of Flick Steel and Carl Siemen's electrical engineers.

Simultaneously, the Gestapo with the help of Wiking-SS commandos provided area protection for the plant, while Heisenberg's most competent physicists, chemists and engineers in nuclear science made steady visits to Vemork.

Their plan was to effectively increase production of the deuterium oxide from less than one ton annually in 1940 to over two tons per year by late 1941.

As October 1941 arrived, the SS-Gruppenfuhrer's Norsk Hydro facility at Vemork, finally began effectively shipping critical inventories of deuterium oxide back to the Sangerhausen research facility.

For the next twelve months, the Vemork facility seemed to be working flawlessly, but because it was not yet practical to build a bomb designed with deuterium, the output of Vemork had been used only as a moderator for the yellow cake Uranium collected from Union Miniere in Katanga. Chief Scientist Werner Heisenberg's team had constructed a heavy-water reactor at Sangerhausen and using the Katanga Uranium, it's output of a small amount of PU-239, bomb grade plutonium, was promising.

However, the same amount of bomb grade Uranium-U235 would, according to most of Heisenberg's calculations at that time, result in the same force of explosive power. Heisenberg was convinced that something else had to be considered due to the difficulty in manipulating and controlling the highly radioactive PU-239.

Since five of his top Nuclear Physicists had reviewed in detail, a theoretical formula scratched out in chalk on a classroom blackboard at Cal Tech during their sabbatical visit in early 1939 to the United States, they all agreed that refined liquid deuterium from the heavy hydrogen facility held the greatest promise.

At that time, the world's superlative expert on nuclear quantum physics, Robert Teller who was then working for Oppenheimer in San Francisco, completely wrote out in his own hand on that chalkboard, detailed formulas and instructions for discussion purposes with his students and the international faculty present.

But back then no one, except his old teacher Heisenberg, understood the need for establishing a veil of secrecy around his revolutionary ideas.

Without any obvious concern for security, by the FBI or the United States Government, the definitive formula for designing a thermonuclear hydrogen based bomb was innocently revealed to Heisenberg's five Nazi scientists and those in the scientific world that understood it's potential, for the very first time.

The difference was that now, in 1942, Nazi Scientists had control of the only sources in the world for one of the two key ingredients; deuterium from the Norsk Hydro facility at Vemork, Norway. While only two areas of the world were known to produce sufficient inventories of yellow cake Uranium; Katanga's Union Miniere Mines in the Congo and the Great Bear Lake Mines in Canada.

It was these facts from the past that now redirected Chief Physicist Werner Heisenberg toward the idea that deuterium from Vemork was simpler to utilize and held even greater promise as an actual component in das Fuhrer's much more effective device.

And besides, the efforts to refine either weapons grade U-235 or the more dangerous PU-239 were going slowly and they needed a larger facility with more cyclotrons, which were considerably more expensive and time consuming to build.

The team's latest predictions for collecting enough U-235 for an effective nuclear explosive device were late 1944, and their estimates indicated that at least twenty to twenty-five kilograms of U-235 would be needed, however U-235 was much more stable and less radioactive than plutonium and the critical mass could be achieved more easily.

By simply using a cannon-like firing device, U-235 masses could be collided into one another at high speed, thus creating an effective atomic explosion.

Teller's theoretical concept of a fifteen to twenty-five kilogram ball of U-235 exploded within an eighty-kilogram liquid deuterium shell suggested a much larger explosion was possible within a much more portable device.

So for the invasion of Russia, the team determined the device could be delivered within a large self-contained remotely controlled panzer tank or in Britain or the US by a remotely controlled U-boat sailed into a pre-selected allied port.

Because of the technical support issues as well as the weight of the device, an aircraft delivery system was initially ruled out. So, as the year progressed, Sangerhausen became pre-occupied with the second task of designing an effective bomb core and support system for Heisenberg's thermonuclear type device, while a more highly refined and concentrated form of liquid deuterium was now being extracted from Norsk Hydro.

Meanwhile, Great Britain and Winston Churchill in particular had become almost paranoid about Germany's potential to create and explode a nuclear device over London or somewhere in England by the early half of 1941. It was assumed, and correctly so, that Nazi Germany was at least a year ahead of Britain and the US in the development of a potential nuclear device, so scientists in both countries set out to make this point very clear to their respective politicians. In the US, Enrico Fermi who had recently left Europe as well as Teller and the Physicist Leo Szilard made it known that Germany might easily be in position to make a preemptive attack with an atomic device as early as 1944.

Armed with these facts from America and the predictions of his own nuclear weapon scientists, Churchill went into a frenzy using double agents of MI-5 within the homeland, and MI-6 internationally to interrogate all their Allies from Europe now displaced onto British soil.

And so the French, the Czechs, the Poles, and finally the Norwegians as well as mainland Europeans still fighting in the underground were used to identify locations that might be hiding Nazi assets planned for use in the production of the Fuhrer's super weapon.

It was finally the Norwegian underground operatives that began alerting British Agents of increasing activities in and around the high concentration dam and power plant at Vemork as early as January 1942.

As a critical priority, Churchill authorized the detailed planning for a raid to destroy the facility, using Royal Engineers of the 1st British Airborne Division.

Unfortunately, imbedded agents from Admiral Canaris Abwehr were able to intercept preliminary details of the planned raid through contacts in the British Admiralty.

Using this information for his own political gains, Admiral Canaris went directly to the Fuhrer with his morsel of critical intelligence, rather than to SSI and the Reichfuhrer.

The result was substantial credibility for Canaris and another potential embarrassment for Himmler and his newly promoted SS-Gruppenfuhrer Horst Deeke.

Chapter 12

The Berghof

Operation Barbarossa, Germany's massive invasion of Soviet Russia, was almost eight months old and the taking of Moscow was dangerously bogging down in the severe Russian Winter and marshes outside of the Great Russian capital.

Now the Fuhrer was under constant pressure from his Generals to make changes from his plan to redirect resources and forces into Stalingrad and to grab the Soviet Oil fields of the Crimea. His only moments to relax the pressure and feel safe were those he cherished at the Berchtesgaden. So this was where they all had come to meet the Supreme Fuhrer of das Vaterland on this particularly cold and clear day, the 17th of February 1942.

As their plane touched down at Ainring Airdrome in the valley below the Berghof, the SS-Reichsfuhrer Heinrich Himmler and SS-Gruppenfuhrer Horst Deeke were unaware that the entire morning had been a major strategy fight between Hitler and his Wehrmacht Generals. Their SS staff car arrived at the mountain summit, and they were immediately directed to a rear parking area away from the mass of black Mercedes command cars overflowing with Wehrmacht Staff Officers awaiting their senior officers who would eventually emerge from the Berghof.

An SS-Sturmscharfuhrer silently met their driver, assisted their exit and escorted them up the rear access staircase to a small anteroom on the second floor. He then addressed them both abruptly.

"By orders of the Fuhrer himself, Herr SS-Reichsfuhrer, you and the SS-Gruppenfuhrer must wait here in the Fuhrer's rear quarters."

As the SS-Sturmscharfuhrer left them, SS-Reichsfuhrer Himmler turned to Horst and spoke in a lowered voice.

"I'm afraid we have arrived into a hornets nest, Herr Deeke, rather than the relaxed atmosphere we had hoped for. With times like these, no man will be safe from the wrath of the Fuhrer."

Horst responded, while cautiously listening for anyone's arrival. "Jawohl, Herr Reichsfuhrer, and the complications of our U235 harvesting at Werner Heisenberg's Nuclear lab at Sangerhausen, are not going to make things any easier for us, than those ill-fated Wehrmacht Generals seem to have it downstairs, with the Fuhrer."

Almost without warning, the door to the inside hallway opened halfway and Adolf Hitler slowly pushed it wide-open.

Both men clearly surprised by the Fuhrer's stealthy arrival cried in unison, "Heil Hitler!" and smartly raised the Nazi salute to their Supreme Commander.

Just as startled in his discovery of them, the Fuhrer, looking somewhat disheveled from the downstairs meeting, stood starring mindlessly beyond them at the snow covered Untersberg centered in the window, behind the two men.

Silence overtook the room until the Fuhrer spoke.

"Heinrich, my god, I'm so glad you're here to get me out of that den of wolves below us. The Wehrmacht are idiots. We have just succeeded in the greatest land invasion in the history of the world and now they are telling me to slow down. We must have the oil in southern Russia now. As you know, Generalfeldmarchall Rommel's Panzer Corps in North Africa have done little to secure critical oil depots for Germany."

The Fuhrer continued without pausing, "Now these imbeciles are letting communist sappers over-run the positions we've already taken to the north and rear of our own Wehrmacht Units.

Only the SS Waffen and SS Wiking units know how to deal with these spineless Russian Mongrel schweinhunds and their Bolshevik whores."

On hearing that, the SS Reichfuhrer responded with enthusiasm, "Jawohl, My Fuhrer!" as Hitler continued.

" Burn them out or annihilate their teaming hordes, as soon as we overrun their cities with our Panzers. Leave no one standing, White or Red Russian, they are all pigs and scum from Hell that we can never trust. Even our supposed White Russian allies in the Right Wing Camp fed us lies before Operation Barbarossa."

Again, the SS Reichfuhrer responded, "Jawohl, My Fuhrer!" but he was cut off again, as the Fuhrer went on preaching in an almost blind madness.

"Stalin has been re-arming and building hundreds of Tanks in caves, a thousand miles east of Moscow deep in the Ural Mountains since 1939 and our successful invasion of Poland. Russian Generals have purposely delayed getting those units to Stalin's front until after our winter stocks are used up this year. Then they will throw everything they've got at us including their new dive-bombers. They are draining Germany's Aryan Manhood with their miles and miles of swamps and tundra. It is now time to activate this "Super Bomb" you have built for me and drive them back into a burning nuclear hell."

Suddenly he stopped, and the room became silent with an ominous sense of desperation. As he looked from the distant mountains and the desolate winter scene beyond to focus directly at their faces, now frozen in panic in front of him. "You do. . . have my Super Bomb ready, don't you Herr Deeke?"

Horst wanted nothing more than to hide at that moment, but this was what they came for, so candidly he responded to Fuhrer.

"My Fuhrer, I would only wish to tell you a resounding, Jawohl, to that question, but we must first explain our complications to this matter."

Flashing his teeth, as the SS-Gruppenfuhrer began his next utterance, the Fuhrer screamed his fury at him with spittle ejecting from his mouth.

"How could you let me down, Herr Gruppenfuhrer, you know full well the mortal consequences of this action."

"With war in Russia becoming impossible, Rommel asking for more reinforcements and Panzers, and the battle in Britain draining my Luftwaffe reserves to protect the cities of das Vaterland, you come here to tell me this! "

"Now that the US has entered the war, it is imperative that we strengthen Europe against any allied invasion on our western front. Russia is draining Aryan manpower that we must have for the protection of the Greater Reich and you tell me the Bomb is not ready! How do you expect me to tolerate this insubordination? Even you, my SS-Reichfuhrer have let me believe that this thing would be at my disposal in this most crucial moment."

Hitler stopped for a moment, but his eyes were widened furiously and his lips still quivering with torment.

At that, realizing only he, could appease the frenzy the Fuhrer was now in, SS-Reichfuhrer Himmler began in a calming tone of voice.

"Again, my Fuhrer, our situation is only a temporary setback." Himmler continued again pausing to judge the Fuhrer's reaction.

"We still have the largest assets in the world in Nuclear Physics, both in scientific manpower and advancement of the project. We are years ahead of anyone in the world on this, but it is still very theoretical in some ways and that is the part that has made us adjust our course.

"Now we are quickly converting the theoretical science into a practical bomb-like device that will exceed all previous assumptions."

"Then we must test it."

"We also know that both the Americans and British have certain assets that we can get quickly, if we need them, through Zionist Scientists we have now recruited with our Bolshevik subterfuge in the United States. As assurance protection, our SSI Agents have captured and are holding ransom certain members of these Jewish Scientists Families in a designated area of Buchenwald near Sangerhausen."

"The Plan is to extract complete allegiance from these scientists in various Institutes of Nuclear Studies at Universities in Chicago and San Francisco, by threatening extermination of their family members. Through this extortion, Operation Sky Club can be used to get whatever we may need, exactly when we need it."

Again Himmler tried to search the Fuhrer's eyes for any indication of soothing. They seemed transfixed a second time, on the winter spectacle created by the imposing Bavarian Alps filling the window. An eerily blinding light glaring through the window pane, held the Fuhrer's attention, as the sun caught a cloud of icy mist boiling up into view from the steep valley below the Berghof.

The SS-Reichfuhrer knew the Fuhrer was building up pressure for the right moment to explode again, yet he continued undaunted, adding information until that moment arrived.

"My Fuhrer, the SS-Gruppenfuhrer's SSI Agents and the Wiking-SS Legion has accomplished much in the past two years since we initiated the Super Bomb project. I must now let him explain the details of where we are in the project so you can again be aware of the timetable we have been working on and the success we have achieved."

At this instant, the Fuhrer again reacted.

"Timetable, the timetable was mine alone to decide Herr Reichsfuhrer."

Himmler quickly agreed, but tried to add the key caveat that established their excuse for the current situation.

"Jawohl, my Fuhrer, that is correct. We had always gone forward knowing that you would need the Super Bomb at the very least, for negotiations with the Allies, and possibly by 1944, but we've never considered it as early as now. The current military events and equipment logistics have never been under our control.

Again the Fuhrer added his response, but this time a little less agitated.

"Yes of course, and neither would it seem that those events are even under the control of my Wehrmacht Generals. . . the idiots! They squabble like young Fräuleins down there giving me excuse after excuse for what is happening outside Moscow. Even the great Blitzkrieg General Guderian cannot seem to understand why I want our energies driven south to control the Russian Oil Reserves. All he wants is another great tank battle and more Oak Leaves for his Knight's Cross for taking Moscow."

The SS-Reichsfuhrer again returned to his comments. "Jawohl, my Fuhrer, you are correct again."

" But with respect to your own directives on the Super Bomb project, the planning deadline for the Super Bomb at the very least, was the end of 1944. Never once had we considered that you would need it in the middle of Operation Barbarossa. My Fuhrer, Nuclear Physics is an ominous force, but its vagaries and the fickle scientific minds that must create the work within it, are unlike you, my Fuhrer. They do not possess the focused and objective strategies that you can foresee for the Reich of the Future."

"You yourself said, the plan could develop until the end of 1944," he cautiously added, " but after that, it would be at your sole discretion to use it or you would personally exact retribution for its failure. I ask you now, at the very least, to hear the alternate plans developed by your top Scientists and presented now by SS-Gruppenfuhrer Horst Deeke for your final approval."

"Without these modified plans," Himmler added, "the OSS and British Commandos as well as other covert American Agencies may be able to destroy parts of our core project before we complete the final Aryan Super Bomb."

Himmler then paused to emphasize the complement hidden within his next point.

"My Fuhrer, their own scientists are telling Churchill and Roosevelt how far ahead we really are and they are clearly worried. Believe me, my Fuhrer, right now the Allies are more afraid of your success, in the development of a Super Bomb than any other clandestine war project in the Third Reich or the World, for that matter."

Suddenly the Fuhrer seemed to focus directly on the SS-Reichsfuhrer's comments. But this time, he had an aire of concern on in his voice as he interjected, "Admiral Canaris has revealed to me that the British are planning a raid on your Norwegian Facilities in the very near future SS-Reichfuhrer," he pulled a letter from his pocket and handed it to the SS-Reichsfuhrer, "so what do you make of that reaction and are you prepared for them?"

"Of course we are, my Fuhrer!" Horst finally returned to the discussion with the Fuhrer, offering a powerful conviction of the Reich's future success, " we knew it was only a matter of time before they realized our potential to use these resources to build the Reich's Super Bomb, my Fuhrer.

My SS-Wiking commandos are awaiting their arrival, and they will be completely destroyed with any tactical ground or airborne assault into the maelstrom we have prepared for them at Vemork!"

Hitler then added, somewhat impressed that the other world leaders had reacted fearfully to Germany's potential overwhelming power,

"Do you think Churchill and Roosevelt are now completely afraid of my Super Bomb program?"

"That they would go to any means to destroy it, my Fuhrer," the SS-Gruppenfuhrer added as he finished the Fuhrer's thought, to the ecstatic relief of the SS-Reichfuhrer who now realized that Admiral Canaris would not get the best of this secret intelligence revelation after all.

This time, the Fuhrer had a smile on his face, as he slumped back into a nearby chair and relaxed at last. Then, with his arms hung limply at his sides, he spoke.

"Well, well, Churchill and Roosevelt so worried about my Super Bomb program, that they would go to any means to destroy it? Maybe you are on schedule then?"

"Exactly, my Fuhrer!" SS-Gruppenfuhrer Horst Deeke responded confidently, as their discussion with the Fuhrer now became an opportunity to gain his support for the Super Bombs next phase, while Horst reviewed his security and the impenetrable nature of Vemork as well as how they planned to derail the British Commando Raids.

Chapter 13

Death of Heydrich

As SS-Gruppenfuhrer Horst Deeke entered the newly constructed Physics Lab at the minus-fifth (-5th) level underground at Sangerhausen, Werner Heisenberg rushed over to enthusiastically greet him. Heisenberg's sequestered team of German Physicists and re-patriated German and French Jewish Nuclear Scientists were standing at a enormous blackboard frantically taking notes on an extensive formula written in white chalk and covering about two-thirds of the surface. Permanently painted above it, in bright yellow stenciled letters were the words,

Achtung!

Do Not Remove any of this Formula

Without the Direct Permission of the Chief Scientist, WH!

SS-Gruppenfuhrer Horst Deeke was the first to speak. "Herr Heisenberg, I must apologize for being so late to our meeting, but a horrible assassination attempt by British SAS operatives has just taken place in the Czech Capital of Prague. The SS-Obergruppenfuhrer Reinhard Heydrich was seriously injured and is now in a medical unit in Prague with a ruptured spleen and possible spine damage. I of course was immediately called to Berlin to handle some classified matters for the SS-Reichfuhrer Himmler so that he could prepare to travel to Prague and direct the retaliation for this horror."

Reinhard Heydrich up to now, had been the most probable choice of the Fuhrer himself for the future replacement of the SS-Reichfuhrer Himmler and at some future point in time, he might even have replaced the Fuhrer as well.

As head of the all-powerful Sicherheitsdienst SD, no one in the Third Reich had moved up the ranks of power as quickly as Heydrich, nor were they as feared and hated as Heydrich.

When Heydrich took over as Reichprotektor in Czechoslovakia from Baron von Neurath in late 1941, his vicious methods and death squads used for maintaining control over the hostile populace, quickly gained him the nickname of the Butcher of Prague.

With respect to the SS-Gruppenfuhrer Horst Deeke, however, his association had always been rather cool.

Both men were highly intelligent and quick thinking in critical situations, but Horst was a true Viking Warrior, battle tested and much more effective in clandestine or direct combat action, whereas the SS-Obergruppenfuhrer Reinhard Heydrich was obviously a crafty politician with a serious flaw for womanizing. Both men kept a proper distance from one another and clearly respected each other's zone of influence and authority.

Instantly interrupting, Werner Heisenberg cried out. "Oh Gott", I have friends in Prague, the fools, the retributions will be incredible," "especially if Heydrich dies. And I can tell you, any type of spleen damage can easily be fatal."

Then, Heisenberg excitedly added, "I must get word to them, to get out now!"

Horst quickly responded gruffly. "Herr Heisenberg, get hold of yourself! These people in Prague are not part of our project. We have much more critically important things to cover now, at this meeting. You and I can discuss these friends of yours later in private, but for now we must quickly exploit this change in the power structure at SS Headquarters and especially with regard to the SS-Reichsfuhrer's weight of authority now placed in my hands."

"We have an opportunity to get more control and additional funds out of the SS-Reichsfuhrer's Bank in Switzerland, but we must act fast."

Werner composed himself outwardly, relaxed his mood and then spoke carefully to the SS-Gruppenfuhrer.

"You are absolutely correct, Herr SS-Gruppenfuhrer. My emotions, as you can see, overcame me. Certainly the increase in your authority by virtue of the circumstances at Prague and your new orders from the SS-Reichfuhrer will advance you my friend."

They both turned at the same time toward the blackboard. There watching them in a state of shocked apprehension was the now silent group of scientist.

Realizing they might have overheard parts of the outburst and trying to re-energize the group's original excitement, Werner smiled at the group and promptly spoke first. "Now, Herr SS-Gruppenfuhrer, let me introduce you to everyone and tell you the news of our great discovery here at Sangerhausen."

Werner was now relaxed enough to explain their results to the SS-Gruppenfuhrer as he and the other scientists seated themselves around the conference room table.

"With Teller's theory," he continued, " as the basis of our research, we believe that exploding a small core of only twenty-five kilograms of U-235, within a round containment well of eighty kilograms of cryogenically cooled liquid deuterium, we can create a massively powerful thermonuclear bomb blast equivalent to over a million tons of TNT.

Horst stood astounded with satisfaction as he reacted. "Herr Heisenberg, this is incredible news for our project. . . continue, please."

"Very well, Herr SS-Gruppenfuhrer," Heisenberg stated with renewed confidence, "the new concept super bomb would be triggered when a smaller core of U-235 is brought to super critical by a chain reaction created using a closed cannon device about twenty feet in length and packed with cordite to fire a bullet shaped pellet of five kilograms of U-235 at a specific rate of speed directly into the U-235 core bringing the event to critical mass. The core would be positioned in the dead center of the newly designed liquid deuterium well. "

Horst again reacted. "This is excellent news, Herr Heisenberg, our project has now been given renewed life and potential, and for now we have the raw nuclear assets and manpower to make it a reality."

And so, throughout the remainder of that day they continued demonstrating their findings to SS-Gruppenfuhrer, as they made extensive plans to redirect their efforts to the new and relatively less complex alternative to building an atomic implosion bomb.

For the first time in the project's evolution, all their resources would now become concentrated on the creation of one device; the world's first liquid hydrogen based thermonuclear bomb.

Chapter 14

The British Raid

Ominously, as the SS-Gruppenfuhrer had predicted to the Fuhrer at their meeting in Bavaria, a British Commando raid was mounted against Vemork in late November.

However the SS-Gruppenfuhrer's forces were well prepared. SS-Wiking had been alerted to the approach on November 19th and German Luftwaffe fighters waited until the British Halifax bombers and their towed gliders were over the Norwegian Coastline before they attacked. Within twenty minutes all of the planes and all known British forces were killed before they got to within forty kilometers of the Hydro Plant.

After the raid, Himmler contacted the Norwegian fascist leader Vidkun Quisling, interrogating him on the possibility that partisans had been involved in the British Commando attack. But it was clear, at least at that time, that no one could be implicated, so no retributions were committed against the local population around Vemork or the town of Rjukan.

Norsk Hydro's location about eighty kilometers west of Oslo in extremely mountainous terrain gave it almost prefect protection from an air attack. So the Brits were forced to use gliders on the first attack to land their men.

The valley in which the Hydro Plant was built rose upward one-thousand feet from a narrow riverbed to the top of a mountain plateau covered by thick pine forests to the north and west. Because of the narrow approach to the valley even paratroopers could easily be defeated from protected fortifications on either side, if they were even able to reach the target.

The actual power plant was situated on a solid rock shelf at the base of a six-hundred foot vertical drop behind the facility housing the massive arrays of water pipelines.

Water rushing downward through the massive pipes at incredible pressures from the mountaintop lake drove the electric turbines feeding power to the two-hundred cell deuterium (D2O) electrolysis tube facility.

Mountainous cliffs behind the main building were filled with pine forests and rock outcroppings further protecting the site.

Horst's SS-Wiking commandos, SS-Security troops and operations personnel were housed in a cluster of cottages and operational buildings that share the rock shelf with the main facility. At the time of the first raid, the British had decided they wanted to approach the target from glider landing zones outside of German control, but their stealth was compromised without their knowledge by agents at the embarkation field in Scotland resulting in the raid's failure.

The forces of SS-Wiking had spent several weeks reconnoitering potential sabotage routes into the valley after the first raid. Horst's Officers felt the facility was almost like a fortress, it was so well protected by it's natural environment. The frontal access along the railroad line was protected on its flanks by a vertical ravine worn by water flowing down the Maan River over thousands of years. Sheer cliffs and thick forests of pine on each flank made perfectly protected machine gun hideouts for the Norsk Hydro's SS-security squads.

The only means to cross the narrow ravine to the Hydro Plant was a seventy-five foot suspension bridge guarded from three positions. Below it, sheer cliffs dropped two-hundred feet straight down to the icy river floor. And contact mines were strategically placed throughout the entire perimeter along routes of unauthorized access in the valley and near the perimeter of the river.

Horst noted that the only area not under constant observation was the rail line. For that zone, they decided that two dog patrols at uneven times during the day and night would allow SS-security teams to maintain effective vigilance over all the lower entrance routes.

At night, several large anti-aircraft spotlights were positioned on the mountainside to cover routes of entry from below as well as cover the sky for potential night assault raids or paratroop drops.

A conventional steam railroad and a lake ferryboat were the two weak links in the system. The train ran through unprotected valleys from Vemork to the ferry dock flanked by steep vertical mountains surrounding the entire length of Lake Tinnsjo. There the Norsk Hydro's ferry carried local people and supplies along with the inventories of heavy water to the railhead at the south end of the deep Glacier Lake. At that point troops were able to guard the rail line as it continued to a sea access at Notodden where a destroyer could transport the inventories onward to the Port of Stettin and southward by secure rail cars into Sangerhausen.

In the past the system had worked flawlessly, at least until the first raid, but now the potential problem was too dangerous for the longer term project and Horst began to consider an alternative plan as the security issues grew along with the brazen will of Churchill and the Allies.

Once the US was in the war, the SS-Gruppenfuhrer knew this site would no longer be safe, no matter how many forces he could station here. But that was not to suggest it couldn't be effectively used as a distraction, while a secondary plan was placed into operation.
Horst returned to Germany to confirm the Reichsfuhrer's financial support and secure resources needed for his zweitens plan. A special team would be assembled to duplicate the deuterium project at Norsk Hydro in Africa; the back-up team would be called 'Klub-der Kongo'.

Chapter 15

Zweitens

As Horst had hoped, the SS-Reichfuhrer Heinrich Himmler secretly approved the Norsk Hydro 'Zweitens Plan' for back up against the possible invasion of Norway, without objection.

It allowed Horst to create an additional team of engineers and scientists to be located in Africa near the Port of Matadi. Klub-der Kongo's Scientists would generate between fifty and one-hundred kilograms of high grade liquid heavy water from the modified hydro-electrolysis site at the St.Niklass Dam on the lower Congo River.

In addition, Horst also would have his Scientists build an exact replica of the Sangerhausen thermonuclear device as a further contingency against potential allied successes in Europe based on Germany's increasingly difficult situation in Russia and North Africa. This device was to be mounted in a modified U-boat housed in a hardened pen beside the unique basin at Matadi.

The deepwater basin at the mouth of the Belgium Congo River was located two hundred kilometers west of Leopoldville. There the massive downstream flow of water was so powerful, that over time, it had carved out a trench, six-hundred meters deep in a basin, where it entered the Atlantic Ocean.

For tens of thousands of years, gold, diamonds, and other precious metals had been flushed downstream into the massive trench by the natural geological flow of the river and more recently from upstream mining operations. The trench was over thirty kilometers wide and it's bottom rose from it's greatest depth at the river's mouth near the Port of Matadi, to within sixteen meters of the surface at the shoreline.

From there, it gradually sloped back down along the edge of the Atlantic Ocean shelf for the next sixty kilometers to a moderate depth of only eighty meters. The deep natural basin provided a perfect escape route for Horst's modified Unterseeboot, and maybe someday they even could exploit it's undiscovered treasures.

St. Niklass Dam had been built by King Leopold and the Belgium Government in the late 1920s to provide electricity for the future development of the capital, Leopoldville and the lower Congo region. From the top of the jungle plateau west of the capital, the Congo River quickly drops two-hundred and ninety meters down to sea level. One hundred meters of this drop was located in a long and narrow twelve-kilometer gorge. There in it's center sat St. Niklass Dam. At the Dam's barrage, several generators would be shipped from Germany that could produced over fifty megawatts of electricity, more than enough for electrolysis of the liquid form of heavy water needed for the bomb.

SSI's architects were directed to design a massive windowless concrete building beside the dam to house the German engineers and scientists. Norsk Hydro's facilities and operations would be entirely replicated there, assuring an uninterrupted flow of liquid deuterium inventory for the new device design, from it's planned completion date in mid-1943 until the end of the war. Shipments from the Dam site would be made by rail, forty kilometers downstream to Matadi.

The final subterfuge would be the ongoing shipments from the uranium mines of Union Miniere. The mines would be required to ship over one-thousand tons of Uranium to Sangerhausen's U235 electromagnetic separation units to further misdirect the Allies from suspecting the St.Niklass site in the Congo, particularly if any breach of Germany's European defenses took place later in the war.

Chapter 16

Poisoned Destiny

The second attack on Norsk Hydro took place in February 1943. Commandos trained in England parachuted onto Norway's massive mountainous plateau, Hardanger Vidda just North of Vemork, on a clear night several days before the end of the month. Members of their highly trained team were successful in destroying most of the heavy water high-concentration cells in the electrolysis plant at Norsk Hydro.

Although many of the SS-Viking defensive fortifications were still in place, the Allied Commandos were able to slip through the sentries and sneak into the hydro cell room undetected to set their charges. Horst Deeke actually considered this attack a subtle victory for SSI, since the Allies apparently presumed that Norsk Hydro was still the most vital point in the Fuhrer's nuclear effort.

However, Horst had since removed his SS-Wiking Commandos and sent them clandestinely to his alternate production facility at St. Nikolas near the mouth of the Congo. The Allied Commandos that attacked the troops stationed at Vemork thought that they were first line SS units because their insignias were hidden under their enormous white sheepskin coats during the cold winter weather of February. In fact, these units had been transferred from Austria under the command of Wehrmacht General Oberst Falkenhorst.

Vemork was still under Horst's administrative control, but because his assets were focused on actual production efforts elsewhere, he knew Norsk Hydro would be lucky to survive for another year now that hundreds of US B-17 bombing raids were destroying major plants all over Germany.

The final orders from SSI's command in Berlin were to rebuild the hydro cells immediately, then ship as much heavy water as possible over the next few months to appear as though they were struggling to catch up.

Norsk Hydro had to remain functional for the ruse to work.

Once again and still fuming after the first raid on Vemork, the SS-Reichfuhrer demanded that Prime Minister Quisling, Norway's Head of the Nazi Party, determine if partisans had been involved in the latest commando raid.

The SS-Reichfuhrer was clearly out for blood and demanded at least the town leaders of Rjukan and the factory agitators along with their families, be taken out and shot immediately.

When Horst found out that the commandos who blew up the hydro cells had neither injured nor killed any German soldiers during the raid, he personally intervened with little time to spare.

As the sole authority, and by order of the Fuhrer himself for SSI's projects, the SS-Gruppenfuhrer Deeke personally contacted General Oberst Falkenhorst to advise him to withdraw any order of retribution against the local Norwegian population. And so, the gentle folk of the little villages of Vemork and Rjukan were spared by a honorable man, that for the first time in his career, exposed a crack in his hardened core of iron will, after years of exposure to the ravages of war in Europe.

On the other hand, SS-Reichfuhrer Himmler was furious as he sat looking at his large gold-framed map of the Thousand-Year Reich hung above his desk in Berlin.

Upon hearing of Horst's countermand of his order, he was literally like a snake spitting poisonous words about his SS-Gruppenfuhrer, as he ordered everyone out of his office after reading General Oberst Falkenhorst's communiqué.

In the back of his mind he knew the Fuhrer would support any action of SSI and particularly the SS-Gruppenfuhrer now that the Russian Campaign was falling apart.

SSI's ultimate device was the only remaining hope of Hitler as the rest of Germany's greatest assets seemed to be slipping from his once powerful grasp.

The SS-Reichfuhrer knew that attacking Deeke's actions now, might prove dangerous even to his own power base, while das Fuhrer's behavior became more unpredictable every day.

Even Hitler's closet confidants had become increasingly fearful of his behavior, as he harassed them incessantly with his unrealistic demands.

For weeks on end, the Fuhrer had remained sequestered, hiding away at the Wolfschanze in East Prussia.

And so, in the deep abyss of Himmler's own mind, Horst's countermand of his order began to seethe within him. He for the first time, felt betrayed by his SS-Gruppenfuhrer.

Himmler would remember this event for a very long time, a very long time indeed. . . and met out his own penalty upon Horst and the SS-Gruppenfuhrer's people in some future diabolical incident, but for now he went on with his work in agitated silence.

Chapter 17

Himmler's Vengeance

By November of 1943, the British and American Air Commands were forced by Churchill to take the Norsk Hydro problem into their own hands.

It was no longer a lower priority commando mission. The 'Most-Secret' British 'Tube Alloys' Project and the 'Top-Secret' American 'Manhattan Project' were now combined at Los Alamos under General Leslie Groves and constantly on Churchill's mind.

He now completely knew the potential of an atomic device and Germany could easily have it sooner than the Allies, if no action was taken at Vemork.

Frustrated, Churchill demanded that a massive bombing raid be launched on Vemork. The final destruction would be left up to Allied Bombers; over one-hundred and fifty Eighth Airforce B-17s with five-hundred pound bombs, using RAF Fighter Escorts to the Norwegian coastline, were authorized to execute a daylight raid to wipe out all of Norsk Hydro and the Nazi's Hydrogen Electrolysis Plant at Vemork.

Churchill obsessed that all shipments of heavy water inventories to Germany 'had to be stopped at all costs'.

So, on November 19th, over seven-hundred bombs were dropped on Vemork and Rjukan.

Although the population was alerted, Horst was advised that a bomb shelter in Rjukan with twenty-one women and children got a direct hit and all were killed instantly.

And so in the end, even his direct efforts to protect Norwegian innocents failed, as the true fear of the Allies grew more aggressive.

It was time to remove Norsk Hydro to the German Alps in Bavaria.

Engineers from SSI at Sangerhausen were dispatched on a Destroyer from Rostock to dismantle the key elements of the hydro cells and electrolysis equipment as well as ship the remaining components of six-hundred kilos of refined heavy water back to Germany.

While the Destroyer waited at the Norwegian Port in the North Sea, a train took the last elements of the Hydro Plant from Vemork to a civilian ferry at Lake Tinnsjo for its trek southward to Notodden by rail.

On the morning of February 20th 1944, under heavy guard from a Wehrmacht security detail, the train arrived at the dock and loaded the ferry with the last elements of the Norsk heavy water plant.

Unknown to it's passengers who included Austrian Soldiers, German Engineers and over twenty-six Norwegian civilians, another sabotage was in progress. Once the ferry reached mid-lake, an explosion ripped the boat apart from it's bow. It sank in under five minutes.

Horst knew the route could not be attacked from the air due to the steep vertical four-thousand foot mountains on either side of the narrow lake. And as a precaution, he advised General Oberst Falkenhorst that sappers would probably try to hit the rail lines or sink the ferry once it was loaded.

But Falkenhorst's Austrians Troops were unfamiliar with boats and chose to concentrate on protecting the rail route instead. Again, the inevitable attack took over nineteen Austrian Soldiers lives, several SSI Engineers, plus at least sixteen more innocent Norwegian civilians.

The ferry captain however, who survived, was later tried by the German Military Governor of Norway and hung for his incompetence.

While in Berlin after reading the incident reports, the SS-Reichsfuhrer simply smiled contemptuously.

This time he wouldn't waste his energy raising the issue of retribution on Norwegian civilians as he prepared to review all of his SSI Files. Norsk Hydro's Chapter for SSI was over and now as far as he was concerned, so was Horst Deeke's.

Himmler's mind focus on the last vital step in his own diabolical equation; how to cover-up the American SSI Agent Network, once Günther Anderssen had delivered his final package. He knew his time and his influence with the Fuhrer would come again soon, now that the SS-Gruppenfuhrer had failed to protect what Hitler assumed was the vital Norsk Hydro Assets.

Vengeance was now his alone, and that event would be set on his terms. As once again the Fuhrer would begin to rely on his expert counsel for the critical matters of das 'Super Bomb'.

For Horst Deeke however, the end of Vemork was inevitable, although the loss of innocent Norwegian lives again sadden him.

But, only he understood why Norway's Norsk Hydro had been the perfect ruse, and only now after this final act, would the Allies believe that they were in *sole possession* of the world's only successful Atomic Bomb project.

PART FIVE

The Dragon Emerges

April 1944

Chapter 1

Gulf of Guinea

UX-506 had traveled almost two-thousand miles in its wide sweep of the deep Atlantic from Brest to Santa Cruz in the Spanish Canaries. The ship was well protected with three of the latest U-boat improvements already installed; the new diesel snorkel system for unlimited underwater cruising, six new magnetic contact torpedoes, and a complete hull rubberizing agent applied to prevent detection from the upgraded British sonar systems.

Even so, Gibraltar had to be avoided at all costs due to the concentration of British and American patrol vessels protecting the entrance to North Africa and the constant convoy traffic arriving from the US. So the wide westward sweep added several days to their south Atlantic journey.

After taking on fuel, supplies, and some local fruits and food stocks, the U-boat turned southeast continuing on to the lazy Port of Freetown in Sierra Leone, somehow untouched by the ravages of the war. A local German contractor topped off the boats fuel tanks before they again picked up Atlantic currents steering them southward. Then, with a full fuel load she ran at a flank speed on the surface, making good time down the western coast of Africa toward her final destination near the mouth of the Congo River.

They ran at seventeen knots on the final leg southeast across the Gulf of Guinea. As evening enveloped its black silhouette stalking low through the waves, UX-506 glided along the surface until it was within thirty-eight kilometers of Pointe Noire. Then without any recognizable markings in the dark starlit night off the African coast, it waited in the calm waters for the rendezvous ship.

At 0400 Hours on the morning of May 15, 1944, the Portugese flagged merchant-ship Kormutan, a disguised German U-boat support ship and raider met UX-506 at the designated rendezvous point off the coastline north of the Belgium Congo. Kormutan then reloaded and refueled the U-boat before escorting her to the protected concrete pens built near the Port of Matadi.

Once secured in it's hardened pen, several SSI agents, nuclear physicists and engineers boarded UX-506 to begin modifications of her aft deck access.

Re-fitting removed the entire inside aft torpedo room and replaced it with a cooling system, massive batteries to support the compressor, and finally the new deuterium shell container for das Fuhrer's Super Bomb.

Only three steps were left to make this U-boat into the most lethal piece of weaponry ever built by any military in world history.

The first variable was the time required for producing the concentrated amounts of weapons grade liquid heavy hydrogen within the St. Nikolas Dam electrolysis generators.

A minimum of eighty kilograms of liquid deuterium was projected for loading into the shell container in the aft section of the U-boat. That part of the device would have to be continuously cooled prior to initiating the bomb's explosion sequence.

Next, the water tight tubular housing located along the exterior starboard deck of the UX-506 would have to be tested repeatedly by loading and unloading the actual firing cannon designed to collide the two masses of U-235. Once the boat was positioned in proximity to the final target, the cannon would have to be re-located by a crane into the U-boat's modified aft hatch located over the deuterium shell casing.

Technicians would then need to test the speed and simplicity of this assembly since the U-boat could become unstable in rough seas with the cannon mounted in the hull's aft deck.

That task and loading the cannon would remain the final events prior to the bomb's initial firing sequence.

The cannon would be mounted with a cordite charge designed to drive a U-235 pellet into an aligned receiver core of U-235 centered within the deuterium shell casing.

Finally, the second variable would be the greatest unknown; timing would be critical to the time of detonation. The success of SSI's agents with the extortion plot on the American nuclear scientists providing the U-235 would be vital. This event would assure the transfer to UX-506 of a five kilogram U-235 pellet and the twenty-kilogram U-235 core. Both of these items would need to be transported from Oak Ridge's Y-12 facility to the rendezvous location on the Eastern Shore of North Carolina.

The remaining process would involve scientist's safely positioning and aligning the U-235 core in the precise center of the liquid deuterium shell prior to initiating the firing sequence.

Heisenberg's team calculated that the U-235 explosion would reach a corresponding temperature of about four-hundred million degrees in that exact instant. The resulting heat and thirty-five-thousand electron volts of power would instantly ignite the eighty kilograms of liquid deuterium or liquid heavy hydrogen into an explosive force equivalent to over six million tons of TNT.

Heisenberg's own projection showed that the same equivalent force using the Allies U-235 'fission only' explosion would require at least five-hundred atomic bombs.

For the next nine months, UX-506 would be maintained at the Port of Matadi's U-boat pen under constant guard by the SS-Gruppenfuhrer's SS-Wiking Commandos, until both variables were ready for delivery. So while it waited, they refitted it, cleaned it and rewired every vital electrical circuit. Then on the morning of April 1st, 1944 they named it, '*The Wiking Dragon*'.

It's deuterium load would be easy, comparatively; Heisenberg's Scientists could install that component at the Matadi pen near the St. Nikolas Hydro Plant.

But enriched U-235 was still the greatest unknown, since the extorted scientists had yet to be confirmed and there was serious doubt that any U-235 inventory could be removed from the highly secured Y-12 plant without radiation exposure or compromising the SSI team in America.

That process became Horst Deeke's greatest nightmare as 1944 became the last full year for Nazi Germany's survival.

Chapter 2

Günther's Bankers

The Louisville & Nashville Railroad had provided connections from Knoxville, Tennessee to Cincinnati and on from there to Chicago. When Günther needed to make certain visits to the Midwest and the West in 1941, he preferred to use the Knoxville L&N Station due to the more direct routes to Chicago, where he could easily transfer via the Milwaukee Road to reach the West Coast. It also gave him time to visit his local Banking associates providing information and advice about opportunities in the local area.

One such situation occurred late that year as word through the local Klan grapevine suggested that a big government operation was picking up support to use the power grid of TVA for a massive plant near Knoxville.

Nothing had been confirmed, but some Federal boys had been observed surveying various farms across from the Clinch River near Harriman in the past weeks.

Armed with that new inside information, Günther Anderssen and his East Tennessee Bankers went about purchasing several plots of land a few miles downstream from the massive Norris Dam located on the Clinch River north of Knoxville.

The area was called Clinton and the bankers and Mr. Anderssen sat on their little nest egg well into August of 1943 before anything appeared to be happening.

By September, America was actively into the war in Europe and initial setbacks in the Pacific against Japan were now beginning to turn back in favor of American Naval forces after Midway on June 6th 1942.

American Naval codebreakers had succeeded in confirming the Japanese codes allowing the US to achieve the most important initial battle in the Pacific War.

That result and the massive mobilization of industry in the US for the war effort astounded and frightened Günther as he realized for the first time, that Germany was probably not going to win the war alongside the Axis powers of Japan and Italy.

Günther had always been a pragmatist as well as a great SSI operative while he supported the Aryan Reich. But the changing times and his intimate knowledge of American industry, willpower and intense passion for freedom caused him to fear the new reality.

The Fuhrer's direction was clear, to destroy the Bolsheviks and Communists within Russia while ridding Germany of the Jews. But Günther also realized that unless a future alliance with America could be established, Germany would lose in a two front war, allowing the Bolsheviks and again the Jews to repopulate all of what remained of the Third Reich.

Germany had to find a way to merge the support of America and Britain. That was essential in Günther's mind, as he again wrote to Horst of his concerns, if das Reich were to survive even for the next five years, much less a thousand.

Chapter 3

Dogpatch

It was not until late in 1942, that General Leslie Groves came down from Washington and began acquiring over fifty-nine-thousand acres of eastern Tennessee land along the Clinch River north and west of Knoxville.

The site was initially named for a small local community; the Clinton Engineer Works. And Günther's land was right in the middle of the main acquisitions just south of the small town. So for the first time since he had arrived in America, a major Government War Project was about to evolve on land he had planned to use to gain insight into the details of the project.

SSI was now in position to contribute to Germany's war effort in a big way, and it was only a matter of time before Günther and his Sky Club team would be activated by the SS-Reichfuhrer.

Unknown at that date, however, the main production factories of the Manhattan Engineering Project were to be located there in the center of a totally self-contained planned community.

With the Cumberland Mountains to the north, the Clinch Mountains to the northeast and the Great Smokey Mountains to the southeast, the community of Clinton and the Engineer Works was protected on all sides by natural geology.

The real question was what was it going to be?

And Günther's connections would assure that answer sooner than anyone in Germany would ever expect.

General Leslie Grove's initial plan was to build at least one large electromagnetic isotope separation plant for U-238.

The plan was to collect bomb grade U-235 atoms at that plant and to build another plant using gaseous diffusion to establish an alternate production method for U-235 collection.

By April 1943, the primary nuclear and chemical lab facilities and community housing the scientists were finished while the incredible twenty-five-thousand man construction workforce completed over three-hundred miles of roads.

In addition they built sixty miles of railroad lines to support materials transport into and out of the area and more roads for internal personnel access to the restricted plants.

Barbed wire and fences were erected with heavily secured gates located at all the critical highway access points. Military Police Guards were everywhere, but the general feeling locally in that hidden wilderness of Tennessee was that the facility was so far inland, that the Germans and the Japs could never find it, much less get there to steal any secrets.

To Günther, that line of thinking was the perfect opportunity to begin using his Cal Tech and University of Chicago contacts developed in the late thirties, to advise him about who the best potential scientists were for recruiting, as soon as they arrived on the scene in Clinton.

General Groves officially named the area Oak Ridge, after a valley that ran the entire length of the research reservation up to the base of the Clinch Mountains, but it was affectionately nicknamed 'Dogpatch' because of the comic strip hillbillies that seemed to resemble the locals.

Soon it was filled with concrete buildings, as the largest became the electromagnetic separation plants, chemistry labs and water and sewage plants. Everything else was metal or wood structures for warehouses, cafeterias, administration, housing, and security.

Scientists and their families as well as contract workers from Tennessee Eastman a subsidiary of Eastman Kodak including federal employees for security and administration filled the area quickly.

The inefficient system was cumbersome, but as time past, the scientists felt that it was starting to yield better results day by day as operations of the massive electromagnetic calutrons, named after Cal Tech, improved.

Groves was still frustrated at the slow progress.

Even when the Calutrons were moved up to continuous twenty-four hour operations, with round the clock maintenance crews and scientists working the production seven days a week, they were still hard pressed to get the results that General Groves needed to build a bomb.

Oppenheimer's team in Los Alamos and the Oak Ridge scientists best estimates still suggested 'only grams per day' of 90%+ weapons grade enriched U-235 could be produced at the Dogpatch.

Ironically, no one in the American Defense establishment realized that the destruction of Germany's major cities and industries by increasingly successful Allied bombing missions were preventing the Nazi's from being able to build equivalent massive electromagnetic separation plants to refine their own stockpiles of U-238 into weapons grade U-235. All they knew was that they had plenty of Uranium and Scientific knowhow to build a bomb.

As a result the German's were now fully dependent on the successful theft of a limited amount of U-235 from America to implement their own 'Super Bomb'. Yet, General Groves and his security teams continued to believe that Oak Ridge was isolated enough to be immune to espionage or penetration by the Nazi's, or any of the other Axis powers for that matter.

Chapter 4

Bruckmann's Vault

As far back as the fall of 1943 the U235 enrichment process at Y-12 remained seriously problematic. The enrichment output was off almost fifty percent per month from the total needed to build the first Bomb Core. In addition, impurity and magnet design problems forced the Y-12 facility to go into hibernation on and off for several months during the fall of '43, while the magnet cores were rebuilt by Allis-Chalmers in Chicago.

During the down time, Mort Bruckmann devised a classified internal plan allowing his Y-12 scientific team to create a greater than fifty-percent enrichment level using the now operational gaseous diffusion process at Nichol's larger K-25 plant in order to later on, complete the final enrichment process at Y-12, once the newer Beta II electromagnetic separation calutrons arrived. The resulting arrangement allowed Bruckmann to beef up the U235 isotopes to 90%+ enrichment purity inside the Beta II units.

The only problem was that he had to store several hundred kilograms of partially enriched U238 in an inventory vault at Y-12 until the new Beta II calutrons were operational. This fact and the inventory vault were never revealed to General Groves at the time due to the hectic push to get the full forty kilograms of 90%+ U-235 ready for the Bomb Core in under fourteen months.

This also drove Bruckmann to create false inventory calculations over the following months in order to hide the real reason why his team had become so efficient. As time went onward, Bruckmann justified his secret inventory of skimmed off unrecorded U-235 isotopes, by planning to use them for other applications or for future Bomb Cores, if Groves needed them.

In any case, his good friend and associate Dr. Harvey Sachs, the lead Nuclear Scientist controlling the combined audits of Y-12 and K-25, had yet to find any inventory shortfall and Mort knew he could adjust for any errors with General Groves, if and when the time came.

No one was given any time off until late November 1943, when Groves was advised by his onsite Y-12 Chief Scientist, Mort Bruckmann, that the projected inventory date could be moved up to less than three hundred days.

This would allow them to meet Oppenheimer's needed projection of forty kilograms of bomb grade U-235. Because of improvements in his Alpha calutrons, the U-235 purification methods were then reaching almost 70% enrichment.

That improvement was based on changes Mort Bruckmann and his team had made to the efficiency of his Alpha enrichment cycles. Then by using a series of secondary Beta II calutrons they were able to further enrich the U-235 to the 90%+ level.

The only other suggestion that he and Ernest Lawrence of Berkley made to Groves to further increase the U-235 production rate was to double the amount of Alpha and Beta II Calutron Units. At an added cost of one-hundred and fifty million dollars, General Groves took that suggestion under advisement.

While these improvements occurred at Y-12, the second process for enriching U-238 to a weapons grade level became more refined at the massive K-25 Gaseous Diffusion Plant as Chief Scientist Charles Nichols made his ominous announcement.

K-25 had almost forty-three acres under roof and the miles of nickel plated pipes could develop leaks at any point in the process. But Nichols finally solved the seal and leak problems with a new plastic material, eventually called Teflon by Dupont, and he also achieved a more manageable operation within K-25 to enrich the U-235 for Bruckmann's Beta II calutrons.

Oppenheimer was now going to get weapons grade U-235 from Oak Ridge in substantial quantities before the middle of 1945.

All that was left, and not exactly a small task, was to build several bomb test devices at Los Alamos from what they knew, and from that choose the best aircraft transportable design for the new weapon; 1944 would be the critical year for both, accumulation of enough weapons grade fissionable material and building the perfect weapon container.

By early 1944, most of the processes at Y-12 and K-25 were becoming routine and the status of day to day U-235 accumulations and recording inventory had become boring.

Only the occasional drill for a security breach, radiation leaks at K-25, chemical poisoning or a Calutron breakdown seemed to break the monotony as everything appeared on the surface to be a smooth flowing operation.

The typical University type scientists working for Groves and motivated by Oppenheimer were considered to be literally robots to be constantly driven by their military administrators and security watchers at the Dogpatch.

From time to time the military drones would issue two or three-day passes. Unfortunately there was little to offer in the Knoxville area for R&R. So with long weekend passes in hand, the big city science brainboys at the Ridge would constantly search for entertainment in the surrounding local towns.

The most prominent of these people needing an outside life became the mature but single Chief Scientist of Y-12, Mort Bruckmann and his young sidekick Chemist from Berkley, the California bred Alan Gross.

With Alan's 1938 Buick Convertible as their chariot and three day passes in their pockets, they visited every nightspot and dance club within a radius of two hundred miles surrounding Knoxville. But the one that they finally got stuck on was up in the Smokey Mountains near Asheville. They called it *The Sky Club*.

Chapter 5

Dancing with the Valkyries

Crystale and Heidi were wearing their drop dead sexiest silver silk dinner dresses with viciously plunging necklines showing off everything, as they anxiously watched from inside at the Sky Club's Auto Entrance while the smaller than usual crowd arrived.

April had been cold that year and the usual Saturday Night member turnout for Count Basie's visits had been sparse for the past two weekends. Suddenly a white Buick convertible with its top up and California tags drove into the roundabout, as Tommy their new colored Valet ran up to greet the new guests. They were both out of the car in an instant and staring towards the glass entrance doors as the girls stood demurely gazing at the duo.

Heidi's dress was bare shouldered as its springtime halter straps held her with a neat bow tied behind her perfectly formed neck, accented only by her long flowing blond hair. Her face was radiant as the sleek dress accented her thin body, small waist and narrow hips. She wore diamond earrings and only one piece of thin gold jewelry on her right wrist.

The dress Crystale was wearing was almost the same style except that her straps were thinner and went over her shoulders to the back of the dress. The two arrival's attention was clearly riveted on the girls as they made their way to the glass and gold entrance doors.

Crystale purposely turned to check something behind her, as the sexy open back of her dress drew everyone's eyes draping down deeply to her hips. Sammy headed for the doorway from his desk as Heidi moved ahead of him.

She turned quickly as she spoke, "I'll get them Sammy, I don't think I've seen these two before, have you?"

Sammy responded in his typical military-style manner, realizing these guys were going to be Heidi and Crystale's new member catches for the evening as he turned back to the empty concierge desk, " No, I don't believe I have, but you go right ahead, Ms. Winters, just let me know if I can be of any help."

She quickly pushed the door forward as Mort Bruckmann and Alan Gross assisted her from the outside and began removing their heavy overcoats and hats as they revealed their New York styled three piece wool suits.

Heidi realized they were professionals of some sort as she smiled with her introductions,

"Welcome to the Sky Club gentlemen," then she paused to give them a moment to react.

"And thank you Miss for your gracious welcome," Mort responded as Fletcher ran up to take their over-garments to the Hat-Check Hostess.

"Oh thanks Fletcher," Heidi said as she reached to shake Mort's hand while he was still distracted by the colored doorman's efforts, "I'm Heidi," she offered as she watched him become awkward while trying to quickly get to her

outstretched hand before it might possibly be withdrawn.

But for Heidi, that stuck-up style would never have been contemplated, as she continued to smile at him, waiting for his readjustment.

Alan had already recovered and decided to direct his attention to Crystale's low cut cleavage as she walked right into his space. She clearly had his attention as she spoke,

"And my name's Crystale, what's yours?"

"Alan. . . Alan Gross," he confidently said as he was drawn into her smile only inches away from the fullest lips he had seen since leaving California, " and it's truly a pleasure to meet you both, Crystale."

Mort was now ready, as he took Heidi's hand in a professional handshake, then added his left covering hers to add a softer touch.

"And it is equally my pleasure to meet you Heidi, and you too Crystale!" Mort looked at Heidi's beautiful blond hair lying softly against her neck; he had always loved blondes ever since his days at Cal Tech in San Francisco, his true home in America, and this girl was simply gorgeous.

Heidi continued to watch him, as she tried to assess the hint of a German accent from his speech.

"Its still very chilly up here in the mountains," Mort added to justify the heavier suits, "and I guess Alan and I haven't quite adjusted to the East Coast climates around here either."

"And where exactly are you both from?" Crystale interjected as she usually did, just to get things moving along while tucking her arm into Alan's as she gently urged him toward the large Mahogany bar overlooking the main dance floor and the massive windows overlooking the scene of Asheville's night lights in the distance. Mort watched them move away for a moment before he realized Heidi was waiting for him to join them or say something,

"Oh, were both from the Knoxville area for the moment, but my real home in America is San Francisco."

"That's interesting," Heidi replied as she grasped his left hand sensing this man might be a more formidable catch then they realized; real home in America, now she was really curious as to where he was from?

"Why don't we join them and have a drink, "then you can tell me all about yourself, Mort."

Several sleek hides moved past them from the entrance and made their way down to reserved tables in the dinning area with assistance from a Concierge, as Mort took notice of the Club's multi-level ambiance.

Some of Basie's Band members were playing some moody jazz sounds creating the atmosphere for a few slow dancing couples moving smoothly across the lower dance floor. It was still too early for the full band to be in action, so the accent sound of silver and chinaware filled the air with background texture for the evening.

A young woman about twenty-five, another blond with shorter hair than Heidi and wearing a medium length dress that fit every curve on her thin body, pushed by them, towing a handsome man in his fifties wearing a dark European styled suit.

"Günther," Heidi exclaimed as the couple moved past them toward a reserved table near the piano,

"I want you to meet, my new friend."

The man turned and realized at once what she was up to as he spoke,

"Heidi, my little darling, and who have you here now?"

Günther was alert as he and Millicent Edmonds waited for Heidi and the new guest to catch up to them, "Uncle Günther," Heidi acted out her part perfectly,

"I'd like you to meet Mr. Mort Bruckmann, he's from the Knoxville area and some place near San Francisco as well, correct Mr. Bruckmann?"

Clearly surprised at how quickly she was warming up to him, Mort felt at ease as he spoke, but he carefully gave the rehearsed response that he and Alan chose to use during their three day R&R trips,

"Heidi's correct, I'm on a sabbatical from a University in California for the time being. Both Alan and myself are teaching at the Engineering and Chemistry department of the University of Tennessee in Knoxville."

Instantly, Günther caught the underlying accent behind his English, 'Hamburg', and a fairly recent transplant as well.

Remembering his earlier discussions with Bill Waterman on the massive secret civil engineering projects at Oak Ridge, this man could be one of the Cal Tech recruits now working on the American Nuclear Bomb Project.

Günther was overwhelmed with excitement, but he knew that it had to wait until he could discuss details with Heidi and Crystale. For the moment, he would remain in the background, but this situation presented his most exciting opportunity since they had arrived in the US. SSI's activation might now produce some serious potential, but Heidi would simply have to recognize his encouragement and be left to her own very capable ways.

"It is truly my pleasure to meet you Mr. Bruckmann, I'm Günther Anderssen and may I also introduce the lovely Miss Millicent Edmonds," Günther shook his hand first then moved Millicent in position to do the same.

"The pleasure is all mine Miss Edmonds and you as well Mr. Anderssen," Millicent nodded as Mort replied looking to see if Alan was anywhere nearby, but he and Crystale were obviously enjoying themselves at the bar with both laughing at a joke he had just told her as her Martini seemed to have tipped into his lap or something.

"Well." Günther added as he subtly winked at Heidi, then grasped Millicent's hand taking her to their private table.

"I hope we will get a chance to talk again young man, once you are a full fledged member of our wonderful Sky Club here in the land of the sky!"

Mort laughed as he spoke,

"Judging from what I've seen so far, I think you are going to see quite a lot of us here in Asheville, for long time to come, Mr. Anderssen."

They all waved walking in opposite directions as Heidi recognized the signal and began moving toward the bar with Mort in tow. A man now absolutely mesmerized by her stunning beauty.

At that moment, Heidi knew she had a big fish, but she also knew that Uncle Günther would need to brief them before anything serious got started.

For tonight, the Valkyries were simply going to have fun, dance, drink and make sure that Mort's good time would surely bring him back for more.

Chapter 6

The Recruitment

Günther Anderssen contacted Horst Deeke as soon as the confirmation had been made with his inside contacts at the Dogpatch. Mort Bruckmann was definitely the Chief Scientist at the Y-12 Plant. Not only that fact, but also his associations within the hierarchy at Berkley and Cal Tech and now Los Alamos top Manhattan Project Managers would make him indispensable to SSI's American effort.

Even Oppenheimer was a close friend of Bruckmann as well as in the past, Heisenberg's top Quantum Physics Student, Robert Teller himself, the unknowing father of Germany's Deuterium Super Bomb that Horst was now completing at Sangerhausen. In fact, Bruckmann's involvement could truly assure the completion of the Fuhrer's Super Bomb before the year's end.

Of course now the true strategy and tactical plan would require everyone's full cooperation. The entire Sky Club team would be appraised on all the steps and even dress rehearsals would be required to make sure no one slipped up. And once they had chosen the course, there was no way to alter it. They must have Bruckmann's undeniable belief that they were who they said they were, and they must be able to get his absolute unwavering commitment, or the entire network would all be taken out by either General Groves Secret Military Force or more likely the SS-Reichsfuhrer's own SSI assassins.

It was early Tuesday evening on May 9th before Günther Anderssen had assembled everyone at the Chateau. The night chill had been erased by the warm fire crackling in the massive stone fireplace as they sat quietly in the Great Living Room waiting for Günther's arrival.

Heidi watched the softly glowing embers in a hypnotic trance, as she thought about the man that had just sent the communiqué to Günther.

A communiqué that had to be transmitted many times until it reached their offshore Nazi U-boat, probably now trying desperately to get away from American Patrol Planes and Destroyers maintaining constant vigilance along the North Carolina Coastline. She wondered what Horst was doing now that the extreme pressures were building against Germany.

There had hardly been a month in the past year when Germany had achieved a success. Even the U-boats were being destroyed in overwhelming numbers every month now and the future of all their efforts seemed very bleak. Sadly all she had now were his letters to remind her.

Günther and Max entered the room together with very serious looks on their faces as the overall strategic plans of the SS-Gruppenfuhrer and the SS-Reichfuhrer were outlined for Heidi and Crystale.

"My sweet Loves," Günther began as he looked down at the translated SSI-Enigma document, "it appears that the highest ranking authorities in all of Germany have once again decided to totally depend on the success of you both, the beautiful Valkyries of our Ultra-Secret Schutzstaffel Infiltration."

Günther paused as he looked at Heidi staring into the embers,

"And only the Great God of the Vikings, Odin himself can help us now."

"What does it mean Günther," Crystal asked realizing there was an even deeper meaning behind what he was about to say.

"My sweet precious child," Günther sounded very solemn as he continued,

"We are the last hope in getting the final element for the Fuhrer's Super Bomb. And as I see it, it is this element that will protect Germany from annihilation by the Allies and Russia."

"If we help them complete the Fuhrer's Super Bomb," he concluded, "we can get the attention of the Allies and sue for an armistice before the Reich is overrun by the Bolsheviks now massing armies against us in Russia. Operation Barbarossa has failed and the Totenkopf Death Squads have only inflamed the Russians into a vicious blood revenge against all Germans."

"The irony of our situation here in America, however is that we must ourselves be portrayed to this Nuclear Scientist, Mort Bruckmann, as clandestine Bolsheviks."

"It appears from research conducted by the SS-Reichsfuhrer's Office of SD, that they have the last two living members of his family in a special concentration camp near Buchenwald."

"His father is a Bolshevik sympathizer and was imprisoned at one time for helping them in Hamburg. The SS-Reichsfuhrer's SD Officers at the special camp called Zelten Jerusalem have intercepted letters between them suggesting that Bruckmann would be willing to work with the Bolsheviks, if they could get his sister and father out of Germany."

"It seems a Post Office run by the SD units censured all in-coming and out-going mail while encouraging the families to communicate to the outside that they were okay."

"Unfortunately they are now in extreme danger and risk being killed unless something is done very soon. If this works, they will be released across the Swiss border near Bern."

"Our job will be to get Bruckmann to smuggle out the secret elements we need from Oak Ridge,"

"In exchange, of course, for the lives and safety of his family."

Silence overtook the room, as the true ugliness of their mission finally began showing it's face. Each of them began to doubt their chances of pulling it off. Only Max seemed unfazed.

Heidi got up and started walking toward the main curved staircase just outside the room.

"Where are you going my darling," Günther questioned as she ascended the first stairs and looked back at them?

"I can't believe it has degraded to this level," She replied weakly with a look of shock on her face as she addressed Crystale as well as Günther,

"It's horrible, how can you both feel motivated to carry this off, I myself have come to love this place, why would I want to destroy it now?"

"Because my dearest," Günther's eyes focused in a narrow squint as he became outraged while emphasizing his point, "failure will not be tolerated by the Fuhrer! It's not option for us here tonight!"

"Without the success of this mission we are all in peril," he shouted back at her, "especially your SS-Gruppenfuhrer Horst Deeke.

"Even while we are here tonight making these plans, the SS-Reichfuhrer is trying to remove the SSI from under Horst's control. "

"If we fail, so does he, and the Fuhrer himself will have him put to death. We ourselves could be next, if the American Agents don't kill us first!"

Günther paused to allow the stunning effect to set in, then he added, "Is that clear to you now Heidi!"

Finally she stopped moving upward and turned to face all of them with a look of ultimate fear and hopelessness in her eyes as Günther again almost shouted at her,

"So get back down here, right now, and let us together set up our plans for this final effort! Only then, will we be able to go back to a normal life Heidi. And only then, will you have a future with Horst."

Günther's plan was simple, it had to be to maintain belief, and to keep everything straight. There couldn't be any mistakes. They had each practiced their roles and all was in readiness as Friday Night, May 12th arrived.

Mort had promised Heidi that he would surely be at the Club that evening, so she arranged to get there before eight to get things ready and was talking to Crystale when the telephone call came in.

It was Mort, and there was a problem.

"Where are you," she asked?

I'm still in Knoxville," he said as he raised his voice to overcome the line static, "but Alan can't make it this weekend, so I'm without a car to get there."

"Can you get the train from the Knoxville Station," she suggested as she sighed to Crystale who realized their plans for tonight were off.

"I'm not sure if I can get over there in time," Mort replied with a sense of frustration in his voice, "but where am I going to get a room after midnight anyhow, the train won't even arrive in Asheville until almost 1:30 in the morning."

"Mort," she seemed excited by an idea," why don't you stay at our place, I'm sure Uncle Günther wouldn't mind and we have lots of room, besides, we don't close the Club until one o'clock on Fridays anyway."

"Oh Heidi, I don't want to put you and your Uncle to that much trouble, maybe I should try to get the train tomorrow afternoon."

"That way I'll be there well before eight and I'll stay over Saturday night at the Grand Park Inn, just like you suggested last time."

"Well suit yourself Mort," Heidi tried to act a little disappointed over the phone, but she wasn't sure it was working, "but it wouldn't be a problem to have our driver pick you up at the main Depot Street Station when the train gets in, even that late."

"That's really nice of you Heidi," he really meant it and she could sense the sincerity in his voice,

"I'll tell you what, I will try to get a taxi over to the station right now. If I succeed, then I'll be there for sure, if not I'll call you from the Station with the bad news. How does that sound?"

Heidi smiled her little crafty grin at Crystale as she answered, "Great Mort, that sounds great! So, if you don't call me, we can expect you at about one-thirty in the morning, Okay?"

"Okay Heidi," Mort replied, "I've got to run if I'm going to make that train, see you soon Heidi!"

"Goodbye Mort, and hurry," she yelled as she hung up the receiver and gleefully hugged Crystale, "he's on his way Crystale, so we better prepare for a change of plans, well just have to improvise this one, but we better talk to Uncle Günther first."

Crystale laughed, "Oh yes Heidi, we will just have to improvise, but boy won't we surprise him with our late night party plans?"

"Lets not get too wild Crystale," Heidi seemed concerned all of a sudden, not at all unrestrained like she usually was, "I don't think" "Mort is the real partying type, he actually seems rather sedate. In fact, maybe we should talk over our plans with Uncle Günther, just to see how he thinks we should approach it."

"Oh that's ridiculous," Crystale reacted zestfully, "and you know it Heidi."

" If this guy is a real scientist, he's basically an icky in his past life that really wants to become a swingaroo or a hep-cat, you know the type. That's why he's hanging out with Alan. Alan told me about things he did in California, and he really is a swingaroo, and that's why Mort hangs out with him. Mort just sits around all day and dreams about girls like us. He's probably still a virgin from what Alan was suggesting."

"I don't know Crystale," she still seemed nervous.

Crystale felt her apprehension was probably from fears building up after Günther's serious talk the other night. That was what had her worried.

"I still think we better ask Uncle Günther," Heidi asked, still unsure of herself?

"For god's sake listen to yourself Heidi," Crystale implored her, " you've got to get back to your old self; beautiful, sexy, and wild. Don't worry about what Uncle Günther says, he's too up tight and serious right now."

Crystale hugged her tight, then looked into her beautiful blue eyes, "God you're beautiful Heidi, let's turn this guy on, believe me, that will get Günther what he wants. With your style and confidence, just act yourself and that will work."

"You're right about that Crystale," Heidi finally seemed charged up again, "we do need to loosen Mort up a little and change his point of view."

"Let face it," Crystale added, "we really are what he wants out of life, he's just never had a chance to take it, or see it for that matter. Heidi, let's really take him for a night he'll never forget, then we can introduce him to Bolshevik Günther," she laughed and hugged Heidi again, "while he's eating right out of our hands."

The telephone rang several times before Nine PM, but Mort never called back, so things must have gone okay. The Sky Club was really busy all of a sudden as the early tourist season was beginning to heat up. By ten o'clock the whole place was alive as sexy vamps and handsome youthful gentlemen seemed to fill every open spot on the upper mezzanine and the areas below near the bandstand.

The Count himself was tickling the keys as he liked to say, and One O'clock Jump was rocking the dance floor for the third time that evening.

Günther had arrived and was standing near the upper bar filled with cigarette and cigar smoke as several young ladies seemed to be enjoying a story he was telling them. Champagne bottles were being re-loaded under the bar by two busboys as the sounds of glasses clinking and conversations buzzing added to the exciting atmosphere.

Heidi and Crystale had decided to wear their shorter jitterbug dance dresses for the evening to show off some new Chicago styled killer-diller moves for the newcomers. Two real swinging guys were dancing with Heidi and Crystale on the dance floor as the Count Basie Band drove the nearby observers crazy with screaming and shouting. Their screams of excitement supercharged the girls to make even wilder splits and twirls while showing off their legs up to their panties on almost every move.

Finally, One O'clock Jump again filled the dance floor with swingers from all over the club as frenzied fans stood around the bandstand watching the Count mystify everyone with his incredible sounds.

It was almost midnight before the girls had a moment to spare as they went downstairs to the kitchen office of Gayle Darling to change.

They were so wet with perspiration they had to strip naked while Gayle brought in some towels to dry them down.

Fortunately, they had brought back-up dresses for the occasion.

After they changed they quickly returned to the upper floor on the elevator with Fletcher operating the controls, just as Uncle Günther was about to enter.

"Hey, what's up Ladies," Günther reacted a little tipsy as the door opened, " and where's Mort Bruckmann and his sidekick?"

Heidi laughed as she realized Uncle Günther was slightly drunk for the first time she could remember in ages, "Are you enjoying yourself tonight, Uncle?"

"Well, yes I am," he stated somewhat perplexed about their guest of honor's whereabouts, "but, I thought we were going forward tonight."

Quickly Crystale intervened before Heidi could let the cat out, "Everything's under control Günther, we just reset our plans for tomorrow instead, tonight Heidi and I will take care of our guest, tomorrow you will have his full cooperation, we can assure you of that, right Heidi?"

"That's right Uncle Günther," Heidi replied unabashed," tomorrow you will have Mort's full cooperation." Crystale was grinning as Fletcher let them out and closed the door chattering away to Günther, as he took him down to the kitchen for his late night snack.

"I believe we did it," Heidi laughed as she walked over to Sammy at the Concierge Desk to reconfirm the time; it was almost 1:00 AM and time to get Max to take them down to the main Asheville Station on Depot Street. They didn't want Mort to be kept waiting.

Crystale turned to Sammy, " Is Millicent here tonight, Sammy?"

"No ma'am, Miss Crystale," he replied dutifully.

"Then could you do us a favor," she asked as she saw Max getting their coats?

"Of course, Miss Crystale," he answered without knowing what he was in for, " and what would that be ma'am?"

"Just make sure that Mr. Anderssen has a ride home tonight, and tell him that we are taking the Limousine to pick up our guest, so be sure not to wait up for us. Is that clear Sammy?"

"Don't worry, Miss Crystale," he confirmed with confidence, "I'll be glad to take him up to the Chateau myself, if necessary."

"Thanks Sammy," both Heidi and Crystale chimed in together, as Max and Sammy helped them with their coats and opened the main entrance door for their exit. In a moment they were gone.

Mort Bruckmann had spent most of Friday morning at his Y-12 lab and had not been able to reach Alan about their trip to Asheville. But he had heard through the grapevine that some unusual meetings had been going on at the Military Police Office for the past two days.

A call he had received from Oppenheimer two nights before from Los Alamos suggested that Oppy's communist friends at Berkeley were causing problems for him. General Groves had developed a new and more concerned suspicion about the Russians, even more so than his fear of Nazi Germany.

He was convinced that the Germans had the technology almost completed, but the Russians were not even close and so would stop at nothing to get it.

General Groves had even commented that the Russians were imbeciles and had no capacity to develop an Atomic Bomb.

Stalin, he stated, knew about it's details from his constant badgering of Churchill and now his spies were trying to steal the Bomb's secrets through contacts with sympathetic project staff members, particularly anyone with ties to Berkley or Cal Tech.

Since May 1st, his ALSOS Team. . . a named derived from the Greek word for 'grove' or the 'secret watchers' as Mort like to call them, had been conducting interviews with selected nuclear scientists and chemists on the Met Lab Project.

It almost reminded him of his days in Karlsruhe and Leipzig in the early 1930s, when Gestapo Officers began following and interrogating known Jewish Bolshevik sympathizers at the Institutes. The overt anti-semitic discrimination festering among students and the Nazi pressures growing throughout Germany had even placed a wedge between Mort and his Professor Werner Heisenberg.

Mort had never had any problems prior to that time because he looked more like his Catholic mother, with blue eyes, very Aryan features and brown hair closely cropped in a military hairstyle. It was of course his name and his father's interest in supporting the Bolshevik cause that got him into trouble with the Gestapo. They always followed him in Leipzig, and if he had tried to shake them, it would have made things worse.

Finally, Heisenberg met with him personally a few days before sending his letter of dismissal from the Institute, and told him that the Gestapo had him on a pick-up list and he should get out of Germany immediately. That was the last he saw of Werner Heisenberg or his own family, but he knew they would have taken him to Buchenwald, if he had stayed any longer.

Now he was wondering if there were the same secret anti-semitic squads imbedded here in America, possibly these ALSOS agents were even their henchmen. Both he and Alan Gross had discussed their tendency towards racial and Jew hatred, obvious in the attitudes and subtle comments of the contract workers at the Ridge.

Both of them had overheard vicious remarks and jokes when the workers hung out on breaks or in their little social work groups.

Coloreds were not even present as cleaning or custodian personnel anywhere on the facility. It was almost like they didn't even exist in this area of the country for some mysterious reason.

The KKK was evident all around the East Tennessee's backwoods, and they had seen for themselves first hand evidence in the bars and nightspots all around Knoxville.

Alan had even commented in comparison, after their first visit, how much more cosmopolitan and international the small community of Asheville seemed to be with it's openness and more liberal social styles at the Sky Club, even allowing a colored band to be the main entertainment. Knoxville had nothing like the Sky Club, nor would they ever allow a colored band in their nightclubs, much less allow them to have the freedom of mixing with the white patrons.

Robert Oppenheimer as far back as 1938, had warned Mort during their days together at Cal Tech and Berkeley, "My friend you must remain politically neutral here in America if you plan to succeed, because they are not yet fully aware of what is happening to the Jews in Germany".

In fact even now, his friend Edward Teller was fearful of the way they watched him at Los Alamos, methods that reminded him of the oppression of Jews in Nazi Germany and the actions of Gestapo Agents infiltrating secretly into Copenhagen just before he left.

Groves' secret watchers were now constantly on the prowl among the entire group of nuclear scientists in recent weeks, particularly since Leo Szilard's protest letter. Dr. Szilard was an old school physicist from Berlin who Groves was convinced was a Nazi Agent.

He was always watched. Leo had immigrated to America via a lengthy stay in England and next to Albert Einstein was the considered the most important senior nuclear scientist in America until 1939. Groves considered his letter dangerous, because it provoked some of the foreign scientists on the Met Lab project to consider another future outcome, if the Bomb was used on a civilian population to end the war.

Mort saw the Szilard Letter as something even worse, an ominous prediction; if, the United States, with its vast resources and the potential for repression with an almost Nazi-like undercurrent of power mongers such as

If General Groves, his unbridled ALSOS Agents, the KKK and other super-right-wing forces in America had their way, the US would be the only country to have the Atomic Bomb. The question on his mind was "could this power" open a future doorway to extreme repression and possibly even the annihilation of certain races from the planet?

Suddenly the sound of his telephone ringing brought him back to the moment. It was almost 1600 Hours and he was still in the Y-12 Lab Office as he answered, "Yes, this is Dr. Bruckmann."

"Mort, its Alan," there was a serious pause, not the jovial kidding voice that usually preceded his conversations as he spoke. "I wont be able to go tonight, and they have impounded my car for some sort of crazy inspection, so you'll have to go it alone, my friend."

"What are you talking about, Alan," Mort sounded incredulous and irritated that they were harassing him, "that's ridiculous, your car is impounded, what's going on?"

"I really can't discuss the details Mort," he was obviously stressed as his voice seemed to break and now Mort was sure his phone was bugged as well.

"I'm sure you will get a report from General Groves' Office, but the ALSOS people want me on base for a follow-up interview tomorrow morning. Just go ahead and enjoy the weekend. I'll join you next time," he again paused to clear his voice," it's okay Mort."

"Very well, Alan," Mort also began to realized he would have to read Groves full report of the interview first, but the interrogations were seriously disrupting the efficiency of his team, and if this proved unfounded, Groves was going to get both barrels when he got to the bottom on this harassment exercise.

"I'll make some calls and get back to you in an hour. Where can I reach you?"

"For now," he added, his voice still shaking, "I'm confined to this so called interrogation area."

"The extension is 4404," he added, " but the operator is an MP over here so be sure and give him your full title before you ask for me, or you'll never get through."

"Oh I'll get through all right," Mort was again fuming as he knew what Groves was obviously doing, "you can be sure of that my friend. Just stay calm and I will be back in-touch soon."

As they hung up Mort was unable to think, he was so angry. The weekend was ruined and now General Groves state of military control was turning this place into a Concentration Camp, if things didn't change, he was resigning from this project, and Groves would have to pay the 'Devil in Hell' to get enough weapons grade U-235 to make one Bomb, much less two by the eight month deadline.

All Mort could rationalize was that Groves was going insane with his state of paranoid fear of the outside world.

After trying, without results to reach Groves at his Office in Washington, to help Alan, Mort decided he was at least going take the night off and to get away from this place and think things over at a martini bar in Knoxville. He located a ride from one of his Associate Engineers at Y-12 that lived in Kingsport, and hopped out of his black 1940 Ford Coupe on Gay Street at fifteen minutes after seven. The sun had set and shadows were beginning to darken most of the buildings.

Mort carried his brown leather overnight bag as he walked toward the center of town.

All he could think about was Heidi and the weekend he had looked forward too, so much.

There was a pay telephone at a downtown Knoxville hotel that he and Alan had used in the past so he quickened his pace to get there before Seven-thirty PM to give her the bad news, he just wasn't sure what he would say. The Blount Hotel was not exactly first class, but it was near most of the dance clubs and bars in town, and within walking distance of the University and the L&N train station.

A few cars and a bus lit up the street with their lights as they past him making his way along the wide sidewalk in the humid sultry air creeping in from the nearby Tennessee River. Very few people were out, but two couples dressed for the evening exited from the Hotel up ahead and crossed Gay Street to a Restaurant on the opposite side.

As he neared the Hotel entrance, he noticed a black car not too far behind him moving slowly along the empty parallel parking places on his side of the street. It's headlamps were out and two figures with hats angled to cover their faces seemed to be watching him as he turned to enter the doorway. A chill shook his body as the figures reminded him of Gestapo Agents stalking Jewish businessmen on the main streets of Leipzig in the mid-30s.

Only the Gestapo had cars back then, everyone else was still too poor to afford one, so it was easy to pick them out.

He recognized the desk clerk from his past visit, as he smiled and quickly recovered a five-dollar bill from his wallet palming it as he shook the man's hand, "Well, it's good to see you again Mister, uh " Mort glanced at his brass name tag, "Holt, this is for your past assistance, and a little help for right now."

"Yes sir," he smartly replied, winking his acknowledgement of the fiver as he offered his services, "And what can I do for you tonight, sir?"

"Well," Mort tried to sound as Midwestern as he could while glancing through the front window to see if the car was still there, "actually, I wanted to use your pay telephone first, before I check-in of course, but it seems that I've got some company outside that could be a problem."

"I see sir," he again answered confidently, while enjoying the idea of a little intrigue on his boring Friday Night shift, "that should be no problem sir." He looked to his left near the staircase. "If you take the doorway under the main staircase right behind me at the EXIT sign, there's a long corridor that comes out on the back street, sir?"

"You know sir," Mort thought as he started to make his move, "why don't you act like you are handing me a key to go to my room, and I'll drop it in your key box as I go around to the doorway."

"That way they might think I was in for the evening and just wait for my return."

"That's okay by me sir," he smiled as he turned and selected a top floor room key, just to give Mort some extra time in case he needed it, "that should keep them busy since the elevators are out tonight, and good luck sir."

"I'll be back again my friend," Mort replied as he quickly took the key and made his way toward the main staircase, turning into a side door at the last moment as he added, "and thanks, Mr. Holt."

The ALSOS men sent to keep an eye on the activities of Mort Bruckmann decided to wait a few minutes before entering the hotel, to make sure they were able to maintain surveillance on exactly which room he was in for the night, without giving away their presence.

Mort was quick and he was also very mad. Again he was sure this was the work of Groves and on Monday all 'Hell' was going to break loose.

Groves had crossed the line into his private life and he was going to pay for that, even if it meant that he would resign from the Met Lab Project. That threat could kill any chance of returning to the high paying job he was now in with the War Department, but he was tired of the new American Gestapo Tactics being used on his innocent and emotionally fragile science team members at Y-12, and now on himself.

These interrogations could psychologically unbalance the team's efforts. General Groves would never get the U-235 purity levels above 90% without the new methods designed and manually employed by Mort's team using K-25s diffusion unit. And, Groves could never have two devices ready by 1945 and maybe not even by the end of 1946.

He would have to deal with these issues and the plight of his friend Alan on Monday, but for now he had to find a telephone to at least apologize to Heidi for the change of plans.

Mort quickly entered another Hotel's entrance two streets further south from the Blount without reading it's marquee as he anxiously looked for a pay telephone.

"Can I help you mister?" a heavily accented southern drawl filled the lobby as Mort hastily looked for the pay booth.

"I need to make a telephone call," Mort reacted without looking at the corpulent bellman that had just spoke while overflowing from a small seat near the elevators, "long distance, right away."

"We don't have a pay telephone here mister," he replied, "but the switchboard lady can put through a call for you."

Within moments Mort had finally gotten connected with Heidi and because of the proximity of the house phone, his entire conversation was overheard by the massive bellman grinning in his direction.

As he tried to decide how far he was from the L&N Station to get to Asheville, the same deep voice filled the lobby again,

"So, you're wanting to go to Asheville, are you mister?"

Mort laughed in surprise as he realized this guy was probably the know it all of downtown Knoxville, so why not put him to the test,

"You are absolutely right, my friend, I'm am going to Asheville. So, how far is the L&N Station from here?"

"Ha, Mister, you're in for a real treat," the bellman seemed please that he had something of a surprise for him, "this is the L&N Station Hotel, and the terminal is just across the back street from us. Why you can walk there, you don't even need a taxi, but I'll be glad to get you one."

"No, that's not necessary, I'll be glad to walk there," Mort replied as the bellman started to get up for the first time to point out the direction through the rear lobby doors, "but would you happen to know the exact train schedule for Asheville?"

"Shaw nuff, mister," he replied pushing the back doors open and pointing to the Station across the busy road, "but then you gonna be close, cause your train pulls out from the other station Mister. That's the Southern Railway Station off the west end of Gay Street. "

"It'll be leav'in exactly Eight-thirty PM sharp, they'll pick-up the steps in 'bout seventeen minutes."

Again Mort was laughing in embarrassment, realizing how messed up he really was as he ran through an opening in the traffic and hailed a taxi in front of the L&N Station entrance.

"Take me to the Southern Station on Gay Street," he said to the driver as he got in and waved to the L&N Hotel Bellman, now laughing away at his silly mix-up.

Within a few minutes he was paying the taxi driver as he jumped out at the Station entrance and realized they were pulling the steps on the forward Pullman Cars.

Instead of running to the ticket booth first, Mort decided not to risk being seen again by his possible tail of ALSOS Agents, so he simply jumped on the forward Pullman Car and headed inside to the first unoccupied seat. To his surprise, however, the car was empty so he moved to a pair of soft first class loungers on the opposite side from the platform to avoid being seen. He would pay the conductor for his ticket once they were underway.

At Eight-thirty PM sharp, the Carolina Special moved slowly out of the Gay Street Station for the mountains of North Carolina; next stop Morristown, Tennessee and by that time, Mort Bruckmann was already asleep.

Chapter 7

Crystale's Magic

The backseat of Günther's Black Cadillac Limousine had provided Heidi and Crystale with a perfect place to fall asleep while Max continued his vigilance waiting in the wee hours of Saturday Morning for the Southern Railway's "Carolina Special" to arrive from Knoxville. Mort had slept most of the way on the train, as it began slowing for it's last stop of the night on the inside platform of the Spanish styled stucco terminal building.

No one had even stepped inside his Pullman car the whole trip. Unknown to Mort at the time, the Knoxville porters had removed the steps early on the two First Class Pullman Cars at the front of the train, because no one had purchased a First Class ticket for Asheville.

And when he made that jump from the platform at the Gay Street Station into the car without the step, he didn't realize he was going to get a free ride. So, as he came down the aisleway from the forward cars to join the small number of Second Class passengers exiting from the steps onto the platform, he completely surprised the Asheville porters assisting the passengers.

"Oh my goodness, sir," the senior porter reacted in embarrassed shock as Mort pushed the forward First Class Pullman door open in front of him to exit with the other passengers," I am so sorry, we didn't know you was up there mister. Can we give you a hand with your luggage?"

"No, but thank you anyway," Mort replied in a friendly response holding up his little leather bag to them, then stepping from the train refreshed, as he walked toward the main terminal hall.

At first he looked up at the spacious dome on the ceiling, then he observed a few people in the seating areas looking for the girls and especially Heidi.

Soft lighting from bronze sconces lit the room while engraved Spanish wall tiles gave it a clean and inviting look as he scanned the exits and entrances for the two beauties, but he saw no one.

Then walking out of the front entrance he saw the waiting Black Cadillac Limousine, just as a uniformed man appeared out of the darkness, catching him by surprise.

"You must be Mr. Bruckmann," Max asked in a deep, but neutral mid-western sounding voice?

Still off guard, Mort appeared startled as he stepped back before he spoke, "Yes, that's right, but I was expecting someone else."

"Of course," Max reassured him as he pointed to the rear of the Limousine, "I'm the driver and Miss Winters and her friend were waiting for you in the back seat, but they fell asleep."

Max reached for Mort's bag as he added, "If you'd like, I'll store your bag in the trunk and you can join me in the front of the car." Max paused for effect as he smiled at Mort watching for his reaction, "or we can wake them and see if they want to make room for you back there?"

"No that's quite alright," Mort said as he tried to avoid his sarcastic grin, handing him the bag while he gallantly chose to sit in the front passenger seat.

"I think they've been put out enough by me already tonight, besides it's so late let's let them sleep."

Max continued to smile as if he knew something trifling was going on with all of this.

Quietly he loaded Mort's bag in the trunk.

In moments he returned and started the powerful engine as they pulled away into the shadows of Depot Street and on to the more brightly-lit streetlights of Cox Avenue.

Mort was beginning to feel relaxed again as he watched the empty late night cityscape slip by them, while the big car elegantly carried them above Asheville and onto the winding ribbon of Town Mountain Road.

He had no idea where they were going, but he recognized the light's of the Sky Club on the mountain to his right as they began to climb upward.

They had been driving for about fifteen minutes and had yet to see another car or street lamp as they continued up the dark mountainside. Max remained in silent concentration as he drove, although he was not driving very fast. Mort at last felt almost serene as he laid his head back into the glove leather of his seat.

Suddenly a sensuous and sexy fragrance filled his nostrils as a pair of soft female hands appeared from behind and began massaging his temples.

"Don't turn around," she said as she began gently rubbing in a circular movement, "well be at the Chateau in a few moments so just relax Mort."

"Heidi," Mort realized it was her as she spoke, "I can't thank you enough for getting me away from the stress I've gone through all day.

I've looked forward to seeing you so much tonight, riding that train and now riding in this car has actually been the pleasure of my day."

He watched the headlights as the car turned into a gravel driveway and stopped at a stone guardhouse before moving up through a thick forest of pine trees surrounding the narrow drive.

He spoke just before they arrived at the rear entrance of the main house, "And, what is that perfume that you are wearing Heidi, it's simply delicious, it smells so wonderful?"

"Ah, Mort, she enticed him a little with her coy answer, "that's one of my little mysteries, my dear, you'll just have to enjoy it, but you'll never know what it is."

"I see," he replied turning to look behind him just as she released her hands helping Max to open their door while she took Crystale's hand and pulled her up carefully.

She got out first and smiled at him, "Well see you in a few minutes, once we've had a chance to freshen up,"
but for now, Max will get you settled into your guest room; bye, Mort."

"Goodnight, Heidi," he said, then he heard her say something to Max as the two girls disappeared into the side door and up the stairs to their bedrooms.

It was almost two-thirty in the morning before Mort had settled into his suite on the second floor of the mansion. Max had told him to unpack his things, take a shower and get into the silk pajamas and nightgown laid out for him on his bed, then he would check in on him again in an hour. Mort did as he was told and got distracted by all the neat gadgets in his bathroom before he realized what time it was. But Max had still not returned.

The Chateau was enormous and Max had given him a simple floorplan map of where everyone's room was, plus where the kitchen was if he wanted a late night snack. Since he was now wide awake and it appeared that everyone else had fallen asleep, Mort decided to look for a snack and something to drink.

Quietly he left his room and found his way down a back staircase to the kitchen where he made himself a sandwich and a glass of milk.

Again he became intrigued with the neat gadgets all over the kitchen and by the time he got back to his room it was almost 3:00 AM.

He knew he had left his table lamp on when he left, but when he opened the door, the room was dark and he couldn't find the light switch.

He was sure Max must have come back to get him and turned out the light when he left.

Mort felt his way to the bed and began sliding in as he heard the distinct sound of someone bathing in his bathroom. Then he realized the door was closed but a faint light coming from underneath guided him to the handle. He carefully pushed the door open and immediately recognized Crystale.

She turned almost nonchalantly as she spoke," I was beginning to wonder when you were going to come up from downstairs Mort?"

Mort watched in surprise as she stepped out of the tub and stood naked in front of him.

She looked beautiful and glistened with water dripping from her smooth skin as she grabbed a towel and began to wipe it down her neck to her tummy. "Could you dry my back Mort," she asked as she turned her back to him and pulled the towel seductively around her shoulders for him to react?

Her thin legs and tiny waist looked so inviting as he watched her hips almost arch back to him as he took the towel. "Well, I must say I didn't expect this tonight," he remarked as he began to gently pat it against her upper back then rubbed it down to her waist.

"I can take it from there, Mort," she responded as she pulled the towel back around and finished drying herself, "and don't make too much from this, I actually had something else in mind to discuss with you."

She slipped into her own full-length silk nightgown, draped over a nearby chair, and tied it closed while he watched every movement she made.

"What next, Crystale," he asked as she began to walk past him into the bedroom.

"Mort, you know that Heidi thinks a lot of you," she paused before she continued as she plopped into a reading chair beside the drapes of the rear window and turned on the nearby pole lamp.

"Actually I'm beginning to feel that way too about her, Crystale," he added, as he looked around the room half expecting someone else to be hidden in the shadows. The light's soft glow highlighted her delicate features as she undid the pins releasing her soft hair strands down onto her shoulders. "And, because she is so young Mort, she is naive and innocent about certain things that you tell her."

Again she paused to give him a moment to catch up to her mentally about the recollection of the story he had told Heidi.

"But Mort, I have lived in Europe and experienced the horror there first hand. And what is left of my family is now in a concentration camp in Germany. So things on the outside of peoples lives in today's world, are not as simple as they may seem, are they Mort?"

He moved directly across from her onto his bed and sat back against three large pillows as he listened, wondering where this was going?

Again, she paused to slowly play with her hair as he thoughtfully observed her seductive movements.

"You and I have a lot in common Mort," she said finally making her move, but hiding her nervousness as she waited for his reaction.

"I see what you mean," he said, still relaxed but curious about what she was suggesting, "you must have talked with Heidi about my remarks last weekend?"

"Well, we 'are' like sisters, you know, Mort," she replied forcefully as she began to dig into his conversation with Heidi.

She knew that Mort and Heidi had actually had several Martinis and were really having fun when something about his accent came up.

By the time Mort and Alan had left that evening for their local hotel, Mort had revealed an incredible story to Heidi about his escape from Germany in 1938, and the fact that his father and sister were still imprisoned there. Heidi knew she didn't want to go any deeper on their first visit, so she wisely chose to change the subject just when he seemed to get emotional; and so, it remained their secret until now.

"And sisters, know when some things are really on a person's mind all the time. You must be in constant pain about your family Mort?"

She tried to imagine what it was like as she made her lies sound very real, "I'm always in pain about it every night. My own little sister was raped in the German camps by those wretched vermin, and only God knows how often. I would kill them if I could get to them, for what they did to her. She was not even eighteen. But now, I may have a solution, thank God for Heidi's wonderful Uncle."

Suddenly she could see a glint of moisture in his eyes as she tried to assess his feelings. He sat forward and cleared his voice as a noticeable tremble made him seem so vulnerable when he finally began to speak, "You know, I wish I had a way to get to my family too."

"I would do anything to get them out of Germany, but I'm afraid it would be too late. I haven't received a letter from them in over five months." She waited for a moment to speak.

"Mort, you've got to talk to Mr. Anderssen, he may be able to help you too. He's a very rich and influential Banker with ties in Switzerland. And I know that his contacts are very powerful leaders in the partisan underground in Europe."

They are working to destabilize Nazi Germany and assure a balance in the future of Europe once the war is over."

"That's how I got out," he offered, as his mind raced back to 1938 when the tragic events on the Swiss border near Zurich shocked him for all time, when the Gestapo Agents caught and murdered the German Jews.

"They were shot in cold blood, right in front of us," he told her impassioned, "several innocent Jewish families just standing in the new fallen snow outside the train car."

Mort had barely made it out, and now he seemed energized by the possibilities she was revealing to him.

"It was actually Swiss partisans in Geneva," he said, almost trembling as he spoke " and French Jews in the Banking and Jewelry Business, that actually helped pay for my transportation on to Paris and then to New York. I was never able to repay them and I've never heard from them again. I was only told they might have been discovered and killed from several scientists that I met in 1942."

"But now," he said, as she came forward and held his hands while both of them sat on the bed in front of each other, " you are telling me that Heidi's Uncle is helping others to get out of the death camps. That's incredible Crystale, I've got to talk to this man. Is he here, will he be here at the Chateau tomorrow?"

"Of course, Mort," she answered softly as she demurely tried to sympathize with him while tears began to fill her own eyes, " but it's still very complicated, and I will have to be sure you understand a critical part of this deep secret you will be require to keep, before I can talk to him and reveal what your situation is."

"And what is that, Crystale," Mort's eyes told her everything as he spoke with true sincerity in his voice?

Then in a hushed tone, he added, as he softly rubbed her hands in his, while looking seriously into her tearing eyes,

" I would do anything to save what's left of my family, Crystale, anything!"

"Mort," she implored him with moisture on her cheeks," you must swear to me that you will never reveal what I'm going to tell you about this man, to anyone else, never. I am deadly serious Mort, this could get him killed, I'm sure of it."

He paused thinking about what she was asking of him as he exploded in an unreserved assurance of his promise, "I will truly promise on my Mother's grave, God rest her sole, that I will never reveal what you are about to tell me here tonight, Crystale."

"Okay Mort," Crystale now squeezed Mort's hands tightly for effect knowing she had him, the tears had worked perfectly she thought. She knew the man's heart was aching as she made her revelation.

"Mr. Anderssen is a Communist operative in America, and he is trying desperately to get loyalists and patriots here and in Europe to help him destroy Nazi Germany. Because of this, he can get your family out, but he will need your full cooperation and help to succeed. "

Mort seemed to gasp as he spoke.

"Oh my God, Crystale," the revelation energized him as he revealed his own background of support for Communism, "my father was a Bolshevik sympathizer himself at the Institute in Hamburg, "
"that's why they took him and my sister Orsi to the Concentration Camp at Buchenwald. They tried to kill me as well, when I made my escape into Switzerland."

"Oh Mort," Crystale again squeezed Mort's hands as she spoke with true excitement, " That's wonderful, I know he will get along great with you, and I'm sure he will want to help you Mort, I'm sure."

"This is such good news, Crystale," Mort was so happy his emotions overpowered him and without realizing what he was doing he leaned forward to hug Crystale. He held her tightly for a while, then aware of his actions moved back against the pillows to recover, as he spoke, "I'm sorry Crystale, I didn't mean to be so overzealous. My happiness with all this, just overcame me."

"I'm sure Heidi would completely understand Mort," she said as she looked into his eyes and moved closer to his lips. Accidentally her gown fell open revealing her right breast as Mort held his breath looking at her.

Without closing the gown, Crystale moved forward and gave him a deep kiss as they both closed their eyes for a moment and pushed even closer together.

In the next moment, she rose from the bed pulling her gown together and moved to the door that would take her into the main hallway, "Mort, you do excite me, but you need to get some sleep and so do I." "So tomorrow morning, you will meet Günther Anderssen. And Heidi and I will find a way to help you get your family home to America, I promise."

"So for now, I must go, goodnight Mort, and sweet dreams."

"Good Night Crystale," Mort said, while in his heart, he longed for her to stay, wondering what might happen to his budding relationship with Heidi. But he knew he could keep that a secret too, as he added, "and thanks Crystale for all you have done. I'll see you in the morning."

The door closed and she was gone as Mort's thoughts returned to the possibilities of saving his family from the horrors of Buchenwald's Nazi Deathcamp. Tomorrow would surely be a new day in his life in America, and he smiled as he slowly drifted off to sleep.

Chapter 8

Günther and Mort

Günther was the last to arrive for the late breakfast as Heidi and Crystale were entertaining Mort with several amusing calamities that had happened at the Sky Club during the last few months. Mort realized he had once seen Günther at the Club, but he hadn't noticed his brilliant blue eyes and brownish blond hair from before. He shook hands with Mort who offered a firm grip and a sincere look in his eyes as he spoke, "Mort Bruckmann, Mr. Anderssen."

"Welcome to our Chateau, Mr. Bruckmann," Günther said as he added, " and I trust you've had a good nights sleep here on our mountain."

"Oh yes, of course Mr. Anderssen," Mort replied, "it was very relaxing and revealing as well. And thank you for your hospitality, sir."

Günther turned and hugged Heidi first then gave Crystale a kiss on her forehead as he greeted each of the girls and took the opposite seat to Mort at the other end of the massive dinning table.

The girls were closer to Mort on either side, but that was Günther's usual chair and the butler assisted him properly as he began drinking his morning cup of Earl Grey.

After about ten minutes of friendly conversation, Heidi and Crystale excused themselves and left the two men to discuss world events and the topic Crystale had assured Mort that he could now broach.

For the next several hours the two of them continued getting to know each other. And by the time the girls returned to find them, they had moved out onto a rear garden terrace hidden by Günther's beloved Norwegian Pines as the sunlight played tricks in their upper branches.

Rays of light intermittently glowed off the Italian marbled tiles in the area they were sitting in, as shadows hid their faces from view.

A warm breeze lifted up from below the ridge as the girls walked up with bright, almost see-through white sundresses with matching French beach sandals and joined them on the chase loungers.

The Butler followed them with a serving cart, four champagne glasses and a chilled bottle of The Dom as Heidi spoke,

"Well, what do you think Uncle Günther, can we open the Dom now, it's past noon and we are overdue for a little fun today, aren't we Crystale?"

She winked at Crystale as Günther responded, "Of course, my dear, he said with a sense of satisfaction from his initial arrangements with Mort, "I think it's about time we relaxed a little, and especially for Mort here, he needs a tour of the Chateau's grounds Heidi."

"Excellent, then," she gleefully replied as she jumped up to take Mort's hand and lead him over to the champagne cart, "pop the top, Jackson, and pour the bubbly, were going to have a party."

Crystale held her glass up first and clinked it into Günther's as he spoke, "Cheers everyone". And they all joined in, "Cheers."

The die was cast as Heidi and Mort drifted away toward the front of the Chateau grounds out of earshot and Crystale sat down beside Günther to see how everything went.

"You've both done great Crystale, " he said as he praised her technique with Mort the night before. "He was fully prepared for our meeting today. In fact, he is completely taken by both of you and his emotions were showing today when I agreed to bring his family out."

"I'm so pleased, Günther," Crystale said as she finally felt relieved that he was again proud of their success.

"Now we can begin to weave the spell that will get him to commit to the project."

"Yes," Günther added, "and he has admitted to what he is actually doing at Oak Ridge, so I now feel he could be ready in less that three months."

Günther got up and checked to see where Heidi had taken him before he continued, pouring another glass of champagne for both of them as he returned to the subject. "Already he has told me of his sympathy for the Russian cause to balance out the Allies, particularly if the war should end quickly because of the Allies' use of the Bomb."

" Obviously some of the other American scientists at Los Alamos are feeling the same way and now General Groves is conducting a witch hunt that is upsetting all of them and actually setting up our situation perfectly. I'm sure he would have no reservations in getting out what we need when the time comes."

"I think they're coming back," Crystale cautioned.

"Why don't you grab the champagne bottle," Günther offered, "and join them out there, we can talk about all of this in private later. Besides, Max and I need to run a few errands in Asheville." Günther smiled to her as he began walking toward the main rear entrance.

"That sounds perfect," she added as he winked to her and headed off, "we need to soften him up a little more today anyhow and I don't want Heidi to have all the fun."

On Tuesday, June 6th 1944 the Allies launched the greatest land invasion in history with their amphibious landings on the beaches of Normandy.

This event shook all of Aryan Germany, the SSI group in America and the SS-Gruppenfuhrer Horst Deeke's assets around the world. It was now only a matter of time before the Soviet armies advancing from Russia and Allies from Western France would plunder all of Nazi Germany.

As these events transpired, the SS-Reichfuhrer was preparing a backdoor, but very few in even the upper echelon of the Nazi Reich outside of the Fuhrer himself knew exactly what treachery was to be intended.

Chapter 9

The Package

In the foothills of Tennessee, Mort Bruckmann was now free to come and go as he pleased from the fortress of Oak Ridge without the intervention of General Groves' ALSOS teams.

In fact most of the teams had been flown into England for entry behind the forward forces of the 3rd Army's advance into occupied France to determine where any Nazi Super Bomb assets might be hidden.

Mort's reaction to the secret surveillance of his people as well as his own embarrassment in early May on his first train trip to Asheville were now only footnotes in the minds of Groves' ALSOS Agents.

The new Met Lab regulation guides had given almost unlimited freedom of movement to the top five at Oak Ridge and Mort was the #2 man.

Mort Bruckmann's face to face meeting with Groves had settled that. His threat to resign and the pressure of Groves' timeline for high quality 90%+ weapons grade U-235 forced a major compromise in the way civilian scientists on the project were treated.

Bruckmann was given the autonomy of movement at a level equal to Groves himself within the Y-12 and K-25 complexes. And orders were established that his personal belongings were not to be bothered with during his frequent visits on weekend passes to the various areas around the immediate two-hundred mile radius of Knoxville.

Even associates that might accompany the Chief Scientist at Y-12 were essentially afforded the same preferred treatment, so now Alan and Mort were able to use his Buick for most of their trips back to see Heidi and Crystale at the Sky Club and the Chateau..

In time, Heidi had become very attached to Mort as well as sympathetic to his causes.

But Heidi had held out with Mort even though Günther had urged her to become promiscuous and ensnare him so that he remained committed, because he said, "January 1945 was a long time off and the critical event was 'transferring the package'."

"Mort must not lose interest", he would say to her, "so make love to this man and give him something to long for every night."

Yet she still withheld herself, until a wild Saturday night in early December after leaving the Sky Club, when she got overly drunk with Mort in Crystale's room. After Heidi passed out, Crystale and Mort carried her to her own suite removing her clothes and leaving her naked in the bed while they returned to Crystale's bedroom and made love into the late night hours.

When Heidi woke at Three AM, she went into Crystale's room and found them lying naked together. Jealous, but satisfied at what Crystale had done in taking the pressure off herself, Heidi decided to remain just a close friend with Mort. From that day forth it was not unusual for the three of them to spend all-nighters together throughout the weekends of late December, yet Heidi still never had sex with him. She only allowed him to watch as she and Crystale made love.

Back in the fall of 1944, secret information was fed to Mort Bruckmann by Günther Anderssen about the work that had begun in 1939 toward the development of an Atomic Bomb in the USSR by a thirty-six year old physicist named Igor Kurchatov.

Günther explained that when the invasion of Russia began in June of 1941 during Operation Barbarossa, it caused a major setback forcing Kurchatov's labs into the mountainous area four-hundred miles east of Moscow to Kazan.

They had access to Uranium, but they lacked the magnetic cyclotrons to separate the U-238, which prevented him from building anything like what the US had developed.

He further explained from Heisenberg's secret memo, how Igor Kurchatov had worked on his project until just recently when they realized they needed to gain control of a limited amount of U-235 just to balance the power curve between the Western Allies and Soviet Russia. Günther pointed out to Mort that both Churchill and Roosevelt did not want either France or the Soviet Union to have access to the Atomic Bomb's assets or secrets.

But he was certain that nuclear scientists in America felt that unless at least Russia had the asset, the future after WWII could become clouded by the powerful American Neo-Nazi Right Wing.

And they might potentially use the bomb to gain world domination over certain liberal political ideologies that would surely imperil the Jews and the Bolsheviks, just as Germany had done for the past ten years.

Mort himself was focused on the letter written by Leo Szilard as he confirmed his decision to help Günther Anderssen. His fear that all this could happen again, if one world power became so omnipotent grew in his mind.

And after the recent experience with ALSOS's Gestapo-like tactics imposed on him and his people here in the US, Mort was further convinced that nothing could prevent an unbridled group of powerful military leaders from taking over the US and imposing their own will on all other races of humanity, just like Hitler had.

People like General Groves, General Hap Arnold and General George Patton were even in the public media taking about the potential Communist threat to the world even before Germany had been defeated.

He wondered 'who would control them' after the war was over?

Sometime in the middle of July 1944, Mort advised Günther that he would provide the package. They had designated a modest amount of U-235 to be delivered by the early months of 1945. His delivery would be limited to two parts; five kilograms of enriched U-235 to be used for a critical mass firing pellet and no more than twenty-five kilograms of U-235 enriched to greater than ninety percent to be used as a receiver core.

Both elements would insure that the Soviets would at the very least be able to demonstrate to the Western Powers that they too must be given a role in the future of world peace.

Mort decided he would use his secret vault to accumulate the extra inventory of weapons grade U-235 until the right moment presented itself.

He chose not to tell Günther about his vault.

And he never mentioned that his vault already held over twenty kilograms of U-235, but that was his private secret and when the time was right, he would use it as his trump card with Groves as well.

In the background of his mind, Mort still had hope. Hope that Günther would come through for him, and once again he would see little Orsi and his father Samuel before the Nazis killed them both.

And in the end, that was all he asked for.

PART SIX

The End of Times

January 1945

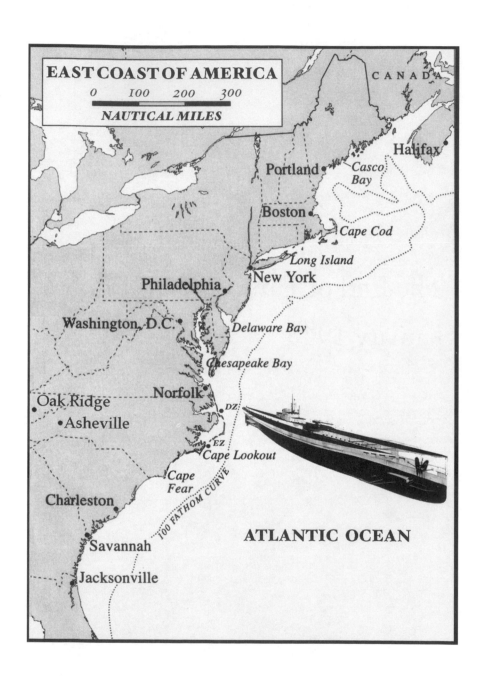

EAST COAST OF AMERICA

0   100   200   300

NAUTICAL MILES

CANADA

Halifax

Portland • *Casco Bay*

Boston •

Cape Cod

Long Island

Philadelphia •

New York

Washington, D.C. • *Delaware Bay*

Chesapeake Bay

Oak Ridge • Norfolk •

• Asheville   DZ

EZ
Cape Lookout

Cape Fear

Charleston •

100 FATHOM CURVE

ATLANTIC OCEAN

Savannah •

Jacksonville •

Chapter 1

Folkers Final Legacy

Heidi Winters began to adjust the frequency dial on the Kriegsmarine Radio transmitter to refine the bandwidth for the midnight outbound Alpha signal to UX-506. She turned and with her exquisitely accented English, spoke. "If you want to observe our procedures, Herr Folkers, you will have to close the black-out door behind you."

The new arrival was quickly getting on her nerves. Her mental torment had been at the breaking point for the past nine months, and now this. Already, being on her own and without Günther's advice for most of January, the basement of the Chateau had become a lurid mountain dungeon only emphasizing her madness not repressing it.

If he prowls around this basement like a caged jaguar any longer, she thought, I will scream. And except for Max at the lower guardhouse, she was all alone with this man.

Günther Anderssen had not arrived on the Southern Pullman from Knoxville as planned and that had her already on edge.

Recently, Crystale had been staying nights with Millicent rather than at the Chateau, so she would not be home to help her tonight either.

But now, with the complications created at the U-boat 'DZ' Drop Zone on the Carolina coast by the American ASW detection, she had a new problem. How to hide Herr Folkers?

She knew Colonel Folkers was a top SSI agent, but his botched clandestine arrival had shot his nerves too. Once again, she would just have to make things work smoothly.

"I understand, you're right", he snapped in German and then prefect unaccented English as he closed the door and walked up behind her.

"Do 'not' call me Herr Folkers again", he seethed in a neutral American Midwestern voice.

"You were informed that my code name would be 'John Wolfe', so you may call me that. Anyway, we should not be so formal in such tight confines as this room, Heidi."

With a tinge of apprehension in her response, she shyly protested in more of the adopted Southern drawl she frequently used on the patrons at the Sky Club.

"I was of the impression that all SSI agents were very formal, after getting to know most of Herr Deeke's men in Berlin, and on many occasions since. . .John."

"In America we need to be obscure and blend smoothly into the background fabric. Besides, there will be plenty of time for formality once we control this damned society of Zionist Lovers, Juden, and Pacifists," Folkers remarked in an obviously nasty reaction.

She continued to work the radio controls without turning to face him.

"Do you really believe we are winning this war?" Heidi responded with a sense of frustration and at the same time a fear of Erich Folkers reaction to her blunt remark.

Erich's eyes glanced down toward the slight opening in Heidi's blouse. When she was naively rushing to get dressed earlier, she hadn't had time to grab her bra or fully button-up her blouse.

Now, as she sat below him at the console, all of the minimal lighting in the operations room seemed to be focused below her face and directly onto her chest.

Her unintended blouse opening allowed Erich's eyes to view her small but well-rounded breasts unnoticed.

He had always had a lustful fascination with young Nordic women, and as a core agent of SSI, none in Germany had ever denied him his pleasures.

At once, he realized his irritation with her comment was beginning to set him off. She was to be the last mark in this mission, but maybe she would just become his first, instead.

With the events of the day and his intensity level at the maximum, he was like a craved animal waiting to attack his small innocent prey. His imagination was fueled with his past exotic images as his eyes were drawn into her unusually deep cleavage.

Enhanced by both her soft skin color and the perfectly formed beauty mark just above her right nipple, his arousal became unbearable.

Lost in the exotic dream, he was now even unable to hear her speaking. Deprivation for so long on the U-boat was clouding his senses.

Heidi continued to work the transmitter dials, as she briefly drifted into thought about her visitor. In a different time and place, she imagined she might have appreciated his Nordic Poster Boy of the Third Reich 'face' and handsome features. But now they were involved in a critical mission that had almost proved fatal already.

With his nerves shot, maybe her remark about Germany's war effort had really unbalanced him or even unleashed his doubts about completing this mission. His young Valkyrie, as Günther always referred to her, knew her smile would warm him up and allow them to get back onto mission planning.

Turning to again face him, she candidly managed a soft smile to ease the impact of her remark as well as to see his reaction toward her.

In the middle of her turn, she was shocked, when she realized his steel blue eyes were now fixated deep within her cleavage.

Erich made a blurred movement of his powerful hands completely grasping Heidi's small waist and lifting her from the chair in one motion. The speed of this movement caught her completely off guard and her exquisitely full lips were parted in a welcoming smile, now by misfortune, as her surprise stimulated his own personal erotic fantasy even more.

His face and mouth moved quickly across her exposed chest as his teeth frantically tore away the remaining buttons of her white-laced blouse.

Erich's massive strength was incredible as he held her motionless. While her blouse fell away, her eyes stared at him in silent shock as her young breasts were fully exposed for his ultimate pleasure.

The brown tipped nipples looked so succulent as his long awaited visual pleasure was fulfilled. He continued to suspend her in the air above him as he feasted on the view he had been starved from for so many weeks in the dark U-boat at sea.

Instantly he sucked her whole breast into his mouth savoring her female taste as he gently pulled the nipple flesh with his teeth moistening her soft skin with his tongue.

Frozen in silence, Heidi still didn't move, she still didn't scream, and she held her breath in fear. There was no one in the house to hear her anyway.

All of this had taken her by overwhelming surprise. She was at once stunned, like a beautiful blond ceramic doll, viciously being unclothed by a wild animal. His face and mouth were all over her.

Finally she began breathing again deeply heaving her chest as her fears drove her body to perspire and waif more feminine odors.

An exotic intoxication filed his lungs as he watched her heaving breasts , driving him even madder than before.

Oh mein Gott, suddenly her primal fear of the unthinkable outcome from this man's erotic cravings, forced her to think clearly in German for the first time in years.

A realization began to evolve in her thoughts; this man might actually try to kill me, even if he does it accidentally in this blind fit of passion. Our whole mission will be compromised. What will Günther do to him if he shows up now? Or worse, what would he do to Günther? Suddenly, Heidi drifted into a state of passive acceptance as Erich moved his face down her chest.

Her thoughts once again tried to justify what was happening. Outside of her world, it was known that Kriegsmariners, Abwehr Agents and SSI Agents became sex-starved masochists while confined to Germany's U-boats, sometimes for months at a time. Without exception, when they got to the mainland, having sex with foreign nationals was forbidden, simply because it might compromise Agents or even an entire mission.

In America, local street whores were often told to report to the Police or even the FBI, if they hooked up with any unusually accented or suspicious persons. So she knew, Erich had to avoid local women for pleasure. That, plus the fear and stress levels that Herr Folkers must have gone through in the last twenty-four hours must have pushed him over the edge.

Reality came back fast. She had kept her eyes closed up to now, but she felt him moving her somewhere else in the room, and she was sure, the next few moments were going to be very dangerous. Her mind was making her dizzy with thoughts of what he was about to do.

How she could avoid it? She didn't want to move, so she remained frozen as he lifted her with his massive arm strength.

Erich carried her to the back wall of the room and mentally savored his fantasy. He couldn't take his eyes off her, as he laid her gently onto the narrow cot.

She couldn't begin to comprehend what was going on in his mind now, and she was too paralyzed with shock, to do anything herself as she tightly squeezed her eyes shut.

Her concern was that she was encouraging him even more, as she got light-headed from the incredible feeling. The anticipation of what this huge man was going to do to her was causing the pressure to build even more.

Erich quickly moved one hand to the green buttons along the side of Heidi's skirt, then moved the other to the garter latch on her left thigh. In one motion he lifted her and removed the skirt.

In the second motion he grasped her garter belt and pulled it along her slender legs dragging her precious nylons and her silk panties along with it, down and off her feet, since she had also not taken the time to put on her shoes as well.

But she still didn't scream as her breasts reflected her heavy panting for air, building the fear within.

Mein Gott, she was in uncontrolled shock, he's stripped me completely naked.

Then she could hear him stripping off his own clothes and carefully kneeling over her naked hips.

She knew what he was going to do as her mind went into frenzy.

Heidi's lips were quivering, as she tried to think of how to handle him.

Finally, she strained to carefully open her eyes, as she found his steel blues looking directly into hers, mad with passion and gleaming at the treasure of her naked body, the tiny hips and her luscious long legs given so freely to Horst, and now outstretched before this mad man.

Blurred from her tears, she could barely see his nakedness now arched and ready over her tiny hips. She tried to glare at him as he moved closer slipping his hand down between her thighs, slowly moving them apart.

With one last effort, Heidi's words came out almost indiscernible in her soft feminine voice. "Erich. Please, please don't do this to me, Please don't hurt me."

He didn't answer. He just shifted her legs further apart and arched her hips upward. In the next moment, he was inside her, as Heidi's eyes rolled back. At once he pinned her hips hard to the mattress with his incredible body force.

Her throat groaned raucously as she had never sounded before in her young life, while a deep scream of pain overwhelmed her.

At first she struggled to reduce the agony as he entered, by grabbing his shoulders and forcing her fingernails deep into his skin to protect herself from his entry, and maybe to make him stop, but he forced her flat time and again. She was all his and he only enjoyed the pain she inflicted on his torn skin.

His heaving and straining inside her quickly made him swell larger, while both his and her pulses became a singular pounding beat, now completely out of her control.

The thrusting and arching became unified in one movement as they drove harder and harder into one another.

But other than the pressure of his weight and his constant thrusting, she could feel nothing below her diaphragm.

She felt it first like a solid fist slamming into her abdomen, then something collapsed within her fragile tummy.

She moaned again with an awkward sound realizing her ultimate horror, oh God, he's ruptured me.

Rolling her eyes in uncontrolled motion, she now began to drift into a truly unconscious dream world thinking he would stop, but he didn't.

Her focus began to blur as the last desperate chance came to her, if I am no longer conscious, then he can't play his morbid game. It's my pain that's driving him crazy, not his own.

Suddenly, Heidi fell back limp onto the bed.

Erich immediately stopped his thrusting and withdrew himself, sliding away from the bed as his own thoughts began analyzing what she was up to. Had she really passed out?

Her soft blond hair was lying almost windblown around her face.

Her eyes were silent and her body appeared flaccid.

The beauty that had made him explode with his maddening sexual arousal was now still. Heidi lay silent in a surreal pose, an artist's re-creation of a nude girl sleeping in a pre-Raphaelite painting.

Folkers then bent sideways and silently removed his SS-Black Knife stiletto from it's ankle sheath. He turned slowly viewing her slender legs, her narrow thighs, and the lifeless naked body that had truly pleasured him.

He wanted this scene firmly etched into his mind's eye as a memento of his final phantasm. The retribution she would now suffer for her disloyalty to the SS-Reichführer and to das Vaterland would be complete.

His orders were undeniable. . . direct from his SS-Gruppenfuhrer and the SS-Reichfuhrer, and he knew they could never be compromised.

The silver gleam of his stiletto with its razor like tip flicked eerily in the light as he moved his left fingers into her opening to prevent any injury to her outer flesh.

Carefully he slid the stiletto in as he held it tight against his forefinger. Her exquisite body had to remain unblemished for his fantasy to be complete. Pressing deep, he quickly found the mound of her pulsing abdominal aorta hidden under the girl's crushed uterus. Like a surgeon, he then moved the stiletto's tip into position. For a brief moment, he stared at her soft eyelids, maybe she was just playing a game with him? His phantasm yearned for her to awake, with her eyes focused on his, as she yielded to the final horror. But she only lay still and unconscious with her soft body lacking any firmness.

Enraged by this denial of his ultimate pleasure, he glared at her sensuous eyelids as he brutally drove the spike of the stiletto through the hard wall of her throbbing aorta. At last he got what he wanted. He could behold his ultimate phantasmal pleasure. The image was now complete.

Heidi's eyes at once sprang open in a bizarre frenzied surprise locking onto his as the stiletto flicked down and across her aorta in grotesque fury. Instantly, her own massive heart pressures gushed Heidi's warm life force out over her opening walls quickly flooding the bed linens in ever-reddening fluids. Heidi could only whimper now in silence at her own stupidity. Mein Gott, I'm dying and I've let him kill me. . . She tried desperately to move and focus her once sparkling blue eyes on the soft lighting coming from near the radio unit at the other end of the room.

But the light faded into red as the room began to spin into a blurring dreamscape.

At that instant, she felt only a paralyzing chill take over her body. Her eyes fixed, and time stood still.

She was gone.

Whisked away into another future and another place.

It was over and Folkers quietly dressed and returned up the stairs to the kitchen where he waited in silence for the SS-Reichsfuhrer's 'final package'.

Chapter 2

Revenge of the Valkyries

The sleek black form slipped through the wave tossed surface of the Atlantic less than five kilometers from Harker Island. UX-506 moved uneasily on the dark seas as salt air blew hard against the face of its Kapitan, Ludwig Hesse. He tightly held his binoculars and checked the coastline a second time for the signal. The First Officer had not signaled from shore since the final radio transmission over six hours ago.

Clouds were low near the surface as the winds began picking up to over ten knots, drifting the boat toward some dangerous shoals located within only two kilometers from the shoreline. It's new snorkel fitted diesels were humming quietly as the Unterseeboot tried to maintain at least eight knots into the rolling waves of the northeast current, also pushing them toward the dangers lurking under the surface.

Kapitan Hesse knew about the events of the past forty-eight hours and was trying to remain alert to possible patrols in the area. But for now at least his updated radar system and the heavy overcast assured him that only surface patrols would remain a problem, at least until dawn.

He had heard the distress call from other U-boat just after the delivery of the SS-Reichsfuhrer's special ops commandos, but UX-506s mission required them to remain silent. Even though U-106 had been rammed and was sinking.

They would all be shot if this mission failed and he knew he couldn't fail his men. So they stayed in place off Harker Island, over one-hundred-forty kilometers south of the botched delivery sortie. At least the radio transmission indicated that one of the commandos got in.

As the swells began to splash more violently against his control tower, his only thought was getting out of this mess and back to Kiel, but that would take at least two weeks, if everything went as planned.

In Berlin, the SS-Reichfuhrer Heinrich Himmler was already aware of the successful delivery of at least one of his newly controlled SSI Assassins. An Enigma transmission received by Admiral Raeder's operations at Flensburg confirmed one commando made it to the eastern coast of North Carolina.

The team consisted of operatives Himmler had removed from SS-Gruppenfuhrer Horst Deeke's direct control surreptitiously within the last few days with the Fuhrer's complete acknowledgement.

And Horst was now in the blind as to what actions the SS-Reichfuhrer was taking with his own men.

Men that still assumed the orders were his, but coming through the SS-Reichsfuhrer's channels due to allied interdiction on Sangerhausen's communication system, now that the American 3rd Army was nearly across the Rhine in several southern penetrations.

It was known in the SS that one of SS-Gruppenfuhrer Deeke's commandos, Folkers, was like a machine, his response to orders was unconditional and his incredible stealth and physical stamina prevented him from failing, even if his wounds were life threatening. Horst had always known this, but now the deep hatred swelling inside the SS-Reichfuhrer's mind became aware of it too.

This man would not fail. He would retrieve the U-235 and eliminate all remnants of the Fuhrer's secret organization in America.

It was the ultimate final act of destruction for Horst Deeke's SSI Network, regardless of who would be killed.

In the end, Himmler knew the pain he would inflict on the SS-Gruppenfuhrer once it was finished and that gave him his only satisfaction, as he sat day after day through the Berlin bombings of American B-17s, deep under his old office building.

Günther Anderssen and Heidi Winters were no more, and the Jew Scientist had to be dead by now according to the last coded message received at the bunker. But the SS-Reichsfuhrer was unaware of the actual details. All he needed was the 'final package' to be delivered to the engineers and scientists on UX-506, then the true power of the Reich would be felt around the world.

His Fuhrer would again rise up and das Vaterland would be saved from further destruction at the hands of the allies. They would be halted in their steps by the fear that New York or Odessa near the Crimea would be next. No one would know how many super bombs Germany had, only that they had proved they could carry out massive destruction on any major allied seaport at will and without detection. This would force them to the armistice table with SS-Panzers and Wehrmacht Armies re-grouping within the boundaries of Germany. All would be saved and a standoff would ensue for the next few years while the Fuhrer's own power could again consolidate the peoples of the Thousand-Year Reich. This was the SS-Reichsfuhrer's dream and the only hope left for Nazi Germany's Thousand-Year Reich.

Folkers outranked Max and had worked with him in Paris some years before. When he arrived at the Chateau early on the first night, Folkers relocated Max to the forward guardhouse where he showed him the orders signed by the SS-Reichfuhrer and the SS-Gruppenfuhrer Deeke. There was no dispute, Max had always obeyed direct orders from the true leaders of SSI and he was equally a machine in certain ways just like Erich.

He knew what had to be done and Max remained at the ready with the black limousine, until Folkers had returned later in the early morning hours.

Still if he had known what had happened to Heidi he might have broken, but that never happened. When Günther Anderssen and Mort Bruckmann arrived about 3:00 AM that morning, it seemed a little odd to Günther that Max was located at the front gate, but until they exited the Cadillac Sedan at the rear entrance, just what that reason was had not become apparent.

Folkers quickly disarmed Günther as he entered the Chateau and tied him to a chair in the kitchen. He then interrogated the Jewish Scientist who was carrying one of the containers and attempted to tie him up as well. As he did so, Bruckmann an athlete himself began struggling with Erich for control of the heavy briefcase like container he was holding and unfortunately for Erich, Mort opened the lead-lined case. The case was one of two they had in the car.

Mort had brought in the heavier one holding the twenty-kilogram ball of U-235 pressed into a black carbon-like packing material.

As they pushed each other closer to the staircase where Heidi's body lay bleeding in the lower room, the bright silver metal ball glowing in it's slot came loose and rolled down the stairs.

Erich forced Bruckmann to the floor and using his stiletto quickly slit his throat. Then as Mort lay dying on the upper stair, Folkers instinctively rushed down to retrieve the ball and return it to the container. As he got to the bottom of the stairs he noticed that the ball had changed colors from bright silver to an almost bluish glow. It's warm feeling when he picked it up reminded him of Heidi's hot blood gushing over his fingers, as he took a last look at the girl's naked body lying in the tepid liquid of what once was her life force.

She seemed to be looking at him with a strange smile on her face as he quickly turned and arrived at the top of the stairs with the ball in his right hand, just as the Jew gurgled a laugh while staring into Erich's blue eyes.

Blood was everywhere as he coughed and whispered out a last phrase, "Shalom you bastard, you're a dead man." His eyes fixed as he died. Erich didn't flinch.

The last words of dead men were common to him. He just looked at Günther who was staring at the ceiling. Folkers placed the ball carefully back into its slot in the case as he noticed that it had changed to a solid plum coloration.

The warmth had changed to a painful burning sensation building throughout his chest and leaving serious blisters growing in the palm of his hand.

Then as he interrogated Günther, he advised him of his orders signed by both the SS-Reichfuhrer and the SS-Gruppenfuhrer Deeke.

When Folkers admitted he had killed Heidi, Günther stated, "Horst Deeke would never have signed those orders. . . he loved that girl more than life itself. It was only the Fuhrer and the SS-Reichfuhrer that could have ordered these murders knowing the Reich was at an end. You're a fool Folkers, you've been tricked!"

He pleaded with Folkers to immediately disband and join him to save what was left of Germany. The money he had stashed away would carry them forever. It was to no avail as he could see from the far off stare in Folkers face.

Folkers right hand had suddenly become immobile as he retrieved his stiletto once again with his left, moving it furiously in one quick and still powerful motion across Günther's throat. Death was instant as he only stared with a look of surprise on his face falling forward.

The drive down the mountain to Old Fort and into the foothills near the Piedmont plains took Max four hours as he past through several small towns finally filling up with gas on the edge of Charlotte. He had been told by Folkers to get them to the coast no matter what happen to him. Just keep driving and don't look back here. The scientists on board the U-boat would know how to handle his illness.

Folkers explained to Max that he had somehow been exposed to something neither of them understood when he had picked up the metal ball.

By the time they were on the outer shores of the Carolina coast near Beaufort it had been almost nine solid hours of driving since they had left the Chateau. It was close to three in the afternoon as they pulled up to the rendezvous, a small beach cottage hidden by some dunes about ten kilometers from UX506's last known position.

Max had tried to make several stops after Charlotte once he realized how bad Folkers condition was, giving him water each time. But Folkers rejected it and told him to drive on. Neither of them knew it, but his entire gastrointestinal system was literally fried by now.

He was unable to control himself as the rear floorboard filled up with his stench. He had swollen up to almost twice his normal size and it took both Max and the U-boat's First Officer over ten minutes to get him out of the Limousine and up the steps into the cottage.

They waited cautiously until dark to send the short encrypted signal to UX-506 waiting submerged with only it's radio antenna mast and snorkel-head breaking the black sea surface near the designated 'EZ' Escape Zone to announce that the mission was accomplished.

The complete 'final package' was now ready for transfer; a lead-line case with a five-kilogram bullet and a twenty-kilogram receiver ball of weapons grade U-235.

Max had decided to stay and take his chances getting out of the US with his friends in the Asheville area, so only Folkers was going back with them.

Max and the Kriegsmarine officer loaded what was left of the once powerful Erich Folkers into the powered black rubber inflatable, as an eerily thick fog seemed to hug the shoreline covering their movements. All Max could think about was how he appeared almost melted with blisters all over his exposed skin and face. There was very little wind and the northwesterly currents were now only driven by the incoming tides.

No one had been seen in the area for the last day and they expected that would hold at least through the evening.

Once they were in the water, Max started to leave the area as he watched the inflatable motoring away to the coordinates radioed back within the past hour.

He immediately set out cleaning the car and the beach house before making the return trip to the mountains. Max knew he was going to have to be careful since he had no idea what condition he would find the Chateau in or what had happened to everyone before Folkers came to get him. He would just have to follow his SSI protocol and clean it up.

All he was sure of was that something had gone horribly wrong and the mission was almost compromised. As he drove away, the bizarre look on Folker's bloated face stuck in his mind. A face full of grotesque blisters making odd gurgling sounds as they pushed the rubber dinghy out into the unusually gentle surf.

Loading took less than ten minutes once they had located the U-boat and the chief nuclear scientist on board placed Folkers in the Kapitan's private head, amidships. He was given morphine and a type of anti-radiation drug, but they all knew 'he was a dead man' .

Methodically they all began their assigned tasks and for the first time in history, a nuclear weapon was now being placed into the first stage of arming. Still only the SSI engineers and scientists on board realized what it meant, as the oblivious Kriegsmariners began the normal tasks assigned to them on what they thought was a homeward bound journey for UX-506.

Kapitan Hesse was summoned just before he opened the sealed orders marked from the office of the Fuhrer himself. As he entered the head, the object in front of him no longer looked like a man. He was clearly dying. Some kind of glob having eyes without color almost white skinned, with blisters on his face and tongue, and hands paralyzed and hanging at his sides. The stench in the tiny closet-like room was overwhelming.

He was saying something about "being placed into the sea with his knife in his hand to die like a Viking," the First Officer explained as the Kapitan stood in the doorway. But it was too late; Folkers had died without the knife and without the Valkyries lifting him to Valhalla. And as his commander Horst Deeke would have said upon seeing his remains, had he known all that had happened, "The Valkyries always revenge their own my friend, as you have truly taken their 'most beautiful' your death will surely be the most vile known to humankind, and your soul will 'never' enter Odin's Great Hall of Valhalla."

Unterseeboot UX-506, according to the now unsealed orders of the SS-Reichsfuhrer, began a strict series of maneuvers, first submerging then running silently with it's new rubberized telescoping snorkel toward the relative safety of the deep mid-Atlantic trench on it's final journey. A long and arduous journey to it's apocalyptic rendezvous with the Viana da Foz, a vessel now at least sixty-two-hundred kilometers away, and trying also to secretly reach the Irish Sea off the coast of Dublin, Ireland.

Chapter 3

Horst's Decision

By early January 1945, the final months of the war and the incredible events leading up to the end of the past year had placed Germany clearly in the vortex of an uncontrollable downward spiraling maelstrom, that would only end at the 'Gates of Hell'.

No one working for the SS-Gruppenfuhrer Horst Deeke knew this more clearly than he did.

Russian tanks were pushing violently across Poland and Czechoslovakia and the Allies were over the Rhine and moving toward the Harz Mountains. And now, with the Fuhrer, the SS-Reichfuhrer, and most of what was the once powerful leaders of the Third Reich huddling in their hardened shelters beneath Berlin, there were very few confidants that Horst Deeke could talk to, face to face, about how to resolve the future of das Vaterland.

Horst had become powerless outside of Sangerhausen. He knew that the ominous actions of his 'Sky Club Team' and the 'Klub der Kongo' Unit during the past two months had been locked-up by the SS-Reichsfuhrer's vengeance upon him alone. The future of the Super Bomb was now operating in a secured sequence of automatic events, taken completely out of his control. And now, he couldn't contact any of his American operatives or he would surely risk fatally exposing them.

He knew General Groves' secret security forces protecting the Manhattan Project had orders to kill anyone suspected of espionage against the project. Groves defense unit was beyond any legal boundaries of even the FBI.

They were equivalent to his own SSI Assassin teams. And that could mean even Heidi and Crystale could be taken out, if they were discovered, and that he couldn't risk..

All of his closest assets in America had been ordered by the Fuhrer to revert to the direct control of the SS-Reichfuhrer. Himmler's orders were to carry out the final U-235 extraction mission down to the last man.

Then, with the Reichfuhrer in final control, UX-506 would be free to strike any port on either side of the Atlantic.

It was to be the final curtain at any cost for the Third Reich; no one could countermand the order, not even the Fuhrer himself, now.

The SS-Gruppenfuhrer was certain that exploding Hitler's horrific Super Bomb now and the resulting human devastation it would cause, would never gain Germany anything.

The only result would be an unthinkable retribution by America and Britain along with their Russian Allies. Horst knew it would mean the total destruction of Germany, taking with it all the Nordic and Aryan peoples he had fought so hard to raise up to the pinnacle of mankind's achievements.

The last night in his library at Sangerhausen, reading the memoirs of Napoleon's Retreat from Moscow, forced Horst to come to terms with his own desperation and the choice he now had to make.

He at once called Frau Bruller over the intercom. "Frau Bruller, get me a secure line to the underground office of Admiral Wilhelm Canaris, in Berlin."

The years he had known Canaris prior to the war made them respectful of each other, although they were competitive for the financial resources of the Reich and the endorsements of the Fuhrer.

Now however even though Canaris command was almost impotent in the final hours of Germany's Third Reich, they were of similar mind, when it came to the future of the German race and das Vaterland.

Horst also knew that the SS-Reichfuhrer Himmler had relented at the last minute to save the old warrior from prison. Himmler had chosen to intervene and return Canaris to Berlin. Otherwise the old spy would have remained under house arrest at the military concentration camp at Flossenburg, after the his alleged involvement with the botched July 1944 attempt to assassinate the Fuhrer.

That fervor had resulted in the subsequent purge and execution of over seven-hundred of Germany's leading military and administrative officers.

Even General Rommel himself committed suicide following his implication in the attempt at the Wolfsschanze in Rastenburg, just fifty kilometers South of Konigsberg in East Prussia.

"Jawohl, Herr Gruppenfuhrer! Frau Bruller exclaimed as she went into action with their secure red phone communication system.

Within minutes she had contact at the underground bunker of Germany's master spy network, as her voice replied through the metal intercom over the library's entrance door. "Admiral Canaris on red line #2, as requested, Herr Gruppenfuhrer."

"Admiral Canaris, I hope you are holding up okay with the pounding the American B-17s are giving Berlin these days." Horst stated with a sense of serious concern in his voice.

"Herr Gruppenfuhrer," the Admiral responded with immediate recognition and a sense of surprise in his voice, almost shouting in order to overcome the line static.

"I haven't heard a word from you in many months. I was concerned that you were having even greater problems in the south, than we are here, deep under what was once my beautiful Tirpizhufer." Horst remembered back to 1936 when the cluster of beautiful 18th century buildings first became the headquarters of the shadowy Abwehr-German Intelligence Service, in the capital city.

"Even the lovely Landwehr Canal across the street has been disemboweled by this senseless bombing."

Canaris sounded weak and broken as he spoke. "Everything from here to the Reichstag is burning now and our beloved city of the arts is a flattened rubble pile of stone and spilled German blood," Canaris added with an apocalyptic aire of desperation in the tone of his voice.

Admiral Wilhelm Canaris was much shorter than Horst, plus with his thick-bodied frame and somewhat portly appearance, he could easily have been mistaken for someone's typical Little German Uncle. The Admiral's signature characteristic, however was his piercing deep set eyes. And, no one in the upper levels of the Reich could ever seem to be sure of what Canaris' mind was thinking, either. His unique power was the complexity of his mind and his ability to keep opponents off-guard in fear of his Byzantine-like reprisals, which he could quickly unleash without warning.

Canaris was old school German naval intelligence, and like Frederich the Great his only allegiance was to das Vaterland.

Even Hitler was not always sure of the true opinions held by the Admiral, since he could create a labyrinth of possibilities in any response to the Fuhrer. But there was never any doubt about his abilities to accomplish the incredible with his private Abwehr Army, Spies and Field Agents whose loyalties were deeply foresworn only to him.

Equally in the eyes of the Fuhrer and the Fuhrer's closest confidants such as SS-Reichfuhrer Himmler, this also became the Admiral's greatest weakness. Some would even try to suggest that Canaris had another network of double agents created before the war, with loyal British contacts within it, that he had developed on his own.

Canaris and his Abwehr thus remained the true enigma within the upper hierarchy of Nazi Germany, and on this particular day, the SS-Gruppenfuhrer Horst Deeke was willing to embrace that enigma, if needed, for the future of what might remain of Nordic and Aryan Europe.

Finally, Canaris delivered his typically condescending question.

"Well my old adversary, how can I assist the renowned Schutzstaffel Infiltration and your Wiking-SS, on this prophetic day?"

Realizing he needed the deepest security on this matter, Horst decided to take the risk of getting Canaris to Sangerhausen, as he spoke.

"Admiral, this situation requires you and I to be together face to face in a protected and secure location. I would like you to join me here, as soon as possible."

With a sense of reservation in his comment, Canaris slyly responded.

"And Herr Deeke, where exactly 'are you', now, that would be safer than my underground bunker here in Berlin?"

"I'm at a hidden underground facility at Sangerhausen, outside Leipzig and about two-hundred meters below the Harz Mountains in a fortress with eleven-hundred Wiking-SS Special Forces and a Squad of eighteen SS-King Panzer Tanks guarding a twenty kilometer perimeter around me. I assure you Admiral, this will be the last fortress to fall if it is ever found, in Germany," Horst commented seriously to get the Admiral's attention.

Somewhat surprised by Horst's comment, Canaris remarked with a little levity in his timbre.

"And why, is this place not on my list of 'Great German Brew Houses', Herr Gruppenfuhrer?"

"That information release, you will have to get from the SS-Reichfuhrer Himmler. But for now, since I am personally inviting you to my quarters, you will be free to verify this facility in more detail when you arrive."

Horst commented, then quickly added, "Do you want me to send my personal pilot, our would you prefer a car?"

Now with the Admiral's full attention, Canaris answered.

"So, you obviously have a concealed airfield at your facility as well. If he can find a place to land near Berlin, I would prefer to fly."

Then the Admiral added,

"You will, of course, have to bring my personal aide, Fregattenkapitan Gerhard Feilbauer, in case of any contingencies preventing my safe return to Berlin in these days of uncertainty."

Quickly and with a sense of relief that the intrigue of his location description had captured the Admirals attention, Horst spoke again.

"Jawohl, Excellency!" Horst addressed him with a seldom used title that had been conferred on Admiral Canaris during his days in WWI as the Chief of the Reichsmarine's Baltic Operations.

And besides, he knew the Admiral enjoyed the title's reference, since one of his own SSI Agents had been planted in Canaris' Map Operations Center, and down there, they always addressed him by his preferred title.

"It is settled then. I will have a car at the Seventy-six Tirpitzhufer Bunker entrance in two hours, to escort you and your Colonel to my Command Focke-Wulf."

"My personal pilot Luftwaffe Major Knut Grimstad will meet you at the Auxiliary Field, #FB-4, and you should be here at Sangerhausen no later than 1800 Hours, just in time for dinner, Excellency."

The Admiral then remarked in a bitter, yet eerily friendly tone of voice, back to Horst.

"First, thank you for being aware of my formal title, Herr Deeke. "

"Clearly, your planning appears to be impeccable, almost as if you knew I would be your willing accomplice in some sinister Post-War plot."

"But never mind," he replied respectfully, "I look forward to our meeting and a chance to avoid the nightly bombing runs over the city, plus of course a fine German Gewürztraminer, if you can find one these days. . . and to celebrate the end and possibly a new beginning for Germany."

"Auf wiedersehen, for now, my friend!"

"Auf wiedersehen, Excellency!"

The line immediately went dead as the high pitched tone hung in the air for a moment before Horst hung-up his own red line phone.

He seemed stunned by both the friendly sign-off of the Admiral, and the seemingly prophetic final comment he made, implying he already knew more of what this meeting was about, than Horst had imagined he would.

How could he possibly have known what Horst had decided to do, just within the past hour?

Maybe that answer would reveal itself tonight, but for now it was time for action and Horst had to get his plane's fuel tanks topped off.

The SS-Gruppenfuhrer jumped up from his chair and called to his assistant.

"Frau Bruller, get my pilot, SS-Strumbannfuhrer Grimstad over to the airfield and have him fuel up my Command Focke-Wulf."

Horst's plane was a modified duel engine command transport aircraft flown by the Luftwaffe specifically for Command and Staff Officers of the Third Reich.

In the case of his Wiking-SS version, it had been updated in 1941 with two Argus AS 10C engines rated at four-hundred horsepower.

Both engines were inverted, water cooled V-8's providing a maximum airspeed of two-hundred and twenty-mph. The six-seat Wiking-SS version also had other modifications for protection that included six MG 15 Machine Guns utilizing the SS's versatile 7.92-mm rounds in two-hundred round magazines and it could carry both wing and internal fuselage bomb racks.

The manufacturer, Focke-Wulf flugzeugbau Gmbh, had been ordered by the SS-Gruppenfuhrer to add a combination landing gear system for his personal SS versions that included wheels for conventional airfields, skis for his Norwegian landing sites, and water floatation for Swiss Lakes or remote Mediterranean landing sites.

Horst added one additional detail to Frau Bruller's assignment as he grabbed his briefcase. "Then have him report directly to me for his flight plan instructions, as soon as possible, is that clear."

"Jawohl, Herr Gruppenfuhrer!" Frau Bruller exclaimed as he was almost at a gallop passing through her office, now on his way to the lower labs to get his Head Physicist, Werner Heisenberg, in on this one. The one thing he needed was proof and pure nuclear science to secure the absolute support of Admiral Canaris.

Nothing could be left to chance, because the future of every man, woman, and child still alive in Germany, was now at stake.

As he entered the main lab, he again wondered if the notorious protest letter unanimously signed by all the scientist at Sangerhausen had been his own catalyst. That letter, given to him the day the allies crossed the Rhine, had precisely detailed the effects over the Continent for the next fifty years. They had tried to get him then, some three weeks ago, to stop this horror from becoming the 'Final Armageddon of Europe'.

Now, knowing the end was near for Nazi Germany, for his part, he was committed. And he knew all the Physicists to a man, would be with him on convincing Canaris, tonight.

All that was left was to somehow get to Churchill, but that would be up to Canaris, and time was turning against them. In the end, he knew that his own people, the best-trained units in the German Military, would carry this action out at any cost, now that the automatic orders to detonate were locked in.

The Command Focke-Wulf touched down smoothly at about 1730 Hours at the camouflaged airstrip just outside the Chateau's grounds.

Then, almost on perfect cue, a heavily armed Wiking-SS security detail quickly escorted Admiral Canaris into Horst Deeke's Hardened Mercedes Command Car. They drove quickly along a road bordered by the Chateau's thick Norwegian Pines and into the massive hardened vehicle entrance within Sangerhausen's main aboveground facility. Once inside, the massive steel doors closed behind the car, and the platform on which the car had stopped began lowering down to the first level of the research facility.

There, the SS-Gruppenfuhrer Horst Deeke, and the welcoming party of several of his key Nuclear Physicists were waiting beside the door of another smaller elevator, for Admiral Canaris to exit the Mercedes.

Personally opening the Command Car's right rear door for the now somewhat overwhelmed Head of the renowned German Abwehr, the SS-Gruppenfuhrer spoke first without saluting.

"Welcome to Sangerhausen, Excellency! It will be my pleasure to provide you with a personal tour of our facilities, but first I would like to introduce you to our distinguished staff of Nuclear Physicists."

"They have personally joined me to greet you, this evening."

The SS-Gruppenfuhrer then turned to face his scientists introducing the Admiral to them, one by one.

Delayed by the formal introductions and now rushing up to his side, a thin balding man, carrying a briefcase and a small box wrapped in silver-coated paper, then spoke to Canaris.

" Excellency, as you requested, the Gift Box."

The Admiral then turned to the SS-Gruppenfuhrer and replied in a serious, but emotion filled manner.

"I must say, Herr Deeke, that I am overwhelmed by this incredible facility and the talented faculty you have introduced me to."

He looked frail and fatigued as Horst watched him clearing his voice before he continued, "And I am once again proud to be in a truly safe German Fortification protected by the most capable soldiers, I have yet to see in the entire Third Reich. An Underground Fortress, that from all outward appearances, could probably withstand the whole Allied Invasion Force on its own. I am truly impressed with your welcome!"

He then turned back to his attaché for the gift, returning his attention to the SS-Gruppenfuhrer as he handed him the silver wrapped box.

"And here, for you my friend, is a small token of my gratitude for your kind hospitality, and the brave pilot you selected to bring me here safely today."

Horst smiled at the Admiral as he took the gift and thanked him. "Excellency, thank you for the gift, but bringing you here is more my commitment for the future of das Vaterland, than it is for any other purpose."

"Now let us join the others in the main hall for dinner, including that very special Gewürztraminer you had requested!"

SS-Gruppenfuhrer Deeke then personally directed them including the Chief Scientists into the large elevator, while the SS-Elevator Control Guard awaited Horst's instructions to close the doors and lower them to the two-hundred-meter level. Following dinner and further introductions, the SS-Gruppenfuhrer requested the assistance of Professor Dresden and Chief Scientist Heisenberg to further detail the entire project for Admiral Canaris as they toured the Nuclear Physics Labs and restricted radioactive cyclotron areas used to build the Fuhrer's Super Bomb. It was nearly 2300 Hours before the SS-Gruppenfuhrer finally had the Admiral alone.

The two of them returned one level up to Horst's Library for Cognac, where Horst could now set the stage for revealing the true purpose of their meeting. Horst initiated the discussion with a very matter of fact approach.

"Excellency, it is now time for both of us to be deadly serious in this matter. I have revealed to you tonight, the Fuhrer's most Ultra-Secret Project. Certainly enough, that less than a year ago, I would have been shot ten times over for telling you any of this. I know you were only vaguely aware of this technology, but now you know it is not only real, but the actual German Super Bomb is only a few short days away from begin detonated in the harbor of Liverpool, England or possibly somewhere else in the Allied world?"

"And if that happens, Germany and all that it could ever be as well as our Nordic people, will be erased forever, by the vengeance of Great Britain and the Allies."

Admiral Canaris spoke at the exact moment Horst completed his sentence in a tone of premonition.

"As I had said before, you will need a willing accomplice to pull this off. And I would like to tell you I have just the man to help you."

"But sadly that is now untrue, since all my Abwehr Agents as of December 29th are either dead or exposed in Great Britain, thanks to MI5 their internal counter intelligence team and Churchill's own Special SAS teams."

Horst retorted in disbelief. "Excellency, it's unbelievable that they were able to dispose of everyone."

"We of course at SSI had no contingency in England or Scotland. Our whole investment, even at the deepest level of our cover and moles, was in America. "

"And now, I've probably lost all of them to the vengeance of the SS-Reichfuhrer Himmler and his orders."

"He had my own agents secretly terminate our operations and begin exfiltration of our deep cover assets in the US to protect the Fuhrer from likely American war crimes retribution."

As if by design, Admiral Canaris added his thoughts.

"The Fuhrer will never see a war crimes courtroom, my friend."

Canaris stared at a map of Berlin on the opposite wall, "As a matter between us alone, if the Bolsheviks beat the Allies to the Mitte District and destroy either the Brandenberg Gate or the Reichstag, which I'm afraid will happen, the Fuhrer and all of those that remain with him, will be dead by their own hands within hours of that final battle for the capital."

Horst then redirected him back on course, to give him another chance to expose anything about his deepest assets in England.

"Excellency, so what options do you think I have in preventing the detonation of our Super Bomb. Is there any way that I can get the direct support of Churchill himself?"

Admiral Canaris decided to reply in a roundabout way.

"Herr Deeke, you are actually one of the sharpest rascals and most challenging members of the New Order in German Espionage, I have had the pleasure of observing, but I will tell you the most clandestine spies on the planet have actually perfected espionage into an art form, and they began their training at the time of the Bolshevik Revolution in 1917 in St. Petersburg, Russia. They are, my friend, the next generation in spy work. But beyond that they were actually taught by the best, and the best came from the old Empire, the Commonwealth."

"They wrote the book in order to control that Empire around the Globe during the time of Victoria. Ever since then, they have continued to perfect it."

" In fact, all of my agents in Great Britain were double agents for MI5 or their international operations at MI6, they even took out their own people to convince me to continue with the others. In the end they had us all."

"Even the Enigma Machine and Donitz notorious Hydra and Triton Ciphers were broken by the OIC at Bletchley Park operations as far back as 1943, Horst."

"Well they missed just one," he mused briefly," and I guess for now that's all you need." Canaris laughed, as he looked at London's street map in the far corner.

"I never activated her, but then again I don't really know if she would be controllable at this late date in the final hours of our Reich."

"Excellency," Horst implored him, "She's all we've got, we must take the risk, I will take the risk myself, and you can remain here at Sangerhausen until the last bell tolls for the Reich."

"I don't expect to return, so I will do whatever must be done to prevent this final mistake. A mistake that every Aryan German living now or during the next thousand years will be held responsible for. We must prevent it at all costs . . . the war is over!"

Admiral Canaris reacted to Horst's comments in a smooth unperturbed way as he spoke.

"Herr Deeke, you must understand that she does not see this the way you and I do, and she fears exposure at this juncture more than her allegiance to me."

At that moment, and with true emotion for the man in his voice, Horst finally rationalized who 'she' was,

"She's yours, isn't she Excellency?" For the first time that he could ever remember, Admiral Canaris froze up. He could not respond to the SS-Gruppenfuhrer. Canaris was completely caught up in a state of personal pain from deep memories now unleashed.

The final desperation of the German People he had watched every day for the last two years, during his afternoon walks along the ruins of his beloved Landwehr Canal; and the impending defeat and final judgment to be meted upon Germans by the now vengeful Bolsheviks rushing to the Gates of Berlin. He thought of his own lost opportunities for family, forever mortgaged to his Abwehr, the now impotent Fuhrer, and the Nazi's Thousand-Year Reich.

And finally today, the guilt he was feeling about having to compromise his last British Agent, an agent that was deeply connected to him personally.

Admiral Canaris finally smiled cynically as he bent down and opened his brief case.

It was if he prophetically knew it was going to happen this way, and so he had brought her dossier along on this final mission. He took the file from his case with the reverence of holding the Hohenzollern's Crown Jewels and looked at the SS-Gruppenfuhrer Horst Deeke .

"Look this over Herr Deeke, and in the morning we will re-establish contact with her. For now, I must retire to my quarters. As you can see, I'm beginning to wear down from the extreme revelations and events of the day. Guten Nacht, Herr Deeke!"

Horst Deeke alerted his Concierge, the SS-Hausmeister in charge of the Officer's Quarters to assist the Admiral in getting settled in his suite, as he responded back, "Und Guten Nacht to you as well, Excellency!"

The SS-Gruppenfuhrer sat down at his main desk and opened her dossier, just after the Admiral left with the SS-Hausmeister.

"Interesting name," he thought out loud as he read the code name of the Admiral's only remaining British asset: 'Sherezade'.

Then, just as he began to dose off, his mind began to imagine what that name actually meant; was it like the tale of the beautiful slave girl telling cliffhanger stories to the King for a thousand Arabian Nights, to prevent her own death?

And what might tomorrow bring from all this?

His last thoughts were crystal clear, the final phase of this impending nightmare had begun, and the only chance he now had left was an unreliable asset in England, but yet more important, could he even get there in time to prevent Germany's ultimate disaster?

Chapter 4

Dragon Slayer

Horst Deeke awoke with a start at about 0300 Hours from the awkward sleeping position he had been in at his desk chair. He immediately called for the SS-Hausmeister to bring him some hot tea, while he began to review the dossier.

As he began reading, he developed a visual image of what this young woman must look like, in the swirling thoughts of his mind's eye.

```
      Top Secret: Dated: December 1, 1942
            Code Name: Sherezade
- Abwehr designation: Trixey Haygood, a twenty-one
year old, single woman, English speaking, living
in Croydon, England.


- Trixey Haygood was born November 28th, 1921 at a
Catholic Women's Clinic in the town of Palma on the
Spanish Island of Majorca. Her mother died in
childbirth and she was raised by Aileen Hausmann,
the mother's sister. Her father (unidentified in
this report) was an Officer in the Reichsmarine
during WWI, but he had never married the mother nor
had he seen the child since leaving Majorca in
early 1921.
- Aileen Hausmann worked for an English landowner
and deep cover Abwehr Agent on the island, Lady
Margaret Anne Gray.
```

- Lady Margaret Anne Gray adopted Trixey at the age of seven in 1928, after her aunt, Aileen Hausmann died of cancer. In 1936, on a mission related to the events of the Spanish Civil War, AWC visited with Lady Margaret Anne Gray and Trixey Haygood.

- A trust fund was then established for the young girl by AWC and he returned several times over the next three years securing a personal relationship with the young girl and setting her up for deep cover in London. When Trixey Haygood was eighteen she graduated from Holy Trinity Girl's Academy in London, England with High Honors. She was also trained for fluency in German, French, and Spanish Languages.

- Trixey Haygood's only Abwehr Preparation training focused on future clerical proficiencies in typing (one-hundred-twenty wpn - English Only), stenographic, accounting and file management. She was never brought inside for Abwehr skill's development by order of AWC.

- The influence of Lady Margaret Anne Gray with British P.M. Chamberlain in 1939 allowed the young girl at eighteen to get an administrative position as a clerk for the Under Secretary of Naval Affairs.

- Later in June of 1942, this became a position within British P.M. Churchill's personal clerical typing staff at the obscure Clive Steps Palace. -

- (CSP) is hidden underground near St. James Park, in the center of Whitehall.

- This modest facility, located within walking distance of #10 Downing Street, is mainly a secure bombproof building used exclusively by Churchill's War Cabinet.

- Final Note: The Agent Code Name: Sherezade has never been activated, by orders of AWC.

    - This file remains Top Secret -

As he closed the file, the SS-Gruppenfuhrer confirmed his assumption as he expected; that AWC was actually Admiral Wilhelm Canaris, and that Officer in the Reichsmarine from the early years of WWI was also the same.

Trixey Haygood had to be his only child, illegitimate as she probably was, and that became the only reason he had always been reluctant to risk her on any mission.

Now, they would both have to trust this untested girl to carry the full weight of Germany and Great Britain's future, by immediately activating her on this final mission.

She would assist them in the first stage of slaying the Dragon.

At 0600 Hours, Admiral Canaris re-entered the Library refreshed and ready for the stressful day ahead. His steel eyes locked onto Horst's as he spoke. "So now you know the truth of what I've been protecting all these years, Jawohl Herr Deeke?" Canaris smirked as he continued.

"All these years, I have been unable to come to terms with myself to let her go and use her for what she was truly prepared for. In reality, she was the only genetically pure German Spy actually placed in England since the Blitz, and she has never been exposed."

"That in itself is remarkable, wouldn't you say Herr Deeke?"

Trying to contain his appreciation for the obvious potential sacrifice of the Admiral's only child, Gruppenfuhrer Deeke spoke in a reserved voice.

"Excellency, the dossier of Trixey Haygood tells an incredible story. But, if she does have your genes in her, then her true Aryan Spirit with come forward, her genius will find a way, and in the end we will prevail in destroying the Fuhrer's Super Bomb before it's detonation can seal the fate of our Nordic race."

Admiral Canaris nodded acknowledgement, then added. "Herr Deeke, it's time to place agent Sherezade into play. Let's get your secure telegraph people in here together with my team right now." Then he added one of his typical brainstorms, "You may need to use Goering's own 'Kampf Geschwader' unit to fly you in under cover to meet with Churchill, if Sherezade succeeds."

Horst knew these units as Special Fight Squadron for Allied Operations, abbreviated as KG-A Ops, and quickly reacted to the suggestion with real surprise for the Admiral's deep knowledge of this other 'super secret' operation.

"Excellency, I'm confident she'll do her part, and I've already got the fly-in under control when she gives us the okay."

"We had our own pilots and KG-A Operations bring a fully refurbished American Army Air Force B-17 into our base here at Sangerhausen last night."

Although Horst was aware that it's operations throughout Nazi controlled Europe were now almost fully destroyed by the Allies, KG-A Ops had once been a fully developed clandestine operations group of the German Luftwaffe created in 1939.

It was secretly controlled and directed only by the Fuhrer and Reichsmarschall Hermann Goering. KG-A Ops was set up to salvage damaged Allied and Russian warplanes as well as training German crews to fly them. It had even built air bases for operations in France, Russia, and Norway throughout the entire Second World War, using them for covert operations and well rehearsed attacks within Allied Bomber formations.

The SS-Gruppenfuhrer then added further details to allay the Admiral's nerves and concerns in committing 'Sherezade' to a potentially failed mission before they even began.

"Originally we were planning to use the KG-A Ops base at Stavanger-Sola in Norway, but the Americans hit it two days ago with a remote control 'Willie Baby', a fully loaded remote controlled B-17. The entire base is now gone."

"The good and bad news for Germany," Horst added, "is that the Allies have moved east so fast that we don't have any Luftwaffe fighters or bases left between here and London to knock down a fully fueled B-17." As they began to move out of the Library and up to the telegraph room, Horst continued assuring the Admiral about his back-up plan.

"So once we have a Green Light on Sherezade's mission, I and the crew will fly from here at Sangerhausen just like any normally returning Allied Bomber crew, right into their designated meeting airfield. With a fully fueled American B-17, we could make the coast of Ireland if needed, in under four hours."

Chapter 5

Rise of a New Valkyrie

It was dark and half-past seven in the evening, when the twenty-four year old girl arrived at the top of the steps from the Tube Station and began walking toward her flat in Croydon along Peall Road. A cold wind was drifting in from the northwest pushing some papers across the street as a misting rain deposited droplets of moisture on the lenses of her glasses, forcing her to quicken her pace.

She was dressed in her only gray wool suit with a full-length overcoat and matching hat, pinned securely to the bun of brown hair stuffed within it. With the heavy overcoat, she was easily able to blend into the office workers and average looking pedestrians returning home along the streets of Croydon. And this particular night, although she had no umbrella, she appeared as nondescript as any other young woman, as her heels clicked along the sidewalk toward her flat.

It was good that she knew her way along Peall Road, since only a few street lights were on at the intersections and dark shadows crept into the road along most of its length. By the time she was halfway up Peall Road however, she was walking alone, and the few people that had exited the Tube Station with her, had as usual, disappeared into their own flats. Fortunately for her and many other single young women around London, the new 'Limited Street Lighting Rule', recently enacted by the Home Secretary, had just removed the 'Complete Blackout Regulation' on January 1st.

The Limited Lighting Rule in nearby cities around London brought back at least a semblance of normal life and safety, following the news of General Patton's Armor Divisions finally crossing the Rhine.

Her flat was located just beyond the mid-section of Peall Road on the second floor of a three story brownstone walk-up, built above a quaint confectioner's shop, named Arthur Bottomsley's Sweets. Once she saw the shop's lighted sign, she breathed a sigh of relief and rushed her pace in order to close the short distance to the safety of her building's front entrance.

Completing her climb up the enclosed stairwell, she caught her breath just as she made the final step and turned to view her doorway.

There facing her and pined under her doorknocker was a brown envelope imprinted with Cable & Wireless Telegram on the upper left corner and a typed description in its cellophane window;

```
TRIXEY HAYGOOD

FLAT NUMBER #2

BOTTOMSLEY HOUSE, 147 PEALL ROAD

CROYDON, SURRY

ENGLAND
```

Her curiosity rose as she removed the telegram and unlocked her flat, closing the door behind her and kicking off her well worn pumps as she fell back onto the only upholstered chair in the room. The room was unlit, but a street lamp just outside the flat's front facing window was bright enough through the silk shears for her to reach the switch and turn on an art deco lamp, positioned near her chair.

Trixey then slowly opened the C&W Telegram as if she wanted to savor every moment of curiosity, before she finally knew, whom it was from. Her interest rose even more, as she carefully slid it from the envelope. Then, opening the single fold, she flattened out the document, adjusted her glasses, and immediately blinked several times.

As she refocused her vision in the dim lighting, she began reading the abruptly typed wording:

27 JANUARY 1945

0900 HOURS GMT

PALMA, ISLAND OF MAJORCA, SPAIN

-STOP

SORRY TO INFORM YOU MY DEAR -
STOP

YOUR AUNT AILEEN HAS THIS
MORNING PASSED AWAY -STOP

HOLDING HER BELONGINGS AND CAT

SHEREZADE FOR YOU - STOP

HER FUNERAL WILL BE TOMARROW -
STOP

YOUR UNCLE WANTS YOU TO ATTEND

THE READING OF THE WILL -STOP

PLEASE CONTACT HIM AT YOUR

EARLIEST -STOP

WITH DEEPEST SYMPATHY LOVE AND

KISSES -STOP

LADY MARGARET ANNE GRAY -STOP

COTTAGE HILL HOUSE-STOP

-STOP

Suddenly it became clear, as she reacted out loud, "Oh, Christ in Heaven, they've found me."

Then with overwhelming fear filling her mind, she realized the dreaded code word 'Sherezade' had now been issued. A chill vibrated down her neck and into her entire body as she tried to grasp the dizzying possibilities of what they would expect her to do.

Trixey had always hoped the war would completely pass her by, as she worked from day to day in her obscure little office below the Clive Steps Palace (CSP) off King Charles Street, right in the middle of Whitehall.

During the past four years, Trixey Haygood had been a typical pool typist often assigned to assist an Under Secretary of the Prime Minister. Up to now, it had been a boring job that simply required her adept typing and filing skills, but now this unexpected event began to revive her greatest fear, activation. Use of her code name Sherezade in any written document clearly meant that she was in play.

Her mind was now in overdrive as she began to consider how to deal with this sudden change of status. She remembered that she would be required to make contact within the next few hours. She also knew that in the telegram, Cottage Hill House was identified.

Cottage Hill House was the code name for an Abwehr safehouse located deep in South Sussex at the town limit of Lewes and not far from Beachy Head on the English Channel.

The code name had been selected by AWC because of Trixey's relationship with Lady Margaret Anne Gray in her early days at the delicate age of seven on the Island of Majorca. Lady Margaret had been an English novelist in London during the 1920s and had rubbed shoulders, not only with Royalty and King George V, but with both of the future Prime Ministers of England, Chamberlain the pacifist and Churchill the warhawk.

She knew their social styles well and maintained correspondence with both of them until the war began in 1939, in order to surreptitiously analyze their personalities on a range of issues. With this knowledge, and as a deep cover agent and personal friend of AWC, she was able to easily prepare the young Trixey, unknowingly, for her later role in London.

Lady Margaret was the ultimate professional spy, but her gregarious personality was infecting and she could easily spin "English Gentlemen" around her little finger with her perfected style of sexual titillation and provocative comeliness.

She realized however that her time in London was growing short as the pressures in Germany grew to put Nazis into the Abwehr in England. She made it clear to AWC that she would have nothing to do with Hitler's Nazi dogma. And so by 1927, she had moved at his suggestion to the town of Palma on the beautiful Spanish Isle of Majorca, writing her novels and entertaining Picasso, Salvador Dali, and a few well known German and English Playboys for the next several years. It was the very next year that Trixey's maternal Aunt died and AWC brought the child into Lady Margaret's fold.

As a favor to AWC, Lady Margaret adopted Trixey and immediately began teaching her the proper manners of aristocratic ladies as well as the art of sexual manipulation and intrigue.

Trixey had no adolescent girl friends to socialize with on the Island.

So, being quite intelligent as well as extremely intuitive at her tender young age, Trixey early on, would slyly listen at the top of the stairs to parlor stories and real experiences being recounted by lady Margaret's male friends from across southern Europe that frequently stayed overnight at the Cottage.

By the time she was ten, she would sometimes be invited to meet these intriguing people, and for attention, Trixey would begin parroting the stories she had learned back to the new arrivals.

Often, she would keep the generally impotent and intoxicated men, young and old, glued to the sounds of her soft virginal voice late into the sultry summer evenings. She would purposely weave intriguing short tales she had heard before, into her own dreams of love, deceit, and mystery. For her, just to have their undivided attention and learn their parlor tricks or sit at their card games, became her early social life and sex education.

Without either a father or a real mother, Trixey became a very precocious young lady often mimicking male only habits of the guests, such as cigar smoking and the indulging in her Uncle Wilhelm's Cognac.

Long after Lady Margaret and her Lover of the Day had departed the gathering to her upper bed chambers at Cottage Hill House, Trixey would often sneak down to the hidden wine cellar below the main house and return to serve Lady Margaret's remaining male guests, nips from her Uncle's famous 1812 Napoleon Brandy and Reserve Cognac.
She would also bring back his private cigars in order to play her favorite game Montecristo, for the new arrivals.

Trixey knew all about Cuban Cigars. They were shipped in at least once a month to the Cottage in small boxes for her Uncle from his friend Rogelio Fortelleza in Havana. The Romeo, Juliettas, Montecristos, and very expensive Cohibas - adillac cigars were always stored in the cellar and she would sneak out entire boxes, just to get the attention of the male crowd. As a reward, the real playboys of the group would demonstrate to her, how to prepare, light and properly smoke them in the unique way of each of their nationalities, English, German, Spanish, and Italian.

Over time she could perfectly mimic the cigar smoking styles of any male in the room. Without exception on these late party nights, after Trixey had taken a few sips of her Uncle's Cognac, she was ready to play her game of Montecristo and sizzle the all male crowd into frenzied excitement as she told them her cigar story.

She would first squat down onto an oversized pillow placed in the center of her all male audience. Once they were up close and watching her precocious impersonation, she would explain that over one-hundred-ninety hand made steps were required to make the best Cuban Cigars and the most critical step was the actual rolling.

"To be perfect though," she said, "a true Cuban must be rolled on the thigh's of a nubile virgin".

At once, with all their eyes riveted on her sensuous little body, she would pull up her tiny sundress, just short of revealing her French styled silk panties, but clearly exposing her beautiful soft thin thighs and long legs to the yells and cheers of her adoring audience.

"May I have a fresh Montecristo, por favor," she would say, as someone in the crowd of cheering admirers would quickly comply. She would then, provocatively roll the Montecristo back and forth, until she had all the guys gazing down at her tender young thighs and holding back their primal urge to touch her soft virginal skin.

But, as soon as Trixey gave one of the guys the now tightly rolled Montecristo, the game was over and she would go back to telling another juicy story for their entertainment.

Over time, as AWC became aware of his niece's social activities and precocious behavior with her storytelling, he gave her the nickname Sherezade. That name of course, much later on when she was finally in place in London, evolved into her code name at Abwehr.

The Cottage Hill House safehouse was located on the higher ground over the Channel and had an excellent radio transmission range due to that altitude.

It also had an enigma encoder and a high frequency radio unit that could make direct contact with Abwehr Agents in the Netherlands.

But what was the chance of exposure and how long could she avoid her office at the Clive Steps Palace, before they would suspect something was up?

All of these questions needed immediate answers and she was clearly alone on this one, so the next step had to be made at the safe house. She realized she would need to pack some things and get a train to Lewes in South Sussex before the 2200 Hours Curfew shut down the trains. Time was of the essence; she must decide now, one way or the other, go or no go?

At that moment, her thoughts began to rationalize their reasoning for making contact with her. It had to be the answer; it was the only reason AWC would use her now. It was Germany's final end game and only Trixey had reasonable access to the key player, to Britain's P.M..

Suddenly, Trixey was clear on why they wanted her. Germany needed a fast way out. It had to be the only explanation. They actually wanted to surrender to Prime Minister Churchill, not the Russians.

During the last two weeks, she had been constantly typing reports at the Clive Steps Palace right in the middle of Whitehall, about the need for the Allies to reach Berlin first. The Russians were burning the German towns, rapping German women, and machine gunning innocent German children, as soon as they conquered each zone of control within Germany.

Even the P.M. was concerned that Monty's Forces in the North and the American Armies to the South could never make Berlin before the Russians. They would capture Hitler and burn the city to the ground before the Allies could accept Germany's Unconditional Surrender.

She knew the Admiral better than most. He had to be thinking that only an Unconditional Surrender directly to Churchill himself would stop the carnage and ravaging of Germany by the Russian Army. At that point, Trixey had to assume for her own piece of mind that she was probably his only Abwehr contact left in England. Maybe the only contact left alive that could arrange a meeting with Churchill. She was now sure that was it!

AWC also knew very well, her little concealment, and he alone knew that she had made personal contact with Churchill on several occasions.

That's why he continued to have Senior Rogelio Fortelleza in Havana, send her boxes of Montecristos whenever a supply convoy got through from Newfoundland in the early years. She loved those cigars, but the greater mystery was that Churchill also loved her to surprise him with a cigar, every so often.

Trixey's mind flashed back to that fateful first time she saw him in person back in late January 1942. A heavy bombing raid had taken place that evening, just after she had arrived for her night shift. Several ladies on her shift were unable to make it in, so the typing pool was short about ten typists. Trixey had a small emergency suitcase that she always kept in her locker in case of contingencies that would force her to stay over night at the CSP Women's Auxiliary Dorm, and this night was beginning to look like an overnighter.

One item she kept in that case besides her bath essentials and fresh underwear was her sealed box of Montecristos.

She had been working for about two hours when a commotion in the nearby hallway caught her attention. The P.M. as they called him for security reasons, had been rushed back to the CSP to prepare his speech for Parliament on February 1st. In his haste to get into London however, his attaché had failed to pack his extra stock of cigars for his overnight at the CSP and he was now explaining this to his undersecretary on duty that night. Somehow, she was going to locate some cigars for him. The poor woman was in a complete state of frustration because no one at this hour could find the supply officer and the canteen had shut down at midnight.

Trixey knew she had some legitimate questions she needed to ask her anyway about a report format regarding The General Auchinleck Communiqué she was forthwith assigned to type. This moment might forever be her only opportunity to meet the Great Man, Winston Churchill.

As Trixey left her desk with the document in hand, she smoothly unbuttoned her top two blouse buttons to expose a little cleavage and removed a side pin from her hair bun to give her a more feminine vogue as she walked out into the hallway and up to the homely looking Mrs. Litchfield.

At once, she distracted the P.M.'s train of thought with her style of provocative yet youthful elegance. Prime Minister Churchill then transformed his demeanor and greeted the young lady as she walked up. In his usual deep voice the P.M. reacted,

"And who do we have here?" The P.M. paused to look her over carefully, then continued, smiling. "Good evening, young miss!"

Then he added in a more relaxed, but kind of jovial manner,

"You wouldn't happen to know where I could find any Good Cuban Cigars around here tonight, would you now?"

Trixey's mind almost went into overdrive as she thought, what an opening, will I surprise him now, as she responded, trying to sound unexaggerated.

"I just happen to have a box of what I've been told are Fine Cuban Cigars in my dorm locker. I was planning, just this week, to post them off to my Uncle in Sussex, Prime Minister."

Immediately, the P.M. perked up in almost disbelief, "Well then young Lady, what say, I impose an executive order, and have them rightly impounded. Would that provide the excuse you need miss, to loan me a few until my Provost arrives in the morning?"

With Mrs. Litchfield now astounded by the exchange, but clearly sensing relief that her impossible task was resolved, she looked down at the report in Trixey's hand. Instantly, she realized why her young clerk was there in the first place. Trixey then replied somewhat coyly to the P.M., "I believe that would do the trick, Prime Minister."

Then she added, "If you would like, I would be glad to go down to my locker right on, and fetch them for you to take back to your quarters. Can you wait here, or do you want me to bring them around?"

As the P.M. pondered her offer, he again spoke eloquently, "Again, young lady, I believe you've saved the day. Why don't you fetch the cigars and meet me in the upstairs map room." Then he hesitated, "You do, have access to that area don't you?"

As she answered, she realized she had never been allowed to enter that area, primarily because it required the next level of clearance, and she was only classified, Secret. "Yes, Minister, but I'm not sure how to get to that room."

Then she added, as she bent forward with her blouse slightly ajar in his direction, to properly display her Official Access Badge, "But, I'm only at Secret Level, Prime Minister."

Churchill squinted through his wire-framed glasses, as he appeared to look carefully at her OAB and secretly her other endowments. Then he turned and focused over the top of his frames onto Mrs. Litchfield, as he commanded somewhat officially to her. "Mrs. Litchfield!

The Undersecretary seemed to almost come to attention as she straightened, looked up and responded to the P.M., "Sir!"

Churchill then continued in a more relaxed manner. "Mrs. Litchfield, have Ms. Trixey Haygood here, upgraded to Level #5, Most Secret, allow her time off to retrieve the items I have now officially impounded, and give her specific directions on how to find my SMOKING MAP ROOM on Level #5!"

Now somewhat perplexed at the instant promotion afforded Haygood, the Undersecretary dutifully answered, "Yes Minister, very well, I will make the upgrade as soon as possible and have her up and on her way!"

Churchill then added further emphasis to his orders as he turned directly into the face of Mrs. Litchfield, "And, Mrs. Litchfield, make this quick, the success of our boys in North Africa against Rommel, my orders to General Auchinleck and the whole of our 1st Armoured Division's future, may very well be resting on my clear thinking tonight, and without my cigars I'm like a King without a Horse, is that clear Mrs. Litchfield?"

Then without waiting for her reaction, he turned to Trixey as he started to walk back to the stair case where a Royal Marine Guard smartly snapped to attention upon seeing him starting to return.

"And, you, Ms. Haygood, I expect to see you at my SMOKING MAP ROOM on Level #5, no later than half-past the hour."

Both Mrs. Litchfield and Trixey stiffened their stance and responded in almost perfect unison, as they stated, "Yes, Minister!"

Once the P.M. was safely out of earshot of her voice, Mrs. Litchfield feeling somewhat embarrassed by the backbiting, spoke in an exasperated tone of voice to Trixey.

"Trixey Haygood, I can't believe you interrupted my conversation with the Honorable P.M. in that way. You know better than to invite yourself into such situations, particularly in a secure MI5 building!"

"Everything must be kept in its proper order," she said with her eyes boring a hole in Trixey's sexually explicit cleavage, "and you were clearly out of order by your actions."

Trixey well knowing this fact herself, just remained silent. She knew she had to take the chance she did, for a cause Mrs. Litchfield was completely unaware of. But that was the risk and fortunately, so far, it had worked. The next step would be getting that security clearance and delivering a few Montecristos up to the P.M.'s SMOKING MAP ROOM on Level #5.

After a pause for her reaction, Mrs. Litchfield resumed her comments. "Now then, Trixey, get on your way to the Women's Dormitory and retrieve that Cigar Box from your locker for the P.M., before I completely loose my temper."

"On your way back by my section office, stop in and I'll give you a temporary 'Most Secret' badge for now. Once my report of this incident is in though, I should expect it will be revoked and you my dear may even be without position in this section, as well."

"So watch your P's & Q's carefully, or all of this could get rather nasty."

Mrs. Litchfield then added, "Oh by the way, what was that question and document all about anyway?"

Trixey without commenting handed her the correspondence she had been holding all this time from the typing pool.

The top of the page read:

MOST SECRET
EYES ONLY - GENERAL AUCHINLECK
- CAIRO, EGYPT -
OFFICE OF P.M. - LONDON
28 JANUARY 1942

An extensive letter was attached to the unfinished typed page in the distinct stenographic handwriting of the P.M.'s First Undersecretary. Immediately, Mrs. Litchfield exclaimed with obvious irritation in her voice. "And what exactly are you doing with this, Trixey?"

Now, Trixey was ready, as she carefully chose her words. "As I am truly sure you are aware, Mrs. Litchfield, tonight's bombing raid kept over ten girls out of the pool at lock-up and I was told by the Provost on Duty, to get everything I could, onto your desk by 0600 Hours. The priority he gave me was MOST, first, then any other urgency level was to be based on the remaining security clearances on any desk in the entire room."

She decided not to take it any further. Trixey then waited for her reaction. Mrs. Litchfield just wheezed then spoke. "All right then, off with you, I'll get someone else to start on this at once."

She almost laughed out loud as she heard that one. Trixey knew everyone in the pool was covered and those that weren't, were down taking tea break by now.

She also knew, she would be given that same assignment, as soon as she returned from the P.M.'s Quarters.

There just wasn't enough people on, to cover the enormous workload and besides, she was the fastest typist in the entire pool. Mrs. Litchfield would eat her words, by morning. She was sure on that one.

Trixey well knew, that she had really stepped on Mrs. Litchfield's toes this time, but her plan was working for now, and that was all that counted.

She had to play these cards first, as Lady Margaret had taught her. What would happen later, would be another matter to deal with further on?

Without another word, and without an official 'Dismissed' from Mrs. Litchfield, she abruptly turned, got her purse and quickly rushed off to the Dorm area and her private locker.

By the time Trixey showed her temporary Most Secret Badge and got past the Royal Marine Sentry stationed outside of the P.M.'s SMOKING MAP ROOM on Level #5 it was almost 0145 Hours.

As she entered the room it had the distinct aroma of a fine cigar that had long been extinguished. The room was not well lit, but there were several larger more powerful lamps hanging from the ceiling, that had not been turned on. In the rear of the large room was a curtained wall and because part of the curtain's center was exposed with part of the drape hanging over a large chair positioned facing it, it was clear that the wall was actually an enormous operations map of Western Europe and North Africa.

She looked around and saw a large planning table, chairs and two work desks piled with documents. As she turned back to the entrance door, she also realized this was a temporary sleeping dorm for the PM.

It had a single cot made up with military folded sheets and a tightly tucked olive drab wool blanket as well as a night chest and lamp next to it. Suddenly, she heard the distinct flush of a water closet privy as she turned toward a door to her right. At that moment it opened and the P.M. himself emerged from the brightly lit privy and walked, oblivious to her arrival, right to the chair centered in front of the obscured map.

Hoping not to startle him, Trixey decided to speak first.

"Mr. Prime Minister, Sir, I have your requisitioned Cuban Cigars. May I approach you, Sir?"

Instantly recognizing her voice, the P.M. graciously asked her to join him.

" Ah, it's you again, Miss Trixey Haygood, pull one of those Naval highbacks over here and let's see what you've got?"

Trixey grabbed one of the command chairs sitting around the staff planning-table and dragged it to Churchill's side.

She then presented the entire sealed box of twenty-five Montecristo Cuban Cigars to the P.M. and spoke." Well Sir, here they are, the best I could find." As Churchill added, "And the very best they are indeed, my dear young Lady." He gazed at the box in triumph.

"These are surely the finest of the fine families of Cuba, the Menendez and Garcia Families of Havana. Have you ever tried one yourself, my dear?"

It was music to Trixey's ears, but she had to play along for a bit, before she went into high gear.

"Well to be honest, Prime Minister, when I was a young girl, I loved the aroma of cigar smoke at my uncle's cottage in Sussex."

"From time to time," she smiled coyly at the P.M. as she added, "he would let me puff a little on his Montecristos."

" Then he taught me how to properly prepare and light one like an English country gentleman would of course."

"Ah ha, then," Churchill mumbled in his deep voice, "you have been well prepared for a night like tonight." He then adeptly removed the cellophane box covering, selected his own cigar, pulled out his cutter, and began preparing the first Cuban Montecristo out of the box. The P.M. began flaming his choice as the perfectly structured ashes began to form and a swirl of intoxicating aromas of cherries and oak trees lifted upward into the map curtain.

The Prime Minister, even at this insanely late hour was now fully awake and clearly in his prime thinking mood, as he spoke with satisfaction in his voice. "Now, that's a jolly good smoke young lady. Would you care to join me?"

The P.M. extended the box over to Trixey and she, as well, skillfully selected, prepped and lit her own Montecristo as the P.M. carefully handed over the various tools of the true cigar lover, just in time for each step in the process, while he made note of her adept movements.

Once Trixey had a proper ash growth on hers, the P.M. added his thoughts.

"So, what do you think, my dear Lady?" Trixey was equally relaxed now as she responded.

"This my dear Sir, is the ultimate pleasure. The only thing I would add is a smooth Cognac, and a good Story Teller, to while away the rest of the evening."

Churchill laughed, "You're jolly right, you know, but in times like these, a good Cognac is hard to come by. Only the Royal Naval Officers up the street at the Admiralty, would keep a cache of Cognac."

"Not these boys over here at the Clive Street Palace, they're strictly MI and straight as a board."

Then he added with a prophetic tone in his voice, "But thanks to you Trixey Haygood, you have made my evening. And, as I said before, the success or failure of our entire North African Campaign against those Desert Panzer Divisions and Rommel himself, might be decided in the next few nights. So with your impounded Cuban contraband, we just might figure out how to beat that scoundrel."

Trixey laughed at his amusing style. She could clearly see why so many people really loved the man and his unwavering effervescent English optimism.

They both just sat there, in the now smoke filled room, relaxed and savoring their smokes a short while longer, in complete silence. Then he turned to a phone beside his chair and requested the night staff officer on duty, to get his commanders up off their arr. . .sses and back up to the SMOKING MAP ROOM. They were urgently needed to finish the planning for the unfortunate task of evacuating the city of Benghazi.

Churchill then turned to Trixey and made a final comment, "Trixey Haygood. . . I and the entire Commonwealth of Great Britain are truly thankful for your actions tonight."

Then he added for her safekeeping, "And don't you mind that Mrs. Litchfield giving you a hard time downstairs in the typing pool. . .I'll personally be checking up on you, and I expect you to join me again if the occasion arises. So for now we must bid farewell and get on with the bloody work of war."

Following that evening, the entire British 1st Armoured Division was destroyed by Rommel's Panzers, and Churchill's Generals faced a steady decline of fortunes in the British North African Campaign of the war.

That was also the last time she saw Churchill for over nine months, except for an occasional chance meeting in a hallway or in the First Undersecretary's Office from time to time.

It was one afternoon, late in October 1942, when Trixey had been working the Day Shift, that she was summoned to one of his meeting rooms because of a shortage of stenographers. She had just finished one of his transmission letters and was asked to bring it with her, for the P.M.'s confirmation, prior to sending it to General Alexander:

MOST SECRET
- EYES ONLY -
GENERAL ALEXANDER
CAIRO, EGYPT
OFFICE OF P.M. - LONDON
20 OCTOBER 1942

EVENTS ARE MOVING IN OUR FAVOUR BOTH IN NORTH AFRICA AND IN VICHY FRANCE. OPERATION "TORCH" IS GOING FORWARD SEADILY AND PUNCTUALLY. ALL OUR HOPES ARE WITH YOU AND MONTGOMERY AND WE ARE CENTERED UPON THE BATTLE YOU ARE GOING TO FIGHT.
IT MAY WELL BE THE KEY TO OUR FUTURE.

GIVE ME THE CODE WORD "ZIP" WHEN YOU START. MY WARMEST REGARDS TO ALL OF YOU.

Within the past three months Churchill had removed General Auchinleck and replaced him with Generals Alexander and later the illustrious Montgomery to try to rebuild British Tank forces and face off with the notorious Desert Fox, Wehrmacht General Rommel and his infamous Panzers. However, the battle crisis in Egypt was growing steadily more precipitous and it was only days until the Great Battle of El Alamein would take place and likely decide the future fate of the entire war, as Churchill had once said to her.

Trixey entered the room alone, while two men were whispering at a Map display on the large back wall of the room. She could barely make out the small script, but she could see a large body of water at the top, some metal tank icons on the left and right of heavy black serpentine lines, and desert sand colors below the lines. She knew it had to be somewhere in North Africa, not far from Cairo, but right on the Mediterranean Sea.

Suddenly, someone tapped her on the shoulder and spoke, "Ms. Trixey Haygood, what a wonderful surprise it is to have you up here with us today."

She immediately took a deep whiff of the cherry and oak aroma now filling her lungs and swirling in the air around her and softly replied, without turning to see him.

"Montecristo, I believe. Does the Prime Minister have a second one for the Lady, or would it be wise, not to reveal her true pleasure?"

Without even a moment's hesitation, the P.M. responded in a deep utterance of supreme authority.

"I believe, the Lady has my complete approval to join me forthwith, in the enjoyment of one of my fine Cuban companions."

Seductively she slowly turned around to look upon her admired friend and supreme commander, face to face, as one of his Royal Marine escorts opened Churchill's personal box of Montecristos and offered it for her to make a selection. While on the P.M.'s right side, the other Royal Marine, an Officer, gave her the P.M.'s cigar clipper and a new gold American Zippo lighter, he had recently received as a gift from President Roosevelt.

Trixey then, in a warm and sincere tone of voice, talked directly to the P.M. as she prepared her cigar and smoothly flamed it creating a nice ash burn while both Marines marveled at her experienced style. "I really have missed these beauties for quite sometime now. I hope we will be able to resume our relaxing pleasures more often, now that the American Convoys are getting through on a regular basis."

"We will indeed, Ms. Haygood, and in the next few days the events ahead in Egypt, may well allow a lot more Englishmen the same opportunity to do this as well. . .just as we here today."

As that month ended, Prime Minister Churchill and the British Commonwealth did, in fact, achieved a great victory at El Alamein. And, many more cigars were lit to the accomplishment of that incredible military feat. Often she would hear Churchill refer to El Alamein as the foretelling of the future of Nazi Germany.

He would often say, "It was the turning, the hinge of fate so to say, where before Alamein we never had a victory; after Alamein we never had a defeat."

Over the next two years, several other opportunities allowed Trixey a chance to tell a few of her own seductive tall tales to the Great Man on various late night visits.

For her, she was always respectful of him.

He was a sincere and admirable gentleman, full of hope and exuberance and sure of the final victorious outcome of the Allies and the War.

Trixey also knew he liked her for her smooth feminine style and their mutual love of the Cuban Beauties as she reverently called them. But she was also sure that her deep sincerity assured Churchill that he could trust her as a person, as well.

Chapter 6

Sherezade

At 2000 Hours Trixey made one last assessment as she thought back to earlier times with Churchill. He was an honorable man who above all others would surely understand how to conclude this final episode in a painful war of men.

Trixey moreover understood her own consequences. She might have to sacrifice herself and the respect that Churchill had surely developed for her, as well as the possibility of life imprisonment for an act of treason. But that was why AWC chose her to arrange the contact and no other. It had to be this way in the final act of a role he had given her, to gain a critical contact and secure the Unconditional Surrender of Germany.

The horror had to end and she believed that with all her heart.

At last her decision was clear. She would have to commit; Sherezade would now be in play.

She was out of her flat and on the subway to Charing Cross Station in less than twenty minutes. The only trains running to Lewes at this hour were coming out of the main train stations in South London. By the time she exited the tube she had less than five minutes to make the connection. She was panting heavily from the run as she stepped onto the entry steps of the second class car. Pushing the car door open, she entered the seating area of the 1930's vintage railcar, hearing the distant whistle signaling their departure to Lewes and then on to Eastborne and Hastings.

A cold wind blew in behind her as the door slammed. The car was empty, except for an old lady in the last row, staring indifferently out her glass at the windowpanes of the opposite train car now slowing to a stop on the ramp beside them.

Exhausted, Trixey settled herself at the first seat near a heater, knowing the door might open several more times before they finally got to Lewes Station, but that never happened.

The train seemed to glide out slowly and then picked up speed as the mesmerizing sound of the wheels clacking against the rail junctions allowed her to drift off into a light sleep.

Each stop was met with the typical squeal of the breaks, a hiss of steam and with only a brief pause before they were again moving toward Lewes. No one entered the car as they continued and Trixey began to dream of happier times on the Isle of Majorca.

Suddenly, something touched her on the back of her hand waking her from her much needed sleep. The old lady was standing beside her moving her mouth as Trixey realized what she was saying. "Oh Christ in Heaven," Trixey screamed under her breath, as she jerked her bag and ran for the door behind the old lady.

Trixey jumped to the platform, with the night train's eerie whistle on it's final call. Then looking up, she was greeted by the overhead signboard in bold letters, LEWES.

Thanks be to God for that old woman Trixey thought. She somehow wanted to express her gratitude, but the old lady was already gone like a shadow into the cold evening mist, maybe in reality her guardian angel, on that fateful night.

Taxis had not operated in the township of Lewes since 1939, but the Cottage Hill safehouse was located only a short walk up a steep hill near the town limit.

Trixey loved brisk walks at night on her own in safe climes. The evening mist had actually warmed the night air as the wind died down to a strange stillness around Lewes. She slowly climbed the last few blocks under some dim streetlights as the fog bank fell away behind her and shrouded the main town in a soft white blanket. At the top of the hill she could see ahead the lights of Beachy Head nestled on the Channel's Coastline below and to the distant southeast.

Even the stars and the clear night sky, gave her a feeling of comfort in knowing she had made the right decision coming to this place.

The key was in it's usual spot under the porch and Trixey had no trouble getting into the Cottage and locating all of the designated equipment stored in the attic.

She adeptly set up the enigma and radio transmitter, dialing in the assigned frequency listed in the codebook for this particular date. As she initiated her sign on code, she quickly hesitated, to re-check the actual transmission time. She would have to wait several hours; it was designated as 0345 Hours with a window of thirty minutes for the acknowledgement response as set for this date.

Trixey went downstairs and made some tea as she began reviewing how she would approach the P.M. about the complex situation as well as revealing her own Abwehr connection, once she returned to CSP. Her fears began to grow ominously . . . And what about his frequently scheduled meetings outside of London?

Where would she likely find him other that the CSP without raising suspicions even further?

She needed the help of an unlikely ally, and that wasn't going to be easy, with time bleeding away.

At exactly 0345 Hours on Sunday Morning, January 28th, 1945, Trixey made her first contact with an unidentified Abwehr Receiving Station in Eastern Holland. Within ten minutes, she was quickly decoding the response document with her own enigma unit:

ACKNOWLEDGED CONTACT

OUTSIDE RELAY TO AWC IN PROGRESS

STANDBY

END TRANSMISSION

The abbreviated information basically told her to stand-by while the receiving station relayed her contact information to a German based facility somewhere near where AWC would actually be located, and probably outside of bomb ravaged Berlin.

It was again another interminable wait for the second location to finally communicate her orders.

At Sangerhausen, following the Canaris telegraph to Agent Sherezade on that fateful morning, both he and the SS-Gruppenfuhrer Deeke had spent the next twelve hours preparing the B-17 crew and gathering the appropriate nuclear confirmation material for the mission.

Everything was designed to convince Churchill of the grave reality of the situation.

However, they had not actually considered how Sherezade would be able to convince Churchill to meet with the SS-Gruppenfuhrer once he was on the ground in England.

Knowing agent Sherezade would have to make contact according to the enigma code books at exactly 0345 the next morning, a final analysis meeting was set at 0200 Hours, just prior to her transmission time, to be ready to respond if she accepted activation. Everyone involved in the mission was told to get at least four hours sleep and be ready in the main staff planning room by that hour.

Horst was standing by the giant wall map of Europe, charting the flight route of his B-17 with his chief pilot, SS-Strumbannfuhrer Grimstad.

His second officer, KG-A Ops Luftwaffe Hauptmann Dietrich Clausen, who had flown over two-hundred hours in KG-A Ops rebuilt and modified American B-17s and British Lancaster Bombers, stood with them.

Horst spoke first, as Admiral Canaris entered the Staff Planning Room.

"Welcome Admiral, I trust you've had enough sleep."

Canaris replied sharply, as if he had rehearsed his lines all night, and without slowing his re-energized gate he walked straight to the map and pointed out the likely air bases around London they would possibly be given authorization to land at.

"If, Churchill accepts our offer for this meeting, Herr Deeke, he will have you land at a British Controlled Base near London, not one of the American 8th Air Force B-17 Bases in Northern England. He will want complete control using his SAS, MI5, and possibly MI6 teams there to fully interrogate you and every individual in your crew.

They will go over that plane with a fine eyeglass and clean every item like it was a bomb, before Churchill gets anywhere near you. Time will be critical, so we must somehow get you and the Prime Minister alone as quickly as possible.

This must happen right after you land, for you to be effective in fully revealing to him our true intention; revelation of the Super Bomb and it's detailed construction."

The Admiral then presented a key question to the SS-Gruppenfuhrer Deeke.

"What could you say or reveal to him that would instantly convince him of your credibility and knowledge of this Nuclear Bomb's technology and impending threat?"

Horst had considered this same problem himself, as he had tossed in stressful sleep at his desk during the past four hours.

Then facing the Admiral with a solid impression of assured confidence, he spoke.

"Three combination word sets will convince Mr. Churchill of what we are there for, only three. We cannot let this out before we meet them though, or they will surely think we have the Bomb in the plane with us. They will shoot our B-17 down before we can cross the Channel, killing any chance to save either England or the future of Germany."

Canaris reacted, "So what are they man, speak out, you have me in utter suspense!"

Horst continued unfettered by Canaris overstressed reaction,

"Tube Alloys, Manhattan Project, Mort Bruckmann".

Canaris seemed confused, but was open for an explanation as Horst continued.

"First, Tube Alloys; that is the designation the British have used all along for their Atomic Bomb Project, now merged with the American program as a result of Churchill and Roosevelt's Quebec Agreement in 1943. This word is considered a 'Most-Secret' British code word, and only Churchill would recognize this right away."

"The Manhattan Project; that is the 'Top Secret' code word for the entire American Atomic Bomb Project being driven by General Groves and the Physicist Robert Oppenheimer at Los Alamos and Oak Ridge . Churchill is aware of this word-set as well from his discussions with Roosevelt."

"Finally, Mort Bruckmann; that is name of the number-two top American Physicist at Oak Ridge and a close friend of Robert Teller that has been 'mysteriously missing' for the last fifteen days in America. We have a communiqué intercepted from Oak Ridge within the last few days that Groves informed Roosevelt and Roosevelt in turn informed Churchill that they believe we have him under our control. Actually, the SS Reichfuhrer may have him sequestered pending the final clean-up at our Sky Club safehouse that has been ongoing since 20th January, just days before our UX-506 apparently sailed on schedule for the Irish Sea."

Canaris then reacted more confidently, "Good, then you have it. That is exactly how you will gain the isolation with Churchill that you will need. He will instantly realize that unless you two are detached from the others at once, a major breech of security will take place within his own command. He will be forced to hear your terms."

But then, Admiral Wilhelm Canaris paused for one of his typical signature moments that caused all within earshot, to hold their breath as he unfolded his next revelation.

"Horst, this is the moment, when not only can you save das Vaterland, England and possibly all of us here in Sangerhausen from annihilation. . .but it will be the only chance you will have to set the term's of acquittal for yourself, the crew, and my own agent Sherezade. Term's that will surely allow all of you to escape the hangman's noose of the British or the other Allies."

"And that my friend, is utmost on my mind following the safe destruction of the coming horror at Liverpool."

Horst agreed with him completely as he looked back to the Map and added, "And, now Admiral, what is the most likely landing area they will offer us in England."

Canaris placed his finger on the map just west of downtown London then dragging it from point to point, he began identifying other sites, as he observed.

"My guess is Northolt in Middlesex first, but this base in Sussex or even this one, further west near Oxford, can each accommodate B-17s and Lancaster Bombers."

Indeed beyond this crucial issue, however, they had not even considered the possibility that the Prime Minister of Great Britain might not even be in London. Horst reacted first as that vital thought struck him.

"What if he's not there? What if he's not even in the whole of England or Scotland?"

Fully aware of that potential problem, the Admiral then injected his own intimate knowledge of Churchill. Canaris knew full well that the man could often be found traveling around the entire Allied War Zone of Europe, more like one his lower ranking military commanders, rather than the Second Most Powerful Leader in the Allied sphere of influence. Canaris seemed to suddenly reveal himself, as he related another one of his cryptic Abwehr tales of intrigue.

"In 1943, for instance, I was completely appraised of, but was reluctant to tell anyone at the Reichstag including das Fuhrer himself, the fact that Churchill was actually in Moscow, meeting with Stalin on how to simultaneously crush Germany from two fronts at once.

Had das Fuhrer or even the SS-Reichfuhrer known what I had known, the SS and the Wehrmacht would have immediately began surrounding the core of Germany including Berlin with their remaining crack Panzer units, rather than play das Fuhrer's game of world domination in Eastern Europe."

Canaris then related that specific 1943 event to the present set of circumstance that he and his Abwehr, the SS-Gruppenfuhrer and his SS-Wiking Units, and the Third Reich now found themselves in.

"Now, here it is late January 1945, and das Fuhrer has over fifteen powerful SS and Wehrmacht Panzer Divisions stranded in far away Bulgaria, Hungary and the mountains of Rumania. With all of these massive Panzer Divisions now out of touch from the Reichstag, Germany and Berlin's defenses are paper-thin. Russia will surely exploit this incredible misfortune with a Bolshevik Blitzkrieg of their own."

"Is it possible then, that all three; Churchill, Roosevelt, and Stalin are meeting somewhere in the US or Canada right at this very moment to divide up the spoils of Europe, Excellency?" Horst cautiously inquired.

Canaris answered without hesitation, " No, not at this moment. Stalin would never leave Russian soil until he has reached his ultimate goal of retribution, the destruction of das Fuhrer and Berlin itself. I know his dossier too well my friend."

He paused, then continued. . . "If they want to meet that vicious 'Bear of the Bolsheviks', they will have to go to him. Besides, if Churchill is not in England now, all is lost anyway, unless you can find another method to destroy that U-boat on your own."

"Herr Deeke", the Admiral thought as he added a critical issue. . ."Have you also considered what my agent Sherezade is thinking about at this very moment?"

Horst stood somewhat perplexed with both of his pilots looking straight at the Admiral, in anticipation of the answer they were sure he would provide for the them.

"You know her and trust her, Excellency," Horst replied. "You alone would understand her reaction to this final mission. And from what you have told me and what I have read in her dossier, all I can assume is that she admires the Prime Minister, she would do nothing to harm him, and she equally believes that you would never ask her to harm him either. The only conclusion she could make at this point is that you want her to be the contact to arrange for our meeting to secure an 'Unconditional Surrender' of Germany."

"You are exactly correct, Herr Deeke," the Admiral reacted. "But the vital question now is, what can my agent Sherezade 'say' to Churchill to convince him to even meet with you at all?"

Again in brilliant style, almost anticipating precisely what the Admiral expected him to say, the SS-Gruppenfuhrer continued his plan.

"We can rule out anything about the impending Thermonuclear Disaster, I will cover that exclusively myself, once I am with Churchill alone."

"To get Churchill to meet with us, we have to give him more than our Unconditional Surrender, we must somehow have Sherezade convince him that we will give him free access across Northern Germany right into Berlin ahead of the Russians fighting on our Eastern Front. If he has that assumption, he will see the opportunity for his future role in how Europe is divided. If he passes this up, both America and Russia will have a stronger position in the spoils. We both know he is a pragmatist and he will exploit any weakness to gain ground for Great Britain."

Then he added, "Surely he must know that both Russia and America will be his future adversaries, at least in economic warfare, if not in ideological warfare. You and I both know he distrusts bolshevism from his past writings as a Naval Commander in WWI."

Horst then concluded. "Excellency, we must code the response to Sherezade simply, and just enough to get Churchill's support. It should state: Unconditional Surrender to Churchill Only - All SS and Wehrmacht Commands West of Berlin will clear and expedite routes into Berlin - Immediate occupation of Berlin by British Forces of Montgomery- Request Occupation as soon as we have met Churchill at selected airfield."

Just as SS-Gruppenfuhrer Deeke finished his comments, the Command Sergeant Major of SS-Wiking entered to room. " SS-Gruppenfuhrer, the command center is ready for your transmission code. We only have a window of thirty minutes."

"Jawohl, SS-Sturmscharfuhrer," Horst replied. "We will have the document in about ten minutes. Have them initiate the transmission codes at once, I will personally bring the final document myself."

Without saluting, the Command Sergeant Major answered, "Jawohl, mein Gruppenfuhrer," and quickly exited back to the radio room. Time was running out, so together, Admiral Canaris and Horst Deeke sat down at the planning table and quickly completed the remaining orders for agent Sherezade.

Trixey's adrenaline had been working overtime all night, keeping her energized, but now she was almost completely exhausted. The wait for what they wanted her to do was mentally draining her, as well. She decided to walk up the stairs to the top of the watch turret, built on the Cottage's south-facing wall.

As she again peered out into the cold darkness of the English coastline from the widow's watch, she gazed at two spitfires launching into the night sky and turning out over the channel on patrol.

There below, along Beachy Head the interceptor airfield suddenly went dark again, after lighting up momentarily for the Spitfires early morning take off. She was wondering if her influence could really succeed in getting Churchill to consider meeting them, just as she heard the signal coming in on the radio unit down below in the attic.

By the time she was at the cipher, the unit was ready to receive the orders message from AWC. She began typing the translation code almost as fast as it came in:

SHEREZADE ACKNOWLEDGED ACTIVE

CONTACT P.M. AT ONCE TO SET UP A MEETING

PREFER AIRBASE IN SOUTHERN ENGLAND / HIS CHOICE

AIRCRAFT INFO NEXT

THIS PART TOP SECRET P.M. EYES ONLY / REPEAT

TOP SECRET P.M. EYES ONLY

AIRCRAFT WILL BE AMERICAN B-17

MOST CRITICAL - MUST MEET P.M. BEFORE FEB 1

UNCONDITIONAL SURRENDER TO CHURCHILL ONLY

ALL SS / WEHRMACHT WEST OF BERLIN WILL SURRENDER

ALL ROUTES TO BERLIN WILL CLEAR

REQUEST ONLY BRITISH FORCES /
MONTGOMERY TO OCCUPY BERLIN
DUE TO RUSSIAN ADVANCE / TIME IS URGENT
ADVISE AIRBASE DETAILS BACK TO AWC AT
2345 THIS DATE
END TRANSMISSION

Trixey was now both relieved and overwhelmed at the same time by the task ahead. But at least some of her greatest fears were finally behind her.

She had been right all along in her hope that this was a call for Unconditional Surrender.

As she returned to the small bedroom below, she thought of AWC and what he must be going through as well, somewhere in war ravaged Germany. She hoped she would see him again, but even her own fate was yet to be decided and that also unnerved her.

For now though, she had to get at least a few hours of needed sleep, until boarding the train out to Charing Cross Station. And on Sunday morning, January 28th, possibly the longest day of her life, that would be no earlier than 0900 Hours.

Chapter 7

Clive Street Palace

Trixey arrived just a few minutes before noon at the interlocking defensive system that made up the massive reinforced concrete underground bunkers and security network of Great Britain's Clive Street Palace. On this particular day she was greeted with a scurry of unusual activity outside the building as she entered. It seemed that all hell had broken loose.

She knew it would normally be a typically slow Sunday morning when she started out, but suddenly, January 28th 1945 was anything but the same place she had left on Saturday evening. A dreadful fear began to grow in her mind, as she was required to pass through two additional entry security checks of Grenadier Guards and Royal Marine Sentries dressed in their wartime uniforms.

Then, as she exited the stairwell and entered sublevel #5, she almost fainted, as she was stopped again by a Provost with two SAS guards at his side.

Both SAS soldiers were armed with Sten Submachine Guns and dressed in their drab camouflaged outfits. Trixey knew these British Special Air Service soldiers, better known as the SAS were easily the most elite fighting units in the allied arsenal. But their missions were usually for work in infiltration behind enemy lines or extraction tactics, not security here at the CSP.

Sten Machine Guns were used exclusively by SAS and other allied special forces because of the deadly combination of firing speed and ammo magazines with thirty-two 9mm cartridges, inserted in their fully charged light weight frames.

Besides, the overt display of weapons like the Sten were generally prohibited below level #3.

Since 1943, the P.M. had decreed that the typing pool ladies and his worker bees be able to carry on, in the most relaxed fashion possible, even if bombs were going off aboveground over their heads.

Churchill had emphasized that below level #3, this zone was to be sanctuary for his most crucial people under all circumstances.

But, something critical had changed. The vital question on Trixey's mind was what it was and how would it affect her present mission? She now had to urgently find the P.M.

As she entered the Undersecretary's Office to get her assignments and begin her furtive search for the P.M., she instantly relaxed her intense apprehension level. A deep voice and the obvious aroma from lingering Montecristo fumes greeted her from the next room.

The door was slightly ajar and the P.M. seemed to be confirming with Mrs. Litchfield that she leave CSP by 0900 Hours tomorrow, in order to complete her packing arrangements at home and report directly to Northolt by 1300 Hours Monday afternoon for security clearance.

At that moment he could be heard moving toward the door, as she tried to appear busy shuffling for something in her assignment pile that had URGENT WORK - P.M. COMMUNIQUÈ on its file header.

Finally she had it and she quickly scanned its contents, just as his pace and the doors opening coincided.

Efficiently, Trixey turned to catch his attention, while he seemed to have his head down in his typical mood of deep thought as a swirl of cigar smoke trailed behind him.

"Minister," she implored him softly, "may I have a very brief moment to clarify this wording to the Commander of H.M.S. Orion on station at Malta."

"Ah yes, you again my dear Miss Haygood. It will be a refreshing break to assist you with that. Come along then with me, as I must return to my SMOKING MAP ROOM for final orders to the Royal Air Staff waiting there."

Churchill then shuffled toward the door as Trixey held her breath, knowing that Mrs. Litchfield would want to know why she was in on Sunday, since her assignment roster clearly read 0800 Hours, Monday 29 January, as her next duty day.

That frightful event never came as she turned and hastily followed the P.M. past his Royal Marine Guard and into the relative safety of the SMOKING MAP ROOM.

As they entered, the room was filled with at least three High Ranking Royal Air Force officers standing at the fully exposed Map of Europe, Mr. Martin and Mr. Rowan and a Royal Naval attaché were seated at the staff table and an MI5 Minister was just exiting the privy. All of them had been talking and joking before Trixey and the P.M. entered.

Someone then announced, "P.M. on board, attention everyone," and suddenly everything went into suspended animation until Churchill himself spoke.

"At ease, Gentlemen." Then realizing they were focused not on him, but the new arrival lingering behind him, he added, "Oh, and this young lady is one of my Secure Clericals and she will be on board for now, to take notes of course."

Trixey went again from ease to a state of absolute panic,

as she momentarily forgot that she actually had her steno pad and pencils stored, as usual, in the bag she was still carrying.

Instantly, she nodded to the officers and shyly took a seat offered to her by Mr. Rowen, on Mr. Churchill's side of the table. She then urgently fumbled down into her bag and, in a moment of pure relief, she raised back facing the table with steno pad and pencil at the ready.

Churchill spotting her anticipation then continued to address the waiting general staff officers.

"From what you have shown me today, Gentlemen, I am confident our planning efforts for Argonaut have included most contingencies, even though as you are all aware, I have strong reservations about the location proper in this very horrid winter weather they are having."

"Even the Black Sea's normally constant weather can be unforgiving in it's Northern reaches at this time of the year."

"What say you, Colonel Fitzwarren?"

Churchill looked at one of the officers near the Map, now using a dead reckoning device to verify some coordinates, as the officer quickly returned his attention to the P.M. and responded.

"Based on tomorrow's climatic projections, we should have no trouble with the weather using the new American Douglas Skymaster provided for your personal flight group by General Arnold, Minister," he replied with conviction.

"From here to Gibraltar, it's variable overcast and on to Malta we should have relatively clear weather. But flying out from Malta using the two converted RAF Lancasters could be a problem since German Panzers still control the coastal areas of Rumania and Bulgaria along the Eastern coastline of the Black Sea. We would be well advised to stay over water on that approach, Minister, with all three transport planes."

"At least until we get over Russian controlled airspace for our approach onto the airfield at Saki in the Crimea."

As he paused, the second RAF Officer beside him was quick to add several technical points.

"This modified over-water approach leg, Minister, will be fourteen-hundred nautical miles one-way from Malta to their airfield, and it leaves very little margin for safety for the Lancasters."

"On the other hand, the new Douglas C-54 Skymaster even with a full complement aboard and five crew members has a thirty-five-hundred nautical mile range at twenty-two-thousand feet making it by far, the best choice, Minister."

Then, to maintain a semblance of his authority on the matter, Colonel Fitzwarren interjected a final tidbit.

"Based on the latest upgrade directives from our 8th Air Force Liaison Officer, the four Pratt & Whitney R-2000 radials on your New Command Bird can produce over fourteen-hundred horsepower per engine. It's really going to be a beauty of a ride to Argonaut for you and your staff, Minister."

At that point Churchill realized the slight competitive edge his technos had over the other commanders at the table on these issues, so he decided to throw in a morsel for the rest of them.

"Well, you know what Hap Arnold and the Americans have code named their C-54 for the President, don't you, the Sacred Cow. What say we do them one better, for our code name? So what will it be Gentlemen?"

At once, creative silence went to work and the spooks at the table suddenly had the edge over the technos.

Suddenly, Brigadier Thorpson suggested they look to the new arrival at the table for her inspiration.

"What say you, young lady, what would you call the Prime Minister's Private Skymaster?"

Trixey already had her thoughts in place, but she would have never mentioned them in this high level crowd, but now they seemed to be playing with her a wee bit, as she spoke.

"General, the Prime Minister is the greatest Knight in our Kingdom at this very moment. Because he is an honorable Knight and he is on a Great Quest for our final salvation here on the homefront in England, his Skymaster should by all rights be named after the chalice that held God's sacred wine. I would name it, 'the Holy Grail'.

The Royal Marine, Brigadier Thorpson reacted with pure satisfaction. "Now, that's a name I think we can seriously put in the mill for true consideration, Aye, Minister?"

The P.M. looked at the surprised faces of all around the room, then he spoke with a grin on his face and sense of jovial satisfaction in her performance.

"My dear young lady, I believe you have spooked my spooks! What say you Gentlemen?"

The entire group began to laugh, then responded to the P.M. in his favorite naval acknowledgement, "Aye, aye, Minister."

Oh Christ, were out of time, Trixey uttered under her breath. At once, Trixey's mind was in a tailspin as she continued to take notes for the P.M., but her fears were growing larger as she began to understand the full dimension of what was going to happen. She had known about the code word Argonaut, from a previous Communiqué of Churchill's to President Roosevelt, which she had been requested to retype the week before for the First Undersecretary.

It was to be called the Triple.

A high level conference meeting of all three leaders somewhere in an Allied controlled area of the Mediterranean where the staffs of all three Allied Powers would meet and carve up Europe, at war's end.

But now she realized that instead of March 31st, as was the original planned meeting date, it had been drastically changed and moved up to February 1st. They probably became desperate, just like AWC was at this very moment in Germany. The Allies were forced to move it up because Little Joe, as the American President Roosevelt like to call Joseph Stalin to Churchill, just might have Berlin and most of Germany under communistic control, before they could negotiate the equal division of Europe.

Churchill's meeting continued relentlessly for another two-hours with everyone in the room speaking at various times regarding, security, extensive details of alternate flight routes, and support logistics.

Finally the grand total of planes and staff that would be flown on from Malta to Saki, and then on by surface convoy through the deep snows in the Russian Crimea down to the hopefully warmer shores of the Black Sea at Yalta was announced by Brigadier Thorpson.

"Minister, I would estimate by the actual day of the Triple Conference you will have two hundred and ninety-five personal from our side in attendance. The initial flight tomorrow will be with three planes, the two Lancasters and your Skymaster. I have purposely left two seats in each plane available for any last minute personnel additions you may need for the Malta meeting with President Roosevelt on the 1st."

The Brigadier then added the final event date. "As for Yalta, Minister, that schedule is set for a late night flight departure from Malta on Friday, February 2nd."

Churchill then rose from the table and looked down at Trixey as she recorded the last of the Brigadier's final statistics.

"I can see by this young lady's valiant effort, that all is now documented and will be ready for transcription to your staffs."

"So, Miss Haygood," the P.M. added as they all cautiously awaited her answer, "what time will everyone here have their copies and their dispatches ready for the remaining staff members scheduled on the flight?"

Not sure how many would need copies, Trixey reacted hesitantly as she spoke in a reserved manner.

"Minister, these transcripts will be ready in forty-five minutes. But, I don't know how many copies will be needed for dissemination or what security protocol will be used?"

Churchill, knowing he personally had no idea what security level had been designated for Argonaut, referred to his provost Mr. Rowen, as he replied,

"Jack, give her the clearance levels proscribed for these documents."

"Sir," Jack reacted without hesitation, "Protocol F and Hush Most Secret, Minister."

Churchill then chimed in, "So there, you have that, Ms. Haygood. And as for the total, what would that be for tomorrows flight, Brigadier?"

Brigadier Thorpson cleared his deep voice and without vacillating gave the exact staff total for Monday's flight. "Minister, the actual number for Malta is forty-five on your Skymaster, and forty each on both Lancasters for a total of one-hundred and twenty-five staff."

Churchill then started for the privy as he spoke,

"Thank you Gentlemen; I will see most of you at 1300 Hours at Northolt tomorrow, packed and ready; the rest of you at the Staff meeting upstairs at 1800 Hours; and you Miss Haygood, stay for a moment so that I may clarify some items for my archive documents."

Churchill added, "Dismissed Gentlemen," as he began to close the privy door.

The group then replied in unison, in the P.M.'s choice of naval protocol for his staff signoffs, "Aye, aye, Sir," as the Brigadier added, "and, God Save The King!"

Trixey kept her head down and continued writing details as the last of the officers filed out of the SMOKING MAP ROOM - Level #5.

No one had bothered to speak to her or to draw the Map's curtain closed as they left the room.

Instantly mesmerized by its vast landscape, Trixey's mind began to race as she realized her whole life was represented in this massive picture, it was clearly a 'God's Eye View of Europe'.

Her thoughts overcame her as she almost began to cry in a sense of hopeless desperation. There was her little island home on Majorca, there was Uncle Wilhelm somewhere in Eastern Germany, there was the Clive Street Palace here in Whitehall, and far in the East was Yalta, headquarters for Stalin's entire military command, now directing troops into the remains of Nazi Germany's thousand year empire. Trixey could now visually see just how far the appropriated American B-17 Bomber would have to fly in order to get the German negotiators to England.

Her mind was racing.

Would they even have time before Churchill left for Malta, or better yet could she even convince the P.M. to even consider meeting with them for this last courageous effort to save what was left of Germany before the Communists ravaged every remaining man, woman, and child.

At that moment, she realized the P.M. was standing right there in front of her observing the strained expression on her face as he began to carefully flame a newly prepared Montecristo.

"Well my dear, if I was a betting man I would say that all of this has gotten to you today, wouldn't you say?"

Trixey knew they were alone and her opportunity for revelation was now at hand. This might be the only chance she would have to catch him in a moment of willingness to understand her predicament. Carefully, Trixey looked into the eyes of this Great Man, somehow hoping there would be compassion for what she was about to say as she began to weave her desperate tale.

"Do you remember when we first met a few years ago, Minister?"

Deciding to remain observant and somewhat aloof, the P.M. puffed away on his Montecristo, and offered only a simple acknowledgment. "Ah my dear, very well I do?"

Trixey then added. "Did you know at that time, who my guardian Aunt was, Minister?"

Once again, he continued to puff away on his Montecristo, and looked somewhat introspectively at the young woman's eyes.

"Ah, as well I do know your Aunt. Lady Margaret Anne Gray of Palma, on the isle of Majorca, I believe."

Trixey now realizing that he knew a lot more about her then she had assumed all these years, decided to play along as if he knew her true story.

"When I lived there on Majorca, Minister, my life was so beautiful. I was very young, but the things Lady Margaret taught me and allowed me to experience caused me to mature very quickly."

"I learned to accept both the unique complexities of people and their oftentimes-unusual sexuality without question or judgment."

"I became very tolerant of people, Minister, of any disposition as long as they were kind to my family and me.

The Prime Minister seemed captivated with her narration and continued to remain calm as he drew another puff, with smoke from the Montecristo rising to the ceiling vent above his head. He then carefully checked it's ash growth as he found his ashtray, then pulled it to his side of the table.

"You know, my dear," he spoke slowly, "this tale is beginning to get exciting, but we have a very long day ahead and I must say, your work load is greater than mine at this very moment."

Trixey implored him, "Please, Minister, I need to get this off my mind, I need you to know this comes from my heart. I beg you to listen just a while longer."

"Very well, my dear," he responded in his deep, but comforting tone, "continue and I will try to be your silent audience."

She continued with a more sultry tone of voice without missing a beat from where she left off.

"I would live every day like I was a fairy Princess and every night I would meet my fairy Princes, rich and powerful, young and old men from all over Europe that were guests and lovers of my Aunt. They were to a man, my other education, teachers and people that influenced my thinking, my philosophy of life, and most importantly my notion of the ideal society for Europe's future.

Churchill at once began to focus on the possible meaning behind her words, almost as if he could divine the path where she was leading would eventually end up. His lips gripped the Montecristo in the corner of his mouth as he added emphasis to his own conjecture. "Ah. . . I see."

But Trixey continued knowing well that she would somehow have to reveal herself soon.

"I would do things back in Majorca that would make men admire me, that would get their undivided attention."

"I was their entertainment, yet I was so alone there without friends my own age, that these men would become more to me than visitors. I even tried to prove that I was their equal or better."

Trixey again looked over at the Great Man as he finally pulled out a chair and lowered himself slowly into position directly across from her. As she now had him at her eye level, she cleared her throat silently, and prepared to tell him the undeniable hidden truth about herself.

"Prime Minister, I was sent to England by Lady Margaret in the mid 1930s, first to be educated here and later on to be developed as a future Agent of Abwehr by my Uncle, his name you will know very well, Admiral Wilhelm Canaris.

It was almost as if Churchill, sensing her human vulnerability as a child, now accepted her idealism as an adult as the reason for her involvement. It was as if he already knew what she was saying to be fact, then without flinching, he replied softly, almost like a Priest sliding the confessional portal open as he spoke, "Go on my child."

Trixey for the first time began to shake and her voice broke with emotion as she continued to her confessor.

"Minister, they never wanted to use me, even Uncle Wilhelm said he never wanted me to be activated. I never saw him much, but when he did visit Majorca, he would bring me presents and tell me that he loved me like his own child in Germany, and since I had never known a father, I accepted him as my own."

She began to softly cry as she continued keeping him mesmerized with her incredible tale, yet he never indicated any extreme reaction, even as her tears began to drop to the tabletop.

He just silently observed her and said, "Calm down now, my child, I'm still listening, so don't worry."

At last, nervously, she knew it was time for her opening. She also knew that someone could be urgently searching for him. Her mind began racing. If they came in now, they would break his concentration. If she could just have a few more moments God; to save them all in Germany; to tell him the purpose of all this, the final revelation. She knew that she was fully exposed now, but she couldn't have risked bringing the actual transmission received at the Cottage Hill Safehouse in Sussex, because there was always the specter of a search at any time or at any security entrance to the lower levels of CSP.

So Trixey had simply memorized the entire transmission from Germany and was now beginning to write it down in detail, as she revealed her true purpose.

She read her notes slowly and methodically as she wrote them and then handed the written page with her fragile shaking right hand to the Prime Minister of Great Britain.

"SHEREZADE ACKNOWLEDGED ACTIVE
CONTACT P.M. AT ONCE TO SET UP A
MEETING
PREFER AIRBASE IN SOUTHERN ENGLAND /
HIS CHOICE
AIRCRAFT INFO NEXT
THIS PART TOP SECRET P.M. EYES ONLY /
REPEAT
TOP SECRET P.M. EYES ONLY
AIRCRAFT WILL BE AMERICAN B-17

MOST CRITICAL - MUST MEET P.M. BEFORE
FEB 1
UNCONDITIONAL   SURRENDER   TO
CHURCHILL ONLY
ALL SS / WEHRMACHT WEST OF BERLIN WILL
SURRENDER
ALL ROUTES TO BERLIN WILL CLEAR"
"REQUEST   ONLY   BRITISH   FORCES   /
MONTGOMERY TO OCCUPY BERLIN
DUE TO RUSSIAN ADVANCE / TIME IS URGENT
ADVISE AIRBASE DETAILS BACK TO AWC AT
2345 THIS DATE
END TRANSMISSION"

Both she and Churchill sat in complete silence while he reread the page a second time. A ring of cigar smoke seemed to swirl out of sight over his head as he focused on his decision.

It felt like an eternity, when as he was just about to speak, his Provost, Mr. Edward Martin entered the SMOKING MAP ROOM and blurted out in a surprised voice. "Oh, Minister, so there you are. We were told to locate you straight away for review of your personal meal requirements on the flight down to Malta, tomorrow.

Churchill spoke in a gruff automatic tone of voice. "Oh that's jolly good of you boys. You know I can't eat heavy meals on long transport flights like this one. You can tell them to pack my Orange Tizer and plenty of Ham and Cucumber sandwiches. And John, that will be all for now, please let me get these archives completed in good order, man."

John replied back, in a matter of fact way, as if the P.M.'s response was typical of the old man when he was down to some serious issues.

"Yes, of course, Minister, as you wish. See you at the 1800 Hours meeting."

"I'll be off now."

Trixey, overwhelmed with extreme gratitude in her voice, broke her silence.

"Prime Minister, I feel so humbled by your kindness to let me speak and I am grateful to almighty God that he has given you this moment in time to listen to the offer of a desperate people in their final tragedy."

Churchill could hold back no longer." Young Lady, you, of all people, should never have been used like this by any man, Uncle, Father, or otherwise."

" I am completely disgusted with all of Nazi Germany and it's Aryan Manhood, and in particular what it has wrought on Germany's youth such as you and all the youth of Europe for generations to come. But, more importantly, I can't even begin to judge you for what you have done. You, Trixey, are like Joan of Arc, an innocent harbinger sent by God, on a desperate mission on behalf of a nation of vermin and just a few humans, desperate to resolve an end to an evil empire that has never before been human itself in it's conduct of warfare; a war that forever will endure for all of history in the minds of men, as the most evil in the annals of mankind."

Trixey continued to shake nervously as she tried to smile at the one man she truly admired, a man having equal measures of strength and compassion.

"Nazi Germany now sends an angel, a messenger like you, to convince warriors like me to stop what they themselves, so willingly began against their own people, my people, and the peoples of mainland Europe over fifteen years ago."

His anger was obvious, but his control was incredible as he then focused attention back onto the now silent courageous young girl waiting willingly for her own punishment in front of him.

"Young lady, you have handed me a most difficult task, but it is actually a very simple one if all emotion and all energies of retribution are removed from it. As pure logic, the answer is quite easy to consider. And, so Trixey Haygood, you above all others will have one opportunity to take back to these people my answer."

"I need Berlin now before I fly to Yalta," his voice became impassioned with fire as he held her spellbound, "I need a secure resolution quickly in this war of attrition and misery for my people, and finally I need to prevent another corrupt ideology from quickly drawing down a curtain while they secretly put another noose around the neck of Europe, preventing the great economic recovery of these lands".

Churchill quietly tapped his Cuban in his ashtray and started to rise up from his chair as he made his final statement.

"Miss Haygood, you will pass along in whatever means you have available the following message. "Start writing, Miss Haygood," he added quite seriously as Trixey still stunned, quickly picked up her pencil and wrote on her pad as he commanded, "that, I will meet them at Northolt Airfield at no later that 1000 Hours, Monday, 29 January 1945, with only a thirty minute window either side of that designated hour. They must taxi their plane to hanger #9 and shut down all engines."

He cleared his voice and sat the Cuban back in his ashtray as he continued, "Everyone must then exit the plane to be searched and shackled. They will then be interrogated by my SAS Team first and turned over to me. They will be given a final opportunity to convince me of their ability to conclude an 'Unconditional Surrender for Germany' with detailed terms that we will demand."

"Finally, my dear. . . you will also report to the Northolt airfield at Hanger #9."

"Your Most Secret Badge will gain you entry and then you will turn yourself in along with these people to my SAS at the same time."

The P.M. then turned and without looking back to Trixey, made one last comment as he picked up his cigar. "May God bless you Trixey Haygood, and may he have mercy on you . . .if any of this mess results in harm to Britain or assets of the Crown of England."

"You are now dismissed."

He then added a final painful reality statement for her own actions, "Turn in the Argonaut work to the Undersecretary on duty. . . and immediately exit the CSP facilities."   "From this moment forth, your final fate will depend on the true intentions of your mission for Germany. . .Goodbye Miss Haygood."

Shocked by the rational and levelheaded reaction of the Prime Minister, Trixey attempted to get his attention one last time before he closed the door on her.

"Prime Minister, again I thank you from my own heart for your decision. I wish God Speed to You, Great Britain, and all the young men out there that may not lose their lives, if this event comes to pass. Goodbye, Minister, you are a truly a great and compassionate man."

Without turning to face her or responding, he closed the door leaving her by herself in the deepest emotional vacuum of her entire youthful life.

Trixey was outside the CSP, in less than ten minutes as she heard Big Ben's deep reverberations signaling the Five PM hour. She felt a deep sense of personal loss as her eyes continued to remain moist from the experience while at the same time an overwhelming sense of relief overtook her, now that her revelation and primary task was concluded.

It was now up to the unknown people on that B-17, whoever they would be, to take this opportunity to the next level and achieve the even greater goal of ending the war. She was on her own to complete the mission and her first stop would be Croydon to get her suitcase packed and to close-up the flat one last time.

If anything, Trixey was always efficient in her personal affairs as well as her work, and for all she knew, she would possibly be spending the next several years in a women's prison for treasonous crimes in a time of war against the British Crown.

As for her belongings, they would have to be stored in a long term place, and that place was in Sussex, where by 2345 Hours tonight the final dye would be cast in the next to last act of this seemingly unending day.

Chapter 8

Flight of the Valkyries

Admiral Wilhelm Canaris had fallen ill that evening and was not in the secure transmission bunker when the message was received just before midnight, from agent Sherezade. The SS-Gruppenfuhrer was immediately notified of the event and he rushed with the translation, in hand, to his Staff Planning Room to locate the airfield indicated in the coded document.

His chief pilot, Luftwaffe Major Knut Grimstad and his second officer, Luftwaffe Ace Hauptmann Dietrich Clausen, were already there, reviewing fuel arrangements for the modified American B-17, as Horst entered the room.

"It's Northolt," Horst stated as he walked purposefully to the Map and without hesitation pointed to a red circled area just west of downtown London.

"That's the busiest airfield in the British realm at this moment, but we know the US 8th Air Force has their hands full at their own bases up in the North of England, so we are clearly going to be the only B-17 in the sky anywhere near London tomorrow, with clearance to land."

Horst looked over his shoulder at his two experts now going over the English translations of specifications on the big American workhorse bomber.

"So, what do you both think of our captured Flying Fortress, as they call it?" Horst said, as he broke their focused concentration.

"Herr Gruppenfuhrer, the KG-A plane we now have is probably the best example of this bomber we have ever recovered."

"It's their latest B-17G with four American R-1820-97 Wright Cyclone nine-cylinder radial engines and their latest exhaust driven turbochargers. They'll generate over twelve-hundred horsepower per engine."

Horst responded almost unimpressed.

"Yes Strumbannfuhrer, but how fast can you get me there, how long will it take, and how much fuel do we need?"

Instantly another voice answered for the Major.

It was Dietrich Clausen, standing upright impressively with his baggy Luftwaffe-style pants and his Ace Luftwaffe Pilot emblem sporting his Iron Cross 1st and 2nd Class above his pocket, while his recently awarded Second Knight's Cross hung around his collar.

"Herr Kommandant, the normal fuel load I have worked with on this bomber is two-thousand five-hundred and twenty US gallons, but your bird has extra fuel tanks which have raised its total fuel capacity another one-thousand gallons. The range to your target at Northolt is only five-hundred and sixty-six nautical miles from our base here at Sangerhausen. Even if we had a bomb load of four-thousand pounds, we could make that range with less than nine-hundred gallons cruising at two-hundred and thirty-eight mph at an average altitude of twenty-five thousand feet. Our time to target at Northolt is two hours and forty eight minutes."

Horst Deeke did not want to offend the young expert, but he needed to make certain things clear, as he paused, then cleared his throat with a growl to speak. . .

"Thank you, Clausen, but I must make both of you perfectly clear on this issue. That is, we will not refer to Northolt as a 'target'. We will be on a mission to save the remaining embers of our beloved Reich."

"And for us, Northolt may well be our final commitment to Germany's future and the ultimate safety of your family members."

Horst then added his own ideas of what would happen . . .

"I'm quite sure, Gentleman, they will probably have some Spitfires on station, to escort us in, once we cross the channel over Dover and they've confirmed that Northolt is our radar vector destination."

Horst turned to his pilot Major Grimstad, as he questioned him. "Knut, what's the normal flight crew size for ferrying that plane in from the US to England?"

Major Grimstad spoke as if he knew exactly where Horst was going with his next thought. "This plane can be flown by a crew of four at the very least, but five would be preferred, Herr Deeke."

Then he added, "In that group would be Dietrich and myself, a flight engineer, a navigator, and a back up cross function engineer, radio controller and navigator. This would assume of course, Herr Deeke, that no tactical action would be necessary by the crew and that the plane would be essentially in a neutral battle condition."

"With all due respect, Herr Kommandant," the young Ace, interrupted. "If you really wanted to neutralize that B-17G sitting out there at our Flughafen for the benefit of the Allies, it would take us over ten hours to gut the thirteen separate Browning Machine Gun emplacements and remove its complete Norden sighting gear."

Horst walked to the table where both men were now standing. "To be very honest with you both," he said, "I don't think it would be in our best interests to let the British think we were armed.

But realistically, the Flying Fortress is a warplane and must at least appear outwardly as if it is fully functional. Therefore, just get rid of the Norden Bombsighting gear, Herr Clausen, and leave the Machine guns in place.

That way if we are sighted by another American Bomber, we would look as though we had injured personnel on board and our gun emplacements were not manned."

Then adding his final comment, but not needing the obvious answer, Horst Deeke spoke again. "Besides, most bombardiers remove their Norden sighting units when they finish their missions, don't they?"

It was a redundant question because the Norden bombsights were one of the most closely guarded classified US technologies, during World War II. The bombsights were the sole responsibility of the B-17 bombardiers, and to a man, they committed to an Oath to guard them with their life.

It had been invented by an American genius named Carl Norden using an array of complex mechanical gyros, motors, gears, mirrors, levers and a telescope to create a sophisticated analog computer.

The bombsight could determine exactly when to drop the bombs from the belly of the B-17 moving at over two-hundred mph in order to precisely hit their ground targets. The version, clandestinely placed into Horst's B-17G, could actually fly the plane through an entire high altitude bombing run, while accurately hitting the fifty yard-line of a football field from four miles up with each bomb-group release.

Luftwaffe Major Grimstad spoke finally in response, more directly to Dietrich than his Commander Horst Deeke.

"What the SS-Gruppenfuhrer is suggesting Herr Hauptmann, is that should the British take us as prisoners of war, it could never be said that we had any intention of bombing or attacking anyone in England, yet we will all be in the proper military uniform of German soldier. Therefore the Geneva Rules should prevail over our mission even though we using an American B-17 for our surrender. Am I correct, Herr Deeke?"

Horst nodded agreement, as they then went over the final details of their flight plan. D-hour was set for 0700 Hours GMT and as much information about the technical aspects of the Nazi Super Bomb as possible had to be provided by Werner Heisenberg's scientists in case Churchill brought in some of his Tube Alloy's people to verify the truth of their claims.

Within about three hours they were ready at the Flughafen's command post making final flight checks on the bomber and loading the last of Herr Deeke's precious Napoleonic Library and scientific data into the belly of the plane. The four-thousand-pound bomb load had been replaced with Horst's personal effects and that of some of his four crewmembers.

Soon they would all join the few other lucky German POWs that would wait out the final hours of WWII on British soil.

At 0655 Hours GMT and 0755 Hours-Sangerhausen, it's moment of departure from the hanger, SS-Gruppenfuhrer's B-17G Flying Fortress the newly named 'Lady Sherezade' weighed in at over twenty-two tons. The plane carried only two-thousand gallons of aviation fuel, however, as it's command pilot, Major Grimstad taxied the massive plane to the end of the six-thousand foot runway.

Each of the four crewmembers and the SS-Gruppenfuhrer had been given nondescript gray flight suites to wear over their cumbersome Luftwaffe and SS-Wiking dress uniforms, on which they wore their rank and all their war ribbons, insignia, and medals in place.

As he looked out over Knut's shoulder through the bulletproof plexiglas windshield, Horst was please to see that an overcast had cleared from the night sky and a soft light was developing in the high clouds to the east.

The young Ace, Clausen then did a communications check with the command tower in a distinct American Midwestern drawl that sounded more like an East Texas Cattle Rancher, than an officer of the US Army's 8th Air Corps.

But for all that bravado, Horst thought he was quite convincing in adding to the possibility of their success. Particularly, if they were challenged by American or British tactical fighters on their flight over Allied France and the English Channel. Knut then turned the big bird into to a ten-knot headwind and set the brakes as he brought up the RPM's and manifold pressures on the four Wright Cyclone engines together pounding out an incredible four-thousand horsepower.

Carefully, he eased off the brakes, while the massive torque thrust began to pull the plane to the left of the runway as it began to pick-up speed.

Quickly the young Ace reminded Knut, "Don't brake those right wheels, Captain." Clausen, with many more hours in the B-17 than Knut, adjusted the yaw effect by leading with the left engine throttles. He advanced them ahead of the two right engines and instantly they were again down the middle of the runway at about eighty mph, as he spoke in his Texan style drawl.

"Okay Captain, you've got full rudder control now, I'll bring em all up to full throttle, on my mark. Now Captain!" Suddenly, a perfectly harmonized roar deafened all sound in the cabin. All four Wright Cyclone engines were now at four-thousand eight-hundred horsepower with full manifold pressures driving the plane into the wind at over one-hundred and twenty-mph.

With expert ease, Knut pulled back the yoke of the giant bomber, as it rotated off the runway with at least eighteen hundred feet to spare.

Sangerhausen and the beautiful Norwegian Pines hiding the mysterious Chateau disappeared quickly beneath the B-17's huge wingspan. They were soon climbing fast into a black sky, and flying west to an unknown destiny, a dream of great men and the ultimate fear of dangerous men.

Incredibly, Sangerhausen was on the same longitude as London so dead reckoning was a snap, as their navigator Luftwaffe Hauptmann Hans Senkelmann gazed up into the empty overhead gun mount.

Their climb out had been uneventful for the last ten minutes until the sudden rush of two high-speed engines whining in a dive caught Horst's attention. Even the weight of the B-17G couldn't prevent it from rocking as their turbulence disturbed the Fortress's right wing vacuum.

To Horst, and his two pilots, the sound was unmistakable, it was two Me-109s from the forward protection squadron at Kassel. Hauptmann Senkelmann jumped into the gunner's seat in the Plexiglas bubble and turned to see where they were, hoping they wouldn't waste their precious ammo on a loan bird returning to England, but it wasn't to be.

Horst got on his mike and called to Knut to give if full throttle so they could possibly outrun them as they climbed up to their planned cruising altitude of twenty-five thousand feet.

Again, the Hauptmann rotated the gun mount and charged the Browning machine guns as Horst arranged the ammo belt for maximum continuous fire.

Below on the open plains of Germany a low cloud cover had blanketed the earth as far west as the edge of the Rhine Valley at Cologne, then as if the wind was pushing it out, it appeared clear all the way to Antwerp and the Netherlands.

Again the familiar high-speed whine grew louder as one of the two planes began firing. Horst knew that some of those rounds were bound to hit his beast, but the B-17G was armored and probably the most formidable battle wagon in the war.

It was well known that even fighters had a hard time equaling the shoot down scores of B-17s which often could single handedly, take out as many as eleven on a bomb run.

But today, this B-17 had no tail, belly, or waist gunners, so they were easy game for the Luftwaffe's last remaining squadron swarming around them.

Just then, the sounds of bullets thudding against metal and breaking plexiglas broke the roar of their own engines. A gush of air seemed to flow in from the tail section and up to the cockpit as Knut angled the Lady Sherezade to avoid being a perfect target in the apparent turkey-shoot taking place outside.

As the lead Me-109 zoomed past his position, Hauptmann Senkelmann fired a continuous burst at its wing and something hit as he yelled,

" I got him in the right wing section, Herr Deeke. That should even the score and make them think again before making another run on us." And so it was, Knut noised down just enough to see that both fighters now running for the lower deck and cloud cover, at about seven-thousand feet.

By now the armored Lady was back to just under twenty-two thousand feet and the time clock was projecting 1012 Hours GMT for their touchdown, at Northolt.

Jumping up with his oxygen canister in hand, Horst climbed back to the tail section to survey the damage.

All of Knut's gauges were reading normal, so they were sure the only problem was the tail gunner bubble.

Those guys always had a rough time because once they were locked in, they were there for the duration of the bomb run. The only less desirable spot was the belly gunner. If the landing gear was out, with no escape route, he was often crushed on belly landings.

They had been cruising at twenty-five thousand feet for over an hour when Knut and the navigator decided to adjust the glide path. Planning to enter the channel zone at about ten-thousand feet, they flew in over Oostende, Belgium and crossed to Ramsgate as they followed the Thames estuary inland.

The objective was to keep the Mouth of the Thames to their Starboard side as they vectored into Northolt. That way there would be no doubt on British Radar where they were heading. If the Brit's planned an escort, Horst and Knut knew they would show up just before the point of Dover near Ramsgate.

Suddenly, as they lowered the bird to the twelve-thousand foot mark on their glide slope, a new and more powerful roaring sound broke Horst's concentration as their Americanized Luftwaffe Ace Clausen, yelled back to him. "That was one of the newer American P-51 fighters from the Squadron at Zeebrugge, Herr Deeke."

"Do you think I should make contact with him just to keep things smooth as 'city slickers', as they say in East Texas?"

Horst responded with a sense of urgency, "Yes. . . yes, get him under control at once and tell him we were shot up."

"Have him check your tail section to see if there's any rudder damage."

The AAF fighter's frequencies had already been logged in by Hauptmann Senkelmann as Clausen, now US Army Air Force Captain Claude Jones adjusted his throat mike and headset as he began to play his role.

"This is #273 - Heavy, out of the 388th Bomb Wing. . . we're shot up bad and need some damage surveillance. . . can you help us Little Man?"

Instantly, an equally foreign voice came over his headset as the P-51 flew in beside them and waved. "Shau nuff, looks like I'm taking to the Little Boss of the Lady Sher..rah..za..dah, the fighter pilot said in a typical Carolina Mountain drawl." Where you from Little Boss. . . out west someplace?"

"Beaumont, Texas, Little Man, how bout yawl?" Clausen added with a little extra twang in his voice.

Without warning, a second voice entered the radio transmission frequency. "Okay you guys, this is a tactical fighter frequency, get to know each other back on the ground. Break off and clear, over!"

At that moment, the squadron ground controller at Zeebrugge, Belgium silenced their friendly banter and the P-51 Mustang slid around to the aft section just above the B-17's slipstream and took a look.

"One final, Little Boss, your ailerons and tail section are fine, but you've got some nasty damage in that tail gunner's bubble, I can't see em, so he must have fallen out when they took out his position. I hope he got his chute open in time. Sorry bout that Luck, signing off now, Good Luck Texas!"

"Good Luck, Tar Boy," Clausen added for good measure.

The P-51 then peeled off and hit at least three-hundred and seventy mph in a quick dive to the deck just over the Western Channel.

As the B-17G dropped down to within five-thousand feet it began it's crossing to Ramsgate where it would enter British airspace.

After that exchange, the Luftwaffe Ace Clausen, timidly added his comments to Horst. "Sorry, I had to sound so damn American, Herr Kommandant, but the performance on those new P-51's is incredible and we didn't want him to get suspicious."

Horst replied back into Clausen's headset. "Good work, Herr Clausen, I actually met the man that got the first order on those Mustangs, as the British first called them, back in 1940."

His family was from Germany and he visited a German aircraft factory in Leipzig, looking over the fast production methods that Messerschmitt was using on our Me-109s.

Last September, my SSI team in the US provided specs on that plane because they had a coastal patrol version looking for our U-boats off the Virginia coastline.

That version of the P-51H he was flying can eat up anything in the sky up to forty-one thousand feet. He was actually just playing with us, when he peeled off and dove down to the deck. With that newer Rolls Royce Merlin V-12 at full out, that thing can hit four-hundred and fifty mph in a controlled dive."

"And they weigh in at four-thousand pounds heavier than our newest Me-109s, so they can effectively dive in under our planes, turn around and come back to meet us face to face, before we make it to cloud cover on the deck."

"So it was really the Brit's that ordered the P-51s in the first place, Mein Kommandant?"

Clausen commented as the command pilot, Grimstad cleared his voice loudly into his throat mike and interrupted.

"Just as you guessed, Herr Deeke, we've got company now at 11 and 2 o'clock straight ahead."

Horst leaned over the shoulders of Knut as he saw the tail insignia of two camouflaged British Spitfires hovering at about one-thousand yards forward and above the B-17's plexiglas nose, running at just about their own air speed of one-hundred and ninety mph. "How should we make contact, Herr Deeke?" Knut exclaimed with some hesitation.

"We shouldn't," the Horst commanded forcefully. "I'm sure they have already monitored our last communication with that American P-51 pilot and wouldn't expect us to say anything to them in our natural language that might spill the beans, so to say."

The SS-Gruppenfuhrer again checked the altitude and navigation charts then turned back to Knut. "I would expect them to peel off the moment we have aligned for our final on Northolt."

At that moment, the Northolt tower controller made a radio check using the previous frequency they had been on.

"This is Northolt Tower - RAF One, do you copy, #273? "

"Repeat, do you copy?"

"Okay, give it back to Clausen, excuse me, US Army Air Force Captain Claude Jones," Horst ordered, as he again adjusted his throat mike and headset.

Clausen again took up his role and keyed his transmission mike.

"This is #273 - Heavy. We copy, over. I repeat, we copy, over."

The Northolt tower controller then made an urgent order change. "#273 - Heavy, squawk frequency 129.825, RAF-One Northolt Airlift Command, Repeat, squawk frequency 129.825, do you copy?"

Immediately their radio expert and navigator Hauptmann Senkelmann had the new frequency dialed in as Clausen waited for his hand signal.

Clausen then keyed his mike again and transmitted.

"Request landing and wind coordinates, we are shot up badly and need immediate priority ground clearance, locate Hanger #9? Repeat, locate Hanger #9, Over?"

There was nothing but silence as the big plane began to lower into position vectoring along the river Thames while building roofs and a railway depot zoomed under the lowering bird.

They were only thirteen minutes to touchdown according to Senkelmann, and Knut had his hands full going through the landing drill with Clausen as he spoke.

"Flaps twenty."

"Jawohl," Clausen confirmed as the 'Lady' descended smoothly into the glide path of Northolt's main one-and-a-half mile runway.

Then the exact coordinates, wind vectors, and wind speed came over the headsets from the tower.

A moment later Northolt added, "#273 - Heavy, you are clear to land runway, Three-North. Taxi clear at first opportunity, go to Hanger #9 at South end of main facilities, and Hold for boarding. . .Repeat, Hanger #9 and Hold for boarding.

"Roger that tower. Clear for runway, Three-North. Taxi to Hanger # 9 and Hold for boarding, Over." Strumbannfuhrer Clausen confirmed back to the tower, as he increased the engine revs with a balance of hand control on the throttles for Knut's approach.

With flaps down, he was carefully slowing the Fortress to one-hundred-seventy mph.

Horst could still see the outlines of Big Ben and Parliament in the far distance to the Northeast as well as some church spires, but nothing of St. Paul's Cathedral was apparently standing, as the silver serpentine of the Thames River below the great bird's wings got closer.

For a moment he reminisced of Heidi and her friend Crystale as the English countryside became a blur under their fuselage, this had truly been the Flight of his Valkyries and he hoped they would somehow see each other again after all the insanity had ended, as he wondered if his own luck would hold out in this desperate mission?

Everyone again checked their safety harnesses as the groaning sound of hydraulics under the wings signaled that Clausen had set the landing gear while he methodically announced events to Knut.

" Wheels down," Clausen checked his lights, "All Green, gear locked, radiators on all engines closed."

They could see the mass of bright green marker lights glowing up from the wide concrete runway as Horst strained to watch through the nose canopy.

The center guide-line was gently coming up to meet them as Knut called out, "Full flaps," and worked his yoke as the nose of the beautiful 'Lady' lifted and he expertly adjusted his trimming knobs, as again he commanded.

"Height and ground speed, bitte, Herr Clausen?"

Clausen had been through the drill many times, but somehow he knew this would be his last flight in one of these great birds, so he called out each increment for Knut with a sense of the true flying spirit, "Jawohl,. . . . . One-Hundred - feet. . .150 - mph,

Eighty. . .120, Sixty. . .110, Forty . . .95, throttles full back,"

then a moment later Clausen announced,

"touchdown, Mein Kommandant, at 1019 Hours GMT."

Both wheels touched at the same moment and the graceful bird was down rolling to a stop within twenty-two-hundred feet from where the wheel marks touched the runway.

Each of them began to look around for signs of activity as Clausen spotted the large number nine, circled in red paint almost like the British RAF Bulls-Eye Insignia on the side of a hanger near a row of Quonset huts.

There parked beside the huts which looked like either flight barracks or operation shacks for one of the Spitfire Squadrons, was a row of military vehicles and several soldiers holding machine guns while guarding the entrance to one of the huts.

Quonset huts had been a mainstay for shelters during most of the build up in England since 1942. Their design used a skeleton of semi-circular steel frames placed in a rib-like configuration, then covered with corrugated sheet metal. The steel ribs mounted on a low steel-frame foundation with a plywood floor gave each hut about twenty feet of width and forty-eight feet of length. Because of the curvature, each small building had only about seven-hundred square feet of usable floor space, but the advantage was that these buildings could be set up or removed quickly in any field of combat, at a very lost cost.

Knut taxied to the first off-ramp and stopped behind a small Military Lorry with an RAF Insignia, blocking their path. At least two SAS soldiers were inside, and one emerged and signaled for the B-17 to follow them.

Again, he revved-up the two in-board engines and the big bird lumbered behind the Lorry until they were lined up with the open hanger entrance.

A signal from the leading SAS soldier convinced Knut to cut the engines.

Once the blades were still, they hooked the B-17 up to the Lorry and pulled it slowly with the crew inside, deep into the hanger well.

Horst and his crew could see the bright overhead lights coming on and in the background hear the massive doors being closed as the sound of stampeding boots seemed to engulf the concrete floor beneath the plane.

At that point, about twenty armed SAS troops could be seen surrounding the entire B-17G, as an SAS Officer came forward with a bull horn and began shouting commands toward the nose canopy, in German and English.

"Achtung! . . Attention!"

"Ab die Bombenflugzeug, nun jetzt! . . .Exit the Bomber, now!"

"Steigern ihrer Hände, hinein die auslüften! . . . Raise your hands, above your head!"

The crew began to emerge, removing their flight suits before they exited from the cockpit hatch on the B-17's forward belly and leaving them in the plane.

One by one, each of them looked around, raised their hands, and walked as instructed by their captors toward a small office that looked back into the gigantic hanger at the now silent Lady Sherezade.

Once all five of them were accounted for, a team of Special SAS soldiers climbed up the access ladder into the big bird and began a detailed search and documentation of the remaining items left on board.

For his crew, this flight and the war were now over. But for Horst, his true mission and his ultimate ordeal had just begun, and with very little time left, only he knew how to see it through to its final ending.

Chapter 9

Northolt

Looking tired and somewhat haggard from the all night effort to secure her facilities in Sussex, Trixey Haygood had arrived at the first of several Northolt Security Checkpoint booths, a few minutes before 0900 Hours GMT Monday morning.

The defense system at Northolt airfield was normally on high alert, but today it was at the top designation level, due to the dignitaries that would soon be departing for the British Island of Malta, and later on the Three Conference at Yalta, deep in the Crimea along the Black Sea of Russia.

Work had begun as far back as February 1943 to extend both of Northolt's runways in preparation for the creation of the RAF's Main Transport Command. It's three Spitfire Wings became the first to operate as RAF Bomber support and tactical combat units over Germany that same year.

Then, because of it's close proximity to the London Operations Headquarters, MI5 and MI6 Espionage Units began placing operatives from flights out of Northolt. Even primary SAS and RAF Tactical and Photographic Reconnaissance Squadrons were regularly using Northolt. More recently, in last few months of 1944, the completion of the new runway, Three-North, made Northolt into London's main wartime airport and the Air Defense Command Center of Great Britain.

Trixey had been cleared quickly with her 'Most Secret' designation, through the first two entry checks of RAF Guards and Royal Marine Sentries, temporarily attached to the Base.

But as she got to her next gate, she was immediately stopped by one of the P.M.'s Provosts who recognized her ID.

She was then loaded in the back, and whisked away in a windowless RAF Transport Lorry with two SAS soldiers armed with Stens, guarding her.

Trixey knew this was her last trip as a free woman. Wherever it was that they were taking her, deep inside Northolt's Command facilities, would signal the end of her final mission.

Several layers of reinforced concrete and steel fortified the bombproof strategic planning room of Northolt's Spitfire Regiment, hidden beneath a Quonset hut next to Hanger #9.

At the ground level entrance of the Quonset Hut, several SAS Commandos holding Sten sub-machine guns were on guard.

Three floors below them, Winston Churchill, the Prime Minister of Great Britain sat in an austere wooden arm chair at the end of the Regiment's strategic planning table appearing somewhat melancholy as he looked around at the staff of officers and an unnamed MI5 Director coded only as M and seated at the opposite end of the table.

An SAS officer carefully entered the silent room and announced, "They've landed, Sir."

Instantly, everyone became animated except for Churchill, as he addressed M indignantly.

"So what does the American OSS and your people have on the Nazi's KG-A operation and that rebuilt B-17 out there, M?"

M rose from his equally austere chair and walked to the Map Wall located behind the P.M..

Churchill turned to observe him as he began to talk and pointed to locations on the Map.

"As you may remember, from my memos in 43, their so called KG-A Gruppe was a massive salvage operation run from about ten clandestine Nazi Luftwaffe bases shown here in various parts of Europe." He then pointed to a base near the coast in southern Norway, Stavanger-Sola, as he added.

"They seemed to have a preponderance of newer B-17E and G versions, plus special Luftwaffe pilots trained to both flight test these planes and to later on, infiltrate American bomber formations returning to England. And that's how they got here Minister, the question is can they deliver a true Unconditional Surrender or are they merely circumventing Hitler and turning Nazi SS and Wehrmacht Divisions in the Western Rhineland into immediate POWs?"

The Prime Minister incensed at his superficial remark, jumped up and faced off with M, cutting off his next comment.

"Good God man, don't you have any sense of where I'm going in the next forty-eight hours. I intend to position Britain in a situation of strength against Stalin, not weakness. Even if this German Agent can only give me control of the two-hundred-mile front, up to the doors of Berlin, we will still be in a better position to protect Europe from a future of absolute Communist domination."

"Uncle Joe, is still the next most dangerous man on the continent, and if President Roosevelt pulls American troops out to fight Japan for the next four years, we will be the only wall against Bolshevism's potential domination of Europe. For that, we had jolly well better have as much of Germany in our hands, before Yalta, then after."

Then without taking a breath he added.

"Without any new negotiation card in my hand, I will have to sit there and watch Germany cut up into four sectors, one of which, the bloody French Sector, will be a jolly good joke to start with.

They will be fortified for less than six months, before General de Gaulle pulls them back to Paris on some economic excuse or political ploy."

Changing directions to return to a more relaxed tone, the P.M. decided to play on M's favorite French derogatory.

"Besides the 'Frogs' are broke, they have no army, and only their wine, cheese, and narcissistic honor really matters to them, as throughout their sordid history it always has."

Laughter and a loud cheer came from the Staff officers as M joined in.

"Here, here, jolly well right, Prime Minister"

Churchill then contained himself as he smiled in agreement with their support.

"So my friends, bring me their commander, after he is thoroughly searched. And bring him with, whatever documents he needs to show me."

The P.M. then turned to the MI5 Director, " M, you're with me until he gets here."

"And, Major Darwin you remain in here, with your two best, just outside. Nothing goes beyond this room, until I've had a go at him, is that clear everyone?"

To a man, they all responded in the P.M.'s favorite naval jargon, "Aye, aye, Sir!"

The SAS and Royal Marine Staff Officers filed out and began the next phase of interrogation on the German B-17 crew, now lined up against a wall in the Hanger #9 Flight Operations office.

Churchill then looked at Major Darwin, "Major, I want you to get someone upstairs to locate that CSP clerk, Trixey Haygood and place her in one of the nearby regiment staff offices, under guard of course."

Then he added thoughtfully, "No interrogation, please. I want to speak to her myself, before all this starts."

Major Darwin bellowed back respectfully, "Yes, S'ah, Minister."

A Royal Air Force special maintenance team had gone over the B-17G in about twenty minutes, checking for hidden doors, and possible booby traps or bombs planted anywhere on the plane.

Simultaneously, several SAS commandos and maintenance personnel unloaded the almost four-thousand pounds of private crew gear and the containers belonging to the Kommandant of Germany's Schutzstaffel Infiltration, including Horst Deeke's Napoleonic Library.

Within that gear they found a large black briefcase with the Kommandant's initials and the Dragons Head emblem of SS-Wiking emblazoned between it's top opening latches.

Following the P.M.'s strict instructions relating to possessions of Enemy Officers involved in an Act of Surrender; they then asked the German Commander himself to step outside and open the briefcase to insure that no bombs or sidearms were in it.

Once the initial interrogation was complete, Horst was then escorted outside to the entrance of the Quonset Hut by two SAS Commandos and an Officer of the P.M.'s Royal Marine Detachment.

It was close to 1115 Hours GMT in the morning, before SS-Gruppenfuhrer Horst Deeke was brought into the makeshift "Surrender" facilities three stories underground in the RAF Regiment's strategic planning room.

Major Darwin bellowed their arrival announcement as he pushed open the metal bombproof door,

"S'ah, Mr. Prime Minister, I bring you the Commandant of German SSI, Left 'tenant-General Horst Deeke."

"General," the Prime Minister spoke first in a moderately formal manner, "I trust that our methods were not too indignant for you, and that you were not personally offended by our security procedures?"

"No, not at all Prime Minister," Horst responded somewhat relaxed in perfectly enunciated English, as he carefully eyed the room's layout and those present.

"On the contrary, Prime Minister, I must say that as an officer and trainer of the finest Military Units in Germany, I was quite impressed with the thoroughness and professionalism of your SAS and Royal Marine Units."

Almost as if he expected Horst's recognition of his men, the P.M. added.

"Rather good they are, those chaps, the finest Special Commandos Unit in the Imperial Realm, General."

"Now, not to be too pressing, General, I have a plane to catch within the next two hours, so I suggest you have a seat," then somewhat unexpected, the P.M. turned to Major Darwin.

"Major, see to those shackles, so the General here can remain comfortable round our table whilst we talk."

Major Darwin again barked his response, "S'ah, yes S'ah, Minister," as one of his SAS Guards was directed to remove the leg irons around Horst's ankles, then he handed the SS-Gruppenfuhrer Deeke's Black Briefcase to the Major.

Now seated in silent observation, they all faced one another at three of the four quadrants of the table in the well-worn wooden armchairs; the P.M., MI5 Director M, and the SS-Gruppenfuhrer Horst Deeke.

"Shall we begin, then General," the P.M. announced as he indicated to Major Darwin to place the briefcase in front of the German General.

SS-Gruppenfuhrer Horst Deeke had mentally rehearsed this moment over and over in his mind. For the last twenty-four hours it was all he could think about, but he never expected it to become as difficult, as it now was.

These people were clearly and hopefully expecting a trump card. A card to play against the other Allies in some up-coming event, now that Germany was on her knees. Their minds were primed, but their patience was surely very fragile, and what he was about to tell them could very easily backfire, resulting in absolute doom for das Vaterland and his mission. Should he flow with his formal approach, or just open up as honestly as possible, and place his life at the mercy of this eternally optimistic man, the true savior of Great Britain.

Horst remembered that the Admiral clearly stated that Churchill always desired as much of the truth or background of a situation as he could get, in any encounter or debate, even if it meant a partial delay in the presentation of the final elements of a course of action.
Churchill liked the concept of 'the process' as much as he liked getting the final results, either good or bad, according to Canaris.

The process was of utmost importance to the Prime Minister and Horst had to somehow use that, to get to where he needed to. That was going to be his approach as he opened with his initial comment.

"Prime Minister, before I expose this briefcase and reveal it's entire contents to you, I must be sure that everyone in this room has your highest level of personal confidence and the highest level of security clearance in your government."

"You can be sure of that, General. This man seated and the others with me here are privy to the uppermost security and paramount covert knowledge, in the realm of England."

"And, what you say here today, stays with us until 'only I choose' to disseminate that information to others. If that is confidence enough, General, then lets get on with this."

The P.M. reiterated, as he seemed somewhat perplexed at the man's preliminaries for an Unconditional Surrender.

"That I shall, Prime Minister," The SS-Gruppenfuhrer Horst Deeke said as he mentally supercharged his mind to begin his methodical presentation of a believable set of events resulting in the more incredible creation of Nazi Germany's Super Bomb, now only short hours away from detonation somewhere in England.

"My role, for the past seven-and-a-half years as the Kommandant of SSI and SS-Wiking was created exclusively by the SS-Reichsfuhrer Heinrich Himmler and sanctioned personally by das Fuhrer himself." Horst began to feel confident he was using the right approach, once he could see that everyone in the room was now focused on his next revelation.

"First, I had sole control over SSI, a separate and independent agent network from Admiral Canaris' Abwehr spy network."

Churchill interrupted briefly and directed a question to the MI5 Director.

"I say then, M," you could hear the drop of a pin as silence held each man in suspense of what was about to be asked, "are you aware of this SSI group?"

"Ah yes, Minister, but only from FBI and OSS re-routes that have just recently arrived, and specifically within the last several months.

I believe, the recent Zodiac memo to you from OSS has a critical issue relating to SSI in it."

Churchill paused. Then remembering cryptically, but with a growing sense of concern in his voice, redirected cautiously back to the General. "Yes, yes, of course Zodiac."

" Well then, carry on, General Deeke."

Horst picked-up where he left off, now with an obvious tension building on the face of the P.M., yet the others just like spies, concealed their emotions, as he again spoke.

" You see, Prime Minister, the SSI network was trained within my own SS-Wiking Units in Germany as far back as 1939."

"Schutzstaffel Infiltration was actually an ultra-secret espionage group that I personally selected from specialists within the Waffen - SS and my own Division SS-Viking Units. Our objective was to clandestinely repatriate or more specifically kidnap nuclear scientists from Denmark, Belgium, France, and America.

Suddenly a chill seemed to cause Churchill to shudder overtly, as he again looked toward his MI5 Director with a serious sense of irritation in his eyes. Churchill, then without facing the SS-Gruppenfuhrer Horst Deeke, bored a visual hole into the forehead of M as he inquired of Horst.

"So then General, are you aware of our SAS and Lancaster bombing raid against Vemork?"

The P.M. knew full well what the answer would be based on the obvious direction the German General was taking. Why else would he be here now?

But Churchill's rage and his emphasis were clearly directed to M.

It was he, who after the final raid on Vemork, Norway in early 1944, had assured Churchill that Germany would never be able to mount a nuclear program against Britain or anyone else for that matter, ever again.

The SS-Gruppenfuhrer knew he had them now. But he also remembered, as the Admiral had advised him, use the process and fill it full of explanation. That was the all-important key to any negotiation or acceptance by Churchill.

"Yes, very much so, Prime Minister," Horst said, then he added.

"In fact that raid on the Hydro Plant at Vemork, and the follow-up by your partisan Norwegian SAS Units, when they sunk the Ferry at Lake Tinnsjo with over six-hundred kilos of Heavy Water bound for our U-235 refinement program, was excellently executed and of course a stroke of luck as well." He paused briefly. . .

"However, Prime Minister, it was truly the turning point for Germany in modifying the final direction of our nuclear program. And, as I look back now, it was probably the worst thing that could have happened."

Now listening intensely, Churchill at once reacted. "And why, would that be so, General?" Churchill had a perplexed look on his face and was hoping that a full disclosure would follow his question.

Everyone in the room was now beginning to realize that this surprise arrival by General Deeke and his crew in a stolen B-17G, was probably not an attempt to give up Germany in an Unconditional Surrender.

Churchill had always feared a German nuclear threat. That's why Vemork was such a high SAS priority. That success was critical to England's safety in Churchill's mind.

Now, with General Deeke's arrival, Churchill could see German technology developing a potential nuclear device using the V-1 or the V-2 rockets against London.

This new situation would recreate the greatest single source of paranoia that had ever existed in Britain's War Cabinet, since the nuclear project became feasible in 1942. It was then, that most of Britain's scientific braintrust had been relocated to America's Nuclear Bomb project at Los Alamos.

Churchill and his staff were silent as they listened to every word.

"At first," the Horst began, "our head scientist Werner Heisenberg believed that we had to get ahead of the Allies in refining U-235." Horst waited for that thought to reverberate around the room. .

"But as far back as 1939 we had scientists at Cal-Tech in San Francisco observing various nuclear physicists working with Dr. Oppenheimer on Atomic theory. One day, a particular scientist named Edward Teller, probably the single most brilliant quantum mechanics physicist anywhere, defined quite simply what could be done beyond the power of a U-235 Bomb."

Everyone was now silent as Horst added. . ."He described on a blackboard at Cal Tech, for all to see, the formula and description of how a deuterium bomb could be built. It wasn't until you first attacked Vemork in 1943, that we realized we would need another source of heavy water. So we built that source in the German controlled Belgium Congo at a Hydro Electric Dam on the Congo River, originally built by Belgium's Union Miniere.

As you were aware, Union Miniere was a Company controlled by us in 1941 within Nazi occupied Belgium. It was there in the Congo, that we produced over ten tons of highly refined deuterium for our new bomb core."

Churchill again reacted as he looked at M. "I thought we controlled at least forty percent of the stock in Belgium's Union Miniere as well M, what happened there?"

The MI5 Director quickly responded. "The Nazis gutted the plants in Belgium and removed all the purified Uranium U-238 to somewhere in Germany."

"Our British holdings were locked up until the war evolved to a point where British controllers could re-evaluate the Company's remaining holdings. Only the Uranium Mines in the Congo were of any concern to us."

"So what happened to the mines, M?"

The P.M. was becoming more and more repressed as the conversation evolved, but Horst simply sat back and observed as it continued between M and Churchill.

"We briefly reviewed this with you, Minister," M said in his icy and controlled manner, "That was in June of 1940; we had a contingency plan, but it was not until Zodiac pointed out the strategic reserves of Uranium in the Congo that we took any action. That's when we started the 'Insecticide Project', aka Worldwide Uranium Control with General Groves' blessing."

"However, you were not advised on the specific action, and the SA Marines and an SAS team from Northolt successfully sabotaged the Union Miniere Mines in the Congo in January of 1942. The mines are still completely flooded as of this date, Minister."

Almost complete disappointment overcame the P.M. as he again questioned M.

"What about this deuterium? Why did we not blow the dam there, as well?"

"The Nazis were not thought to be using any part of the Congo then."

His methodical mind and knowledge was even beginning to amaze Horst as M added minute details to his comments.

"So, we abandoned all other action there, to concentrate on events in North Africa and Egypt, as you were aware, Minister. Besides, our arrangement with the local tribal elders and partisans required that the Dam stay in place to maintain electricity to Leopoldville.

Without the obvious Uranium assets, the Dam became only a local issue, so it was left untouched. Zodiac never advised us of potential Deuterium production, so we never inspected the dam for a Hydro System."

"Very well then, continue General." Again, Churchill had a sullen look on his face as he waited for more revelations.

Horst continued forcefully, now exposing the enormity of his SSI projects.

"Then, as more of Germany was destroyed by your Allied bombing effort, we finally realized we would be forced to remove a small amount of the needed U235 from both the Y-12 and K-25 facilities once they were fully operational in America."

That caught even Churchill by surprise as the benefit of SSI in America became clear to all of them. . .

"By the end of 1943 we had direct feedback from an operative close to General Groves as well as Dr. Bruckmann on the Oak Ridge Manhattan Project team. . . that Groves' real intention was to create far more U-235 than was needed for either two or three bombs and possibly up to ten, so we made a decision to skim a little at a time from the lower percentage enriched product."

"My God General," added Churchill with an extreme sense of concern, "Your people were up their bumms in Tennessee, deeper than any of my people were up yours, in Germany or much better right here in England."

Horst waited for him to vent his frustration in his joking style, realizing it was time to close the loop. Time was becoming very critical and Horst needed to carefully finalize a plan with Churchill, as he began speaking again.

"Dr. Bruckmann worked out a way, that if he was caught he would just reload the stolen kilos of U-235 and claim it was lower percentage grade, needing a higher level of purity."

"It worked, and he walked out with a total of thirty kilograms under our control on January 5th. That Physicist, Dr, Mort Bruckmann, is now exfiltrated or possibly dead at the hands of SS-Reichfuhrer Himmler's operatives."

Horst now got very serious as he spoke and tried to control the direction of this final phase of explanation. Everyone sensed that he was getting to his decisive conclusion, so no one moved or spoke.

"Prime Minister, this type of bomb needs only a small amount of U235. In reality, the limited amount of U-235 Bruckmann procured could only result in an explosion equal to about a five thousand tons of TNT."

"However, as I said earlier, the course of our efforts changed after the Vemork incident and we became focused on a Thermonuclear Bomb concept using a small core of about twenty-five kilograms of U-235, within a round containment well of eighty kilograms of cryogenically cooled liquid deuterium. . . The bomb is actually triggered when the U-235 core is brought to super critical by a chain reaction.

This is done using a closed cannon device about twenty feet in length. The cannon is packed with cordite and armed to fire a bullet shaped pellet of U-235 at high speed directly into a second mass of U-235, positioned at the dead center of the liquid deuterium well.

The Prime Minister could hold back no longer.

"Okay General, you have my full and complete attention, as I'm sure you had intended you would, when you arrived at Northolt."

"Why in God's name," he questioned, "have you chosen to reveal this to us at this moment, today?"

"And, how can I prove that what you have told us is not a fiction, from your own mind, a theory so to say, and not an actual nuclear. . . uh, thermonuclear bomb?"

As he looked up from the table, Horst took a deep breath and spoke directly into the face of this Great Statesman and Allied Leader. A man that now had both the future's of England and Germany looking him in the face.

"Prime Minister, you and your Director of MI5 have heard me mention several highly classified Allied code terms today. The final one I must add is yours. "

" We must immediately get one of your Tube Alloy's scientists over here to prove that these documents in this briefcase are what I say they are. Then and only then will you be justified to act. You will need to fully understand the massive extent of the absolute horror that is about to happen. . . "

"A horror that I must avert from happening, to forestall you and your Allies from completely annihilating the remainder of my beloved Germany from the face of this planet."

Horst then added, "Werner Heisenberg and every scientist in the German Nuclear program have signed a letter I have here with me today."

"They are to a man, committed to end the Fuhrer's Super Bomb Project and prevent it from ever being used on humans. I myself, as well as all my men have come here today, to betray the Fuhrer and the SS-Reichfuhrer, because we now feel in their final hour of desperation, it is they that have chosen to betray our Aryan Nation and das Vaterland itself."

"The war is over for Germany and we must now try to prevent any further horrors that will force you and America to seek the total elimination of Germany from the face of Europe, forever."

"If this Bomb succeeds, Minister, then my people will die with my entire country and me."

Churchill spoke first, as each man in the room seemed to emerge from a disorienting dream, "Major, what time is the planned departure for Operation Orion?"

Major Darwin snapped to attention, "S'ah, it is now 1230 Hours, departure is scheduled for 1430 Hours, plus or minus thirty minutes, Minister."

The P.M. then barked out more questions. "Director, how quickly could we get Professor Geoffrey Greenewalt over from the 'Insecticide Project' lab? And, of course, would he be the one to verify these documents and give us a direction?"

M looked as though he needed no further convincing, but he yielded to the P.M.'s request with a sense of serious urgency as he spoke.

"Minister, the next closest expert, so to say on these heavy water matters is in Glasgow, so it's my firm inclination to go with Geoffrey for now."

"Besides if this one is as hot as I think, I want this Herr Deeke here on board with my SAS Operatives to squelch it, right off, before it blooms into it's next iteration.

Churchill agreed with him, then directed the Major to act on getting the agreed expert, "Major, have operations dispatch Professor Geoffrey Greenewalt over here from the 'Insecticide Project' lab at Richmond, post haste."

As he sharply complied back to the P.M., "Yes S'ah, Minister, right away." Major Darwin opened the doorway briefly to advise his Master Sergeant of the orders to fetch Greenewalt, then closed the door as he stepped back in, and walked over to the P.M. to stand guard.

The Director of MI5 then turned to Horst Deeke, "Herr Deeke how are they planning to deliver this bomb, anyway, by air or by sea?

"Director, because of the excessive weight of the combination of the eighty kilogram Deuterium container, a cooling system and a massive cannon used as a firing mechanism, it can only be delivered by sea. U-506 was originally selected as the delivery device and was modified in Brest, France in 1943 and then further modified at the Belgium Congo facilities in December 1944. It was then re-named UX-506. The only thing that made sense was using a U-boat, if for no other reason than to acquire the final kilos of U-235 in America, prior to arming the device and delivering it to a seaport in Europe."

"And what is your best estimate of the time left to shut this thing down?" The Director inquired, as at the other end of the table, Churchill seemed distracted by added worries, now that the flight times for the Three Conference were only a short two hours away, and this matter was clearly taking center stage.

Horst again responded as if on cue, "Director, on 26 January, I received a coded communiqué from the Kapitanleutnant of German U-boat X-506. That was the final enigma message they were to transmit once at sea and at least thirty kilometers off the Carolina Coast. Assuming they sailed directly for their primary rendezvous, a Portugese Supply Ship within twenty kilometers east of Dublin in the Irish Sea, they would be ready to activate the bomb around midnight tomorrow night."

M then questioned Horst again, "Herr Deeke why would they take so long at sea, they could cross on the surface in three days, possibly four if they had to submerge for security around Royal Navy or US Destroyers? That would have them at or near Dublin by tonight, would you not agree?"

"Two things must be considered Director; first, their schedule calls for the final assembly of the arming mechanism by scientists from the Supply Freighter, they would wait to make that rendezvous with very little exposure and the work to assemble it could take several hours even in mild seas."

"And, second the U-boat must remain on the surface to activate the bomb, and the massive weight of the firing cannon can cause the U-boat to become unstable at over eight knots in rough seas."

"Actually, the firing system includes mounting the closed cannon barrel assembly onto the stern of the U-boat."

"It's position is over a hatch that holds the bomb well. . . and within that hatch is the U-235 core centered in the well of liquid Deuterium."

Horst then added,

"That well unit completely fills the modified rear torpedo room and it's kept cool by a cryogenic refrigeration unit driven by the U-boat's extra batteries."

"What happens next General Deeke?" the Prime Minister broke in needing a true sense of how long they had in order to prepare for any contingency.

"Minister, their intention is to sail her into the harbor of Liverpool under a flag of surrender. That shouldn't take but a couple of hours from the time the UX-506 leaves the assembly area. Of course, no one would recognize the bomb's firing device, so the Unterseeboot could probably get to within a few kilometers of the center of the main harbor of Liverpool before the bomb detonated."

Horst then added his two final cautions. . .

"Once the firing process has begun however, nothing will be able to stop it. Also, their primary target is merely planned to be Liverpool, and that's not guaranteed to be the final target."

"So you must understand that with radio silence and the fact that the SS-Reichfuhrer personally relieved me of this command on January 15th, it is possible that he has also changed my directives and selected another target."

"The SS-Reichsfuhrer's foremost concern," Horst said, "has always been to protect himself and the Fuhrer from any implication in this matter, by either exfiltrating or possibly assassinating my entire operatives team in America."

"Furthermore," he forewarned, "the crew of the U-boat is not aware of this bomb's potential. So once, the bomb is armed and the sub has surrendered to the Royal Navy, the crew just intends to get off the sub and let it blow-up and sink."

"Their orders are the same as any other Kriegsmarine Crew; protect any Top Secret devices left on board at all costs, even if it means sinking the ship."

"The diabolical bastards!" the Prime Minister injected, as he seemed completely frustrated now, just staring into the overhead lighting.

They continued talking for a further fifteen minutes before another British Officer arrived at the underground Staff room.

Royal Marine, Brigadier Thorpson, the Prime Minister's Chief of Staff entered with little fanfare as he went directly to the P.M. and spoke quietly into his right ear.

His secret conversation confirmed to the P.M. that General Leslie Groves code named 'Zodiac' had sent a memo to President Roosevelt requesting assistance from the P.M. on the Bruckmann affair.

Following that tight-lipped exchange with the P.M., the Brigadier then turned and sat down himself, to hear the expanded comments.

Finally, a disheveled man of about thirty pushed his way into the room with the assistance of a Royal Marine Command Sergeant Major sporting mutton chops and a massive Scottish mustache, waxed at the tips and forking it's auburn color just beyond the lower portion of his mouth.

Horst realizing time was of the essence now, halted his commentary and looked toward the newcomers.

Then, recognizing his lead-in, the Royal Marine Command Sergeant Major announced the new arrival with vehemence in his powerful voice.

"S'ah, Mr. Prime Minister, Gentlemen, I present you Professor Geoffrey Greenewalt of His Majesty's St. James University at Richmond."

The diminutive man with a bushy tangle of brown hair spreading almost to his shoulders was a mathematical genius, besides being a nuclear physicist.

At the age of eight, Greenewalt could multiply six digit numbers casually in his head and became the center of parlor parties at his parent's home in Colchester.

His past background included extensive studies with Niels Bohr in Denmark and more recently with Enrico Fermi in a joint project at an American Nuclear Lab at the University of Chicago.

Now, it was up to him to quickly analyze for the first time by any Allied Scientist, the true possibility that Germany had in fact, the Bomb, but not just an Atomic Bomb, something much more devastating and clearly more sinister; a device they were capable of deploying in some mobile form for use against almost any port in Europe or America.

"Professor Greenewalt," the Prime Minister spoke first, "we have a very serious contingency regarding the tube alloy's project.

The German Military Officer you see with us today is General Horst Deeke. He is the administrative head of Werner Heisenberg's Nuclear Bomb program in Germany and I believe it is safe to say he has brought us the entire baby.

Churchill then looked at the SS-Gruppenfuhrer and directed the next statement to him.

"We have a very short time line for me to conclude a course of action, that may require the mobilization of every RAF pilot and every SAS Commando left in England.

Needless to say we are at critical on this Professor". . . He paused to detect any reaction from the professor, then continued.

"General Deeke here will now show you what he has. Try to stay neutral emotionally and politically, but be as thorough as possible. Your assessment of what he has will allow me to make a quick and final decision on this, understood?"

"Now," the Prime Minister added, "everyone except for the Professor, General Deeke and Major Darwin with his security team, will join me in the Level Two Briefing Room."

Horst Deeke then unsnapped both locks on his briefcase and began removing a group of pre-set numbered folders prepared for the technical eyes of an assumed expert Nuclear Physicist. Dr. Heisenberg's nuclear scientific team had meticulously prepared for just this sort of situation.

Horst then sat back, as Churchill and the others exited the Regiment Ops Room.

Chapter 10

Affirmation

As the door once again banged shut, the Major and his NCOs took up guard at the inside entrance and observed the proceedings as Professor Greenewalt, who was also fluent in German, began his readings in earnest silence.

Horst did not speak, but he could see the man was growing small beads of perspiration on his forehead, as he quickly went from one file to the next, making notes and putting number sums in the margins of his note pad. It was almost as if, he was calculating formulas in his head rather than on the paper in front of him. At one point, he uttered a panicked remark, "Oh Christ", but Horst realized it was only a reaction to the incredible reality now becoming clear in his mind, so he didn't respond.

Minutes turned into hours as the process continued with very little interaction, except for an occasional German word clarification for the Professor. Horst now realized that Churchill's flight had probably been delayed or even postponed as a result of this incredible situation.

Major Darwin heard the knock first as he pushed open the door allowing Brigadier Thorpson to enter the Ops Room.

Horst was looking over some written questions that the professor had asked him to translate as the Brigadier sat down beside him.

"I think you need to read this my good man," the Brigadiers deep voice seemed to suggest a solemn occasion for his surprise arrival, as he gave the document to Horst in an almost venerating fashion.

The tension was incredible in both men while Horst's hands began to tremble as he carefully pulled open and read the document;

MI/SIS - DOCUMENT ENVELOPE
"MOST SECRET"   "MOST SECRET"
FROM: PRESIDENT - UNITED STATES
TRANSFERRED TO: P.M. - GREAT BRITAIN
RE: POSSIBLE NAZI ACCESS TO TUBE ALLOYS
DATE: 29 JANUARY 1945
SUBJECT: "TOP SECRET" ONGOING EVENTS
OF MET LAB THEFT

TO: PRESIDENT ROOSEVELT

CC1: GENERAL LESLIE GROVES
        MET LAB PROJECT
CC2: COLONEL FRANK MATHESON
        ALSOS TEAM - EUROPE
CC3: LT. GENERAL ANDREW MACMILLEN
        OFFICE OF STRATEGIC SERVICES

FROM: FBI DIRECTOR H. HOOVER
        WASHINGTON, D.C.

-       IT HAS ALWAYS BEEN MY PERSONAL
FEELING THAT YOU LEFT US OUT OF THIS
SITUATION FOR TOO LONG MR. PRESIDENT.

- THAT BEING THE CASE, NOW THAT ALSOS AND GENERAL GROVES HAVE BEEN KIND ENOUGH TO ADVISE ME ON THIS MATTER. . . .

MY MEN HAVE BEEN ABLE TO UNCOVER THE SORDID DETAILS OF THIS PLACE AND THE EVENTS OF WHAT HAPPENED.

- FIRST ANY REMAINING NAZI OPERATIVES HAVE LONG SINCE GONE AND IT APPEARS THAT ONLY ONE GRAVE WAS APPARENT ON THE PROPERTY AT ONE PATTON MOUNTAIN WHEN MY MEN ARRIVED ON 25 JANUARY 1945.

- THE GRAVE WAS HIDDEN UNDER SOME THICK PINE TREES AND THREE BODIES HAVE BEEN IDENTIFIED: ONE MALE APPROXIMATELY 200 LBS. - SIX FEET TALL DANISH OR NORWEGIAN FACIAL CHARACTERICTICS BLOND HAIR AND POSSIBLE BLUE EYES - DEATH BY THROAT LACERATION AND BLOOD LOSS - TIME OF DEATH ON OR ABOUT 20 JANUARY 1945.

- SECOND MALE APPROXIMATELY 180 LBS. - FIVE FEET NINE INCHES TALL GERMAN FACIAL CHARACTERICTICS BROWN HAIR AND POSSIBLE BROWN EYES - DEATH BY THROAT LACERATION AND
BLOOD LOSS - TIME OF DEATH ON OR ABOUT 20 JANUARY 1945.

-      ONE FEMALE APPROXIMATELY 105 LBS.
- FIVE FEET EIGHT INCHES TALL DANISH OR NORWEGIAN FACIAL CHARACTERICTICS LONG LIGHT BLOND HAIR AND POSSIBLE BLUE EYES - DEATH BY ABDOMINAL ARTERY LACERATION AND BLOOD LOSS - TIME OF DEATH ON OR ABOUT 20 JANUARY 1945.

-      WE BELIEVE THE FIRST MALE IDENTIFIED WAS A NAZI AGENT, POSSIBLY NAMED GUNTHER ANDERSSEN. THE SECOND MALE IDENTIFIED WAS CHIEF OF Y-12 OPERATIONS, NUCLEAR SCIENTIST MORT BRUCKMANN
THE FEMALE IDENTIFIED WAS THE OWNER OF A NIGHTCLUB IN THE AREA, HEIDI WINTERS.

-      ALL OF THE DECEASED WERE INVOLVED IN SOME WAY WITH THE REMOVAL OF THE TOP SECRET U-235 ELEMENTS FOUND TO BE RECENTLY MISSING FROM THE Y-12 FACILITY ON OR BEFORE 19 JANUARY 1945.-

-      THE INTERESTING ASPECT OF THIS CASE THAT WE HAVE FOUND SO FAR IS THAT DR. BRUCKMANN WAS ESSENTIALLY IMUNE FROM SEARCHES AT OAK RIDGE UNDER ORDERS FROM GENERAL GROVES. OWING TO THE NATURE OF YOUR MISSION AT THIS FACILITY, MR. PRESIDENT, I WOULD NEVER HAVE ALLOWED SUCH FREEDOM FOR A

KNOWN GERMAN NATIONAL EVEN THOUGH HE WAS OF JEWISH ORIGIN.

-         MAYBE HE WAS UNDER EXTORTION BY THE NAZIS OR MORE LIKELY HE WAS A SYMPATHIZER. WE WILL PROVIDE FURTHER FOLLOW UP ON THIS CASE MR. PRESIDENT, BUT SUFFICE IT TO SAY THAT THE PREMISES AT ONE PATTON MOUNTAIN AND ALL BANK ACCOUNTS OF THE KNOWN NAZI HAVE BEEN CLEANED OUT.

END REPORT

Horst's mind was blurring as he returned the document to the envelope and stared at the uneven patterns in the wood tabletop as the Brigadier silently took the envelope and left the room. Horst's heart sank to the deepest point it had ever been in his entire life, as he could only think of how his beautiful Heidi must have died. Oh Odin, how could you have taken away my only true love, he thought, as his hand's shook with emotion and anger. His pain was unbearable as tears began to fill his eyes.

Why had Heinrich done this to such a beautiful woman? He once even told Horst that she was truly the ultimate example of Aryan Womanhood; beauty, intelligence, and resourcefulness, that was Heidi. But in the end, Horst knew why. It started with what he did in Norway and kept growing. And now the insanity had taken Heidi with it. Horst had no family left, she was everything and Himmler knew it. That was the only way he could exact vengeance on him. Everything else he had in Germany was already gone.

He could see her smiling at him on that bright sunlit afternoon at the Berlin Olympics, the girl that every man in the Reich wanted, if only just to touch her on that glorious day for Germany. The beautiful woman that made him always long for a future even now in the darkest days of the Reich"

"The viscous bastard! "

Horst knew he must have used his own men. He probably fabricated their orders and used SSI's own assassins. Assassins that would follow only Horst's orders even to their own peril or death, never failing in their mission.

Failure was never an option and now as he began to think about their motto, that phrase would likewise become his personal creed in the destruction of the Fuhrer's Super Bomb.

His pain began to evolve into anger and then into his absolute resolve. This mission would end in either his own death or the destruction of the SS-Reichsfuhrer's Ultimate Weapon. Now there could be no choice, as his hatred and focus became one fused objective.

Suddenly, some muffled sounds could be heard in the hallway as the door was again pushed open and the P.M., his Director of MI5 and Brigadier Thorpson re-entered the Ops Room.

As Churchill entered he looked long and hard at the SS-Gruppenfuhrer to detect what effect that document had had on him. He couldn't begin to realize the level of pain it had generated within Horst, nor the level of commitment it had given him, but he knew there was something overpowering the SS-Gruppenfuhrer, as he saw the man's eyes.

Horst Deeke had become singularly focused in a way only the pain of lost love could energize.

"Well, Professor Greenewalt," the Prime Minister turned back to the Professor, while at the same time he seemed stressed as he spoke, "we have run out of time. The Brigadier here has chosen to delay my departure until 1630 Hours. But that is my final window of opportunity."

"Tomorrow," he spoke with a sense of frustration in his voice, "a serious cold weather front will be pushing winds down from Liverpool at up to forty knots by Tuesday night, so I suppose you will just have to make an intelligent guess as to what we have here."

Greenewalt cleared his throat before he spoke, fearing that his somewhat high pitched voice, might being to squeak or break as he became nervous with his presentation.

"Prime Minister, the Werner Heisenberg Nuclear Bomb program is a very real system. They have a strong background in quantum mechanics theory and have used the Teller concept to create an actual device of immense magnitude, although I am quite sure they cannot effectively deploy it over the channel by plane or rocket due to it's unstable nature and excessive weight."

"Would they be able to deploy it by some type of naval vessel, Professor Greenewalt?"

The Prime Minister offered, obviously knowing the result of his question, but wanting back-up agreement.

"Prime Minister," Greenewalt replied, "it is quite feasible to move this device in or on a large, but stable naval platform as long as they have ample cryogenic refrigeration support on board to maintain stability of the liquid deuterium within the bomb core for as long as it may take to get it to the detonation target."

"How much U-235 would you estimate that they would need to activate this device, Professor?"

Again the Prime Minister probed hopefully, but not sure of what the answer might really mean.

" Minister," Greenewalt began stressing as his voice rose an octave, "I'm out of my element on this question."

"All I can safely say is that Dr. Teller is a theorist," his voice quivered with self-doubt as he spoke, "not an engineer nor did he ever prove his theory at Cal-Tech. What the German's have in all likelihood is an atomic bomb at the very minimum, capable of producing an explosion with their current assumed U-235 weight of twenty to twenty-five kilograms, equal to about four-point-eight kilotons of TNT.

If on the other hand, their physical application of the Teller Deuterium and U-235 Theory is proved correct, then we have a wholly different hypothetical event."

"And what would, that hypothetical event be, in terms of raw explosive power, Professor?"

This time even the Prime Minister himself became outwardly nervous as he used his handkerchief to wipe moisture off his face. They all waited tensely for Greenewalt to write several numbers on his note pad and begin to mentally calculate the outcome.

"First of all," Professor Greenewalt began slowly as he spoke, "deuterium is an essential component of Heavy Water; second it is much easier and considerably less expensive to separate from hydrogen than U-235 is from U-238; and third, theoretically eighty kilograms of liquid heavy hydrogen ignited by a small atomic bomb detonation could explode with a force equivalent to at least one million tons of TNT and possibly more. . . that same explosion would require about five-hundred atomic bombs of the size we are now working on at the Los Alamos Labs."

The room was suddenly frozen with imagining the enormous potential of the Nazi designed Deuterium Super Bomb.

Professor Greenewalt then continued down a more philosophical path, "To ignite the liquid deuterium, my estimate corresponds with theirs at thirty-five-thousand electron volts or about four-hundred-million degrees of instantaneous heat."

"Only an atomic explosion," he pointed out emphatically, "can generate that much heat on earth. But, I am still skeptical how this can be accomplished with any system, not just theirs. Its never been proven. There are those that believe that this atomic explosion effect could trigger the detonation of nitrogen in the surrounding atmosphere of our planet or even the hydrogen in the ocean. That would be the ultimate catastrophe. Better to accept the slavery of mankind than run the chance of it's absolute destruction and all life on the planet as well."

"My God, Professor, is this the kind of council I would be getting from Oppenheimer or is this just your obvious skepticism drawn from our earlier Tube Alloys opinions?"

The Prime Minister was clearly incensed by the remarks that he himself had been advised on by his close friend and Nuclear Physicist Dr. Lindemann, as far back as 1944, about the real effects that would be realized when the first atom bomb test is proven.

"Very well then, Prime Minister, so let's accept the fact that the bomb is proven containable," Professor Greenewalt cleared his throat once again as he carefully spoke.

"Detonation height and weather conditions will always have a direct relation to the yield and effective range of damage of these devices, if they successfully detonate."

He paused as he looked at his notes and final calculations, "What we may,. . . uh probably have in this bomb is a resulting thermonuclear blast at nearly the surface level of the water, if using a naval vessel.

The design they have shown, Minister, is what is called a gun bomb and once the cordite fires the five kilogram U235 bullet down the barrel and into the target core of twenty to twenty-five kilograms of U-235, that nuclear explosion event could then generate a secondary explosion within it's eighty kilogram deuterium core of a magnitude equivalent to from one to up to ten-million tons of TNT."

Churchill's eyes were as wide as saucers and the others at the table were dead silent, as the P.M. shouted for the answer to what it meant.

"My God Man, so what does that mean in terms of destruction power?"

This time the Professor realized this whole thing had to be real and these men, the most powerful leaders in Great Britain were actually scared of what he was telling them.

"Prime Minister," he implored, "even our current Tube Alloys team in Los Alamos, Oppenheimer or even Teller himself could not give you anymore than theoretical answers to this question. So anything I say from this moment forward is simply a projection, a guess at best."

Churchill focused on his wild hairstyle, as he finally seemed to relax his composure.

"Professor, settle down, no man in England at this moment could fault you for what you have done, and no man in the world of science would fault you for an estimate that may be just slightly off the mark. So give it a go, and let us decide what to make of it, Man."

"Very well then, sir," Professor Greenewalt then took his best projections and began unveiling a comprehensive list of compelling reasons why all of Great Britain, might be at risk in the next twenty-four hours.

Finishing his assessment, the Professor's chilling summary horrified both the War Staff and Churchill himself, while they starred in a state of shock into the stale air re-circulating in the bombproof basement. Each one of them envisioned their own separate fears for the Imperial Kingdom as the Professor's high pitched voice filled the room with the surreal sound of foreboding. . .

"The fireball of the initial explosion will rise about five miles over the target site. That cloud, depending on the weather patterns, could spread lethal radiation over a three-hundred-mile area and life limiting radiation over another fifty to seventy-five miles beyond that." He paused briefly. . .

"As I have calculated with these documents gentlemen, the German deuterium bomb's thermonuclear explosion plume would be the equivalent of a minimum of two-hundred times and a maximum of five-hundred times greater than that planned for the American Uranium-235 only atomic bomb capacity. "

"The results," he concluded, " of this horrific explosion would be the leveling of all structures within eighteen miles of the actual zero radius point. Finally, anything biological, human, animal, plant, and wooden structures would be completely incinerated at up to twenty-five miles, plus exposed humans would have "5th degree tissue burns over seventy-five-percent of their bodies at up to fifty miles. The rest of the explosion area outside of a one-hundred and ten mile radius would be collateral damage that would be equal to the fire storms that raged over Hamburg and Berlin during our most recent one-thousand plane raids."

The room was now eerily silent for at least a full minute after the Professor completed his comments.

Before anyone of the stunned men could speak, Churchill, exhibiting a true sense of humility turned and looked directly at the SS-Gruppenfuhrer.

A new aura of respect for this man's proven faithfulness to his cause of destroying his own Nazi Super Bomb was evident to everyone, as the Prime Minister spoke to Horst Deeke in his most compelling style.

"General Deeke, until this menace has been neutralized from the face of Great Britain, you and what men you might need from the crew of that B-17 are, effective immediately, part of my emergency mobilization team code name, Red Viking."

Churchill then added, "Do I have your word of honor then, to actively join us in this single mission, to destroy this bomb once and for all?"

Horst Deeke's energy finally came forth, as the heaviest decision in his career had now been lifted from his shoulders by a man that would now assure the completion of his personal duty to save the future of Germany and partially revenge the death of his true love.

"Prime Minister, you have my word of honor and the honor of my men to actively join your forces in the successful destruction of das Fuhrer's Super Bomb."

The P.M., now more than ever since the day had begun, felt a sense of triumph and relief as he firmly replied. . .

"Thank you General, for that commitment. Neither I nor England will forget your efforts, if this is truly a success."

Horst Deeke then said, in his most assured tone of voice, "Prime Minister, you have my personal promise, it will conclude with that bomb destroyed and the device that carried it, at the bottom of the Irish Sea.

This is now my sole duty, to assure a future for my homeland and that of Aryan Europe."

Again the room was silent, as the P.M. seemed to loosen up,

"Well then, General Deeke, that takes care of the formalities, I believe."

Churchill then turned to the Major, as he added.

"Major Darwin here will see to it that you and your men are outfitted properly for this specific mission, immediately, with uniforms and weapons of your choice."

Just then the P.M.'s stomach rumbled loudly and caught everyone's attention, as he added somewhat jokingly,

"And of course, all of you, including General Deeke's Men, will be fed just as soon as these proceedings here are concluded."

With everyone's emotions on edge anyhow, they all jumped in with a loud emotional response and laughter, "Here, here, Prime Minister!"

Churchill then smiled his agreement and turned to C.O.S. Royal Marine Brigadier Thorpson, "Brigadier, as we discussed upstairs, you will head up Red Viking in my absence and will utilize my highest authority to resolve this matter in any way you see fit". . .

Churchill paused as he looked around the room.

"Use these facilities here at Northolt as your planning base. I will personally leave word with RAF Air-Marshall Tedder, to provide you with any command or tactical aircraft you may designate, and place sufficient crews on immediate standby for Red Viking's sole discretionary use."

As the Brigadier nodded his acknowledgement, of the already agreed plan they had worked out during the break upstairs for operation 'Red Viking' , Churchill then turned to M.

"Director, how many SAS assets can you spare for this mission?"

"Minister, I have thirty assigned to the Hanger 9 Mission already. Since those are some of our best, why not re-assign them to Red Viking under the Brigadier, since Herr Deeke's men are now folded into Red Viking as well and the Hanger 9 Mission has officially ended."

The Director of MI5 added as he looked obediently toward the Brigadier.

"And, as always, I will be on standby for the C.O.S., if needed, to activate my field agents in Liverpool."

Once again, Churchill turned to the Major. "Major, what is the current updated departure for my Skymaster?"

Major Darwin snapped to attention, "S'ah, I have current GMT now at 1542 Hours, with departure for your Skymaster scheduled for 1645 Hours, Minister."

"Excellent! Well Brigadier, have you any other thoughts for me before I go to visit the President and Uncle Joe?"

Royal Marine Brigadier Thorpson had been planning to discuss this next issue with the P.M. at a later time, but the present moment seemed most appropriate.

"Minister, as your newly appointed authority here in the homeland, I felt it most important to keep you and Mrs. Churchill together as well as Sarah and Mary, on this one. I took it upon myself to have them packed and ready at your Skymaster's Terminal with the official party. Mr. Martin and Mr. Rowan are waiting with them just now. I'm sure they all deserve a relaxing trip to the blue seas of the sunny Mediterranean and the beautiful isle of Malta, wouldn't you say sir?"

Churchill realizing his magnanimous intention in protecting the future of Britain and the Royal Realm at all costs, simply thanked him in his typically roundabout way.

"As is always the case, Brigadier, your timing is impeccable. I couldn't agree with you more, and of course you will always be my conscience in these matters it seems. I'm sure Mrs. Churchill has provided adequate thanks to you on this one, so of course I need not add further flourishes. Well then, is that all for now?"

"There is one other of course, the matter of the young CSP Clerk," Brigadier Thorpson added as he continued.

"It seems that we have had her sequestered with some reading material in one of the Regiment offices on level one, since early this morning."

Instantly remembering the poor girl's plight, the P.M. smiled with silent pleasure, intimately knowing he was going to let her go, as he reacted. " Ah, yes Brigadier, Miss Trixey Haygood. Well, well, what should we do with Miss Trixey Haygood?"

Without hesitation, the Brigadier answered. "I'd say we jolly well pin the Victoria's Cross on her chest, and tell her to be off, Minister!"

The Prime Minister himself started the group into a fit of almost uncontrolled laughter as he responded in surprise to the C.O.S.'s apparently sincere suggestion.

" Ah, Brigadier," Churchill replied, "we needn't go just that far with Miss Trixey Haygood, should we now." He then looked to General Deeke who was clearly enjoying the outcome of the entire situation including the opportunity to complete his promise to the Admiral in defense of Miss Haygood.

"And you, General Deeke, what have you to say on Miss Haygood's behalf?"

"You know of course, Minister," Horst replied cautiously, "that I've never met Miss Haygood."

"But it is truly obvious, that without her ability to arrange this meeting, and by her direct contact with you Minister, we are now in a position to eliminate this menace from England before it is detonated."

Just at that moment, the Royal Marine Command Sergeant Major sporting his muttonchops and waxed mustache, pushed open the outer door and again his powerful voice instantly stopped the conversation.

"S'ah, Mr. Prime Minister, your Skymaster is ready for final boarding now, and the weather is beginning to grow worse."

"Yes of course, Sergeant Major, we mustn't keep the Gods of Destiny waiting any longer," Churchill replied.

"Gentlemen, God Speed your success, on this greatest of missions for the safety of England. I now know, you will prevail." Churchill then turned to the Brigadier and winked as he added, "And, on the subject of Miss Haygood, Brigadier, I believe an RAF flight back to her previous home on Majorca, might just do her a bit of good."

At that, the Command Sergeant Major grabbed Churchill's attaché case and pushed open the heavy metal door in front of him as the Prime Minister turned back, eye to eye with Horst Deeke for one last comment.

" For the future honor of England and your homeland General, don't let us down."

Immediately, standing up to a position of attention, the SS-Gruppenfuhrer Horst Deeke presented the British Styled Officers 'Hand Salute' in respect as he answered back to the P.M.,

"We will not let you or our homelands down, Minister."

"We have the most highly trained Marines, Commandos, and SS-Wiking Warriors anywhere on the planet working together for a common duty, failure will not an option!"

Horst's words, his strength and his conviction to this ultimate duty, put a glow on Churchill's face as he turned, and in the next instant was gone.

Chapter 11

Viana da Foz

At about 1520 Hours on the afternoon of 29 January, an MI5 agent making his regular crossing on the ferry leaving Dublin to his station on Anglesey Island in Wales had reported a Portugese Flagged Freighter about forty kilometers off the Irish Coast, drifting slowly Northward. Very few ships traveled through the harsh seas of the St. George's Channel in winter months, unless they were heading to Dublin or Liverpool on the Eastern Shore of the Irish Sea. So, his comments were made because the ship did not appear to be trying to make either port. In fact, the agent had transmitted back to London; it appeared to be a rendezvous of a sort that should be looked into by our boys.

The Portugese Flagged Freighter Viana da Foz, with LISBON printed in dull lettering on the curved metal hull plates of her stern, looked as though salt water had repainted her over the years with dark brown rust stains, as she slowly ploughed into the growing whitecaps of the St. George's Channel.

The wooden planks of the main superstructure deck were loaded with barrels of diesel fuel and lubrication oil, bound for some local destination.

Two gantries and booms were positioned on the forward deck area and another single gantry with it's booms lashed to the second deck's superstructure was located on the aft section. An even higher third and fourth deck superstructure were positioned about two-thirds from the bow and held the pilothouse with the captain and several officers milling about.

Above all that, the uppermost structure held a single black smoke stack with it's middle painted over by the barely discernable green and red color bands of Portugal, now caked with the residue of diesel fumes from months at sea.

Several transmitting antennas were located on that upper area as well, and only three guide wires secured the stack to the deck floor, while a fourth lay broken as its upper portion whipped against metal in the direction of the billowing smoke.

A distant Ferry crossing to Wales had sighted the Freighter from a good distance several hours earlier, but nothing had seemed to be in the channel now as the light began to fade and the ship's dim navigation lights began to glow in the dark sea mist.

They were now only about three kilometers from the rendezvous point, but no one had observed any vessels or unusual activity south of their position, so they began to slow to five knots as they made plans to drift the Freighter to coordinate zero.

First Officer, Oberleutnant zur See Vitor Santos, one of the few actual Portugese speaking Officers aboard, was on the aft deck supervising two seamen.

They were adjusting a winch on the rear gantry to eventually hoist the disguised Cannon Barrel from its storage hold on the U-boat, as one of the SSI Officers, SS-Hauptsturmfuhrer Gustav Lemp, exited a latched door and carefully held the handrail as he maneuvered out over the slippery deck to talk to Santos.

The sea began to roll the ship more unevenly as he looked over the side and saw a signal light flashing in the dark about three-hundred meters east of their present position.

"Hey, there they are!" Lemp shouted trying to yell over the increasing noise made by the combination of the straining motor and howling wind.

Santos understood, but was unable to do anything with his concentration focused on the complicated maneuver as he yelled back.

"Herr Lemp, you will have to advise the Korvettenkapitan to Stop Engines now, and signal them. Hurry, I can't leave these men in this predicament, or well loose the winch."

The SS-Hauptsturmfuhrer turned and made it to a phone box mounted near the door portal he had just left, then dialed up the pilothouse and shouted into the black handset.

"Kapitan, Kapitan, this is Lemp, I have spotted our U-boat at the 3 o'clock position off the stern of the ship. Can we flash a signal to acknowledge?"

Korvettenkapitan, Siegfried Winkler, had been a U-boat Officer until 1943, when his own U-boat on a night mission in the English Channel began rushing on the surface to catch a British Freighter.

Unfortunately, it struck a mine off the Dover-Cape Gris field before it could get off even one torpedo. All but three of his crew drowned, and he was able to survive until their sister U-boat trailing them, found him at first light the next morning. He was half-dead in the frigid water still holding on to his two dead seamen. From that day forth, he vowed to stay on neutral surface support ships, to try to save as many of his brothers as he could until the war ended.

Korvettenkapitan Winkler started barking commands as soon as he hung-up the handset with Lemp, bringing the bow of the Viana da Foz to within one-hundred meters of the U-boat.

The waves were very treacherous now, and getting worse as the storm front quickly pushed down from Iceland and into the Irish Sea. They were certainly not concerned about spotter planes because the ceiling was little more that fifty to seventy-five feet above the stack, and even the hardy PBY flying boats would not venture out on a night like tonight, even to rescue the bloody King of England.

A new plan began to spring into Winkler's mind as he personally flashed instructions to the crew of UX-506.

Winkler knew the potential hazards of trying to work with heavy equipment at sea between two boats even in mildly rolling conditions and he realized the complex nature of what they would have to do to prepare the sub for it's final mission.

The mission planners in Germany had not considered that this little body of water off Ireland, even in good weather, could get so mean. It was time to visit an old friend.

The Brit's always had a running feud with the Welch and especially the real Celtic Island folk around the Irish Sea, at least that's what his grandfather use to say.

So, if you ever needed a friendly cottage in which to hide in the British Isles or a safe Harbor for your damaged U-boat, you could always look to the Welch or Irish Coastlines in your time of need.

Had it not been for his mother's side of the family, Winkler would himself be without a plan. But back in the early 1900's before the Great War, his mother's father, a Danish Construction Engineer, worked on a project to build a Copper Mine on a remote island in the Irish Sea called Anglesey Island. A British firm needed some experts on mining copper and his grandfather's Danish Engineering Firm joined them in the survey and design.

In times past, the predicament it seems, was not how to get the ore out of the rich mother lode found in Pary's Mountain on the northern tip of the island, but without a railroad over it's difficult mountain-like terrain, the problem was actually how to get the ore shipped to the smelting furnaces in Blackpool, an industrial area north of Liverpool on the English Coast.

To further complicate things, the only town near the mine, Amlwch, was situated on cliffs over looking the Irish Sea. And, because of that rugged mountainous geology, it had no natural harbor to use as an alternative to hauling the ore overland on dirt roads to the train depot at Bangor, on the mainland of Wales.

His grandfather had built several hardened concrete seawalls for the Germans in their massive Naval Port of Kiel just south of Copenhagen in 1905. With his experience there, he was able to devise a unique walled harbor for the Copper Mine at Amlwch to load their ore ships without fear of sinking, even in the harsh winters along the Irish Seacoast.

The system had used locks and concrete gateway devices to raise and lower the water levels, while protecting the massive ore boats that were to be loaded there back in the early 1900's, regardless of the tidal level of the sea.

Now, falling back on that past built by his grandfather, Korvettenkapitan Winkler knew that the engineered harbor at Amlwch, could easily accommodate a seven-hundred and fifty ton U-boat and a twenty-two hundred ton supply ship side by side, if need be for several hours in relative calm and without prying eyes, while all transfers and modifications were made to the UX-506's hull.

The first step would be contacting that old friend his grandfather had known, or at the very least a next of kin that would remember that old family friendship.

Those kinds of memories were always past down in the Celtic Islands from generation to generation.

Kapitan Winkler decided to use the last name of his grandfather, Bjorn Tronstad, for the communication, rather than his own to simplify things for the radio transmission to the island.

The place where his grandfather had stayed for over two years during the Harbor and Mine Engineering project was only known as the Stag Inn. He loved to hear him tell the stories of his travels, but these people in Wales and their Celtic folk stories always reminded him of the Viking tales he loved to read. Even the odd sounding name of the young lady, Branwena, his grandfather Tronstad had known there and her father Culh Hergst, owner of the Inn, sounded like names from his own folk heroes.

Since most harbors and fishermen in the area monitored distress channels, he decided to take a chance and play on the locals to get the correct frequency for the Harbormaster in Amlwch.

After about three tries, a fishing boat out of Barmouth gave him the harbor frequency and he made his call.

"Amlwch Harbormaster, This is Captain Tronstad of Denmark, requesting safe harbor, Over!"

There was no response.

Winkler tried several more times, then he decided that even though they would be closer to possible radar detection from coastal patrols, he had to move both boats to within ten kilometers of the harbor entrance and try again.

It was very slow going with both boats almost getting swamped by following rogue waves as they made the forty kilometers due eastward to the approximate coordinates north of Amlwch Harbor.

Finally, just before 2200 Hours, they were due north of the entrance, and Korvettenkapitan Winkler gave it one more try.

Suddenly, someone came over the receiver in an almost Gaelic-French accented tone of voice, obviously a woman.

"I would be the Harbormistress of Amlwch, of whom do chi know in these parts, over, to chi mister."

" My grandfather designed and helped build your harbor walls, and knew the owner of the Stag Inn many years ago, over," Korvettenkapitan Winkler, then added.

After another, very long pause, a man's voice came over the receiver in a much heavier almost garbled, but probably Gaelic tone.

"How large a vessel are chi sailing mister. And what's chi beam, tonnage, and draft?" Then after another brief pause he added, "And mister, give us the flag chi be a'flying? Over."

The more serious male voice sounded ominous to Winkler, but he decided to take a chance on using the Portugese Flagged vessels information for the official harbor record.

"This is the Portugese Flagged Freighter Viana da Foz, and we have a crew of thirty-four with a tonnage of twenty-two hundred gross. Our draft is sixteen feet and our beam is forty-two feet."

Then he added somewhat cautiously, "We are also towing a disabled boat of eight-hundred tons with a limited crew on board. We intend all vessels to depart at first light for Liverpool, over."

After a short pause, the female voice returned and took over again with a warmer and friendlier response.

"Aye then mister, chi are clear to enter the harbor entrance narrows."

"Watch the surf direction as chi line up with the navigation lights and the harbor beacon, chi have a two-hundred foot gateway, but the swells can make that very tricky."

"And mister, once chi have cleared the harbor entrance with both badau, cut the engines as chi throw off the ropes. "

"We cah'noot close the harbor gates 'til chi cut the engines. Over again, to chi mister."

Winkler then acknowledged the approval, as he then barked his orders to his men.

"Both crews place guides to the port and starboard bow areas and make ready to enter Amlwch."

Unknown to even Winkler, the fully loaded Ore boats of the early 1900's needed over fifty feet of draft, so the engineers had dredged the harbor entrance to a depth of seventy-five feet to make the channel entry stable enough to navigate, even in fairly choppy seas.

As they positioned the boats in line, they were fortunate that the windspeed and the surf height had abated some, as they made their way carefully between the massive one-hundred-foot hinged dam walls that held back the Irish Sea.

They slowed to less than five knots, yet still maintained half-full on their engine speeds to correct for any possible collisions with the harbor walls or each other. But without incident, they slid carefully between the green and red navigation lights and along the massive walled dykes protecting only about ten fishing boats. None of the fishing boats were larger than forty-five tons, as they drifted tied to individual concrete walled slips slotted on the east side of the Harbor Channel.

The place was reminiscent of the massive U-boat pens at Brest, France, except that there was no overhead concrete cover, and cliffs blocked the view on one side, while a few dimly lit houses filled the apparent green hillside at the south end of the harbor's darkened channel.

Watching them for handouts, the local gulls and sea birds seemed to be grounded in small groups for the night around the concrete ledges sheltered below the wall dykes, just as sheets of rain started pulsing loudly like hailstones on the sheetmetal of the Freighter's Pilothouse.

They threw off ropes and again began to sway a little as the wind picked up across the bow to about thirty knots, and to their rear, the diesel engines driving the gate hydraulics pushed a wave of seawater against their sterns.

The massive harbor dams closed in a mysteriously eerie silence, locking them into either a grave or a safe keeping for the duration of the wintry blow.

As instructed by Korvettenkapitan Winkler, both crews began to silently tie off all ropes to the dock cleats on the west side of the Harbor Channel in order to leave room for Amlwch's tiny fishing fleet to navigate around them, if they chose to leave before dawn.

The crews then quickly moved back below decks to avoid any further observation.

Once everything was secure, Winkler, now as Captain Tronstad of Denmark, stepped ashore to hopefully meet some friends from his grandfather's past.

Icy raindrops began to hit his exposed neck as he was almost pushed along the well-worn path by a strong northwest wind coming down the coastline.

Winkler could see some light coming from a small cottage at the south side of the Harbor, and it's large transmission antenna was rattling ever louder in the increasing wind.

Ah. . . that had to be the Harbormaster's house, he thought as he looked about carefully.

It was a strange kind of almost mystical place, that time and the war had left untouched.   He could see why his grandfather had often referred to it as a land of fairies and sea gods, that would sometimes help you and sometimes trip you up just for their own amusement. He would often warn his workers," You'd better keep a sharp eye out for unusual things, in this ancient place, men."

Suddenly an enormous hulk of a man with a salt worn face and a tangled red beard was standing in front of him. Winkler, was startled by his appearance from out of nowhere, as he asked himself, 'Speaking of the most weird things, how the hell did you get here mister'?

"I welcome chi to Amlwch," he grumbled in a foreign Gaelic accent unfamiliar to Winkler, then added, "God bless all chi here on this Winter Nos."

Winkler responded uneasily, hoping he understood what was said, "And to you as well, kind sir."

The man was wearing an old wool cap and a reefer coat as he continued to look over at the two boats now moored in the harbor.

"And a fine job of maneuvering those badau through the jetty gates, with all the wind and sea pushing bout, as well."

A Portugese Flag was flying over the Freighter, but for security reasons, there were no markings or numbers on the UX-506, just the SS-Wiking emblem of a Prow of a Dragon Viking Ship meticulously painted on either side of the periscope tower.

The old man spoke again as he carefully eyed the 'Viking Ship' emblem painted on the U-boat, " Ah, and it looks to me like chi found a stray Norseman lost in that vicious Irish gale out there? We always have had a time taming the Irish chi know."

Then very insightfully, he turned and went quickly inside the cottage, motioning to the Captain to follow, as he disappeared into the doorway.

It was a comfortable room with very low beams of dark hand hewn wood and a brightly burning fire in a stone hearth against the back wall. Several chairs and a desk with a radio transmitter in it's center were the room's main fixtures.

A door to another room with some light coming out was the only other entrance.

This time, as he turned back to the desk, he was bewildered by a young woman, standing directly in front of him.

"And chi must be the Captain Tronstad of Denmark, are chi not?"

Winkler almost forgot, as he stuttered agreement in a confused Danish-German accent,   "Ja, Ja, that I am, young lady, that I am. And who might you be?"

The young woman paused for a moment and considered how she would answer him.

"Well, if daid Bjorn is your grandfather, then I'd surely be, to the mister Captain Tronstad o' Denmark, a furst cousin. Myfi name's Colleen Mawr, myfi grandmum' s Branwena Tronstad."

Once more, Winkler, was shocked by this mysterious place, and the new revelation as he thought to himself, Well, I always had a feeling something had made a passionate impression on grandfather, after two years of isolation on this obscure island.

Now it appeared that he had a second wife besides his grandmother, and at the same time as well.

Then he thought, somewhat compassionately toward his grandfather's indiscretion, but that was a long time ago and look what we have here.

Besides, looking at this young girl with the long dark hair and stunning almost Nordic-like features, he thought, I'm sure her grandmother Branwena had to have been a very beautiful and inspiring Celtic woman as well.

For the next hour or so they made small talk, as he learned more than he needed of his grandfather's legacy on Amlwch. He felt as though the girl was comfortable, with him being there, and she clearly did not appear to be a threat to the mission.

The main thing that he was clear on was that the Brit's never ventured into this part of the Island. They only hung out down at Holyhead Island where the lighthouse and British patrol boats were located, some twenty kilometers to the southwest overlooking the St. George's Channel, and over some very mean roads overland.

So for now with plenty of cloud cover and the massive concrete walls hiding their boats from any sea patrols, they could probably begin preparing the U-boat and split off into their various directions by the break of dawn.

At least that sounded like a reasonable plan.

She had also told him that they did not have any telephones or telegraph to the mainland, and that the locals only used the Post or the radio transmitter here at the cottage, but that was very infrequently.

His only concern was that someone in Amlwch might get a little funny and try to transmit over to the one of the homeland guard stations in England or even to Holyhead.

So, just in case, he was going to fix the radios on those fishing boats, and likewise probably remove a tube or two on this one here, at the cottage.

By the time anyone noticed what was up, they would be well on their way to finalizing the mission.

Chapter 12

Merseyside

It was raining hard at Northolt early on the morning of January 30th as the converted British RAF Lancaster Bomber took off for the airfield outside of Birkenhead just south of the Merseyside estuary. For the tactical mission team, after the P.M. had left, C.O.S. Royal Marine Brigadier Thorpson selected only ten of his top operatives and General Deeke from the Germans, for Red Viking.

All eleven wore standard SAS camouflaged uniforms and carried Sten sub-machine guns because of their deadly firing speed and light-weight frames.

RAF Air-Marshall Tedder had re-assigned a hot Lancaster from a previously scrubbed mission to provide them with a fully operational tactical delivery aircraft for the Red Viking mission.

Merseyside was an estuary formed by a wide-open bay at the end of the Mersey River flowing into Liverpool, Britain's largest seaport. The Mersey ran down from the hills of South Yorkshire and along a narrow L shaped channel thirty miles long until it reached the Irish Sea. Liverpool had been protected by it's geographic location, almost one-hundred and seventy miles northwest of London, from German Air Power throughout most of the airwar since 1943. And, as a result, it had become more commercial than ever before by late 1944.

That fact was actually a problem for the Red Viking mission, since the U-boat could probably get lost within the maze of ships waiting to be offloaded into the harbor of Liverpool.

It's distance from Germany also created a complacent attitude among the officers of the British Admiralty about the protection of Liverpool and as a result, the amount of fast attack craft assigned to the area were very limited.

Only one Royal Naval craft of any substantial size or tactical benefit could be located for the mission as both MI5 and Churchill's Special Operations Executive attempted to secure equipment for the mission.

The choice was the HMS Juno, an eleven-hundred ton escort destroyer of the Royal Navy's Hunt-class design.

It was fast enough with an over twenty-eight-knot flank speed to catch a U-boat, but the search area was over two-thousand five-hundred square miles and recent bad weather had forced all search aircraft to be grounded.

Only a surface ship could be used to locate UX-506. But at least the Juno had the latest radar and underwater detection gear recently installed.

Armed with General Deeke's original final rendezvous coordinates, the Red Viking team boarded the HMS Juno and began a westerly course toward the north of Anglesey Island, fifty miles west of Liverpool.

HMS Juno was told to hug the Welsh coastline just in case they were hidden in one of the coves on the way to Anglesey.

Brigadier Thorpson and General Deeke were meeting with the ship's Captain Howard Durham as a weather report came into the Command Bridge.

Several maps of the Irish Sea north and south of Holyhead were spread out on a charting table in the center of the bridge.

"S'ah, Sub-Lieutenant Tidwell reporting from the radio room."

"Aye, aye Tidwell, at ease," Captain Durham replied in his usual tone of voice, "what have we in the forecast for the coordinates north of Amlwch?"

"Heavy fog ahead S'ah, with wind speeds reaching up to twenty knots and temperatures holding at forty-four degrees Fahrenheit, Barometric Pressure holding at twenty-nine-point-five inches."

The young officer then adjusted the report sheets, "Do you still want the report for the Liverpool docks, S'ah?"

"Aye, Tidwell, but first how thick is the fog estimate from Holyhead Station," Durham asked.

"S'ah," Tidwell again barked out his report in an automated fashion, "Holyhead reports less than one mile visibility, but two ships north of there have reported they are all stopped, in visibility of less than one-hundred yards."

"Well man, let's have the Merseyside Report," the Captain directed.

"The fog bank is moving south into our current zone of operations at about ten knots from the north northwest and according to this new report from Royal Naval Operations at Birkenhead, S'ah, it has already reached a line less than four miles west of the docks at Merseyside."

Brigadier Thorpson interrupted," How can this stuff be so thick with an almost twenty knot wind pushing us around out here Captain, shouldn't we be getting some relief or at the very least some dissipation of this stuff?"

"Tell the Brigadier, Tidwell," Captain Durham again directed.

"Aye, aye, S'ah," Tidwell snapped to attention and faced the Brigadier.

"At ease man," Brigadier Thorpson spoke in a deep voice, " so break the news to us young man."

"Aye, S'ah," the young officer relaxed again as he explained, "over the sea where there is less frictional turbulence then there is on the land, fog can form into thick bands even when wind speeds are quite strong, even up to thirty knots or so. Adjoining warm and cold currents in the sea effect wide differences in the overrunning air masses, and it's more of a problem if the air is already unstable from industrial dust and humidity at one-hundred-percent. The result is very thick fog. And that's what we are currently in now, S'ah."

Suddenly Horst Deeke realized an opportunity as he entered the conversation, "Lieutenant Tidwell, can you get the coordinates and the identification of the two ships that reported to Holyhead?"

"Aye, aye, S'ah," Tidwell again snapped to attention this time turning to General Deeke, "it could take a few minutes, S'ah, but I'm sure Holyhead could relay that back to us while were underway."

"Brigadier," Horst addressed him specifically, but included all of them as he spoke, "if we had their coordinates and identification, maybe I could determine from memory if either of the ships were on the SS-Reichsfuhrer's U-boat replenishment list. I can't remember all the names, but if I heard one, it just might jog my memory."

"Excellent, General," the Brigadier remarked as he looked at the Captain, " well Captain Durham, make it so, and to cut the time as short as possible, set our course at flank speed to the nearest coordinate. If that one turns out to be a dud, well still be only a short distance from the real target."

"Aye, aye, Brigadier," Captain Durham reacted then turned to his junior officer, " off with you man, and get it done quickly, this is high priority!"

"Jolly right S'ah," Tidwell reacted and was out the doorway in an instant as the Captain ordered his First Officer to sound General Alert and make Flank Speed to the projected first coordinates about twenty miles northeast of Holyhead.

The claxon went off as everyone donned his helmet and Horst and the Brigadier quickly set out below decks to inform their tactical commando platoon on what they might soon be up against.

The time was now almost 0600 Hours and they were running westward along the north coast of Wales at twenty-eight knots just twelve miles southwest of the Merseyside docks.

They were projected to intersect the first target at 0720 Hours GMT, if the target remained stationary. Time was now their greatest enemy; the fog was their second.

Their assets were stealth, the best radar in the war, the finest commandos under any allied command, as well as the fact that Horst Deeke knew failure was not an option.

Chapter 13

Due West of Liverpool

Except for Winkler and five designated SSI and U-boat volunteer crewmen, all hands on board UX-506 were evacuated to the Portugese Flagged Replenishment Freighter Viana da Foz. Both ships flashed signals in the early morning of January 30th, and turned away from each other disappearing in opposite directions into a thick fog bank, now surrounding their locations about eighty kilometers west of Liverpool in the Irish Sea.

The newly reconfigured UX-506 with what appeared to be an aft mast rising skyward near it's stern, remained on the surface as it slipped slowly eastward through the waves at about twelve knots; final destination, the Merseyside estuary at Liverpool in approximately four hours and thirty minutes.

In the winter months, this part of the Irish Sea was usually a very treacherous body of water. Channeled evenly between England and Ireland, the Irish Sea rises from depths of over fifteen-hundred feet to less than one-hundred feet as it meets the English Coastline near the Harbor of Liverpool. It is also a very cold body of water.

Korvettenkapitan Winkler knew that his U-boat was very unstable now that it had been fitted with the black four-ton cannon barrel projecting into the air over the stern storage hold.

He took his binoculars and inspected the fittings at it's base as someone climbed up from below. One of the remaining SSI Officers still on board, SS-Hauptsturmfuhrer Karl Bergen, now stood beside him on the boat's conning tower lighting a cigarette as they moved silently through the unusually thick fogbank due east toward their target.

"This is the thickest fog I think I've ever seen, Kapitan," SS-Hauptsturmfuhrer Bergen blurted as he tried to make out something floating by off the starboard side of the boat, " even in the Baltic, we could at least see a boat's length out there, but here it must be less than fifty meters."

"You know Herr Bergen," Winkler commented matter of factly to make small talk as they both knew their mission's end was very near, "fog is actually a cloud whose base has come to rest on the sea. The difference between a cloud and the fog is that the cloud forms from rising air that expands and cools, while Fog is cooled air remaining on the earth's surface."

"Fog this thick is likely to be with us until we get to Liverpool. And unlike the Baltic, Karl, this part of England has this problem because of the dust and smoke from Ireland's factories mixing with the warm air that comes across it from the Gulf Stream running north to Iceland. Because of that, this sea has some of the thickest fog banks anywhere on earth"

Karl just smiled as they both suddenly realized that the item floating by them was an old mildewed life jacket from a probable allied freighter sinking in the area during the recent past, as Winkler grimaced and looked below into the conning tower without acknowledging the trash floating by. But the SS-Hauptsturmfuhrer seemed concerned as he spoke, "I hope that sinking hasn't got them riled up over there in Liverpool, Kapitan, they'll think we did it and probably try to sink us before we can surrender this boat to them."

"I don't think so Karl," Winkler said without much excitement in his voice, "that harbor is so busy these days they probably wouldn't even notice a missing freighter even if one of our boats was lucky enough to get through the underwater mines surrounding the harbor."

Just then, someone called from down below to once again announce negative contacts on all four quadrants as Winkler had requested. He wanted reports every fifteen minutes regardless of their speed, to prevent a possible collision while visually blinded by the vaporous white curtain.

"Jawohl, carry on!" Winkler shouted down to them, then he added, "The fact that they will not see this boat until we are ready to give it to them because of this fog bank, makes our task even easier."

Winkler pulled out a waterproof envelope and removed a silk map of the harbor area to re-locate the rendezvous location near Bootle, just north of Merseyside.

"Do you think your people will have the speedboat ready Herr Bergen," Winkler questioned the SS-Hauptsturmfuhrer, somewhat uneasy as he again thought about the explosive power of the bomb they were carrying?

They all knew the scientists were no longer on board because they had completed their designated mission of building the arming device and setting the timers for firing. The only men selected to remain had to be expendable military forces or U-boat crewmen, not the Reich's nuclear scientists.

Still, Winkler had a gnawing feeling about the device now that he had seen the massive container and cooling units taking up the U-boat's entire rear torpedo room and crews quarters.

The SS-Hauptsturmfuhrer looked at him quizzically, "Why should you be concerned Herr Kapitan, you know I was able to reach them last night from the Island and they are in place as agreed by the SS-Reichsfuhrer's orders."

"Maybe it's not so much whether your people will be there Herr Bergen," Winkler replied in a serious tone of voice, "but whether or not they can get us far enough away from this thing, before it blows up more than Liverpool itself."

"Yes, I agree Herr Kapitan," Karl turned to him as the faint light of morning began to brighten the fog bank, but did little to change it's thickness even though a constant windspeed of over ten knots from the northwest was being registered on their instruments.

"But I'm certain they considered our distance from the blast once we get north of Blackpool." Karl added as he tried to assure himself, as well as the Kapitan.

"The facts given to me by both of the chief scientists showed we would be in the clear at only twenty kilometers away. . . Blackpool is almost forty."

"I agree Karl," Winkler replied still unsure of their real safety, "but remember, neither of them have anything to lose, since they are both on my freighter returning safely back to Portugal."

Chapter 14

The First Target

Fog was clearing from the coastal areas as they moved to the northwest of the small Welsh village of Amlwch into another thick fog bank.

Holyhead had finally identified the coordinates of a Portugese Flagged Freighter called the Viana da Foz out of Lisbon and General Deeke had confirmed it's identity as German. Plus the Juno's radar was sweeping out to over forty miles when the target blip had clearly showed up on their screen. Quickly they slowed to less than ten knots as they approached to within one-thousand yards of the freighter.

Viana da Foz was not equipped with radar as sophisticated as the HMS Juno, but they clearly knew they were spotted when the Viana da Foz's foghorn echoed it's eerie moan into the sea west of their position. Their engines were running but they were only idling in the water as Horst and the Red Viking team members spotted them.

The plan for the commandos was to be positioned east of the target as the HMS Juno came within view on her port side at one-hundred yards, where it would maintain a standoff position until the Viana da Foz was secured.

Captain Durham was to hail the ship in an attempt to distract them until the Red Viking team went into action. Two of the commandos donned their frogmen gear and placed charges on the bow and stern to add to the confusion once the team had boarded the ship.

At 0745 Hours all was in readiness.

Horst and an Irishman named Liam were the first to reach the midship superstructure as she slowly rolled back and forth on the growing waves. He could see several barrels of diesel fuel as they quietly made their way along the wooden planks of the deck.

Within moments six more of their men with their Stens at the ready were positioned forward near portals to the lower decks.

At once they could hear someone yelling into a bullhorn from the pilothouse toward the dark form of the HMS Juno now exposing itself on the port side, while several Portugese crewmen stood along the railing watching the British Naval vessel.

Horst and Liam moved higher near the Pilothouse observing the ship's captain and several officers milling about. None of them had guns in their hands, but they were all armed with pistols. Horst gave Liam orders to quickly climb up to the overhead deck and set charges to take out the transmitting antennas before they commenced the attack. As he got to the stack deck beside the antennas, the warped metal floor gave away his movements.

An authoritative voice bellowed to the officers in the pilothouse, "What was that Lieutenant Santos?"

"Someone's on the radio antenna deck, SS-Hauptsturmfuhrer." Santos yelled as he ordered his First Mate to check it out, "Rudy get up there, now!"

But it was too late.

Captain Lemp, exited the pilothouse door right into the barrel of Horst Deeke's Sten and was pushed back into the pilothouse knocking Rudy to the floor behind him.

Rudy rose just as the charges went off at the bow and stern rocking the ship violently.

Shots ran out around the lower decks as Red Viking commandos of the SAS fired several shots killing some of the German and Portugese fighters with all hell braking loose down below.

Rudy pulled his revolver and aimed it at Horst's leg as Liam crashed through the forward window firing his Sten into Rudy and the Officer behind him that was also trying to reach his gun to fire at Horst.

Within minutes the entire ships crew and it's German Officers and SSI Scientists not killed or dying were brought on deck to be offloaded onto the Juno.

Horst looked at Gustav and spoke, " Well my old friend, it seems you almost made it to Liverpool."

"My god it's you SS-Gruppenfuhrer," the shock on Gustav's face was genuine, as Liam yelled at them both.

"Aye General, we better get below quick, or m'ah charges are gin to giv ye a'real Irish headache!"

They all made it to the wooden floor of the main deck before the top of the pilothouse blew off, taking with it the rusted smoke stack and Viana da Foz's transmission antennas.

Everyone ducked to the port side as the mass of metal groaned and went over the starboard handrailing into the growing sea swells below.

"What is going on Herr Gruppenfuhrer?" Gustav spoke in a state of total confusion as they led him to the makeshift pulley hauling the captured crew over the water between the two ships,

"And why are you here in a British Commando's Uniform with these attackers?"

Horst and the Brigadier had already decided that the crew and SS on board the Viana da Foz would be in a communications void from the current events in Germany.

Their plan was to lead them into thinking the Reich had split into two factions; those that were still fighting to protect Germany from the Russian Communists and those that had already surrendered to the British and Americans to save what was left of Germany before the Bolsheviks had raped and burned it into oblivion.

It was this explanation that worked on the senior SS Officer, Hauptsturmfuhrer Gustav Lemp, as he was taken to the HMS Juno's holding area for interrogation.

The rest of the Red Viking team remained on board to search the old Portuguese hulk before setting charges to sink her while Horst joined the Brigadier in the holding room of the HMS Juno to finish interrogation of the SSI Scientists that survived the attack.

What they uncovered was Himmler's undeniable apocalypse.

Chapter 15

Rush to Valhalla

All of the Scientists were standing, smoking cigarettes in the confined room on the lower deck when Horst and Brigadier Thorpson entered. The smoke was almost enough to asphyxiate a bear as they found seats around the backside of a small operation's table centered below two portholes at the far end of the room.

After seating himself, the Brigadier gruffly cleared his throat and spoke first in text book German, "Gentlemen, your interrogations did not go smoothly as I'm sure you realize. Now it's time for myself and General Deeke, excuse me SS-Gruppenfuhrer Horst Deeke, Commandant of all worldwide Nazi SSI Operations as well as your Fuhrer's renowned SS-Wiking Commando Forces, to bring you into the light of day, so to say."

It was almost 0930 Hours by the time the meeting with the Scientist started and the HMS Juno was again underway. They had all stood on deck earlier to observe the charges going off on the Viana da Foz as the final members of the Red Viking team reboarded the Juno.

Explosions were heard as rumblings at first, but not seen, until large gushes of seafoam and bubbles rushed out from under the water line at three points along the ship's portside. Then the old hulk rolled over on her starboard side and within a minute, stern first, slid back into the foam and rising currents of the dark Irish sea as several fifty-five gallon drums of oil marked the only remaining evidence of her grave; a grave hundreds of feet below them, on the rocky sea bottom.

Again the Brigadier sized up the audience carefully as he continued in a neutral accent, "You may not realized what the consequences are, but the SS-Gruppenfuhrer and I will need your full co-operation now that your Reich has agree to side with England to save the lives of millions of innocent Germans."

Brigadier Thorpson looked at Horst to begin his remarks, "Please explain SS-Gruppenfuhrer for their benefit as to what we are up against."

Horst knew only one of Werner Heisenberg's men now standing in the huddle of confused nuclear scientists in front of them as he began, "Rolf Petersen, you know me, you know what I have stood for, and you know why I am here on board this British ship with you right now." He paused to see if the others seemed willing to accept his opening, as he waited for Rolf to answer, but he was silent.

"Every Physicist at Sangerhausen," he dug into his briefcase then returned his gaze to them, "when I left there less than three days ago, agreed we must destroy the bomb to save Germany from complete annihilation, which I can truly assure you will happen gentlemen, if this explosion is successful." Horst shook the document he had taken from his briefcase at them and continued.

"Its all in here, signed by all of them. Read it for yourselves."

Again he paused pushing the document to the center of the table, "The British and the Americans along with the Russians, who are now almost to the Brandenberg Gate will dissolve every remnant of the Third Reich and our Aryan culture from the face of this earth forever, if you allow this to happen. I know you are all committed to the Reich even to the end, but in the name of your families and friends in Germany, you must tell us how to stop this horror, assuming we are successful in even locating Unterseeboot UX-506 in time."

Finally it was Rolf Petersen who broke the silence, but none reached for the document, "Okay SS-Gruppenfuhrer, you yourself know that we all signed the orders that the SS-Reichfuhrer handed down to us. And we all know that nothing, not even the hand of the Fuhrer himself is to interfere with this countdown."

"You as well, must know these facts Herr Deeke. And that penalty is just as severe as what you are suggesting, even if we do nothing. They will shoot us well as every member of our families now living under the hand of the Gestapo in Germany."

"If we break these orders, they die!"

Seeming to tighten up physically, they grouped together like wounded sheep surrounded by wolves from all sides. They felt any option would still result in sure death to all.

"And that's truly what would happen if they were still in control, but they are not. Their power is gone! The Reich has already split into two factions. Berlin and the Fuhrer, the SS-Reichfuhrer, and his personal staff are out of touch with everyone in the rest of the Reich now. In fact, Admiral Donitz and several SS and Wehrmacht Commanders are all that's left in charge, west of the Brandenberg Region."

"Even Sangerhausen itself, is soon to be under the control of the Russian Communist Brigades driving through Dresden, burning and raping our people as they go. The only reason I am here is because we would rather side with the British and Americans than give the rest of Germany to the Bolsheviks. Admiral Donitz is now surrendering his Unterseeboot forces across the Atlantic to the British and Americans to save what is left."

"All we can hope for is the salvation of Western Germany and the Rhineland before the Bolsheviks get there to defile our people and lands into oblivion."

After an interim of silently watching Horst, someone whispered to Rolf.

"SS-Gruppenfuhrer," Rolf looked at his colleagues as he spoke, "give us a few moments to confer privately, then we will give you our answer."

"Very well Rolf," Horst offered as the Brigadier nodded agreement and both of them returned to the door hatch to leave, "but don't let us down. And don't let your family and what is left of our Reich down, Rolf. You must help us, we need a plan to disarm it."

Horst closed and locked the hatch as he ran up the narrow stairway to the Command Deck to get an update on the possible position of UX-506. The Brigadier chose to remain and stood guard with two of his men near the windowless door hatch.

"Captain Durham," Horst yelled in a state of panic, as he rushed into the bridge after not finding him on the Command Deck, what has happened to our speed? We have slowed to almost a crawl? And where is the U-boat's location? Has the radar room even caught sight of them yet?

"Aye, General Deeke," the Captain announced matter of factly to his mass of questions, "we've had to slow to fifteen knots because of several ships spotted ahead of us, at less than ten miles out from the Merseyside Docks. But that's not a crawl at all, S'ah. If we continue at flank speed, we may not be able to avoid a collision with one of them in this pea soup.

We have less than two-hundred yards visibility, General, and we would never be able to turn in time to avoid ramming another ship of possibly ten times our tonnage.

There's freighters out there at over fifteen-thousand tons loaded with ammunition, oil, and armaments."

"Okay then Captain," Horst was still not satisfied as he tried to stay calm, "what is the latest radar coordinates and possible identifications? We've got to find out where the U-boat is by a process of elimination, do you have that yet?"

"Absolutely, General," the Captain again reported, but now he had unexpected support as Tidwell entered behind him from the lower radar room, "we've actually been working it that way General and we only had one ship left to identify."

Let's see if Sub-Lieutenant Tidwell has it now?" As he turned and was immediately surprised realizing Sub-Lieutenant Tidwell was already beside him, "Tidwell!"

"Aye, aye, S'ah, you're Jolly well right," Tidwell shouted after entering the Bridge and overhearing the Captain's comments. . . ."the large one is the Nyholt Norwegian out of Boston with a load of tanks and ammunition outbound for Normandy."

"All traffic has been advised to make way in the channel, S'ah."

"An alert has been posted by the harbormaster because someone spotted a German U-boat moving on the surface ten miles off Formby Point."

"Sound General Alert and hold this speed Commander Heath." Captain Durham shouted to his First Officer as he turned back toward the ship's wheel, "make your coordinates for five miles northeast of Merseyside."

Then he lowered his voice as he again spoke to the Sub-Lieutenant, "Get me the latest coordinates on that unidentified target Tidwell, and make it fast man!"

"Aye, aye, S'ah," Tidwell was off the Bridge and down a flight of stairs in an instant.

The wild scurry of activity had almost thrown Horst off his original interrogation plan as he realized he needed to get back downstairs for critical answers from his captive scientists. As he turned to leave, people came onto the Bridge from all directions helmets donned and firearms belted at their sides.

"Keep me informed Captain, and maintain a protective standoff once you are sure that's the one, I've got to get those physicists to tell me how to disarm that monster."

"Excellent, General Deeke," Captain Durham shouted out as Horst ran for the lower deck, "we'll locate him for you, S'ah, don't worry about that!"

As Horst reached the interrogation room, the door hatch was open and the Brigadier was just coming out shaking his head as he caught him, "Brigadier, what going on down here?"

"They're gone, General," Thorpson exclaimed as his demeanor showed his depression and outrage all at once, "the whole bloody lot of them, they're all dead, the cowards!"

Horst was frozen in shock as he spoke, "How did they do it?"

"Cyanide capsules," he replied, " buried in the bloody cigarette tobacco," as if he should have known where they kept them, but his boys had already checked their mouths and teeth."

"Damned Nazis they think of everything when it comes time to leave. Look at the mess they've made for us."

"May your God and mine take revenge on those bloody bastards, wherever they end up!"

"What else could happen?" Horst placed his face in his hands as he tried to think, then he saw movement out of the corner of his eye as he ran over to Rolf who was still conscious, but dying.

"Your wife and children you fool," Horst held up his head and looked into his eyes as the chemical finally ate through some bread he had eaten earlier and was now reaching his gut and blood stream. Don't let them die with you Rolf, for God's sake man, the war's over.

If this bomb destroys Liverpool, the Allies will disembowel every man, woman, and child with an Aryan heritage for a thousand years. Rolf talk to me and tell me what to do?"

Suddenly a gurgle uttered out of his mouth as he tried to speak, "the timer has already begun," he coughed, "it's useless, save yourself, Horst, they'll blow by noon." Then he was gone.

"The timer", Horst said out loud as he finally rationalize how he could stop them, "that bastard Himmler ordered the Scientists to set the timers before UX-506 left the tender ship, that means the crew on board the U-boat isn't aware that they have no chance to escape before the bomb detonates."

"Maybe that's our opportunity, General," the Brigadier offered, "is there a way you can communicate with them and let them know they are doomed?"

"Only one way, Brigadier," Horst said as they made their way to the Bridge, " we need a bright ship's signal light with a yellow filtered lens on it."

"How's that General?" he questioned as they entered the Bridge to get the current bearings of the target.

"All of our U-boats have boat to boat flash signals at certain times of the day." Horst answered, " Before 1200 Hours it's yellow. And, we need a bright light to be seen through this heavy fog."

Captain Durham greeted them with the new coordinates as they arrived on the Bridge Deck.

Two Petty Officers were peering through the windshield with binoculars straining to see beyond the two-hundred-yard limit as rain droplets formed on the thick glass.

The First Mate was steering the new course heading to the northeast, as Sub-Lieutenant Tidwell confirmed they would intersect the possible target, in less than twenty minutes.

It was now almost 1100 Hours and the tension was building in everyone.

Several scenarios had Horst's nerves on edge; What if the target wasn't UX-506 after all? With zero options, that scenario was the worst. . . . yet how could they confirm it now, that was also impossible? And what if the timer was set before noon, how much time would they really have before disaster struck?

Horst again advised the Brigadier, "You will need to send the message nonetheless, to distract them Brigadier, while your frogmen and I get on board the U-boat from the opposite approach. That way we've got two methods to hopefully dissuade them."

"Just keep the code signals simple, General," the Brigadier added, "that way we'll be able to keep repeating the warning until you have full control."

"And if you don't, do you want me to ram them, General?" Captain Durham chimed in with a sense of final frustration.

"That's a tough one, Captain," Horst pointed out, "for, if they sink with the device intact, the cannon can still fire and the bomb can still reach critical mass becoming a water borne thermonuclear explosion instead of a surface one. The results can reek just as much devastation and maybe more, no one really knows, do we?"

"So what's our final option, then General," the Brigadier queried as a last resort?

"Two things," Horst answered, "first, we've got to prevent the chain reaction from starting."

"We've probably got to blow the firing device, 'the cannon' that is, off the U-boat's deck with our plastic explosives, maybe even with a round from your five inch gun Captain, if nothing else works or if we are taken out before we can set the explosives."

"Then the entire boat will have to be towed into deep water and sunk, with it's batteries removed, otherwise the radiation and the liquid deuterium core could become unstable and cause a future problem to the area."

Again Sub-Lieutenant Tidwell ran up the stairway and entered the Bridge, "Less than seven minutes to the target, General."

"Thanks Lieutenant" Horst answered as he turned to the Brigadier, "Are you clear on everything Brigadier Thorpson?"

"We're clear here General, you get on with it man," he confidently responded as a Petty Officer in charge of the ship's signal lamps led him out on deck to the equipment near an anti-aircraft gun emplacement.

In moments two frogmen with plastic explosives, several Red Viking commandos with charged Stens, and the SS-Gruppenfuhrer were into a fast twenty-six-foot modified whaleboat used for clandestine SAS water borne attacks.

As they launched from the HMS Juno, a third set of frogman's gear was donned by the Horst himself while they made ready to drop-off ahead of the U-boat and wait to board her on the rear deck in the growing fog bank.

The mid-engine craft was extremely stealthy and capable of up to thirty-knots fully loaded with ten commandos on board.

Their approach was set to cross the wake of the U-boat now traveling at twelve-knots within three-hundred yards of it's stern, then rush ahead to drop off the frogmen into the projected path. They would then have time to throw their rubber-insulated grappling hooks and silently pull themselves on deck while the U-boat remained underway and unaware.

The commandos would later join them or be ready to pick them up once their water proof-lights flashed the appropriate signals.

Everything had been timed down to the wire with Horst breathing a sigh of relief as his lead operative finally whispered an announcement, "We've just crossed the wake of a submarine type craft, S'ah."

HMS Juno's Chief Petty Officer had control of their modified whaleboat as he motioned to them to make ready for the turn, due south along side the U-boat's port side.

They quickly reached a point almost four hundred yards ahead of the boat where the three frogmen dropped silently into the black waves and aligned themselves to swim alongside the U-boat's hull as it past their stationary locations. Each of them remained in neutral buoyancy, hovering at about twelve-feet deep to conserve energy as they soon spotted the prow of the U-boat moving rapidly into their positions.

Timing was critical as they surfaced with the aid of the grappling hooks once they were hidden by the hull's curvature.

Horst was the first to see the massive cannon structure in place on the stern as their hooks were locked on and they each of them began to surf alongside the boat's hull abruptly pulling themselves out of the water and onto the UX-506's rear deck. Fog still hung heavy enough to give cover as it hovered over them like a thick shroud.

Silently, Horst removed his Sten from the waterproof bag. He charged it and dashed to just below the conning tower watching for any movement.

Tenaciously he was able to sneak with his rubber dive boots, up to the only man on watch as his two frogmen set their plastic charges around the base of the critical mass firing cannon. The man was intently watching the bow cut through the fog as Horst came up behind him.

Rather than take him out though, he chose to confront him once he knew both the divers were clear and back in the water.

First, he marked the location of the whaleboat in the fog at about one-hundred yards off his left shoulder and signaled them to hold position as he again checked the time, 1121 Hours.

Chief Petty Officer Lewis affirmed the hold signal and swung the whaleboat behind UX-506 to retrieve both frogmen.

In an instant they were completely hidden by the white blur of the fog as Horst moved closer to his prey.

In one movement he had his man in a death grip as he softly assured the frightened sailor in German who he was, and that he only wanted him restrained and mute; He would do the talking.

As he explained quietly what he was about to do, he moved the man to the edge of the deck until he could see the bow of Chief Lewis's whaleboat pulling in behind UX-506's port flank. Horst again signaled, then threw the wide-eyed Kreigsmariner overboard into the surf.

They caught him and dragged him in as the whaleboat pulled parallel to the U-boat's conning tower at about fifteen yards out.

Horst grabbed a line they threw him and tied it off as five Red Viking Commandos briskly made their way onto the U-boat's deck and charged their Stens. At that moment Horst signaled the frogmen to fire their charges.

Nothing seemed to happen, then all of a sudden the entire rear deck raised up in flame as the explosion and blast concussion knocked down two of his men standing alongside the tower.

The groan of the deck ripping apart held everyone in awe as the immense metal cannon, weighing almost four tons leaned to one side.

It's weight began pulling at the deck plates as it finally broke off and crashed into the rolling waves disappearing in a few seconds beneath the dark surface.

Horst and everyone else had taken cover either in the conning tower or on the forward deck.

Screaming crewmen started climbing up the periscope hatch as Horst's men pulled each of them hastily from the conning tower and down to the deck to be off loaded on to Chief Lewis' boat.

Deck hatches on the bow and mid-ship opened as three more crewmen were subdued.

Everyone was now accounted for except for the Kapitan.

Horst shouted in German for him to come up on deck. He even tried to explain what was happening, but to no avail, no one answered.

By now the HMS Juno was alongside the U-boat's starboard hull as Horst realized the engines had stopped, and the boat was gliding slower in the water with every wave across it's bow.

Crewmen from the Juno were already throwing lines over to attach for towing as Horst made his decision to go below.

What he found was frightening. But it provided an answer for the intense emotional pain he was struggling with over the loss of his beautiful Heidi, his true Valkyrie and the woman that was to be his future family.

Korvettenkapitan Winkler had been checking the rear storage batteries when the deck charges blew. With the rear batteries also under the deuterium holding cell, the explosion forced support mounts on the cell to give way and collapse the entire unit into the battery storage area crushing Winkler in the twisted wreckage.

When Horst found him he had already perished, but the acid continued to burn his flesh into a grotesque black form, giving off obnoxious odors as it mixed with the toxic chemical fumes from the batteries.

The lower deck reeked of death, but as he began to get out he came upon the sealed hatch of the Skipper's Head near the Control Room.

On its door was taped a single SS lapel pin of a Nazi officer with an inscription in German carved by knife into the metal.

Horst was finally able to imagine what had happened to Erich as he turned over the SS pin confirming the inscription SSI-EF and sadly placed it into his pocket. He knew the sinking of this boat would carry him on to his grave at the bottom of the Irish Sea, but not to Valhalla where the chosen Viking warriors would live on to fight for Odin in the final battle of Legend, not if he had any hand in the destruction of his Valkyrie.

And Horst was now sure he had.

As the SS-Gruppenfuhrer climbed out onto the conning tower, fresh sea air purged his lungs from the acid fumes growing in the U-boat's lower deck.

The fog was beginning to lift and he could just barely see the docks of Merseyside in the distance to the east, not more than five miles away.

The Horror was over.

Within less than two hours the HMS Juno had reached a point almost forty miles due west of Merseyside in fifteen hundred feet of water as both boats began to drift with 'all engines stopped' in the moderate afternoon swells of the Irish Sea.

It had towed the dying U-boat holding the most lethal device ever built by any nation on earth as Horst took a last look at his own creation, before he buried it forever.

Charges were set to blow at 1630 Hours, but no coordinates were recorded to mark the spot where they scuttled the P.M.'s 'Most Secret' captured device, the seven-hundred-ton German U-boat UX-506 holding the world's first Hydrogen Bomb.

Only a footnote would remain in the diaries of Winston Churchill, but the men that carried out the Red Viking Mission, would remember this event until their dying day.

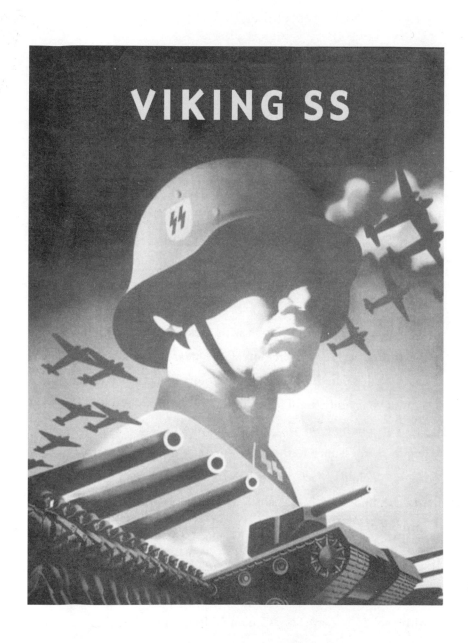

EPILOGUE

HMS JUNO - September, 1972

Jost Van der Vort Island - BVI

It was getting late when both Lieutenant Codrington and his SAS counterpart Lieutenant Ian MacDonald began knocking at the main door. Both had been previously advised that Colonel MacCurry was not to be disturbed until the Royal Navy escort destroyer HMS Juno had arrived in the area. The sun was turning a deep orange in the western horizon as the Juno anchored in a shallow bay between Jost Van der Vort Island and Coopers Island about a mile to the northeast. The Colonel had been scheduled to join Lieutenant-Commander Philip Wickes for dinner on board.

As he opened the door, with dark shadows beginning to hide the turquoise blue watercolor of the nearby shallows, Lieutenant MacDonald saluted and spoke first. "Colonel MacCurry, Sir, the Juno is 'now at your ready' and Lieutenant-Commander Wickes has requested that you join him onboard. A crew is awaiting you at our dock to taxi you by motor launch to the Juno."

Colonel MacCurry held a small flight bag in his left hand, and responded with his salute to the 'camouflaged' dressed SAS Lieutenant.

"Well gentlemen, let's all get over to our host and finish up this bottle of the MACALLAN, what do you say?"

Unexpectedly invited by the Colonel, both officers responded with a solid, "Aye, aye Sir" as Colonel MacCurry locked the main door behind him and walked in the direction of the waiting crewmen.

"By the way," he added, not expecting a response," have either of you ever attended a Viking warrior's funeral? MacCurry paused, then spoke. . .

"You know, the Vikings would place the honored dead warrior on the pyre of a Viking Dragonship and launch it out to sea against the backdrop of a setting sun."

"With a single flaming arrow launched to ignite it's pyre, the remaining warriors would then watch it burn to the waterline and sink into the sea at sunset."

Again the Colonel's unusual remark caught them both by surprise, as they quizzically looked at each other, with only Lieutenant Codrington responding, "I don't believe so, Sir."

Colonel MacCurry continued on towards the dock undeterred.

"Well, just keep that one under your hat for now gentlemen," MacCurry emphasized as they climbed aboard the Destroyer's motorlaunch.

In minutes they were onboard the Juno and Lieutenant-Commander Philip Wickes was on deck for their informal welcome.

"Sir!" Codrington faced Wickes with a quick salute, I would like to introduce
Lieutenant-Colonel MacCurry."

The Lieutenant Commander saluted. "Welcome aboard HMS Juno Colonel."

Wickes then shook hands with the Colonel and looked back over his shoulder at the two junior officers.

"Looks like we'll have a full complement for dinner tonight, aye Colonel!"

Lieutenant-Colonel MacCurry responded in an agitated and somewhat sarcastic tone of voice, "We sure as hell will Lieutenant Commander, and we've all got lots to talk about regarding the security procedures at Lord Sunderland's Castle."

MacCurry then faced Wickes sternly and held out an official document for him to scan as they walked to the Bridge, " Lieutenant Commander, are you familiar with these orders and the protocol afforded them?"

Wickes nodded his head as he carefully read the document's highlights, while scanning the signatures of the Head of Section, Viscount Dalton Ramsbotham of British Military Intelligence and Admiral Albert Henry Harrwood, the Senior Sea Lord and Operations Admiral in the Atlantic and Mediterranean for the Royal Navy.

"I see Sir. . . . it look's as though you are requisitioning my ship, aye Colonel!"

Lieutenant-Colonel MacCurry responded again, still sporting a biting tone of voice, "That's quite right, Lieutenant Commander. . .And are you equipped with maps of the area around Palma on the Spanish isle of Majorca?"

Again Wickes looked at the two junior officers quizzically, "I'm sure my staff can get that arranged easily enough. . . and for now, I know we have maps of the Mediterranean, Colonel."

At last, Lieutenant-Colonel MacCurry seemed pleased with his answer and the obviously improved attitude of the Commander, as he finally managed a grin,

"Well then Commander, as soon as we've had a proper send off for the remains of Lord Sunderland, we'll be making headway to visit that sunny isle in the Mediterranean, ... within the next few days of course."

MacCurry's cryptic comments where meant to hide his real interest in what Trixey Haygood had been up to all these years since the Northolt incident in '45 with Churchill, and now with a fully operational Destroyer at his command, he intended to find out?

"I've got some unfinished business to complete regarding this assignment, and that's where I believe it finishes up."

"Aye, Colonel," Wickes seemed relieved that the testy part appeared to be over, at least for the moment. "Then let's be off, sir."

Ominously curious, Wickes turned the latch on the forward door and silently led the group, as they all disappeared below decks and into the main officers galley for a round of well needed drinks.

Epitaph of Horst Deeke

"There through some battlefield, where men fall fast,
Their horses fetlock-deep in blood, they ride,
And pick the bravest warriors out for death,
Whom the Valkyries bringback with them at night
to Heaven
To glad the gods and feast in Odin's hall forever."

- Balder Dead
Matthew Arnold